Children of the Flame

Mike Jefferies was born in Kent but spent his early years in Australia. He attended the Goldsmiths School of Arts and then taught art in schools and prisons. A keen rider, he was selected in 1980 to ride for Britain in the Belgian Three Day Event. He now lives in Norfolk with his wife and three stepchildren, working full-time as a writer and illustrator.

SCIENCE
FICTION
FANTASY

MIKE JEFFERIES

Children of the Flame

HarperCollins*Publishers*

HarperCollins Science Fiction & Fantasy
An imprint of HarperCollins*Publishers*
77–85 Fulham Palace Road,
Hammersmith, London W6 8JB

This paperback edition 1994
1 3 5 7 9 8 6 4 2

ISBN 0 586 21749 5

Set in Stempel Garamond by
Rowland Phototypesetting Ltd
Bury St Edmunds, Suffolk

Printed in Great Britain by
HarperCollinsManufacturing Glasgow

TO SHEILA,
whose perception lit up the darkness
and drew aside the veils that hid
all those other lives.

Winter 1942

CHRIS OSTIC DIDN'T need to use the car's headlights to find his way along the narrow, winding English country lanes even if the blackout regulations had allowed him to. He couldn't shake off the sensation that something was following him, a dark shape, a fleeting, pursuing shadow. He kept catching sight of it in the rear view mirror, gradually gaining on him. Fear drove him – he knew he could find his destination blindfold; his soul was driven by the urgency of its task and his heart by the depth of its sorrow. He had to help Stephanie escape.

He barely noticed the distant fires that were raging through the streets of London, lighting up the skyline for twenty miles or more with a livid orange glow. He threw the big car along the lanes, the tyres screaming in protest as it slewed around the corners. He crashed the gearbox and ignored the protest of the engine as it strained in the dark rural silence. He braked only when he saw, some way ahead, the interwoven archway of branches formed by two gnarled oaks crowning the top of Bovingdon Hill, etched in leafless black lacework against the burning sky. Journey's end had come upon him all too soon. He shifted through the Humber's unfamiliar gears and slowed the car. He wasn't sure he could keep his promise.

The open gateway ahead to the right came up fast and he braked and reached out a gentle restraining hand to stop her from slipping off the seat, using the heel of his hand to keep her head up as he spun the wheel and drove into the empty field. The heavy car bumped and rumbled over the tough tussocks of frozen grass, filling the interior with the powerful, heady smell of aviation fuel as the hastily-stacked cans in the back tipped and spilled. Slowing down, Chris drove the remaining distance more carefully and gently brought the vehicle to a halt.

This was the place: it was time to fulfil his promise. He turned the ignition key and killed the engine, holding his breath as he hunted the rear view mirror for a sign of their pursuer, but the dark gateway of the field stood black and empty. The deep stillness of the place was broken by the distant rumble of the anti-aircraft batteries along the far-off river. He sat and watched for a moment as the clusters of searchlights stroked the thick under-sides of the clouds. One of them caught and held the wing of a German bomber and the other slender pencils of light converged, sweeping through the fiery darkness to trap and illuminate the aircraft. Anti-aircraft shells burst brightly against its black belly and slithers of shrapnel punctured its fragile skin. It would die as surely as a moth caught in a candle flame. All around the stricken bomber the vast armada of death ploughed relentlessly on, the drone and throb of their engines fading into the night as they turned for home. The destruction of the bomber brought him little satisfaction: it might have been the one that had brought his happiness to an end but he felt as remote from its drama as if he were in another world.

As he got out of the car the cold night air frosted his breath white and he shivered, turning up the collar of his flying jacket. It was quiet now and he imagined he could hear the crackle of the frost forming on the branches above his head. A rustle of fallen leaves close by made him concentrate on the darkness, but he heard nothing more.

It took him only a minute to saturate the inside of the car with the aviation fuel and then he stood back, the box of matches ready in his hand. His eyes never left the slender dark form in the passenger seat.

He reached in and touched her birthmark, identical to his own, letting his fingers trace the pattern of the labyrinth carved in deepest blue and remembering how she had touched his own mark as she died, whispering how it bound them together and how it must be destroyed by fire, how the watchers and their beast must never be allowed to touch it. She had said that when his own moment came and the shadow of death fell upon him he must destroy his mark as he destroyed hers, or they would be separated forever.

He felt the coldness of her skin through the watered silk of her blouse. The outline of her face against the flickering light was beautiful, death having smoothed away the terror of those last, frantic moments amongst the falling masonry, the smoke and the fire. For a moment time stood still as he looked at her and the memory of the intense love he felt for her filled him utterly, taking his breath away. He remembered the six months they had spent together, the glimpses of strange images that she had awoken in his mind, images he had no way of understanding. He remembered yearning for a future together after the war. For six months he had felt he was with someone he had known and that they were destined to be together always. Now desolation overcame him and he felt completely alone.

'Oh God, I can't do this!'

His promise suddenly seemed crazy. He slammed his fist into the dashboard. The sharp stab of pain focused his mind and at once he remembered that familiar, uneasy sense of being haunted, the feeling that someone – or something – was always watching them, following them, hiding in the shadows in their footsteps. A feeling

3

that Stephanie had spoken of, that he had experienced even before they had met. Suddenly he sensed the watchers, and knew that they had found the car in the gateway.

He struck the match. The flame flared brightly between his fingers. 'Goodbye, sweetheart, until we meet again.' His voice was heavy with tears as he tossed the flame through the gap in the driver's window.

There came a faint scuff of footsteps running over the frozen grass and the panting breath of something huge was magnified by an eerie silence. The lighted match spun and fell inside the car.

'Burn! Damn you burn!'

The fragile flame thinned and elongated, turning a blue-white before seeming to vanish as if extinguished by an invisible breath. A knot of panic tightened in his stomach. A twig snapped behind him and he heard a howl as something huge launched itself at the car.

His fingers trembled and in his haste he dropped the box and the contents spilled onto the ground around his feet.

'Damn, damn, damn,' he sobbed, ducking down beside the car and frantically searching the dark, frosty grass for the scattered matches.

A vast, shadowy, three-headed beast sent him sprawling to the ground as it leapt up onto the bonnet. But the match that landed on the saturated leather seat of the Humber was not entirely dead. The pinpoint spark that still glowed in its blackened head rekindled and a flame spread suddenly from one end of the car to the other.

The sudden heat of the blaze shattered the windscreen and sent a column of flames shooting across the bonnet, sweeping the creature away in a howl of pain. Chris scrambled to his feet and backed away, using his right arm to shield his face from the heat as the inside of the

4

car became a raging inferno. He had the briefest glimpse of Stephanie, her clothes and hair a mass of flame. Behind him in the darkness wailing shrieks rent the air making him spin round, his fists clenched.

Two shadowy figures rushed forward. The dancing light of the flames illuminated their flowing, black robes and their faces; they were women, their skin skeletally white, their features distorted with rage as they cursed the demon dog and drove it back toward the car to pull Stephanie out . . .

'The watchers!'

They advanced in leaping strides. Chris stepped backward and, looking around for something to attack them with, caught his foot on a fallen branch. He reached down and picked it up, gripping it with both hands as his anger boiled up inside him to replace the fear.

'Come on, you ugly bastards!' he shouted, running past the car with the stick raised. 'Come on! I'm not afraid of you!'

The huge dog snarled and leapt at him. Chris brought the branch down with all his strength and struck out at one of the creature's heads. There was a splintering crack of wood on bone and the force of the blow sent a burning pain up his arm. The beast howled and scuttled away into the shadows. He swept the weapon in a swinging arc at the closest figure only to stagger and almost lose his balance as it scythed through empty air and struck the metal body of the car. They melted at his touch, vanishing into the flickering darkness only to reappear a moment later. They seemed to be everywhere at once, trying to pull at the locked door handles, shrieking and cursing as the hot metal burned their fingers. They attempted to clamber onto the bonnet and the blistering roof only to be driven back in a blaze of sparks, stamping their smouldering boots on the frozen ground before cursing the dog and goading it to renew the attack. In a demented rage they began to hurl broken branches at the smoke-blackened windows as if trying to smash the glass closest to where Stephanie sat engulfed in the flames.

Chris caught a glimpse of the huge dog as it circled the car and knew he had to do something before the window shattered and it was able to jump úp and reach in to grab at her charred body. But what could he do? He didn't know how long he could beat off the dog's attacks. His thoughts raced: he could see the shadowy, cloaked women but he couldn't touch them. They couldn't be ghosts – ghosts wouldn't have been afraid of the fire. Then he remembered Stephanie's dying words: she had said that fire was their only protection from the watchers, that must be why they had that salivating monster with them, to pull Stephanie out of the flames. Perhaps, if the fire was fierce enough . . .

'Fire! I must ring the car with fire, there must be enough fire to keep the dog back!'

He hurled the branch at the approaching hound, sent it scuttling away, and looked desperately around him for anything he could set alight. Beyond the circle of light from the burning car he saw the bulky shape of a fallen wind-blown oak, its broken branches scattered across the ground. 'A ring of fire!'

He ran to and from the fallen tree, shouting and cursing at the ugly creature, throwing stones at it every time it tried to approach, sending it back to the two shadowy figures who haunted the firelight. He gathered as many of the branches as he could carry and pushed their thickened, broken ends into the ground as near to the burning car as he could get until he had built a continuous circle. Tongues of flame danced out of the shattered windscreen and licked amongst the closest twigs, making them shrivel and crackle as they caught light. Slowly the flames leapt from branch to branch until the car was completely encircled in a ring of bright fire.

Chris gathered a final bundle of fallen branches, as many as he could carry, and placed them as close as he could to the burning car ready for him to use to strengthen his circle of fire if any part of it threatened to collapse. He felt drained and empty of emotion as he sank down onto his knees on the cold wet ground to keep his lonely vigil yet as he watched the roaring flames he sensed that he had done it all before and there was triumph over the darkness, but the memory was dim and clouded – it belonged to other lives, no more than images on the edge of consciousness. The pictures misted his eyes, blurring the shapes of the two shadowy figures with their dog running at their heels who leapt and spun around his makeshift barricade of fire in their futile attempts to break through it. There was nothing else he could do now but sit there and guard Stephanie's soul until it had vanished in the flames.

The heat from the burning car rose in a shimmering haze, distorting the flickering firelight, blending and merging the dancing shapes, lulling and mesmerizing him, transforming reality into vivid, shifting images. He could smell the reek of other funeral pyres and hear unfamiliar sounds, mournful wails and funeral chants, the creak of leather and the beat of hooves over cobbles. He could see sun and moonlight, each in their turn, reflecting from a ring of silver blades that were sometimes set about the burning pyres. The images swam closer and he saw the mark of the labyrinth on the bodies of the corpses and always, in every shifting kaleidoscopic vision, the two shadowy watchers goading their hideous dog to maul at the ashes, trying to reach and pull out the dead.

Chris blinked, pulled up his sleeve and touched his birthmark, wondering what the Hell it all meant, then the images changed and intensified, drowning him. He wasn't kneeling on the cold wet earth beside the burning car any more: he could feel his body but he couldn't see it – he was in a different time, a different place.

A loud explosion suddenly rocked Stephanie's burning car. The seals on the petrol tank had finally ruptured in the intense heat of the fire and the fuel had ignited, forcing the filler cap to fly off in a gushing fountain of burning liquid. Parts of the makeshift barricade of branches were burning through and collapsing, sending ribbons of dancing sparks swirling up to vanish amongst the shrivelled, blackened twigs in the overhanging oaks. The sound made Chris jump and broke into the images that were filling his mind, confusing them, blurring them together and pulling him back into the present. He tried to cling onto the melting shapes wondering what they were, what they meant. One moment they had been so vivid and the next they had faded beyond reach.

For a muddled moment he knelt there staring at the burning hulk of the car. He couldn't remember where he was or how he had got there. The sound of the crackling flames was somehow blending in his head with other melodic sounds that he couldn't quite focus on. Slowly he became more aware of the charred and blackened body engulfed in the flames inside the car and the bleak, awful reality of why he was keeping this terrible vigil on the top of Bovingdon Hill struck him in the pit of his stomach.

'Stephanie. Oh, my God, Stephanie, what have I done?' He tried to scramble to his feet and run to the car only to fall back onto his knees. There was nothing he could do but kneel there, his fists clenched helplessly as he watched the cremation.

A movement on the edge of the firelight and whispering, goading voices beyond the funeral pyre caught his attention. His eyes flicked toward the two shadowy figures on the rim of darkness as they sent their beast charging at his burning barricade. He stared open-mouthed as it tore at the lighted branches with its teeth and claws, its reeking hide smouldering and catching light before it fled howling into the night. The two figures rushed forward through the breaks in the barrier and tried to get at the car, but fell back with shrieking curses, defeated by the crackling flames. Their fingers and the sleeves and hems of their robes were covered in sparks. Who were they? What were they doing?

Then it all came flooding back. He recalled the terror the two watchers had brought into Stephanie's dying moments; he remembered her begging him to burn her body so they couldn't get to it. But why? Who were these creatures who had pursued her to the threshold of eternity? Where in Hell's name had they sprung from? His anger boiled as he watched them rush away into the darkness stamping and beating at the fire that still clung to their clothes. Then they renewed their frenzied attack.

His anger turned to rage. He scrambled to his feet, punching the air with his fists to drive them away. 'Get the Hell out of here you goddamn . . .'

His words died on his lips as he caught a clearer glimpse of their faces in the firelight and it sent an ice-cold shiver of panic up his spine to prickle the hair on his scalp. He knew these women: there was something unnervingly familiar about them. All at once he realized he had known them all his life – they had dwelt in his subconscious, inhabited his dreams, never quite in focus yet always there, a soft ache, a constant itch.

Now the sight of them, the sound of their voices, stirred up long-forgotten memories, fragments and echoes from other lives that he had lived, other times and places that he had forgotten; the rush of water falling in a hidden gorge, the cry of eagles hunting in the crags, the smell of the mountain pines. Other things began to fill his head, the babble of strange voices, the rumble of iron-shod wheels, the reek of busy summer streets, all took their place in the dancing flicker of the flames. The fire inside the car began to mesmerize him and again reality was clouded as he was drawn back to the very beginning, to the start of things in a distant medieval town.

Shadows of Evil
Summer 1347

BRIGHT SUNLIGHT REFLECTED from the steep, weather-bleached roof tops and cast elongated shadows from the crowded houses and balconies that leaned across the cobbled streets below. A forest of pencil-thin church steeples and the soaring cathedral spire rose above the castellated walls of the town to shimmer, grey-pink and crystal white, in the noon day haze, a stark contrast against the backdrop of sombre, wooded shoulders and narrow gorges of the mountains. But for all its isolated beauty and tranquillity, Aurillac was filled with an air of impending catastrophe.

Rumours of a new and terrifying plague which was ravaging the lowlands beyond the mountains to the east had been brought into the city by the journeymen and travelling merchants who traded through the mountain passes. They had brought, with their bales of silk and jars of spices, horrifying stories of a mysterious disease that had laid waste whole towns and villages, killing everyone it touched with purple blotches, evil, suppurating swellings, or a ring of rose-coloured spots upon their skin. They would huddle closer to the fire and in whispering voices they would call it the Black Death and tell how it had spread in a noxious, deadly wind from the very bowels of Hell. They would swear that there wasn't a healer or a leech doctor in all Christendom who knew of a cure for those unfortunates who fell beneath its shadow, and, in the startled silence that followed, they would bare their arms and legs to show that they were clean, untouched by the disease, before they were assaulted by a barrage of questions.

The town was alive with the rumours and seething with speculation in the face of its impending doom. The bishops declared it to be a visitation of the plagues of Egypt sent to purge the sinners of the world and they warned their congregations, bidding them to make themselves ready, and then began a brisk trade in selling privileges. The town elders, sensing the rising panic, imposed a curfew and ordered baskets of columbine and valerian to be burned continuously at the gates of the town to ward off the plague should it come. And then, to make it worse, the town was struck by the longest heatwave anybody alive could remember.

For twenty days the weather had been unbearably hot. The sun had beaten down relentlessly, killing the crops in the fields long before they ripened, and cracking the cobblestones in the narrow, airless streets. Farm animals, small babes-in-arms and the frail and elderly began dying in the heat. The rivers and wells that provided the town with water began to dry up, the shallower ones rapidly shrinking into brackish, stagnant puddles. The familiar summer stench of overflowing midden ditches and the heaps of rubbish that littered the gutters, humming with the buzz and drone of the blowflies that were drawn to them, began to hang over the town in a choking, invisible fog.

Gradually the weak summer breeze died away to nothing amongst the tall silver-headed trees that grew on either side of the town gates, their leathery leaves feebly spinning in the last evaporating breath of air before they hung limp and still while the noon-day bells struck out the hour.

The sharp crackle of untended flames, the dance of firelight on the soot-black chimney walls and the acrid reek of herbs boiling dry and burning in the bottom of the cauldron made Mother Zem, the ancient soothsayer and healer, stir and start awake where she dozed in the gloomy corner of her kitchen beside the chimney. She sniffed and sat upright, her eyes watering in the thin haze of bitter yellow smoke that was beginning to rise above the rim of the old, black cooking pot.

'Daughters, where are those useless daughters? The town's seething with the talk of plagues and I'll soon be run off my feet. I can't even trust them to brew the simplest of syrups for curing the itch – what am I going to do with them? They're not even fit to tend a herd of swine.' She cursed and the wrinkled, leathery skin around her sunken mouth twitched and tightened with anger as she rose unsteadily from her stool and shuffled forward to kick cold ashes over the fire to smother the flames.

She leaned down and peered at the withered, black-ened mess of hyssop, whitlowgrass and wormwood leaves in the bottom of the cauldron. 'Aglia, Harlonis – you have ruined the syrup, you useless daughters. Where are you? Come here this moment and help me!'

Mother Zem moved away from the chimney mutter-ing under her breath as she searched the jars and pitchers that filled the crowded cupboard shelves, pushing aside the thick bundles of drying herbs and grasses and faded flower heads hanging from the iron hooks that had been set into the low, wooden beams that criss-crossed the kitchen. Eventually she found the heavy stone pitcher of distilled coltsfoot and dragged it across the earthen floor to the hearth. She spat on the rim of the cooking pot and watched as the spittle bubbled and hissed, wait-ing impatiently for the cauldron to cool before ladling three measures of the liquor into the ruined syrup. She stirred the blackened mess and tasted it gingerly, pucker-ing her mouth at the foul taste. 'Ruined! Utterly ruined,' she grumbled.

A noise from beyond the open doorway, whispered voices in the street outside, made her turn and pick up a knobbled threshing stick and hurry out as fast as her crippled legs would carry her. The old woman's angry mutterings turned to apprehension as she caught the sound of Aglia's voice rising into a chant of magic. She was using words that would brand her as a dabbler in the Black Arts. Then she saw both of her daughters squatting a mere pace beyond the threshold of their dwelling in the dust of the alleyway, surrounded by a growing crowd of curious onlookers and ragged children.

'You'll be the death of us all. They'll burn us for dabbling in the ways of the Devil,' she hissed, hobbling out into the glare of the midday sunlight, gesticulating wildly with her stick.

The crowd edged quickly backward out of her way as Mother Zem hurried through them, but she was already too late to stop her daughters' foolishness. Aglia was hunched forward scratching the last of thirteen spidery rows of tallow runes in the dirt with her left hand. Her other hand was raised in the act of scattering bright cockerel feathers and broken chicken bones to fall across the runes as she chanted the magic that would help her predict the future. Harlonis heard the shuffle of feet as the crowd opened out behind her and glanced up to see their mother bearing down on them, her face a thunderous mask of black anger. The shadow of the raised threshing stick and the white, knuckled hand that held it fell across her face and she barely had time to cry out a warning to her sister or raise her own arm to ward off the savage blow that was aimed at her head.

'Foolish, addle-headed women! Get back to your chores at once – at once do you hear!' Mother Zem began to shriek as she wielded her stick first at Harlonis and then set about Aglia's shoulders.

14

A hot, dry wind rustled the trees and riddled the dust of the town's alleyways, slamming doors and shutters, swirling and catching at the onlookers' robes and sending a stinging cloud of dirt up into their faces as it took the cockerel's feathers. It moved the chicken bones and scratched out the spidery drawings until there was nothing, not a trace of Aglia's magic in the baked earth.

'It is a sign, an omen of the future!' somebody called out from the crowd.

The wind died and a deathly hush spread through the gathering as they stared down at the empty space where once there were tallow runes. An elderly iron master and a group of washerwomen made the sign of the cross and began to hurry away, whispering against the Devil's works. Angry murmurings rose amongst the crowd but other voices clamoured for an answer from the strange magic they had just seen the women perform. They called out, demanding satisfaction.

'What did the wind foretell? Will the Black Death sweep through our town or will we be spared? What must we do to avert its black shadow?'

Mother Zem smelled the danger of heresy in the questions and didn't give Aglia a moment to draw breath. If she answered and tried to interpret the spell she had cast she would condemn herself as a practitioner of the Black Arts. She knocked her daughter roughly off balance with her threshing stick, sending her sprawling in the dirt.

'She can tell you nothing. The heat of the sun has addled her wits!' Mother Zem cried, stooping over her and scuffing at the dirt where the runes had been before crushing and trampling on the feathers and bones until they were a broken mess in the gutter. She looked up at the hesitant and uneasy crowd. 'Go! Go about your business. You'll learn nothing here about the Black Death – you have my oath on it. My daughters are honest, God-fearing girls and will pray for your souls when they do their penance for trying to entertain you with such foolishness. There are no spells or magic in my house; there is nothing here for you save wholesome lotions for the itch or syrups for the common fevers, or perhaps you wish for oils for the cough or purges against the pox?'

Gradually the crowd began to disperse in ones and twos, but they were clearly disturbed by what they had witnessed and muttered as they drifted away into the town.

'What madness do you call this? Who has put such notions into your heads? Have you been consorting with the Devil or meeting with demons in the dead of night?' Mother Zem hissed at the younger of the two cowering women when the alleyway was completely deserted.

'I heard voices, words in the dark...' Aglia began, but the old woman's anger cut her short.

'Voices? You fool, don't you realize that we live on the edge of dark and dangerous times? Do you want us to carry the blame for bringing the pestilence that is spreading its shadow toward us, because if it enters this town that is what will happen to you if you're foolish enough to dabble openly in the Black Arts. We will all be tarred with the brush of the Devil.'

'We meant no harm by it – we would never consort with the Devil,' Harlonis tried to explain, scrabbling awkwardly away on her hands and heels, her skirts dragging in the dirt as she reached the safety of the doorway's shadows.

'It was only a harmless chant!' Aglia called out, rubbing gingerly at the angry weals from the threshing stick that were already turning blue-black across her forehead. 'I don't see what all this commotion is about. We were only trying to infuse some good luck into the syrup for the itch that is bubbling in the cook pot over the fire. We thought you would be pleased with us.'

The old woman frowned in bewilderment, and she looked from one to the other of them as Harlonis continued quickly. 'We were only copying the picture that we found in that old Book of Knowledge that you keep hidden away in the hole at the side of the chimney. The picture of the old woman sitting at her hearth stirring a cauldron of herbs and scattering bones and feathers over a mass of signs drawn on the ground at her feet. We thought she was summoning up good luck so we copied the runes as best we could, but Aglia had to make up most of the chant because we couldn't understand more than a handful of the words.'

'Thought? You don't have enough brains between you to think,' Mother Zem muttered, letting the knobbly threshing stick fall to her side. Then her wrinkled face paled to deadly white and she clutched the door post for support as she realized the terrible implications of what her daughters had done by looking secretly in the Apothecaries' Bible and meddling with powers they didn't understand. She glanced anxiously across her shoulder to check that they were not being overheard and then shuffled closer, drawing her daughters to her. 'You were very stupid to touch the forbidden book. The "Clavicles de Saloman" contains much evil and it is not for the eyes of empty-headed women like you.'

'But we often see you consulting the Book of Knowledge and those rolls of manuscripts before you prepare your lotions and remedies. Surely if the book contains so much evil . . .'

The old woman shushed Harlonis' question into silence and fixed them both with a long, searching look, turning over and over in her mind how much she dared to tell them, cursing herself and wishing now that she had instructed them more thoroughly years earlier so that they would have known the Apothecaries' ways by now. At length she drew breath and spoke. 'I fear you are not yet ready to be burdened with the knowledge and your foolishness today warns me that you may never have the wits to understand the awful power that lies amongst the secrets that are written in that book. But I must tell you a little and warn you not to touch its covers again until you have enough of the knowledge to understand it. For now it is enough for you to know that it is not all evil: amongst its dark secrets lies the fountainhead of all that is good. For those who can unravel its wholesome wisdom it will reveal the four bodily elements, the cardinal humours and, most importantly, the cause and effect of everything medicinal that has been discovered since the beginning of time. All this knowledge has been passed in an unbroken line of succession through the healers of this world until it came into my safe keeping. But I fear that it will only be passed onto you if you can prove yourselves worthy of guarding it and using it wisely.'

'Do you understand everything in this book, Mother?' Aglia gasped, her eyes wide with wonder and fear. 'Was the woman in the picture a witch? Was she trying to raise a storm? I'm thinking of the wind that came and blew away the signs I had drawn into the dirt . . .'

The old woman shook her head and the ghost of a smile softened her puckering lips. 'No, she was no witch. I broke the spell's power before you finished uttering it, but be warned never to meddle again in what you do not understand . . .' Mother Zem hesitated, wondering if she should tell her daughters what real danger they had been in or how close they had come to summoning up a swarm of demons by drawing the signs for the compounding of the sorcerers' unguent, the most secret of preparations. For there was no quicker way to unlock the doorcrack of Hell, no faster path to the witches' Sabbath. And that unnatural wind was not a freak of nature: she knew better than that – the stinging clouds of dust that had rubbed out her daughters' scratchings had been the draught of a horde of demons passing over the town, searching for the spellbinders. The only reason her daughters had escaped their evil eyes was because she had been quick to break the chant and scatter and trample the feathers and bones into the gutter.

'Beware, my daughters,' she hissed, glancing up into the cloudless sky to check that they were not being watched or overheard. 'There are so many facets of good and evil: real knowledge and the measure of wisdom is knowing how to use them. Never forget that you were born to be healers, born to have the skill to leech and to bleed and to draw out ill humours. Yours are not the ways of witches or sorcerers: you must not try to unravel the mysteries of the black arts nor fathom the secrets of the pentacle. And you must always always remember this . . .' The old woman paused and clutched at their arms, drawing them down so close to her that her lips almost brushed against their ears. 'The Devil is always listening, waiting to hear the slightest rustle of those dark pages and that whispered sound, less than the summer's breeze in the trees, that will summon him to haunt your threshold and then claim you as his own to burn in Hell forever!'

The two women were visibly terrified and clung to one another. 'Forgive us, Mother, we will never, never touch the book again!' 'You can pluck out our eyes if we break our pledge!' Their voices rose in a chorus.

'But you must, you must! How else will you learn all there is to know of the healer's art and carry it forward into the future? It is I who must make the pledge to teach you from this book and I who will put an end to your ignorance. I must start today while the liquors and syrups simmer in the cauldron.'

The distant sound of the town coming to life as the

noonday hour passed made the old woman pause and listen to the rumble of cartwheels on the cobbles and the songs of the hawkers crying out their wares. She frowned. Something was different in the bustling, dusty streets. Her gaze rose beyond the sun-baked roofs, the turrets and towers and on toward the silent, tree-clad slopes of the mountains that hemmed in their world. She tilted her head slightly, stretching her neck as she tried to catch and hold the sounds that she had heard – the everyday, familiar noises that had momentarily swelled into a wailing cry of torment. It was as though she had caught the reek of bitter ashes and heard the church bells rising into a clamorous peal only to fade away into the mournful tolling of the death bell.

Mother Zem took a blind, hesitant step forward, her head snaking as she chased the vanishing echo, but it was gone. She shivered, her bony fingers worrying at the smooth, ebony beads on the hemp string that hung in knotted loops from her apron pockets. 'The Black Death!' she muttered. 'May the Saints preserve us.' And she quickly rubbed the sign of the cross across her forehead with her thumb nail.

'Mother, what is it? What's wrong?' Harlonis asked anxiously.

The old woman blinked, her eyes snapping back into focus, and she almost told them what she had glimpsed, the Black Death sweeping through the town. She had seen it through the shrouds that cloaked the future and heard the relentless tread of its passage through the mountain passes. But she knew all too well the curse of fuelling panic. 'It was nothing, daughters, nothing but the sound of a passing carriage that distracted me, nothing at all really.' She swallowed the vision and clapped her hands briskly at the two startled women. 'We've had enough of this foolishness for one day – go, take your baskets and gather wild hyssop, whitlowgrass and wormwood to brew a new syrup against the itch to replace the one your meddling magic allowed to burn dry. Cut fresh galingales and daynum, horehound and vetchling. Fill your baskets with every wholesome herb and flower that you can carry because I fear that we may need every leaf and berry and all our healing skills to infuse and blend them together.'

'You saw something just now,' Aglia insisted, refusing to move. 'You glimpsed the future and it disturbed you.'

The old woman raised her threshing stick angrily. 'Go, go at once without another word of argument. Only gather in the wild and secret places that I have shown you. There is rumour that Lord Cerventis has stirred up the other lords who live in the foothills and their stewards will set their hunting dogs on anyone who dares to trespass on their land lest they carry the plague. Take care only to walk on the common path.'

The old woman watched as they collected their baskets and left but she stood in the doorway gazing along the empty alleyway long after her daughters had vanished from sight. The glimpse of a black shadow enveloping the town burned inside her head, thrusting aside all thoughts of the ordinary things that usually set the measure of the days; now there was a gnawing knot of dread tightening in her stomach.

'The vision was a sign to prepare. I must teach the girls all I know or this plague will touch us all.' She retreated into the darkness of her kitchen and pulled the heavy Book of Knowledge out of its hiding place in the chimney. 'There must be something here, some secret lotion to treat the plague: there is no wiser book in all the world.'

Slowly she turned the pages, averting her eyes from the sorcery and allowing the magic to slip beneath her fingertips.

*   *   *

'Wait, Aglia, wait and let me rest a moment. I can't keep up, you climb too fast.' Harlonis stopped and slumped down on an outcrop of rock, sending a basking lizard scuttling into the undergrowth of brambles and bracken. Puffing out her cheeks with a loud sigh she set the heavily laden basket of newly-gathered hyssop and vetch down on the ground between her feet before using her sleeve to wipe away the trickles of perspiration that were running down her forehead and into the corners of her eyes. Sweat was wetting the lank curls of hair that clung to the back of her broad neck. She frowned and looked back the way they had come, not recognizing the path at all, which was steeper and more overgrown than the one they usually used. She could barely see the roofs and towers of the town that should have been immediately below them, and she was beginning to wonder where her sister was taking them when a shriek of laughter made her look up.

'You'd be nimbler if you weren't so fat, sister!' Aglia's taunt cut her to the quick and she half rose, shielding her eyes against the harsh glare of the sun to see Aglia standing above her, silhouetted against the rugged skyline of rocks and trees.

'It's easy for you to mock,' she retorted angrily. 'You aren't so lucky to have been born thin – there's nothing of you but skin and bone. Anyway, you made me carry the heaviest basket, so I need the rest.'

Aglia shrugged and retraced her footsteps down the steep, narrow sheep-path. 'Rest here as long as you like, sister, but the hunting dogs will tear you apart if they get wind of your scent,' she sneered.

Harlonis gave a startled cry and leapt to her feet, grabbing at the woven handle of the basket, scattering a loose bunch of hyssop across the ground. 'Dogs? Hunting dogs? Where in God's name have you brought us? Mother warned us not to trespass.'

Aglia laughed, seeing her sister close to tears as she gathered up the scattered herbs. 'I am taking you to a special, secret glade where the best whitlowgrass grows beside a tumbling waterfall, where the scent of the horehound will make you dizzy and banks of daynum sprout ten feet high.'

Harlonis began to protest but Aglia cut her short. 'You're always creeping around our mother's apron strings, doing her bidding, saying *yes, Mother* to this and *no, Mother* to that. You would never have looked in that book and seen all that magic if I hadn't taken it out of its hiding place in the chimney, would you? And without my help you would never have seen the wonderful things that make up a real spell.'

Harlonis shook her head miserably. She was afraid of being savaged by the dogs and listened anxiously, searching the trees and rough scrub on either side of the track for any sight of Lord Cerventis' hunting hounds. 'But we were wrong to look in that book and to meddle in the magic. You heard Mother say how dangerous it is. We're healers, not dabblers in the Arts, and that mysterious wind that blew along the alleyway and rubbed out the signs you had drawn in the dirt really frightened me. And . . .'

'Be quiet! Stop your babbling – there is someone moving through the trees below us. Quickly, follow me and don't make a sound.' Aglia ran back up the narrow track and disappeared amongst the outcrops of rocks and trees on the top of the ridge.

Harlonis caught the faint sound of baying hounds, the shouts of the huntsmen and the clatter of their horses' iron-shod hooves as they scrambled for a foothold over the rough ground somewhere amongst the trees below her. She let out a strangled cry of fear and, clutching her basket tightly in her arms, climbed as fast as her legs would carry her, snagging her skirts on the brambles and stumbling through the banks of thick bracken as she tried to follow the path that Aglia had taken. Puffing and panting, her heart pounding in her chest, she reached the top of the ridge and stared wildly about her.

'Aglia, Aglia, which way? Where are you? The sounds of the dogs are getting closer, where now?' she gasped between laboured breaths.

'Keep quiet, I'm down here you fool,' her sister hissed. 'There's a way down to your left between those tall rocks. Be careful, it's very steep.'

Harlonis scrambled through the gap in the rocks and then came to an abrupt halt. She had to clutch at the rough bark of a spindly pine tree to stop herself falling as her feet sent a shower of loose earth and stones cascading over the crumbling lip of a sheer cliff that dropped away directly in front of her. 'Aglia, I'll never get down there, it's impossible. I'll plunge to my death!' she cried, leaning out as far as she dared and peering down. She caught a glimpse of a sparkling waterfall and heard the roar and splash as it cut a gorge through the rocks and trees to vanish beneath the thick canopy of tree-tops that lay in shadow in the valley below.

There was mocking laughter in Aglia's voice as it floated up to her. 'The dogs will get you if you don't hurry.'

'I can't get down there, it's impossible.'

The shouts of the hunters told her that they had arrived at the bottom of the slope that she had just climbed. The noise suddenly grew louder and she realized that the hounds must have found their scent and were racing up toward the top of the ridge. The riders were breaking the undergrowth with their iron-tailed whips and spurring their horses up after them.

'Help me, Aglia, help me!'

'Work your way around the outcrop of rock on the left – there's a narrow ledge that leads down to the

Giant's Steps. There's nothing to be afraid of if you don't look down.'

The baying of the hounds seemed almost on top of her. Harlonis' fear of the dogs was greater than her terror of plunging to her death and she began to edge her way out around the rock, gripping hard into every crack and crevice that she could find. Her skirts and apron snagged each time she moved and the sharp granite made her fingers bleed. Sweat trickled into her eyes but inch by inch she moved her right foot, searching the empty air until she found the narrow ledge with her toes.

'Hurry, sister, those cursed dogs are as nimble as mountain goats!' Aglia urged.

Harlonis could hear the dogs' panting breaths as they reached the outcrop of rock and began to scramble over it, dislodging dirt and loose stones that rained onto her head. 'Hurry, you've almost reached the first of the Giant's Steps.'

Harlonis felt the narrow ledge widen out beneath her feet and glanced down. She could see the second step further to her left beneath it and she began to reach out with her foot when a snarling hound directly overhead made her look up. She screamed and almost lost her grip. An enormous fawn dog was slithering down over the rocks toward her, its lips curled back to reveal a cavernous mouth of snapping fangs. Loops of saliva hung from its jowls and she felt its hot, fetid breath on her face as it lunged at her. She ducked instinctively and pressed herself against the rock face, clinging to it in desperation and screwing her eyes firmly shut. The blood-curdling snarl turned into a yelp as the dog lost its footing and its jaws snapped shut inches from her face as it clawed frantically at the surface of the rock for purchase. The huge dog struck her shoulder, its claws tearing through her sleeve as it overbalanced and fell, letting out a wailing howl as it lunged downwards, turning over and over as it plunged into the valley below.

Furious barking and howling broke out as the rest of the pack of hunting dogs swarmed to the brink of the overhanging rocks. They had the scent of her now and were searching for a way down. Harlonis could see their savage jowls and powerful forelegs above her as they stood against the skyline barely a yard away. They snarled and milled about, scrabbling for a foothold as they bayed for her blood.

Suddenly the air was full of the whistling crack of iron-tailed whips as the hunters spurred their horses along the ridge, cursing and driving the hounds onto the lower ground to prevent them all leaping to their deaths.

Sheer terror made Harlonis cower away and scramble backward as fast as she could down the Giant's Steps. She grazed her shins and cut her elbows as her feet slipped on the weather-worn, granite ledges. She dared not look down and clung with desperate fingers onto every exposed root and withered branch, crack and crevice on her perilous descent.

'You idiot! You fat fool! You've really done it now!' Aglia cried as her sister slithered in an avalanche of loose rocks and earth and came to a halt on the step beside her. 'Why did you have to take so long getting down from that ridge, it's not that difficult! We could have vanished among the trees and been in the valley ages ago if you hadn't made such a fuss. Those huntsmen wouldn't have bothered to chase us for long if you hadn't killed one of their cursed dogs. They'll make sure they hunt us down now – they won't let us escape. When they catch us they'll probably flay us alive, or worse, then they'll hang our bleeding skins on the town gates as a warning to everyone else who tries to trespass.'

Aglia paused. The overhanging rock hid them from the huntsmen. She frowned – it was too quiet – and looked up, straining her ears to hear the sounds of the pursuit. She had expected one or more of the huntsmen to try to follow them down but there was no one. Her mind raced: they must be going back along the next valley: there was a chance they could slip quietly under the Withenthorpe Bridge at the head of the valley long before any of the hunters reached it, but they would have to be quick and keep to the stream to throw the dogs off their scent.

'But I didn't kill it, it fell . . .' Harlonis, purple-faced, tried to answer Aglia's accusations but she couldn't find the breath to form the words and it came out in a strangled gasp.

'Keep quiet, stupid. The sound of your babbling is loud enough to wake the dead!' Aglia snapped. She scanned the trees below and tried to make up her mind what they should do. 'Listen, sister, there is a chance we can escape but to do it we have got to reach that stream hidden in the trees below before the riders reach the other end of the valley where they'll see us. We haven't got time for you to be afraid or cling to the cliff while you whine and dribble, do you understand?'

Harlonis nodded bleakly. She wished desperately that she hadn't left the safety of her mother's kitchen. Aglia's face softened. 'Don't look down, it isn't far and I promise I won't let go of you. Here, give me your hand, I'll lead the way.'

Harlonis kept her eyes tightly shut as she shuffled awkwardly sideways, her basket swinging and banging against the rocks, scattering the last of the hyssop which fluttered and spun away below her in the hot, still air. Her mouth was dry and trembling, every nerve and muscle in her body ached. The sun beat relentlessly on the back of her neck and somewhere high above her the piercing shriek of an eagle broke the summer silence. After what seemed an age Aglia whispered, 'You can open your eyes now.'

Harlonis blinked and breathed a sob of relief. They had reached the bottom of the tortuous goats' trail and were standing at the top of a steep slope of broken rock and debris that the previous winter's avalanches had brought down into the valley. Twenty feet below them the trees began: tall, straggling pine and dense copses of mountain ash and silver birch.

'Come on – we've got to reach the bridge before the huntsmen do,' Aglia urged, grabbing her sleeve.

Harlonis hurried after her, losing her balance and slipping and sliding on the steep slope of loose shale in her effort to keep up. 'We would never be in this mess if you hadn't brought us up here. Mother warned us not to trespass,' she muttered miserably as they reached the cover of the trees.

'Be quiet and listen!'

Aglia stopped abruptly. Far away she could hear the sound of barking coming from somewhere below them in the mouth of the valley.

Harlonis came to a shambling halt beside her. 'We are never going to get away. It's all your fault.'

'Shut up! They haven't caught us yet have they? I know of a hundred dark and secret hiding places where the knapweed and water pimpernel grow beside the stream. Come on, we'll follow it down and try to slip past these huntsmen. They can't be everywhere at once and the dogs won't be able to scent us if we keep in the water.'

Harlonis couldn't see any choice other than to follow her sister down through the trees and she gathered up her torn skirts. The sparse mountain grass gave way to a thick carpet of pine needles and it grew dark beneath the canopy. The ferns deadened the sound of their footsteps and elder bushes and blackthorn grew in wild profusion. It took Aglia a few troubled moments to find the goat track they should follow and then, with a rustle of sharp thorns and waving bracken fronds, she vanished with Harlonis close behind her. It was hot and airless beneath the trees and insects hummed around their heads as they followed the meandering path down through the thickening undergrowth. The rush and gurgle of water running over stones and falling into secret pools grew louder and vivid patches of moss and lichen covered the rocks beside the track. The brambles and bracken gave way to high banks of knapweed and woundwort and the heady scent of garlic and wild rosemary filled the air.

'I have never seen so many herbs growing wild together like this,' Harlonis whispered. 'How did you find this place?'

Aglia slowed, picked a sprig of snakeweed and laid it in the basket. 'Birstort, the wheelwright's son, brought me here once, years ago. He showed me a way down the Giant's Steps.'

'You came here alone, with Birstort? What would Mother say if she found out?'

Aglia shrugged off the question. 'You can pick all the plants you can carry here, sister, we'll not return home empty-handed.'

'But it's Lord Cerventis' land.'

'Yes, of course it is, but he didn't plant them did he? They just grow wild here. Now keep quiet and do as I tell you. Those huntsmen are getting closer and they'll be sure to catch us if you don't stop your constant whining.'

Harlonis fell silent, fearing to argue. She was discovering a wild and dangerous side to her sister that she'd never seen before and it frightened her. Instead she listened, listened for the sound of pursuit and kept close to Aglia. She tried to busy herself by refilling her empty basket, picking from the profusion of lush vegetation that grew on each side of the track, but her heart wasn't in it and she gathered nothing of value. The sudden jingle of bit rings, the creak of leather harness and the dull, rhythmic beat of horses' hooves from a couple of paces ahead of them made both women stop and duck down. Aglia crept forward and parted the tangled undergrowth with her hand to watch the horseman ride away from them along a wide, grassy path. The track they were following had brought them too far down into the valley – she had wanted to get to the stream higher up where the ground was wilder and the undergrowth more impenetrable, where there would have been less chance of the hounds picking up their scent. Now they would have to try to dash across the path ahead of them to reach the liquid, silver glint of water that she could see through the trailing curtains of creepers and low branches.

'I wish we had never trespassed up here, or looked into that cursed book: it's brought us nothing but trouble,' Harlonis groaned as the sound of the dogs grew closer.

Aglia glanced back at her irritably and then the beginnings of a cunning idea stirred in her mind and a smile thinned her lips. She gripped Harlonis' arm. 'We've got to get to the water quickly but the magic in that book might help us to escape if the dogs do get on our scent. I looked at pictures of people flying and vanishing up chimneys – perhaps the magic could help us to fly out of these woods. I think I can remember some of the words.'

'No, no, it would be madness.' Harlonis' eyes were round and frantic with fear as she crouched down, refusing to move.

'This is not the time to argue, you fool – with or without the help of the magic we've got to make a dash for the stream now, before the dogs reach this part of the path and scent us!'

Aglia tried to haul her sister to her feet and drag her out through the screen of undergrowth that had hidden them and onto the path but she cowered back.

'You can stay here, you fool, and be torn apart by the dogs for all I care!' Aglia left her and ran for the stream.

Orliak, Lord Cerventis' chief steward, heard a rustle in the undergrowth somewhere ahead of him. He spurred his horse forward and trotted around a sharp bend in the shadow-dappled path just in time to see a woman dressed in ragged commoners' clothes break cover and run across the wide path toward the stream. He gave a shout and hollered up the hounds who were hunting in the trees and undergrowth behind him, and blew short blasts on his hunting horn to warn his master that he had sighted the quarry.

Harlonis felt the terror of being left behind and glanced wildly around as she heard the piercing note of the huntsman's horn. The baying voices of the hounds drew closer and she scrambled after her sister. She saw the huntsman and dogs bearing down on her and cried out as she stumbled in her haste to escape. She would have fallen beneath the horse's hooves if Aglia had not ducked back onto the path and grabbed her arm, pulling at her. 'Run! Run!' she shouted, dragging her sister to her feet.

The path was suddenly full of horsemen and barking dogs drawn by Orliak's call. They were breaking through the undergrowth, trampling everything underfoot, converging on the two helpless women from every direction. The dogs had their scent now and had surged forward, snarling and howling as they bounded along in huge, leaping strides. Aglia staggered as the leading hound leapt at her throat. She barely had time to raise her arm to protect her face as its razor-sharp fangs tore at her flesh. She cried out desperately as another dog leapt at her. 'Gorgo, Mormo, Olet, Olet, Hecate, Alis Ku, make us fly. Banchal, spirit us away. Cerberus, Cerberus, help us! Help us!'

'No, no! Do not say it, the Devil will hear you. We're better off dead!' Harlonis screamed, frantically covering her head with her arms as the pack tore at her clothes and began to overwhelm her and pull her down.

But it was too late. Aglia, in her ignorance, had called out words she did not understand, words from the Book of Knowledge, dark, secret words that stirred and awoke Hecate and Cerberus, the dog demon, in its subterranean caverns. The rough ground beneath their feet trembled and then shook violently, the hounds' savage baying turning to yelps of fear. The hunters reined in their mounts in panic as shadows shrouded the bright sunlight casting a deathly black gloom underneath the trees.

The stifling silence was broken as the ground shook again, buckling and rippling. And then, with a crack that hurt their ears, the earth split open in zigzag fractures and out of the fissures a foul, stinking, hot wind began to rise. It stirred the leaves and bushes, bleaching them leprous-white, and scoured the bark from the tree trunks and overhanging branches. It rose into a howling gale full of demented, shrieking voices. It tore and thrashed at the ferns and brambles, trampling them flat as it sent the hounds whimpering and whining, cowering away on their bellies. The huntsmen's horses reared and plunged, neighing in panic, their eyes ringed white with terror as their riders clung helplessly to their necks. Orliak cried out to his master, begging him to keep back, to escape while there was still time, but the shrieking wind drowned his voice.

The ground convulsed, widening the crack near the women's feet and turning it into a gaping chasm. Clouds of choking, yellow fumes and tongues of sulphurous fire spewed out as the shadowy figure of Hecate, the witch-queen, cloaked in livid flames, emerged. The grass and undergrowth shrivelled to ash in front of her as a hideous dog, straining at a leash of iron links, clawed his way up out of the fire-pits of Hell at her feet. Cerberus snarled and shook its maggoty hide, rippling the rotting flesh that hung from its bones, twisting and turning each of its three savage heads and sending drools of glistening strings of fire from its jowls toward the cowering hounds.

'Who has summoned me and my hearth-beast Cerberus to devour and kill, rend and tear, to savour the taste of living flesh?' the woman hissed and the monstrous dog snarled, baring its fangs, eyes glowing with pinpoints of fire, and as it leapt forward ready to begin the destruction, shadows of death spread out from its outstretched claws, enveloping and swallowing the helpless victims and muffling their screams.

'I . . . I . . . I did.' Aglia struggled to her feet, sick and terrified at what she had done. She grabbed at her sister's hand. 'Get up, Harlonis, quickly – we must escape before Hecate or that creature turn on us.' And she tried to pull and drag her sister toward the stream.

Harlonis tried to run but her legs were paralysed with fear. She clawed at the ground, crying and sobbing, desperate to escape from the terror.

Lord Cerventis waited impatiently astride his charger standing on the Withenthorpe Bridge. 'What in God's name is Orliak up to? It shouldn't take him this long to comb the valley for those trespassers.'

The leash of his black mastiff, Solomon, hung loose across the pommel of his saddle: the hunt was taking too long and he had a host of important matters to attend to. His huntsmen seemed to have spent hours beating the dense undergrowth of the narrow valley and all to no avail. 'We've wasted time enough – those hounds must have the noses of sheep to have let the quarry get clean away.' He waved an armoured gauntlet in irritation at the cloud of insects that buzzed and droned around his head. Gathering the reins, he rode toward the centre of the bridge, the dog trotting lazily at the horse's heels, and called out to the two archers he had stationed at the bottom of the steep bank close to the surface of the fast-flowing stream, ordering them back up onto the road. 'I'll have them flogged raw,' he grumbled as they left the bridge and rode higher up the valley.

Suddenly the sharp notes from Orliak's horn echoed through the trees and one of the archers laughed. 'They've not escaped Orliak, Eagle-eye. We'd better get back onto the bank of the stream, sire, in case they drive them down toward us.'

'No, wait!' Cerventis frowned as Orliak's warning shout came faintly through the trees almost before the sound of the horn died away. He pirouetted his horse back onto the bridge and stood in the stirrups, shading his eyes with his hand against the low afternoon sun and listening for the sounds of the hunt as he anxiously scanned the trees.

'By all the saints, what infernal deviltry is that?' A thick cloud of yellow smoke mushroomed up and hung in the tree-tops less than sixty feet away from them. He heard the furious baying of his hounds turn to yelping howls and the shouts of his hunters became screams of terror.

'There must be more of them than we thought. It's an armed band and the huntsmen are under attack. Come quick, they need help, follow me!' he shouted to his men, slipping the leash of his dog and using the handle of his hunting whip on his horse's flank spurred it into a gallop onto the path beside the stream and followed the huge hound into the undergrowth.

The frantic cries of his huntsmen, the screaming

neighing of their horses and the yelps of the hounds were loud and piercing at one moment and then became mysteriously faint and muffled and seemed to be far away. The stench of sulphur was becoming stronger the further Cerventis ventured along the track. A riderless horse, its reins broken and flapping around its forelegs, its flanks a mass of torn and bloody flesh, burst through the undergrowth a stride ahead of him and a terrified hound which bounded between its legs made it stumble and lose its footing. The horse pecked and ploughed up clods of loose earth and stone with its nose before regaining its feet. It snorted, nostrils flared, eyes white with fear, and banged heavily against Lord Cerventis' horse, leaving livid smears of blood on the lord's knee and almost tipping him out of the saddle as it fled toward the bridge. Another hound broke cover, yelping as it followed the bolting horse.

Cerventis cursed and fought to control his terrified mount as it careered off balance and then veered off the path through the gap the riderless horse had trampled in the undergrowth. He barely had the time to draw his sword before the sound of an unearthly, bellowing roar shook the trees. His horse sensed the danger and tried to shy away, rearing and plunging as it cut a new path through the almost impenetrable tangle of brambles and briars. Cerventis hauled on the reins and raked his spurs across the horse's flanks, forcing it to turn back, and with a brutal crack from the hunting whip, he urged it on. The horse flattened its ears and surged forward through the thorny, overhanging trees, making Cerventis hunch low along its neck as the leaves and branches whipped and cut painfully across his face. He raised his sword arm to shield and protect his eyes as he shouted for Orliak, but his voice was suddenly lost, muffled by a gloomy, reeking darkness that smothered the trees and bushes in claustrophobic silence. His horse faltered, its mouth opening in a silent scream as it reared up, throwing Cerventis out of the saddle as it thrashed at the foul, stinking air with its forelegs before turning and fleeing.

Lord Cerventis hit the ground hard, his sword flying from his hand, and rolled over and over through the dense brambles and bracken until he came up against the gnarled trunk of a mountain oak. The silence was shattered by another, louder, snarling roar and bright tongues of fire lit up the false darkness. He scrambled unsteadily to his feet and gave a wounded, strangled cry of terror before falling back, helpless with fear, against the tree trunk. Less than a dozen paces away a huge, diabolical creation, a hideous, monstrous mockery of a dog with three savage, snarling heads was moving through the trees toward Orliak who lay trapped beneath his fallen horse. It was mauling the bodies of two of his hounds with its enormous claws, dragging them through the dirt while crushing and greedily devouring another, crunching flesh and bones in one set of its cavernous, drooling jaws. Cerventis sank down, a knot of fear clutching his stomach. He felt so alone, so helpless, and his blood ran cold as a pitiless shriek of laughter echoed through the trees and he looked behind the monstrous apparition to see the tall, shadowy figure of a woman clothed in a cloak of dancing flames. Her voice rose, urging the beast forward to kill and feast on the fallen rider lying helpless beneath his dead horse.

'Kill! Kill! Gobble the flesh and gnaw at his bones!' she shrieked, slipping the leash of red-hot glowing iron links from around its neck. The huge creature bounded forward, fire and steam boiling from its mouths.

'Hecate and the hell-hound, Cerberus,' whispered Cerventis. He had seen pictures and heard fearsome stories of the dog-demon and his hands trembled as he desperately searched the undergrowth for his sword. He had to try to do something, anything, to stop this creature and his mistress from Hell. But his sword was lost, buried somewhere in the rough grass and trampled undergrowth beyond his reach. He had nothing else to fight with against this dog-demon except his bone-handled knife.

Orliak screamed and frantically tried to ward off the monstrous creature as it leapt on top of him. He flailed his arms and beat against its fire-wreathed heads as it savaged and clawed at his chest, tearing his doublet to ribbons. Cerventis cursed under his breath and rose to his feet. He could not cower and hide no matter how helplessly afraid he felt. He could not watch while his friend and steward was mauled by this monster from Hell. He reached back to unsheathe the dagger from where it hung from his belt and he felt something tug hard against his wrist. He glanced fearfully down not knowing what to expect and saw that a coil of the long, iron-tailed whip that he carried had somehow wound itself around his wrist as he had been thrown from his horse.

'By God's great mercy!' he cried, as he unwound it. He gripped the thick, hide-bound handle firmly in his right hand and yanked the other end free from where it had snaked through the bushes, snagging and curling amongst the tangled thorns. His hands trembled as he quickly gathered the long leather-woven whip, threaded with fine silver wire, and wound it into six tight coils.

'God give me the strength,' he whispered, pinching the armoured iron tail between thumb and finger, ready to hurl it at the monstrous hound. Summoning all his courage he cried out and charged forward across the burned and blackened ground. 'Get back you reeking beast! Get back you foul despoiler of the sunlight! Get back and return where you belong in the infernal fire-pits of Hell!'

Cerberus heard his shout and dropped Orliak, snarling as he spun round toward Cerventis and arching his back in readiness to leap at its attacker. The witch-goddess Hecate turned her head in fury that anyone would dare to challenge her and shrieked, cursing him and lifting her hands to stir up a gale of burning hot ash from the fire-pits below that rained down, scalding and burning him as he ran.

Lord Cerventis' desperate onslaught against the powers of darkness faltered. He staggered to a halt screaming and almost blinded by the hot, stinking deluge that enveloped him and set the undergrowth around them alight. It scorched and burned his face and singed his hair. Dimly through the swirling particles of fiery ash he saw the beast Cerberus rush toward him, looming bigger and bigger with each leaping stride. The hell-hound's snarling, cavernous jaws stretched wide, ready to tear him to pieces when Solomon leapt upon the beast from the burning undergrowth, sinking his teeth into its throat, sending it crashing to the ground. Cerberus snarled and threw the mastiff off, then charged. Lord Cerventis hurled the iron-tailed whip high into the choking clouds of ash above the advancing monster's heads. He knew he had to wait until the unwinding coils had stretched taut before cracking it and he had to fight down the impulse to turn and run and use those last precious moments to escape the shadows of death that were swarming across the ground to engulf him. He felt the slight tug on the handle of the whip and, gripping it with both hands, he jerked it backward with all his strength, making the flail crack and sing as it scythed down through the putrid air, crying out for the power of God to come to his aid as he did so.

The spinning flail seemed suddenly to burn white-hot in the swirling sulphurous darkness, as if blessed with the pure light of St Elmo's fire. It struck the oncoming beast with such force that it almost pulled Lord Cerventis off his feet. The huge creature floundered and crashed to the ground a pace in front of him, sprawling on its side upon the blackened, burning earth. Solomon immediately leapt on top of the creature, savaging its throat. Cerberus writhed and clawed at the ground, its jaws frothing and snapping open and shut, its bellowing snarls turning gradually into howls of pain. Bright fountains of yellow, silvery slime oozed up from its torn windpipe and bubbled across the ruptured skin where the iron tail of the whip had cut through its maggot-ridden hide, shearing deeply into its rotting flesh and crumbling bones, unravelling the spells and dark, venomous secrets that bound its sinews together.

Hecate screamed, her shadowy face seething with rage as she watched her beast so easily brought down. She cursed and wove new spells through Cerberus' shuddering body and then raised her arms, brewing up boiling streams of molten rock to spew out of the fire-pits and spread in a shimmering, bubbling lake all around her. She stabbed her finger up at the sky and drew down jagged bolts of lightning that she hurled into Cerberus' flanks, driving the dog-demon into a savage fury. 'Kill! Kill! Rend and tear, gnaw his bones!' she shrieked, forcing the beast to rear up and shake the mastiff off.

Lord Cerventis quailed beneath the ferocity of the attack. He stumbled backward, pulling as hard as he could to free the whip from the monster's body. The end of the whip broke free and snaked back toward him. 'Get back, you hound of Hell! Get away from here!' he shouted, making the sign of the cross against the black shadows that were engulfing him as he strove to drive the creature away, sending the flail sailing amongst the trees high above Cerberus' three snarling heads.

The whip streaked out and the iron tail dropped faster than a stone, striking the monster between its shoulderblades, shearing through its putrid flesh, making the huge beast bellow with pain and reel backward, its back rigidly arched as it clawed at the empty air above Cerventis' head. The dog-demon staggered on its hind legs as it towered over him and the reeking stink of scalding saliva that drooled from its gaping jaws made him choke and gasp for air. Solomon, torn and bloody, made a last, desperate lunge at the beast. Slowly, with a terrible, wailing howl, Cerberus began to topple forward, its claws rending the air as it tried to crush and smother him as it fell.

Lord Cerventis leapt backward as the huge creature crashed to the ground. Its long, curved talons struck his breast-plate, gouging and peeling long, jagged tears through the thick layers of beaten silver and sending him sprawling onto his back amongst the brambles. The force of the blow knocked all the breath out of him and he lay there for a moment unable to move. Frantically gasping for air he struggled to get up, brandishing the whip and sending the iron tail in a whistling, shrieking arc around his head. Cerberus, his bleeding body shuddering and convulsing as the mastiff's teeth hung grimly onto its rotten flesh, cowered away, defeated, as the flail blazed white-hot in a glowing circle above their heads. The hell-dog whimpered and broke free from the great hound's grip to drag its oozing carcass back across the burnt and tortured ground to plunge over the lip of the yawning split in the earth. It howled mournfully at its mistress as it vanished in a billowing cloud of yellow smoke and fire back into the subterranean pits of Hell.

'I curse you, Lord Cerventis. I shall pluck out your eyes for the worms to devour and your flesh shall burn forever!' Hecate shrieked, her shadowy form rising above the ground and advancing on him in waves of writhing shapes of fire that kindled the leaves and set light to the branches as they spread toward him through the trees.

Cerventis cried out and spun the whip faster and faster around his head to ward them off, stirring up such a wind that it caught at the advancing apparitions, folding and crushing them together and sending them spinning away from him in a blazing cyclone of fire that shrieked and howled as it glowed hotter than the mouth of a furnace. Suddenly the column of fire exploded into a blazing ball that fizzed and sparkled as it drifted away to nothing on the evening breeze.

The blackened ground trembled and the yawning fire cracks snapped shut. Hecate and her demon-dog had vanished completely but the echo of her voice lingered as the smoke and fumes slowly cleared and the early evening sunlight began to filter through the gloom. The words were clearly audible. 'From this day forward, the House of Cerventis and all who dwell within it are cursed. Cursed to burn for all eternity.'

Lord Cerventis knelt, exhausted, his hand upon Solomon's bloody flank, comforting the trembling dog as it tried to struggle to its feet. He listened with a shudder of fear, hearing the dying echoes and knowing in his heart that the words would stay with him forever, that he would never be free of their memory. He made the sign of the cross as he prayed, rubbed his hand across his forehead and climbed wearily to his feet. A movement on the edge of the path caught his eye and he saw Orliak, his steward, struggling to pull himself clear of his dead horse.

'Orliak! Thank God you are alive!' he called out, coiling his whip in his hand as he crossed the burned clearing and hurried toward him.

'Master, look behind you!' Orliak cried out suddenly. 'The two women, the ones we were hunting, the ones who called up that demon and her monstrous hound – they are getting away.'

Solomon growled and limped toward them as

Cerventis spun round, his whip hand raised, to see the two ragged women. The smoke fumes had almost hidden them from his sight but he could see them clearly now, scrambling to escape through a break in the dense under-growth, hurrying down to the bank of the stream. 'Stop! I command you to stop!' he shouted angrily as he began to run toward them.

Aglia looked quickly back at the sound of his voice. 'Come on, he'll never catch us now!' she cried to her sister, leaping down the steep bank into the stream.

Harlonis threw herself through the gap, but her skirts snagged on the thorns. She cried out and struggled to free herself. Lord Cerventis aimed his whip as he ran, and as the woman's skirt tore free of the thorns and she began to slide down the bank away from him, he sent the flail singing through the air. It struck the side of her face, cutting through the flesh on her cheek, opening it up in a bloody line. He stumbled, his foot catching in the brambles, and he pulled hard on the handle of the whip to keep his balance, brutally jerking the iron tail free from her face.

She screamed as the flail hit her, the searing pain exploded inside her head as it was torn free. She toppled forward into the fast-flowing water of the stream, her head striking a mossy boulder, knocking her uncon-scious. Slowly turning in the current until she was face-down she began to float away in a widening streak of blood. Lord Cerventis reached the break in the under-growth and caught hold of Solomon's spiked collar. He saw the woman floating away in the stream and thought her dead. He hesitated on the bank as he heard his stew-ard calling out to him. He turned back, coiling his whip, and went to help his friend.

Aglia, who had been hiding beneath the overhanging bank, splashed out through the shallow water and waded after Harlonis. She grabbed her bloody head and held it above the water to stop her from drowning. Tears of rage coursed down her cheeks and anger boiled up and darkened her heart, and she swore that Lord Cerventis would pay dearly for what he had done.

The Black Death

AGLIA DRAGGED HER sister's body out of the water and hid beneath a tangle of briar bushes, crouching down, hardly daring to move or breathe in case they were discovered. The sounds of the hounds crashing through the trees and undergrowth were getting dangerously close. Then she heard Lord Cerventis calling them back, ordering them to abandon the chase and get the uninjured huntsmen to safety. She waited until long after the sounds of the hunting party had receded before whispering to Harlonis and shaking her fiercely. Her sister groaned and cried out as she regained consciousness and Aglia knelt down to examine the wound in her cheek, covering it with wet rags to stem the bleeding. The gash was ugly but it wouldn't prove fatal: what really worried Aglia was how she was to explain the day's events to her mother when they arrived home. The huntsmen were sure to have spread wild stories of the witch-queen and her hell-hound – they were already talking of it as they passed.

'Harlonis, get up, we've got to get back before the gates of the town are locked for the night. Come on, hold my hand, I'll lead the way.'

Aglia let out a sigh of relief as they reached the main road that looked down on the town; she could see that the gates were still open. The lamps on the walls illuminated a group of travelling merchants who were shepherding in a slow-moving caravan. The heavily-laden pack animals had stirred up a thick, hazy cloud of dust which was fogging the lamplight and making the drovers choke and cough.

Aglia linked arms with her sister and hurried her down to join the tail end of the caravan. They mingled with the drovers and slipped between the weary pack mules that had unknowingly brought the Black Death with them through the high mountain passes, hidden in the swaying corn bins, lying in the sagging flour sacks and pressed in amongst the thick bales of silks. Together they all passed in a long procession through the gates and the two girls made their way back to the Apothecary's Quarter.

There were stifling days when the air in the narrow streets grew so hot and heavy it became difficult to breathe; but the town bustled with frantic energy despite the weather. Crowds thronged the market-places and filled the alms houses and taverns, ignoring all the precautions issued by the Council of Elders which had been devised for their protection. They jostled and pushed together, tasting the sweetmeats and sampling the wondrous rarities the merchants' caravan had brought to them through the mountains. Shouts of barter rang out at every merchant's stall, yet the plague was not forgotten. Anxious voices asked the journeymen for news of the Black Death at every opportunity. Which towns and villages had it already struck, how close was it, how many had died? The travelling apothecary was besieged with questions and his cures and lotions for every malady were sold out before the first day's trading was half done. He laughed and assured them of their good health, ignorant that the plague's terrible shadow already lay across them.

Twice during those frantic market days there were sudden commotions amongst the stalls when hordes of black rats were discovered amongst the merchandise. Squabbling urchins accidentally overturned an almost empty corn bin and spilt open a spice drum and on both occasions the crowd scattered as rats tumbled out of their hiding places and escaped, scuttling away in every direction – running across the cobbles, darting between the feet of the startled crowd to disappear into the maze of dingy alleyways and lanes surrounding the markets.

The merchants cursed at the vermin and swore that although they had seen hundreds of the rats in towns and some in the countryside, they had never known them to invade a travelling caravan in such numbers. They declared it a mystery and reluctantly pledged to take back any of their goods the rats might have soiled. They added, in their worldly voices, that they had passed whole villages who were close to starving, riddled with the Black Death, who would have been glad to feed from the crumbs the rats had left.

Whispers of uncertainty rippled through the crowds, a sudden realization that the merchants, by virtue of their trade, rubbed shoulders with everyone in their travels. They stood next to the sick, the poor and, perhaps unknowingly, even those afflicted with the plague. The mood of the crowded market-place turned against the travelling men and many of them were stoned and driven out beyond the gates. Their corn bins, their bales of silk and drums of spices were thrown into a huge heap in the centre of the square where they were set alight.

The sight of so many black rats scattering across the cobbles added fuel to another darker rumour that was being told and retold in every ale house and hostelry throughout the town: the story of how Lord Cerventis' huntsmen had unexpectedly come upon two women, ragged women from the poorer part of town, trespassing on the lord's lands. When Orliak had challenged them they had summoned up a hideous three-headed demon hound and its ghostly keeper from the bowels of the earth and had laughed and shrieked and spat venom that had made leaves shrivel. It was said that the creature had defended them and had struck terror into the horses' hearts, causing them to rear and cast their riders to the ground. It had savaged and killed many of the lord's hounds and none dared to approach it. It had mauled Orliak near to death before Lord Cerventis had arrived and, with the help of his hearth-dog, Solomon, and his hunting whip, he had driven the monstrous creature back into the foul pits of Hell. The worst part of the story, the part where the teller's voice fell to a whisper and the crowd huddled closer, was that although their lord was sure he had killed one of them the other had escaped. Their lord insisted they were local hags and that the surviving one must be hiding somewhere amongst them – somewhere in the town. An unnatural hush would spread as the teller finished and reached for his ale.

Furtive whispers would pass through the crowd, speculation was rife. Someone mentioned Mother Zem, but someone else called out, 'You'll only find good, wholesome cures in our Apothecary's Quarter. Old Mother Zem doesn't hold with witchcraft or consulting with the Devil. She brews all manner of wonderful cures and lotions against all the evil humours.'

'Yes, you're right, the old woman made a fearful fuss a while back, she beat both her daughters with a stick for making signs in the dust. I have heard tell she made them do penance for their foolishness.'

'Well she's keeping them busy now: they're all brewing potions and syrups against the plague. They sell the best medicines in the town.'

Mother Zem had forced her daughters to tell her the truth of what had happened in the forest and had wrung her hands in despair when she had heard of Aglia's foolishness. She cursed her stupidity for meddling with the

Black Art despite her warnings and she made her do a thousand penances. She prayed that God would forgive her because if he didn't then the Devil or his emissaries would be waiting, dwelling in the shadows for their time to claim her. She banished the two girls to the chimney-hearth and set them to watch over the cauldron, ordering them to keep out of sight until the rumours of the witch-queen and her demon-hound had died away.

Ever since that dreadful day Lord Cerventis was gripped by a great fear. He couldn't shake off the echo of Hecate's words as she had vanished back into the pits of Hell. He was afraid of her power, of the black magic she would surely use against his family. He was sure she could make his cattle and horses sick, poison his wells and wither his vines and he had masses and special prayers sung every morning and night. But the more he thought about it the more he became convinced that he had to get to the root of the evil. He had to find the woman who had escaped in the woods.

He sent Orliak and his agents to mingle with the market crowds and listen in the ale houses. He was sure that the tavern gossips would eventually lead him to her. He summoned two priests from his private chapel to accompany them into the town and charged them to search through the Apothecary's Quarter to find the woman who had summoned the witch-queen. But the search was never begun.

Orliak was riding at the head of the small company as they crossed the Withenthorpe Bridge and he looked down at the town spread out below them. Black pennants hung from the gates and every church tower and cold dread fell upon him. The plague had struck. He turned around and shouted to the company, ordering them to retreat and galloped back over the bridge in a blaze of sparks eager to tell his master that the shadow of the Black Death had reached the town and he must lock his doors and shutter his windows against it.

The plague struck first amongst the journeymen and merchants who had been driven out of the market-place and had set up a temporary camp outside the walls of the town. The sickness gradually showed itself during those busy days while the travellers were preparing the caravan to move south into the lowlands. Many of the merchants and their mule drivers began to complain of feeling light-headed, some felt sudden chills and giddiness that brought them to their knees: others were burned up with fever, their joints swelling so much they were unable to move. During the third or fourth night a drover and a journeyman suddenly died. A great shout of fear went up when their bodies were stripped for burial, for the purple swellings of the plague were discovered in their armpits and groins.

Panic followed the discovery faster than fire through summer grass. Pandemonium broke out as the travellers who thought they were still healthy shunned the sick. By morning all those who could travel had abandoned the camp leaving the sickly to the mercy of the people of Aurillac. Word that the plague was rife amongst the merchants and that some had been left to die reached the townspeople early in the morning. The Council of Elders, terrified that the pestilence now loomed so close, ordered the gates of the town be shut fast and locked against travellers and, on pain of death, that none should be allowed to enter or to leave. Fire-baskets of juniper, vine leaves and rosemary were to be burned continually upon the walls to ward off the evil vapours and prevent them from settling over the town.

The people of Aurillac were forbidden by their Council to help the people in the abandoned tents – they could do nothing to alleviate their suffering. They covered their ears to block out the cries of the sick and dying as they went about their business. Within days they had to carry perfumed apples of amber or mixtures of black pepper and red and white sandal-rose leaves with camphor to mask the growing stench of unburied corpses that had begun to putrefy in the unnaturally hot weather. The buzz of the clouds of flies and the stink of death that hung over the temporary camp grew worse by the hour. The travellers' pack animals dragged and broke free from their picket lines and wandered unattended on the road, foraging for themselves and trampling the crops in the fields.

The church bells were rung continuously and masses for the people's deliverance were said from morning to night. The townspeople hoped and prayed that by isolating themselves, by locking out the dying merchants, they might escape. But the plague had already breached the gates and spread secretly through Aurillac, carried by the rats that had travelled with the merchants' caravan. They had taken the pestilence with them as they scattered across the crowded market-place into every courtyard, street, house and hovel. The plague ran unchecked, burrowing through the rubbish that littered the narrow lanes and alleyways, multiplying and breeding in the rank, stinking midden ditches. It had already invaded every dark corner and secret hiding place it could find.

The diseased rats began to die and the swarms of plague-infected fleas that had lived on their bodies began to migrate to seek new sources of food and softer, smoother skin to bite silently with their kiss of death. They would leave minute puncture wounds that would ripen and fester as the hot summer days went past and become the hard, purpling boils and suppurating swellings of the Black Death.

For three agonizing days and sleepless nights the town waited. The watchmen listened as the cries of the dying merchants beyond the walls grew gradually weaker and weaker until the travellers' tents and booths lay utterly silent. The quiet was broken only by the harsh cries of the flocks of carrion crows attracted by the smell of rotting flesh as they strutted and pecked and fought over the dead.

For another hot, unbearable day the travellers' bodies lay where they had fallen, swelling and turning black in the heat while the Council of Elders argued and became more undecided about whether they should burn or bury the corpses. The townspeople were afraid to venture near the camp and wanted it burned, along with the bodies and everything else the merchants had brought with them. But the priests and doctors warned against such foolishness, insisting that to burn the corpses would release the evil vapours of the plague still trapped in their bodies and send them up into the air amidst the smoke and ashes to fall and settle on everyone who lived nearby and infect them with the disease. They were adamant that the travellers must be buried deep in the ground, their bodies covered with thick layers of lime and earth to stop the plague from spreading.

Eventually, as night was falling, the Council agreed to bury the bodies. The gates were unlocked and a party of grave-diggers were sent out to dig a deep pit, to throw the bodies of the merchants into it and cover them with a huge mound of earth. Altar candles were burned late into the night in every church as a thanksgiving for their deliverance. Prayers of gratitude were given and there was such an air of relief that hardly anyone noticed the first trickle of deaths in the town. It was only later the next day and even more the day after when the bills of the dead were posted in the market square, showing that six people had already died, that the awful reality struck home. Despite all the prayers and litanies they had sung in the flickering candle-light, despite all the selfless actions of the priests who had swathed themselves in sackcloth and covered their heads with ashes, despite the baskets of burning herbs set so carefully along the walls, despite everything that had been done by the Council of Elders, the plague had come to the town.

The Black Death crept silently, relentlessly amongst them. Nothing, not one of a thousand repeated rumours or travellers' tales, not one verse from one book, no matter how well or how vividly told, could have prepared the people of Aurillac for the violence, the suddenness, of the disease once it had begun. Nor would they have believed the speed with which it raged unchecked through the streets, smoothing its hideous shroud over everyone who stood in its path.

The town was thrown into chaos. Public order dissolved into panic as that first trickle of deaths became a flood. Assurances from the doctors, apothecaries and brewers of lotions, that their wholesome cures would halt the plague, were all swept away in the next few, terrifying, days. Their words disappeared faster than empty straws in a gale. Their ointments of calamine, vinegar and rosewater and their powders of myrrh, saffron and damascus did little more than perfume the pervading odour of death. Their bleeding and their leeching wet dishes and blunted knives but it did not cure the sick. The wailing laments of the dying grew louder and louder as the shadow of the plague engulfed whole neighbourhoods.

The Council of Elders met in emergency sessions and gradually managed to restore a semblance of order. People were dying in their hundreds, too many by far for the authorities to cope with, and many of them were left undiscovered in their houses until the stench of putrefying flesh became so unbearable that the neighbours were forced to drag them out into the street. The Council ordered that each and every house infected with the plague must bear the mark of a red cross and that searchers would visit those dwellings during the hours of darkness and bring out their dead. Grave-diggers were ordered to dig vast grave pits beyond the walls as they readied themselves for the death count.

All night long the streets of Aurillac echoed to the slow rumble of the death carts and the mournful tolling of the bell they rang to herald their coming. The carts swayed and creaked beneath the weight of the corpses as they slowly trundled out to the waiting buriers. To the helpless townspeople, the plague seemed to drift invisibly from street to street, invading every house and hovel. They could not feel its touch as it passed amongst them nor see the inevitable, indelible fingerprint of death upon their skin until it was too late.

In desperation many who survived those first nightmare days began to search for ways to stay alive, trying every lotion and cure they could lay their hands on, even dabbling in magic and turning to soothsayers for help. They squandered their possessions on zodiac signs and words written in the shapes of magical pyramids to scrawl upon their doors, words and numbers they didn't understand. But a rumour began to spread that held more hope than all those magic charms and signs, a rumour that the Black Death had not spread through the gloomy alleyways of Gedney, the area that lay on the far side of the Apothecary's Quarter and that Mother Zem and her daughters and almost all who lived close to them neither sickened nor died of the plague.

A rumour that there must be some magic, some power, in the potions they brewed so that the pestilence was passing them by.

Daily more and more people began to gather outside Mother Zem's door begging loudly for cures, choking and rubbing their eyes in the acrid smoke and fumes that belched continuously from her chimney.

'Aglia – come out here, you lazy, useless daughter.

Come out at once – there are neighbours, good people, clamouring at our door, calling out for the wholesome medicines we brew against the plague. Come out now and serve their needs.'

Aglia appeared in the doorway of the cubbyhole, her face tight and drawn, with a dark shadow of fear and fatigue around her eyes. She let the rough hemp curtain fall back into place behind her and turned slowly towards the rows of jars and vessels holding potions and cures which filled the huge kitchen table and the shelves that lined the walls of the room.

'Tell them there will be a newly-prepared syrup of camphor veined with silver ready to drink by sunset,' the old woman called after her, blinking her watery eyes in the haze of the stinking, yellow smoke that issued from the dying fire. She riddled the ash with her foot before digging her hand into the earthenware pitcher beside her and throwing another handful of quickblaze onto the dying embers and watched thoughtfully as her secret mixture of sulphur, arsenic, saltpetre and antimony burst into bright yellow flames that curled up to lick greedily around the bottom of the fat, soot-black belly of the cauldron. The glutinous surface of the thick syrup began to bubble as the old woman fed more fuel into the fire.

The moment Aglia reached the threshold dragging two of the heavy stone medicine jars the crowd began to shout and surge forwards. She hesitated, sensing that something was different in their voices, there was an edge of anger, a violence she hadn't heard before. Reluctantly, unsure of the milling masses, she stepped out into the street, setting the two jars down beside her. A hush spread through the crowd. She frowned and bit her lip as she began to reach for the wooden measuring cup that hung from her belt. Suddenly an accusing shout froze her.

'She's not a healer! She's one of the women I saw in the woods. She's the one Lord Cerventis has been looking for. She's the woman who called up that monster, that demon-hound! My lord will give anyone a purse of silver for her!'

Aglia gasped and stepped backward, covering her mouth with her hand to strangle a scream as one of the huntsmen began to thrust his way toward the front of the crowd.

'Leave her be!' cursed a tall iron-master. As the huntsman tried to push past him he gripped his shoulder with a huge callused hand to restrain him.

'It wasn't me. I . . . I haven't left my mother's hearth, I've been here all the while helping her to brew the lotions. I have wholesome syrups . . .'

Suddenly other voices sneered. 'We want the secret ingredients you put in your potions and powders, woman. We want to know how you protect yourself against the plague.'

'But . . . but . . . there isn't anything . . .' she began, but another voice shouted her down.

'There must be something, some secret, some magic you use to protect yourselves. We can all see there's nobody round here dying of the plague. We want your magic!'

Aglia stared at them, speechless, as a chorus of voices demanded and chanted. 'We want magic. Weave a spell to drive the plague away.'

'No, no, I cannot!' she cried.

A single harsh voice in the front of the crowd cut across her denial. 'Give us some real magic, dearie, or we'll hand you over to Cerventis' men and burn your home to the ground.'

The crowd surged forward angrily, their faces set hard. Somebody pushed against one of the heavy stone jars and it toppled over, spilling the contents in sluggish yellow ripples that soaked slowly into the trampled dirt. Aglia looked frantically at the sea of advancing faces. She had to do something. She had to think quickly.

Her mother's voice called out anxiously from the gloomy darkness of the kitchen. Aglia had no time to answer her question or call for help – the mood of the crowd was turning against her. A sharp stone thrown from somewhere in the press of bodies struck the clay wall close to her head quickly followed by another. Instinctively she ducked and threw up her arm to shield her face.

Voices began to rise in an ugly chant. 'Magic! Magic! Give us your magic. Give us your magic or we'll stone you to death!'

A hail of missiles, filth and rubbish from the gutter, peppered the wall and some of the objects hurled at her struck her chest and arms making her scream and stumble backwards. She was terrified and cowering down, too frightened to deny their accusations, too weak to placate them, too afraid to do anything to stop the rage that was about to destroy her and her family. The huntsman struggled and shouted at the crowd, trying to call them off. He broke free from the iron-master's grip and burst to the front of the mob, making a grab for Aglia's wrist and then turning to shout at the people.

'No! My master will give a whole purse of silver for her alive.'

The crowd began to shuffle to a halt. She could see their anger turn to greed and it made her realize that her only escape lay in her magic. If she could weave a spell, something so powerful it would ward off the plague and strike down her pursuers she would be safe. But what? Her dabbling in the Black Arts had been accidental and her mother had watched her like a hawk since that disastrous incident in the woods and had kept the forbidden book firmly locked away. Pulling her wrist free she cried out the words she had read in secret, words she did not begin to understand.

'Gorgo, Mormo, Rondmo, Sator Zoros Rondmo!'

Symbols, words and images from the book suddenly filled her mind and she began to shriek. Demonic voices and scuttling whispers clouded her sanity and she threw back her head as words surged up her throat. Her piercing cry abruptly stopped the advancing mob and suddenly they saw a shape in the doorway beside her. It was part-human, part-beast, but it seemed no more than half-formed, shrouded in windings and muslin rags that blended and merged as it vanished through the pores of Aglia's skin. For a moment Aglia crouched in the doorway shivering, her skin turning a livid, leprous white, her eyes burning with an intense, penetrating stare that sent a ripple of fear through the onlookers. Slowly, the dark powers of the forbidden book possessed her, devouring and blackening her soul, infusing her mind with madness, flooding it with strange, vivid images of the dark powers she had summoned to save her.

The crowd shrank back becoming mere formless shapes in the gutter, while in their place it appeared that brilliantly coloured serpents slithered and writhed in, out and through a carpet of bleached white bones. Horned beasts, satyrs, black-robed witches and all the hideous creatures that dwelt in the half light capered and danced in a circle, treading the bones back into the dusty earth around her. Aglia felt light and empty, as if she would float and the slightest breath of wind would carry her up to soar and glide with the carrion flocks that circled endlessly above the grave pits. She felt as if she could walk through fire and pass unhindered through any wall or obstacle that lay in her path. She felt the power of the magic tingle her fingertips, making her want to throw back her head and shriek with laughter, to spit and shout at her persecutors, to curse them and strike them down with searing daggers of magic. But the dark, shadowy figure that had possessed her forbade it. The voice of Hecate scratched painfully at her ears, hungry for revenge, and made her listen to the howling cries of the beast, Cerberus, as it licked at its wounds deep in the bowels of the earth.

As she knelt in the dirt, Hecate's voice was as soft as rustling velvet, whispering as it fed her anger and showing her new images, vivid pictures of Lord Cerventis playing with his two infant children: carrying them upon his shoulders, wrapping them in their downy swaddling clothes. They were so healthy – not a mark nor a blemish upon their skin. As each picture faded Aglia saw vivid images of the pestilence raging through the town and the stink of the grave pits choked in her throat.

'They must be punished. They must burn!' Hecate's voice was now at the very centre of her soul.

Abruptly, the serpents, witches and beasts vanished. Aglia was aware of the crowd pressing in, watching with bated breath, waiting for her trance to pass, waiting for the magic. There, standing in front of her, reaching out to grab at her, was the huntsman, Lord Cerventis' servant. Aglia focused on the man and the hatred stirred inside her soul, turning her eyes into cunning, glittering slits that made him hesitate and try to escape.

'I will not weave my spells while he is free!' she said quietly, pointing a quivering finger at the terrified man.

A mass of hands reached out and caught hold of the huntsman, wresting him to his knees. Aglia shivered as she watched, her lips thinning into a hissing sneer of triumph. Then suddenly her body convulsed and she leapt high into the air above the startled faces of the crowd and began to cry out in strange, unrecognizable tongues, strengthening the spells that held sway over the people. She landed lightly on her toes and cavorted around the crowd, almost dancing before dropping to her hands and knees, snatching up handfuls of refuse and excrement from the overflowing midden ditch and hurling it up into the air. The power of her magic shrouded the eyes of the mob and they imagined that a flock of blackbirds and singing thrushes had fluttered down to perch upon their shoulders. Suddenly she became statue-still, her mouth gaping open, her eyes shining and staring blankly ahead. The spectre of Hecate filled her and her voice, hollow and echoing, poured out dark, mesmerizing words of magic, bewitching, trapping and entangling them with her power.

Now she stole softly from person to person, filling their ears with poisonous whispers, feeding on their weaknesses and their terror of the plague. Visually she unfolded each of their feared things, stripping away their defences, making them choke and gag at the reek of the unburied dead, dragging them down into the claustrophobic darkness of the grave pits to burrow with the fat, white worms through the putrefying bodies of the dead. As their cries and screams for deliverance from these dark, sinister visions rose, Aglia/Hecate soothed and promised them her magic, promised to weave a spell so powerful, so absolute that it would protect them and their loved ones from all the horrors of the Black Death and explained how it could so easily and simply be theirs if they were to seize Lord Cerventis' children and sacrifice their infant innocence to the flames.

Abruptly Hecate's voice fell silent and she withdrew her dark, elusive shadow, dissolving it back into Aglia's body where she watched with human eyes and took satisfaction in knowing that the seed of her evil took root and flourished.

The Curse is Laid

LORD CERVENTIS TWISTED and turned, crying out fitfully as he slept. He was trapped, lost in the same recurring nightmare that had plagued him since the day he had driven the demon-hound, Cerberus, back into the Underworld. The darkness of the dream was suffocating, full of choking sulphur and the creature's reek. There were always more terrifying monsters pressing in all around him, touching him, scratching at his skin; and as their grip tightened, the wet, leafy earth beneath his feet erupted and slithering, scaly tentacles entwined themselves around him, reaching up out of the black void of his nightmare to strangle him. Sometimes he could hear voices in the darkness, howling, screaming voices that seemed to get louder and louder. Suddenly he started awake.

For an instant he lay huddled beneath his sleeping rug, gripping at its crumpled corners, disorientated and shivering. His face and hands were wet from the nightmare's terror and he waited for the images to vanish back into the darkness, waited for the howling to fade, but instead the sounds of shouting grew louder and closer. He half rose in the bed, pulling back the heavy drapes and turning his head towards the shuttered window. He saw the faint reflection of lights dancing across the ceiling of his chamber and smelt the acrid smell of pitch and burning rush torches.

Throwing aside the thin, summer sleeping rug, he

snatched up his sword and ran to the window, pushing open the shutters.

'What in God's name is this?'

He stared down at the frenzied mob besieging the gatehouse below. They swarmed up and over the walls, attacking the guards who tried to prevent them from reaching the house.

Faces in the milling crowd looked up as the hinges creaked open and then the mob saw him in the window. Their voices rose to screams of madness as they demanded that he deliver up his children for the good of Aurillac. Behind him he heard the door to his wife's sleeping chamber swing open and his children's voices cried out in the darkness. His wife hurried in to him over the threshold and the light from her candle cast a soft glow across the room.

'What is that noise? It has woken the children. What is happening?' Lady Ilyer called, her voice was small and frightened as she glanced anxiously back at the nurse who had lifted their babies out of the cradle to soothe and comfort them.

Cerventis backed away from the window, his face a white and trembling mask in the light of the candle. He spun toward her, the blade of his sword humming through the air.

'Snuff out that flame! Keep the children quiet. The people of Aurillac are possessed with an evil madness tonight – they are crying out that they will sacrifice our babies, and burn them at the stake! Go, get away, Ilyer, take the children to the monastery of Heratius – they will be safe there. Go now, escape while there's still time, my guards cannot hold back the crowd for much–'

The sound of splintering timbers and a triumphant roar from the courtyard below cut across his voice: the doors had been riven and there could now be no escape.

'Quickly, wife, get the children into the inner chamber with Solomon. Be quick, barricade all the openings. Solomon: stay, guard them with your life!' Cerventis shouted, desperately running toward the main doors to try and throw the heavy iron bolts before the first of the rampaging mob reached the stairhead.

He was too late to stop them. Hecate possessed them and drove them with screaming frenzy up the winding stairways and along the low, stone-arched corridors until they burst in through the door with such a fury that they tore it from its hinges and sent it crashing to the floor. The seething mob spilled out across the chamber, overturning and trampling on everything that lay in their path, advancing in a solid, engulfing wave of hatred. Their faces were distorted, cruel and hideous in the flickering torchlight and their eyes burned with evil as they shouted for the sacrifice.

Cerventis fought desperately, trying to stop them before they reached his wife and children in the inner chamber. Crying out across his shoulder he begged her to bar the door and jump from the window as he stabbed and slashed with his sword, hacking at the advancing mob, cutting off hands and arms as they thrust and stabbed at him with scythes and pitchforks.

Pace by bloody pace they drove him back across the chamber, trampling on their own dead to reach him until he was pressed hard against the inner doorway. Exhausted and gasping for breath, he raised his sword arm defiantly against the onslaught. The hilt of his sword was slippery and wet with their blood but they seemed senseless to pain, driven by some madness. With one last cry begging God for strength, he tried to sweep the blade of his sword across their faces as they overwhelmed him only to feel the sharp tines of a pitchfork pierce his body, skewering him to the door.

The blood gurgling in his throat choked his scream as

the final tine pierced his heart; the shadow of death folded over him and he glimpsed the wild, demented figure of Hecate break free and emerge from the seething crowd. He smelt the reek of sulphur and heard the echo of her voice. She reached out to claw at his face but her fingers melted as they touched him and her image shrivelled and was sucked wailing away into the growing void of darkness that surrounded him.

The ferocity of the attack smashed the locks of the inner chamber and forced it open. The door swung slowly inward and Lady Ilyer screamed as she saw her husband's body brutally skewered upon it. The crowd hesitated and paused. They were bewildered and confused, the madness had deserted them and they stared in at the huge, black mastiff guarding the two women who sat huddled in the corner of the room trying to conceal the crying infants. The dog snarled, its hackles raised along its back as it crouched ready to spring. Ripples of movement swayed and jostled the bloody throng, chafing and rubbing their elbows and shoulders together. Their momentum pushed and squeezed them, edging them together and moving them relentlessly forwards through the open doorway of the inner chamber to surround the crouching women.

Lady Ilyer looked around desperately but there was no chance of escape. She turned and faced the advancing horde defiantly, closing her hand on the hilt of the dagger she had hidden beneath her robe.

The whispers of madness that had brought the mob to rampage and kill, the dark shreds of Hecate's evil began to rekindle. The screams and cries of the two infants seemed to echo the wailing voices of the plague victims, re-awakening the crowd's memory of their terror of the Black Death and in that hot, airless chamber they smelled the reek of the death pits and heard the endless toll of the death bell. They remembered the powerful magic they had been promised and they were sure that it could save them.

Voices began to call out from the throng, urgent demanding voices that rose in a howling chant, screaming for the two infants to be offered up for sacrifice.

'Hold the children still for me,' whispered Ilyer to the nurse as she unsheathed the dagger. 'They shall not take my babies alive: I'd rather kill them myself first.'

To the crowd she shrieked, 'You shall not take them: they are God's children!'

Solomon leapt up, snarling and biting at the mass of arms and faces only to be clubbed to the ground and his body hacked to pieces. Lady Ilyer, tears of anger and helplessness coursing down her cheeks, raised her knife and turned to plunge it down into the hearts of her twin babies but as the blade swung through the air the crowd surged forward and overwhelmed her. Rough, brutal hands grabbed at her arms and fingers clawed at her neck and face, tearing out her hair as they jerked her backwards and away from the screaming infants. The knife was knocked from her hand and sent flying across the chamber, its blade flashing in the torchlight as she was beaten and cruelly thrown to the floor before being kicked and trampled and left for dead.

The two screaming babies were snatched from the helpless nurse's arms and tossed high into the air where they were passed roughly from hand to hand before being carried out at the head of the chanting, torchlit procession that wound its way back down towards the gates of Aurillac.

Feathered tails of dawn-dark mist clung silently to the steep weathered roofs and gutterings of Aurillac, ghosting the walls and rutted cobblestones of the narrow winding lanes and gloomy alleyways with cold, glistening beads of moisture. Thicker, denser patches of the mist lay along the midden ditches, masking their filth, and drifted in eerie, smothering shrouds over the litter of corpses which the searchers had found during the night and dragged out into the streets to await the arrival of the death cart.

Lady Ilyer heard the rumble and creak of the cart's wheels and the mournful toll of the death bell. The mist swirled and parted and almost directly ahead of her she saw the flickering light of their torches and then the shape of the horse and high-sided cart as it emerged through it and travelled straight towards her.

'Nobody must see us,' she whispered, gripping at the nurse's arm as she looked round frantically for somewhere for them to hide. She saw a dark doorway on the left of the narrow street and beckoned the nurse to follow her as she stepped over a row of bodies and slipped quickly into it, immediately crouching down and drawing the hood of her cloak up over her head, wincing as the heavy material touched her raw bruises. She was trembling uncontrollably, her heart pounding in her chest, her breaths coming in short, ragged gasps from her effort to reach the town before they killed her children. The carters must not see them. If they realized who she was they would know why she was there and they would stone them to death. The bundle Adzine was clutching beneath her cloak began to wriggle and faint squeals and snuffling sounds began to come from inside it.

'Keep them quiet!' Ilyer hissed, pressing herself back into the shadows as the clatter of the horses' hooves and the rumble of the wheels of the cart stopped almost immediately beside them.

She heard muffled curses and the sound of something heavy being dragged across the cobbles. There were gasps of effort as the bodies were lifted and, one by one, deposited in the cart. 'I won't be sorry if this is the last night of gathering up these stinking corpses. I hope that magic works!' One of the carters muttered as they threw the last of the bodies up into the cart.

'Magic!' scoffed the other carter. 'I don't know if it will be much help, it's very unreliable.' He slapped the horse's rump and tolled the death bell as they moved slowly on down the street.

Ilyer half rose, straining her ears, trying to catch their receding voices.

'My mother once went to a witch to have a wart removed from her nose,' continued one of the carters. 'It cost her her two best hens. Well, she did everything the old hag told her to do and within a week three more warts had grown beside the first one.'

The other carter roared with laughter. 'Well, believe in the power of magic or not – I don't care, I'm going to watch the magic as the sun rises over the market-place. I'll even help to nail up the fire sacks containing the ashes of those babies on to the gates of the town if it will rid us of this pestilence. You should see the pyres they're building beneath the fire baskets – it'll be some sacrifice. We'll pass them on the way to the grave pits, you'll see.'

Ilyer let out a whisper of relief. 'The children are still alive. Quickly, we must follow the cart.'

She caught up the hems of her skirts and left the shadow of the doorway, keeping the death cart just in sight, guessing that few would want to look out of their windows at such a mournful sight. When the slow, rumbling cart reached the edge of the market-place and turned through a small gate towards the vast line of grave pits that had been dug outside the town she slipped into a dark doorway, pulling Adzine in behind her and looked out across the square. She caught her breath and stifled a cry as she saw the small, pitiful fire sacks lying in the iron fire baskets above the pyre of sticks and

66

branches. As she moved closer she could hear the wailing cries of her frightened children inside the sacks; but something stemmed her instinct to run out across the open market square. To be discovered now would serve no purpose. She would need cunning and stealth if she was going to rescue her children and thwart this hideous sacrifice.

She watched the slow procession of figures emerge through the swirling grey mist on the far side of the square as they piled more kindling onto the pyre. The shivering guard paced backwards and forwards in front of it and an idea began to form in her mind.

'Keep very close to me and do exactly as I do.' Moving silently around the edge of the market square through a low archway they came upon a huge pile of firewood and saw that people were tearing out bundles of kindling and carrying them to the pyre. Pulling her hood over her head she gathered a bundle of firewood and slipped in amongst them to wait for her turn. She felt Adzine move in close behind her and prayed that nobody would challenge them.

'Stop you two!' A heavy-set guard waiting at the base of the fire pointed a filthy finger directly at them as they leaned their bundles of wood up against the others. 'That's no good – it's too spread out – it will never burn properly. Take your bundles up onto the top of the pile and spread it out directly beneath the fire baskets. And be quick about it – the sacrifice will start as soon as this cursed mist lifts.'

Ilyer could have wept with joy. She had been troubled about climbing to the top without being noticed, but now they had been ordered to do it. Keeping her hood pulled down over her face and grasping the bundle of twigs and sticks she scrambled quickly onto the pyre, hearing the snap and crack of the spindly bundles under Adzine's feet who kept a short pace behind her. They climbed fast, their feet slipping and sliding on the smooth, loosely-stacked branches, their skirts and cloak hems snagging and tearing on the sharp twigs and thorns. Dizzy and breathless they reached the top and Ilyer gripped onto the nearest of the two baskets to steady herself. She was so close to her children now, she could hear their whispered sobs. She saw to her horror that the square was filling up, shadowy figures were converging around the pyre, appearing through the mist. The crowds were gathering in readiness for the sacrifice. They were looking up, staring quizzically at her, waiting for the sunrise.

She began to spread out her bundle of kindling, her mind racing. Should she retrieve her babies now while she had the chance, could she get them out of the fire sacks without the crowd seeing her? The cold morning mist blew gently against the stray strands of her hair, sticking them to her forehead. She glanced around and offered up a silent prayer. Billowing swirls of mist were drifting across the market-place blanketing everything with a grey-white shroud, but the sky above her head was lightening and pale sunlight was beginning to touch the roofs and turrets of the town-houses. She realized she only had a few precious moments before the rising sun burst out of the mist. She had to act now.

'Quickly – open the sack beneath your cloak!' she whispered to the nurse. Her heart beat furiously and her fingers trembled and fumbled as she attacked the drawstring woven through the throat of the fire sacks. 'Faster, woman, faster!' she hissed, as she held the two babies in her arms. She let out a sigh of relief as the knots came undone but the piglets in her sack began to wriggle violently, trying to escape. Ilyer slipped her hand into the sack and caressed their ears, trying to soothe them.

'No sound. Not even a murmur. Thank God for it!'

she whispered as her two babies settled snugly into the sack and she drew the drawstring tight.

'Come on down, you two, they're about to light the fire. What are you doing up there? Do you want to be burned as well?'

The guard's impatient voice joined with shouts from the crowd and floated up through the thinning mist as they cursed their slowness. Ilyer did her best to disguise her voice and, mumbling their apologies, scrambled down the side of the fire keeping her head bowed, not daring to look across to Adzine, expecting her babies to cry out at any moment. She began to squeeze and push her way through the gathering crowds as they tried to get to the back of the square.

'Wait!' shouted the guard, grabbing at Adzine's arm. 'Don't you want to watch the fun? You've earned a place here at the front.'

Heads turned and Ilyer sensed a dozen sets of eyes watching them. The hair on the nape of her neck prickled. She had succeeded beyond her wildest hopes – she had her children back, she had thwarted the evil ritual – now all she wanted to do was to run, as far away as she possibly could; but she forced herself to stop and turn and she saw the panic in Adzine's eyes. To her right she glimpsed an old woman bent almost double, her body withered and crippled.

'Mother! She'll miss the sacrifice, please save our places, we must fetch our mother, she's very frail.'

Ilyer forced herself to walk, keeping a tight grip on Adzine's arm as she threaded her way to the back of the crowd and reached the edge of the market square. She breathed a sigh of relief as they turned beneath the low archway that would lead them to the gates of the town only to come face to face with a noisy, chanting crowd who filled the narrow lane.

'Quickly, in here!' She pressed herself into the nearest

doorway, pulling Adzine in roughly beside her. The approaching throng was led by a young, dark-haired woman who was shouting and stirring up the crowd, behind her mother, leaning heavily on her stick, was being reluctantly helped along by her other daughter who had an ugly gash on the side of her face.

Aglia noticed the two women slip into the doorway, noticed something about the taller one that troubled her. She slowed and almost stopped as she drew level with the doorway and for the briefest moment the two women's eyes met. She began to turn and reached out a hand to pull her into the lane.

'Leave them be, girl. Do you want to drag every poor wretch into your web of evil?' Mother Zem shouted angrily at her daughter, still trying to discourage her, cursing at Harlonis as she pulled her along. 'This sacrifice is nothing but madness, mark my words, nothing good will come of it. Leave them be, they're nothing to us!'

A great shout for the magic erupted in the market-place as Aglia hesitated, sneering at the two women in the doorway as they brushed past them and emerged through the low archway. She hurried forwards, lifting up her arms and crying out, uttering a jumble of rhymes and words from the forbidden book, fragments of dark, powerful spells she didn't wholly understand.

'Bring our mother forwards, she must share in this moment with us!' she cried, lifting a flaring torch to light the pyre.

Aglia was deaf to her mother's frantic voice as her sister dragged her through the market-place. She refused to hear her warnings. She would not allow the children to live. She grabbed at her mother's wrist, forcing her to become a part of the sacrifice.

By now she was giddy, drunk with power. Every face in the crowd was turned eagerly towards her and today she would show them real magic, dark magic, magic that Hecate had whispered inside her head – if only she could remember the words.

Ilyer brought her hand up to her mouth and watched helplessly from the shadows of the archway as the shout went up. 'God have mercy on your souls for what you intend to do this day,' she whispered as the column of thick, black smoke and ribbons of dancing sparks billowed and swirled above the rooftops, staining the clear morning air with its evil. She made the sign of the cross on her forehead and was about to hurry Adzine away to safety when she heard the shrill, squealing screams erupt from the fire sacks as the flames licked up around them.

The chanting stopped abruptly and an awful silence spread across the crowd. Ilyer held her breath as one of the sacks burst open and a piglet's head appeared, wreathed in smoke and flame. She silently thanked God that she had the sense to bring them with her to exchange for her tiny infants but she brought her hand up to her mouth in horror as it struggled and fought before it broke free of the sack and escaped, screaming as it tumbled down the steep side of the blazing pyre. It fled through the startled crowd with its skin sizzling and crackling, before vanishing down one of the narrow alleyways.

Aglia watched helplessly, her mouth hanging open as the other sack burst apart and a second piglet tumbled over and over, down through the flames, and ran straight towards her making her leap aside as it fled. She felt a knot of panic tighten in her throat. She didn't under-stand, what was happening? What had gone wrong? Had she used the wrong words? Had the children been transformed into piglets? She tried to shout, to call out the words she could hear echoing inside her head but nothing came out – her mouth opened and shut silently.

A low murmur of fear rippled through the crowd. The sudden shock of seeing the two piglets escape had brought them to their senses, making them realize the horror of what they had nearly done. They had been hypnotized by this woman and her sister; they had killed their lord and his lady and they had nearly sacrificed two helpless children. They had been fools: they should have known better than to follow practitioners of the Black Arts. The huntsman must have been right when he said that he had seen them consorting with the witch-queen Hecate and her demon-hound: they had drawn them into their evil. A murmur rose and quickly turned to anger. They would all be punished, their souls damned for all eternity, they would burn in the fires of Hell.

'Those two women must burn!' a priest cried out, breaking free from the restraining hands that had held him prisoner at the back of the crowd. He forced his way through the crush and prodded Aglia viciously with his staff sending her staggering backwards towards the flames. He turned to the people. 'You will suffer eternal damnation for what you have done! These women have consorted with the Devil and blasphemed against God. They have brought his wrath down upon us in the shape of the plague. The metamorphosis of those babies is a sign that you have defiled his benevolence.'

There was a shocked silence and then someone at the back of the market-place shouted. 'Burn them both!'

Perhaps it wasn't too late. Perhaps if they made amends. The shout was taken up and spread faster than the leaping flames of the pyre.

'Burn them! Burn them! Burn them!'

Aglia cowered away like a trapped animal encircled by huntsmen. She looked around her, desperate for a way to escape. Now she knew that the magic had deserted her and she felt utterly alone. She cried out for

Hecate to rescue her, she cried for mercy, for forgiveness, she promised the crowd cures for the plague and all the potions in her mother's house – anything, everything if they would only spare her life. But the faces of the advancing people were bleak and unforgiving, their eyes hard and without pity as they bore down on her, raising their staffs and cudgels to beat her into the flames as they chanted. 'Burn them, burn them, burn them.'

There was no escape. Mother Zem tried to reach them and plead for their lives but she was pushed to the ground and kicked aside as the crowd advanced. Harlonis screamed in terror as she tried to turn, raising her hands hopelessly to ward off their attackers.

'Run, sister, run for your life!' Aglia caught hold of her sleeve and tried to make a dash for a small gap in the advancing throng but the space closed and with a roaring shout the mob swirled around them.

Harlonis felt her sister's hand torn from her arm and she cowered helplessly as hundreds of hands and staves stabbed painfully at her, pushing and jostling her towards the searing heat of the fire. She screamed as the leaping roar of the flames scalded her flesh and she tottered on the brink of the fire, her clothes a mass of bright sparks. One final push from a rough stave and she fell backwards, arms thrashing in desperation. Aglia fought and cursed beside her, clinging to a dozen stakes and cudgels that were relentlessly forcing her into the fire. A huge, muscled iron-master lunged at her with his staff, catching it in the soft flesh beneath her rib cage and making her gasp with pain as he lifted her up and hurled her onto the top of the roaring pyre.

'Burn in the fires of Hell, you evil hags!' voices in the crowd shouted.

Aglia let out a long, wailing scream of agony as she fell amongst the burning branches, sending up a shower of sparks and flames. Her skin blistered and began to shrivel and blacken as she sunk lower into the heart of the fire with each wild, thrashing movement of her arms and legs. She cried out Hecate's name, cursing her for deserting her, her voice growing weaker and weaker with each word. Harlonis' body slipped sideways and rolled out of the fire, blackened and charred, her corpse sending up the sickly smell of burnt flesh and bones.

Ilyer stood in the shadow of the archway, transfixed with horror, watching the two young women burn to death. She had never wished for this. She bent down and kissed her babies as they lay in Adzine's arms, then took the two children from the nurse. They moved restlessly and began to wail; thin cries which floated up on the morning breeze, cutting through Aglia's death screams, tearing at the shreds of Hecate's magic that still lingered in her heart. The sound echoed down through the cobblestones and deep into the bowels of the earth where the witch-queen dwelt, tending to the wounds that Lord Cerventis had inflicted on her demon-hound Cerberus. In that instant Hecate knew that even beyond his death Cerventis had thwarted her. She knew that her simple servant had been tricked out of the sacrifice that would have tarnished all of Aurillac with her evil. She, the Queen of Darkness, had been denied her revenge.

Seething with rage, Hecate rose up through the damp, wormy earth, shattering rock and splitting stone in a howling gale of hatred that erupted through the core of the fire, sending up blazing branches and a hurricane of white-hot sparks high into the air. The crowd cried out in terror and shrank back as they saw the shadowy figure of the witch tread through the raging inferno and touch Aglia a second before merging with her, entering her through her blistering, blackened skin. They had become one again, she had merged with the girl's burnt flesh, resurrecting her, using all her dark powers to bind together her shrivelled, charred body.

'You shall have your revenge on the House of Cerventis!' Hecate's voice hissed and echoed inside Aglia's head.

An inner force jerked the girl upright and opened her melting, bubbling eyes to focus them on Ilyer. 'You must have the souls of those babies – they shall be yours to torment in the fires of Hell!' The voice goaded her to rise and she raised her burning arm, her charred, quivering finger pointing at Ilyer across the market-place.

Aglia, wreathed in smoke and flame, began to climb down out of the roaring fire. Her jaw fell open and the blackened skin of her lips split and fell apart as flames licked at her teeth and curled over her exposed cheek-bones as she spoke.

'Sator, Daudalem, Sator – give me back what you have stolen, Cerventis' woman!' Aglia's voice rasped and hissed in a vaporous stream of smoke and flame that struck terror into the hearts of everyone cowering in the market-place. She leapt out of the fire and staggered two paces away from it, shedding sparks and burning embers of skin as she beckoned Ilyer with her charred fingers. Aglia's voice rose to a piercing shriek, her fingers cracked and split across the knuckles as she flexed them, and she stirred up a gale of foul wind that pulled and tore at Ilyer's clothing, drawing her step by helpless step, towards the terrible figure.

'By all the carrion eaters and gabares that haunt the darkness and gnaw on the bones of the dead I command you to give back my sacrifice!'

'No! No, I won't! I will never let you touch my babies with your vile evil, never never never!' Ilyer cried. She clasped her arm protectively around the babies, and fought against the force that was drawing her, inch by inch, towards the hideous, burning figure in front of the blazing pyre. She tried to cling with her free hand onto the rough stone of the archway but the power of Hecate's magic tore her fingers away, making them bleed. She stumbled and fell to her knees but even as Adzine tightened her grip on her arms she could feel both of them being pulled across the cobbles towards the fire.

Aglia's voice rose in triumph. She took another shuffling step. 'Their souls shall be mine to torment and consume in the eternal darkness. Their blood shall stand still and their flesh shall fall from their bones. They will wither, shrivel and become as nothing in my embrace.'

'NO! I'll never . . .' Ilyer screamed as she violently struck the wheel of a cart that stood in her path. The brutal force of the magic knocked the breath out of her, sucking at her as it tried to pull her through the thick wooden spokes of the wheel. Dragging and scraping, the heavy cart slid sideways across the cobbles, threatening to tip over at any moment.

Suddenly another voice cried out across the marketplace, frail and yet fuelled by anger. Mother Zem struggled unsteadily to her feet and advanced, brandishing her threshing stick at the burning figure. 'Enough! You are a wicked harridan, Hecate, you hagbound Queen of Darkness! Leave my daughter's body alone – stop using her for your revenge. Begone, you evil witch!'

Aglia stopped abruptly, the gale of hatred that was sucking Ilyer and the nurse towards her faltered as she turned her charred skull towards the old woman. 'Get back – grovel in the dirt, you dried-up maggot!' she snarled, her blackened eye sockets glowing with lurid, yellow light. She spat a glob of boiling spittle into the old woman's face which splattered and scorched her skin.

Mother Zem staggered but held her ground fiercely. The rage at what was happening to her own daughter boiled inside her. 'You don't frighten me, you ugly grave-wraith! Your powers are forged through vile corruption, fear and diabolical rituals. The webs of your magic are rotten and diseased. I know of you, Hecate, I know of the evil you weave. I feared for my daughters' souls and I hoped beyond hope that they would listen to my wisdom and turn their backs on you but they chose to tread this dangerous path to eternal damnation and follow your shadow. I may be powerless to change their fate now but I will not stand by and watch you murder these innocent babies. I have read the Grimoires and I have studied every page of the forbidden book. IH . . . IHUIT . . . IHUIT!'

Hobbling in an erratic dance she held up a frog's heart that hung on a hemp string around her neck. 'I can conjure up angels' spirits to defend these helpless children and then I will drive you back beneath the ground where you belong.'

Aglia began to laugh, directing her whole attention to the old woman's antics. 'Dance then, dance, you fool!' she hissed, clapping her charred hands together, unaware that Ilyer and the nurse had got to their feet now that the wind had abated.

Aglia's hands slapped together and Hecate cried out as the charred flesh and bones crumbled and fell apart. The old woman had distracted her for too long – her webs of magic were wearing dangerously thin. She swayed and tottered unsteadily, scattering burning embers of rag and bone onto the cobblestones around her as her magic weakened. Hecate cursed the old woman's cleverness in a voice choked with ashes and tried to direct her failing powers back against Ilyer as she sensed her quarry escaping. With a wailing scream she turned, her burning body collapsing onto its knees as her feet and shins fractured into pieces of charred bone. She flailed her blackened, shrivelled arms and cried out with such a piercing rage that it froze Ilyer beneath the archway, the children safe in her arms, and forced her to turn back and face the disintegrating effigy.

'Zoros, Delmusan, Surmy, Dandalen, Sator!' Hecate shrieked. 'I can see beneath your cloak. I know you for who you are, there is no escape! No matter how far you run, Ilyer, no matter where you try to hide Cerventis' vile offspring, their souls are mine. The House of Cerventis is cursed forever, my gabares will hunt your children to the ends of the earth and beyond. They will follow them into eternal darkness and they will wait, silently haunting all their nightmares; they will hide, cloaked in the shadows of their fear, and in the moment of their deaths they will pounce and reveal themselves. At that moment they will devour them and cry out my name as they suck out their souls and bring them into my eternal night.'

'No, oh no, you will never have them!' Ilyer cried out defiantly.

Aglia's failing voice cackled. 'The curse is laid, Lady Ilyer, your children cannot escape it no matter what you do. Remember, my gabares will be waiting to claim their souls on the threshold of eternity.'

'They don't deserve to suffer your evil: God will protect them. I will pray for his mercy; he will take care of them, they are only helpless innocents.'

Aglia's body fell slowly forwards, collapsing in a blaze of sparks. As it vanished Hecate's voice whispered, 'Their souls can never be cleansed of this curse, Ilyer: even if they escape from me with the help of some greater power than mine my grave-wraiths will be watching, waiting, watching and waiting. Remember, the House of Cerventis is cursed, their souls are damned, condemned to the eternal darkness, damned . . . forever . . .'

The echo of Hecate's curse faded into silence. The air beneath the archway seemed to grow shiver-cold and gloomy with shadows as if the grave watchers were already gathering around her, haunting the sunlight.

'What are we to do?' Adzine cried.

'I'll find a way to save them,' Ilyer whispered, edging backwards towards the town gates. She was about to turn and run when Mother Zem spoke: 'Perhaps I can help you—'

Ilyer's face flushed with anger. It was all her fault – all this meddling in the unknown, teaching her daughters to look for secret cures and magic potions. In fury and misery Ilyer raised her fist, clenching it ready to strike her, but then she hesitated and let it drop to her side. Anger dissolved into pity as she watched Mother Zem try to lift the two hideously burned bodies of her daughters into the cart. The departing crowd spat at the old woman, beating her with their sticks as they hurried out of the market-place. How quickly they had forgotten all her potions and medicines that had cured them over the years – how eager they were to blame her for their part in the hideous ritual.

She watched and saw how weak and helpless the old woman really was and remembered how much courage she had shown when she had confronted Hecate. She watched with tears in her eyes, realizing that Mother Zem was an old lady who didn't even have the strength to lift the charred corpses of her children into the cart and give them a decent burial.

'Guard the infants with your life. Let no one touch them!' Ilyer whispered to Adzine, and walked back through the angry crowd into the square, many of them looked away and made the sign of the cross as she passed.

'Here, let me help you,' she spoke softly and reached down to help lift Harlonis' body into the cart.

Mother Zem coughed as she fought to swallow back her tears while Lady Ilyer helped her to lift the second, more badly burned, bundle of rags and bones that had once been her daughter, Aglia, and place it carefully into the cart. One of Ilyer's babies cried out fretfully from the archway. The thin, piercing sound made the old woman freeze and then glance anxiously across the emptying market square as if she was searching for something, or someone, she dreaded but could not yet see.

'You must not linger here a moment longer, good lady. You must get away, far away from this cursed place. Your children are still in mortal danger,' she whispered, gripping Ilyer's arm so fiercely that her crooked fingers pinched and bruised her skin.

Ilyer stared at the old lady and saw the terror mirrored in her eyes. 'But where can I go? Who will dare help me? Indeed, who can help me break the curse that Hecate laid upon my children? Do you know of someone . . .'

'Be quiet!' Mother Zem hissed, hunching her shoulders and bringing her fingers to her lips, silencing Ilyer as she drew her closer. 'Hecate's grave-wraiths are already gathering – can't you sense their presence? Can't you smell their evil in this market-place? Run, run for your life now, while you still can.'

Ilyer took two hesitant steps, calling out to Adzine, commanding her to follow through the low archway and the narrow lane that she knew would lead them to the outer gateway of the town before her progress faltered. The way ahead seemed dark and shrouded with moving shadows. She tried to move to the left and then to the right but every exit looked dark and foreboding. Eventually she turned back and reached out imploring hands towards Mother Zem who she could barely see in the gloom.

'We are already hopelessly lost. I cannot find my way out of here.'

Mother Zem shivered and shook her head. She knew

only too well how dangerous the witch-queen was. She sensed her power stirring in the glowing ashes of the fire. She laid her hand on the charred bodies of her two daughters and felt the emptiness and pain of her loss. 'No, Hecate,' she murmured, her anger rising. 'You are vile and vengeful, an unnatural creature of the darkness. No, I will not stand helplessly by and watch while you steal those infants' souls as easily as you seized my daughters.'

She fumbled beneath her skirts and loosened the knot of her secret belt. There was something she could do to help the Lady Ilyer and protect her children, one precious thing that she could give her. She had gathered and woven it more years ago than she cared to remember and she had carried it with her for so long it almost seemed to be a forgotten part of her. 'Stand perfectly still,' she called out to Ilyer and chanted an ancient spell to dispel the gabares' darkness while she hurried to her side.

'By all the powers of the sun and the cold blue light of the moon. Eko, Eko, Aradia, melt the shadows and tear aside the tangled webs of darkness from this place . . .'

The morning sunlight streamed for a moment across the market-place, catching and reflecting all the hidden beauty of the talismanic belt that the old woman had withdrawn from beneath her skirts. It was thickly woven with a thousand secrets. Tiny leather pouches of sweet aromatic herbs hung from it, dark fragments of dragons' teeth, glistening petals of stone, brightly-coloured shells that whispered of the sea were sewn in there with precious crystals of kyanite, chalcedony and golden beryl, wolfsbane and widowhead bound around the edges. She motioned to Adzine to hold the babies up while she passed the talisman around them before tying it twice around Ilyer's waist beneath her cloak and knotted it securely. 'The belt is hung with good, wholesome magic that will protect your children and light your path, but use its powers sparingly and scatter the talismans across your road one by one only when the grave-wraiths are hunting their souls. Whenever they darken your way use a sea shell: press it against their ears so that it may shut out their howling cries and comfort them. Remember this: never, never utter one word of where your journey will end or you will find these evil creatures are there already, waiting, haunting the shadows. Now run! Run for your life!'

Mother Zem reached beneath Ilyer's cloak to snatch a slither of imperial topaz from the belt before giving her a push. 'Run!' She smashed the crystal at her feet.

The topaz shattered into a thousand fragments, sending off a golden, yellow light that clung to Ilyer's feet and the hems of her cloak and gown. It spread out in a glowing halo around the two women, illuminating their path as they fled across the market-place. The gabares screamed and howled as they tried to claw at their hair and flying cloaks with their skeletal fingers only to collide, blinded and confused by the brilliant light.

'Run, run as fast as you can!' the old woman shouted after her. The ashes of the fire erupted in a blaze of white hot sparks as the shadowy form of Hecate rose menacing and terrible to hover above Mother Zem.

'Twice, twice now you have dared to challenge me. For that your daughters will never rest . . . NEVER!'

An Antidote to Evil

THE WALLS OF the monastery of Heratius rose
bleak and inhospitable, etched coldly black
against the fading light. Its barred window-slits
and crumbling towers stared blindly down across the
steep slopes of broken scree and wind-bent, stunted trees
into the empty valleys below. Night and a thick rising
mist smothered the desolate landscape with darkness.
Lady Ilyer sank down wearily on her haunches upon
the worn steps of the monastery and wept with despair.
The scrape and echo of the small grille set in the door
slid firmly shut against her and the harsh voice of the
monk denying her entry still rang in her ears.

'My children are in mortal danger!' she had cried as
the father had opened the grille. 'The witch-queen
Hecate laid a curse upon their souls in the market-place
of Aurillac. Let me in, quickly, you must let me see the
Abbot!'

'Aurillac?' the monk had repeated, his voice sharpening with fear.

Ilyer had heard him shuffle backwards a step and
smelled the sweet, slightly sickly odour of calamine and
camphor as he brought an aromatic apple to his nose.
'Word has reached us that the plague is raging in Aurillac.' His voice was muffled now but Ilyer sensed it hard-
ening against her.

'We are not touched with the plague. Quickly, please
let us in or my children will suffer a far worse fate than
that . . .'

'The monastery is closed by the Abbot's order. He forbids all strangers to cross the threshold until twenty days after the Black Death has left the surrounding countryside. You will find bread and water in a basket by the outer wall, to give you strength for your journey. May God go with you, child.'

'But you *must* let us in!' Adzine shouted angrily, crowding close to the grille. 'There is nowhere else we can go and my mistress's children will suffer eternal damnation! Please, please, I beg you, do not turn them away.'

She hammered fruitlessly on the iron-studded doors until her knuckles bled and her calls fell on deaf ears long after the monk's shuffling footsteps had faded to nothing.

'What can we do now, mistress?' she wept, gently rocking the two babies in her arms to comfort them.

One of the horses they had been riding snorted with alarm from where it was tied up at the bottom of the steps. It turned its head, pricking its ears as it heard a noise from somewhere close in the thickening darkness. It made Ilyer catch her breath and stifle her despair. She thought she saw the briefest flicker of soft light, perhaps a flame reflecting through a smoky lantern glass, and she distinctly heard the sudden scrape of footsteps approaching along one of the rough, stony paths inside the monastery grounds. The sound made Adzine hide the children quickly beneath her cloak. Ilyer stood, loosing the dagger she carried, her heart pounding. She ran down the steps, a cold knot of fear tightening in her stomach. The people in the last village had warned her of bands of robbers who preyed on travellers to the monastery, advising her to wait until the next large group of pilgrims passed through before they ventured into the wild, desolate lands, but she had waved their warnings aside and ridden on. Twice in the last three days she thought that they were being followed by figures that she had glimpsed silhouetted against the tortured skyline, and they had ridden hard to get away from them, keeping to the open ground all the while. Now it seemed that they were closing in, but they were wrong if they thought they could prey on their helplessness. A hooded figure was becoming visible through the gloom.

'You will not take us easily. We'll not be taken without a fight!' she cried, trying to control the tremble in her voice as her fingers tightened around the hilt of her dagger. 'Come no closer or I will slit your throat!' She brandished the blade nervously.

The approaching figure came to an abrupt halt a few paces away and a gentle voice filled the darkness. 'You have no need to fear me, my lady. I am Brother Ralph and I am a simple pilgrim travelling in peace.'

The monk drew back the heavy folds of his cloak and held up the small, flickering lantern that he carried to illuminate his path. The dancing light revealed his coarsely-woven and travel-stained robes and the worn wooden sandals on his feet. His face was partially hidden by the deep shadows of his hood but Ilyer sensed him smile and saw his honest, penetrating gaze soften as he observed the other woman behind her on the step.

'It is late and dangerous for two women to be travelling these mountain roads alone, my lady. Surely you have knocked to seek entry and a safe bed for the night?'

Ilyer laughed harshly, her mouth thin and bitter, her eyes blinking back the tears. 'Oh yes, we have knocked upon this door, but no one here will give us shelter, no shepherd in this monastery cares for his flock.' And she took a step towards the horse.

The monk caught a glimpse of her tears in the lantern light and he stepped forward, reaching up and putting his hand on the halter ring. 'Forgive me, my lady, but

I will not see either of you venture out alone. There is a darkness in the air tonight that chills my heart.'

Ilyer pulled at the rope but the monk's grip was firm. 'Please, let go! We have journeyed from Aurillac where the plague rages through the streets and death's hand overshadows everything. We are not afraid of the darkness.'

'Yes you are, my lady,' Brother Ralph replied softly. 'I heard you weeping in the doorway as I entered through the gates of the monastery. I fear you carry a great burden and you are lost and alone – and very afraid.'

The monk's gentle and perceptive words had touched the heart of her despair and Ilyer buried her head. Her silent tears glittered in the lamplight as they ran unchecked down her cheeks.

'What are we to do? How can I save my babies' souls now that the Abbot has turned us away, father?' she whispered between her sobs. 'We have been shut out, abandoned, and no one in this world can help us.'

A bell began to toll somewhere in the depths of the monastery, its mournful sound calling the monks to evensong. Brother Ralph frowned as he let his gaze climb up the cold, inhospitable walls and barred windows of the Abbot's fortress, then he shook his head. 'While on my travels I have heard rumours that this Abbot is consumed with a terror of the Black Death. It fills his mind with a selfish madness and keeps him and all his disciples prisoners. But do not judge them by their actions – they are but mortals, men whose strengths and goodness are overcome by their fears, and I doubt that any man so overwhelmed and distracted could have given you the council you seek, whatever it is. But come, good lady, we will travel together, there is a greater safety in numbers. We will find a sheltered place to build a fire and while we sit beneath the stars and eat the bread that has been left in the basket at the monastery gate I will ease your burden if I possibly can.'

'Perhaps we should stay here and rest, mistress. We need to feed the children.' Adzine looked at the monk suspiciously.

'He is a man of God, we have nothing to fear from him.' Ilyer studied the man's face. 'Are you not fearful that we might have carried the plague with us from Aurillac?' As she voiced her question, bitterness and doubt crept back into Ilyer's voice.

The monk began to lead the way towards the outer gate, his wooden sandals clattering over the rough, stony ground. 'Yes, my lady, I am afraid, as any mortal man would be, but I try to be a good shepherd whose lamp is always there to light a path for those who need to find their way through these dark and troubled times.'

Silence crackled in the firelight mingling with the bright ribbons of sparks that swirled and danced into the darkness to vanish into the canopy of stars that were strewn across the night sky: Ilyer told her story to the monk and explained what had driven her to seek the Abbot's help. 'You see, father, I must find a way to protect my children. I must find someone who can break the witch's curse,' she concluded, reaching out to gently caress the two infants sleeping in Adzine's arms.

Brother Ralph nodded and sat staring thoughtfully into the fire for a long moment before he answered. 'Perhaps . . . perhaps you need something more power- ful than an Abbot's blessing to ward off this evil.'

'What are you saying?' Ilyer cried in alarm. 'You are a man of God – would you advise me to use unholy means? Would you tell me to enter into diabolical rituals?'

'No . . . no . . .' The monk interrupted quickly. 'You go too fast, Lady Ilyer, I would never council you in the ways of the Devil, nor would I speak of them here in the wilderness.' He glanced anxiously around him into the darkness before continuing with a lowered voice. 'Remember there are more good powers and wonders in this world than we could ever begin to understand, and there are those who spend their lives harvesting this knowledge. I know of one, perhaps the wisest man in all the world, and I would urge you to seek him out. I know the Abbot would call my advice blasphemy but there is no one better qualified to help you. He is a healer and an alchemist called Wenceslaus.'

'What could a healer and a dabbler in broths and potions do to put things right?' she questioned angrily. 'It is because of those cursed healing women in Aurillac and their meddling with evil to ward off the plague that my children are under this curse. My husband would still be alive, my babies safe . . .' Ilyer's voice trailed into sobs.

'I'm so sorry, Lady Ilyer, but sometimes the best advice is not what we wish to hear.' Brother Ralph's voice was soft and persuasive. 'But remember this, for almost every poison there is an antidote, so for every black curse that is uttered there should also be a counter-spell, or a ritual that will unravel it. And if there is any wise man alive who knows of a way to break that evil witch's claim upon your children's souls then the Master Wenceslaus will. Go to him. Beg his indulgence and go to him.'

Ilyer shook her head fiercely and sat mute, huddled in misery. The warmth seemed to have gone from the fire and the darkness pressed in all around them. She hated and abhorred the idea of seeking out more magic.

A faint noise in the rocks and scrub beyond the weak circle of firelight caused a snort of alarm from their horses and made Ilyer scramble quickly to her feet as she reached beneath her cloak for one of Mother Zem's trinkets. She pulled free a small turquoise scarab and drew her arm back to cast it into the night. Brother Ralph was quick to snatch up a stone from beside the fire and throw it in the same direction. There was a brief flash of pale blue light as the scarab shattered, followed by a weird yelping cry that grew fainter and fainter as the creature that uttered it vanished into the darkness. The babies began to cry, disturbed by the piercing shriek.

'What in God's name could that have been?' Brother Ralph's voice was frightened and uncertain as he searched the shadows before building the fire up to a roaring blaze.

'I think it was a grave-wraith,' Ilyer whispered, shuddering with fear as she moved closer to the flames, feeling with trembling fingers the remaining smooth shells, precious stones and tiny magic trinkets that were still woven into the belt around her waist. She plucked off two shells and passed them to Adzine to hold against the babies so that the whispering melodies would lull them back to sleep. Suddenly she felt ashamed of what she had just said for without the old woman's gift they would never have escaped from Aurillac or reached this monastery.

'Where can I find this alchemist?' she asked in a small, breathless voice.

Brother Ralph gestured out across the desolate land-scape and the broken rocks and scrub that stretched away into the mist that shrouded the valleys, gullies and ravines below the monastery. 'The hermitage lies to the east. If you look carefully you can see its light from here on a clear and starry night.' He directed her gaze across the silent mountains, black monoliths that seemed to march away to the edge of morning. 'There, can you see it?'

Ilyer followed his pointing finger and searched the bleak, cold darkness. Then she saw it; a tiny, fragile blink of light. It was more like a fallen star that seemed to balance upon a sheer black precipice of rock, clinging precariously onto the far horizon of night. 'It looks so far away. Is there a clear road for me to follow, father?' she asked hesitantly.

The monk turned thoughtfully towards her and shook his head. 'It is but a two-day journey, but there is no easy road, Lady Ilyer. Master Wenceslaus is a solitary man who does not readily welcome visitors.'

'How do we know if he will give us assistance even if we can find that solitary tower?' There was an edge of hopelessness in Ilyer's voice as she sank down beside the fire.

'We'll find it, mistress,' Adzine said firmly. 'We haven't come this far to give up now.'

Bending her head she began to sing a soft haunting lullaby to soothe the babies back to sleep, holding the sea shells gently against their ears. Brother Ralph listened for a moment. It had a gentle tune, as old as time itself, yet the words were powerful, strong enough to keep out the darkness. 'I will lead you there, good lady. The road we will take in the mountains runs through . . .'

'Shush! Do not speak of it!' Ilyer hissed in alarm. 'The grave-wraiths must not hear it.'

Ilyer shivered and helped Adzine to settle the two babies safely in their cradle and away from the biting wind. The nurse began to feed them while they waited in the outer keep of the hermitage as Brother Ralph had instructed. They were worn out and dishevelled from their circuitous journey through the mountains where they had had to search out a road that would lead to this dark, cold tower of granite. She rubbed her hands together and stamped her feet, constantly glancing down at the infants and praying for help as she slowly paced backwards and forwards trying to keep warm while

Ralph sought to gain her an audience with the alchemist. 'He is an eccentric recluse: let me speak to him first, he has helped me before,' the monk had whispered as he hammered on an inner door.

Faintly Ilyer caught the sound of raised voices inside the tower. She moved closer, pressing her ear against the door. 'Why do you plague me, brother? Why do you come here with these holy matters: you know I do not have the time to explore half the mysteries set before me let alone deal with this hysterical threat of dark magic!'

The alchemist's voice was lost for a moment but Ilyer was sure that she heard Brother Ralph utter the evil witch's name.

'Hecate!' Wenceslaus repeated, his voice quickening with interest. 'Did you say the Queen herself laid this curse?'

Ilyer barely had time to straighten her back and move away from the door before it was thrown open and the alchemist crowded the threshold. He was much taller and thinner than she had expected, and older. He wore a long, flowing gown of watered silk and his mane of silver-white hair was as fine as gossamer; his wrinkled skin was so parchment dry that it looked ready to crack. His eyes were azure blue, and hard, and they held her still, frozen by their gaze.

'Ah, Lady Ilyer. Forgive me for not greeting you on your arrival.' He blinked and released his prisoner before turning on his heel. He peered into the cradle at the babies, bending slightly to look closely, his forehead furrowed in thought. 'Please, please, step this way. Time presses so heavily on the hour-glass and there is always so much to do. Come, sit by the fire – my assistant will bring you food and drink while you tell me of this black curse.' His eyebrows rose in owlish arches of anticipation as he showed her to a seat.

Ilyer caught her breath as he led her across the

threshold into the tower. She felt as if she had entered an enchanted cavern filled with the warm, heady scent of alum, saffron and myrrh. The vast, circular room was illuminated by flickering flames from the enormous fire in the hearth where squat, black-bellied cauldrons hung by iron chains and brimming crucibles of precious metals sat side by side waiting to be put upon the glowing coals. Leather bellows, fire-blackened tongs, long-handled salamanders and polished brass measures and scoops of every shape and size cluttered the hearth or lay, half-buried and forgotten, in the ash and cinders. She let her startled gaze travel through the chaos over the worn stone-flagged floor, past heavily-laden chairs and long wooden tables overflowing with piles of opened books, scrolls and illuminated manuscripts to the dimmer outer edges of the chamber where tiers of shelves and open cupboards had been built haphazardly on top of one another to climb up into the raftered darkness of the roof where they vanished from sight. Every shelf seemed to be crammed with books, jars, bottles, boxes and dishes of every size and shape imaginable. Crowded in amongst them were all manner of oddly shaped brass and copper tubes, funnels and apparatus that reflected back the firelight.

'Come, sit down, Lady Ilyer, do not be distracted by the toys of my craft,' Wenceslaus laughed, dismissing the chaos and clutter with a wave of his hand as he guided her through the maze of earthenware pots, tall stone jugs and baskets of herbs that littered the floor and steered her to a chair at the fireside. 'Put the cradle down by the hearth,' he ordered, giving Adzine a vague wave of his hand, 'and sit, sit down.' His face grew grave as he swept a pile of parchment scrolls to the floor. 'Now tell me the manner of this black curse – and I warn you to leave nothing out, not a single word or gesture.'

He sprinkled a mixture of sulphur and saltpetre onto the fire, uttering, 'The sun is the father of daylight. Keep back the shadows of night.'

A spectacular whirlwind of flames roared up the chimney, filling the chamber with brilliant light, making the babies cry and move restlessly. 'Speak of it now, Lady Ilyer, while the fire still burns. Let nothing distract you.'

Ilyer told him everything. It all came pouring out in a breathless, frightened rush while the flames hissed and crackled up into the chimney hole. She willingly unburdened herself of everything that had happened since that fateful, hot afternoon when her husband's huntsmen had unexpectedly come upon the two women trespassing in the forest above the Withenthorpe Bridge.

Wenceslaus' eyebrows drew together into a deep, worried furrow as Ilyer reached the end of her story and fell silent. 'This is indeed a black matter, my lady, far, far worse than I had imagined.' His voice trailed off into whispered mutterings as he rummaged through his piles of books and scrolls, sending up thick clouds of dust as he scattered them along the wooden tables. His face became paler and more fraught with each page he turned.

'Zoros, Delmusan, Surmy, Dandalen, Sator, Sator, Dandalen, Hiamintho. There is no escape!' he whispered. Suddenly he paused, his long, bony fingers hovering over a dense page of erratic, spidery hieroglyphics that sprawled like the fingers of night across the open parchment. He had to turn the page upside down to read it all and he expelled a short gasp as he realized that he had come upon the exact words of the curse but that they were arranged in two separate pieces with a warning to whoever read them out loud never to link them unless they were prepared for the powers of darkness they would release. Quickly he closed the book, clearing the visions that threatened to engulf him. He gathered his courage before repeating the second part of the curse. He had to know if these were the exact words that Hecate had used. He held Ilyer's gaze as he whispered, 'Listen very carefully. Did either of the burning effigies chant these words – Zoros, Delmusan, Surmy, their souls shall be mine to torment and consume in the eternal darkness. Their blood shall stand still and their flesh shall fall from their bones. They will wither, shiver and become as nothing in my embrace.'

Ilyer shivered and nodded bleakly. Even though only half the curse had been spoken the light of the fire seemed to shrink and die back and the chamber filled with formless shadows. Wenceslaus threw more salt-petre and sulphur onto the fire but his words struck an icy chill into her heart.

'Lady Ilyer, there is no antidote, no escape. There are no words of ritual written that I can perform to break this black curse. Hecate's evil is absolute and beyond my power to undo. I fear your children's souls are condemned to be with her. They are lost.'

'No! No!' she cried out in agony, rising from the chair. Her frantic voice and sudden movement wakened the two infants and they screamed and wailed, grasping at Adzine's hands as she tried to soothe them, lifting them up one by one, whispering their names with words of comfort. Ilyer begged the alchemist and pleaded with him. 'Look, look how helpless they are. You have so much knowledge . . .'

In desperation she tore free the belt that Mother Zem had wound around her waist and thrust it awkwardly at him. 'Even the old healing woman whose daughters were burned to death for meddling with the evil tried to help me. Even *she* had some small power against Hecate's curse. I heard her shout defiantly at the evil witch as she promised that she would not stand by and watch her steal my children's souls and the magic in her belt has kept them safe thus far.'

Wenceslaus sighed and shook his head as he gently took one of the babies from Adzine. 'Yes, yes, good lady, her magic has indeed protected you on the road but what will happen when it runs out? How many precious crystals are there left?' His face softened as he rocked the infant but as he gave the baby back to Adzine his gaze darkened.

'I fear Mother Zem has put their souls in even greater danger. By helping you she stirred up Hecate's anger to such a pitch that she also laid a curse on the old woman's daughters. She has damned them and forced them to be the ones who will hunt your children to the ends of the earth and beyond. Of all the grave-wraiths she resurrects those two have the greatest cause to hate your children and want their revenge upon them. They will never tire of watching, never rest until they have seized them. I fear that Mother Zem has unwittingly strengthened the original curse.'

'But they are only babies, so helpless, so innocent – look at them, how can you say there is nothing you can do?' Ilyer cried, wringing her hands together.

'Lady Ilyer, calm yourself lest there are listeners beyond the door. I said I could not break the curse but . . .' The alchemist paused and drew close to her, his dry lips barely moving as he whispered. 'But I didn't say I wouldn't try to help you. I think there are ways, secret ways that I can use to arm them against this evil.'

'But how will you do it? What can you do? Will it be enduring?'

'Have patience, my lady,' Wenceslaus muttered as he moved back to consult the mass of books and scrolls. 'The secret ways are the most difficult and the most elusive.'

The alchemist turned away from her and beckoned Brother Ralph to assist him as he began to prepare ink and a sharp quill before becoming absorbed in his search. Wenceslaus hummed a tuneless dirge to himself and absently cracked his bony knuckles one by one as he pored over his dusty manuscripts and journals of magic. He paused occasionally to mark a word, to raise an eyebrow and underline a passage or to copy out a sign or mystical symbol. He whispered whole strings of numbers and recited secret alphabets as he consulted the marvels of the world, the sacred magic of Abra Merlin or the oracles of Zoroaster.

'Have you found a way?' Ilyer cried, leaping to her feet in joy.

Wenceslaus hissed her into silence as he took up the ink and quill and began to make a mass of calculations upon a scroll of parchment. Both Ilyer and Brother Ralph crowded anxiously forwards, watching and holding their breath as the spidery arithmetic spread erratically across the page. The alchemist suddenly threw down the pen in disgust as he crumpled the paper between his fingers.

'There is a way to break this curse, a mantra so obvious, so simple. It is hidden in the words themselves. If the children recite both halves of the curse, one backwards and one forwards, one thousand times their souls will be free of this black shadow. But it is impossible, they cannot use it.' He reached for the Grimoires of Mascous in the vain hope of finding another way.

'But I can recite the curse backwards or forwards one hundred thousand times, or more if you want – that is not impossible,' Ilyer said hopefully.

Wenceslaus snapped the heavy book shut and laughed harshly, a brittle sound that could have shattered crystal. 'It is your children, Lady Ilyer, it is your babies that the witch-queen cursed and it is they, not you, who must recite it. By my calculations of the astrological clock they must perform the mantra between tomorrow's cock-crow and the first cry of the night owl in one month's time.'

'But they cannot speak – they are far too young. Is there no other way to use what you have discovered? Is there no other time they could recite those words when they are full-grown?'

The alchemist frowned and then nodded, reluctantly. 'Yes, yes, there will be other times, times when the brief windows of magic will open and close as the great clock slowly turns in the sky, but . . .' With a sharp intake of breath he scanned his calculations again and threw up his hands in despair, 'the next alignment will not be for a hundred years. There is no way to break the curse, no way on earth – unless . . .'

He fell silent and rubbed his chin thoughtfully, chafing the dry, wrinkled skin with his thin fingers as he returned to the long table and bent over the piles of books. There was something in the calculations that had caught his eye, a recurring pattern, as if life travelled on beyond death. It was something he had thought he may have glimpsed before when he had tried to explore the logic of time. 'I wonder how frequently the moment will occur? Why does that particular window open so far into the future, and how often will it occur after that?' he mumbled, smoothing out the crumpled scroll of parchment as he continued with his calculations to put up Galea's chart.

'But surely, Master Wenceslaus, it is only necessary to protect their souls until they die and while they are on their journey to heaven – after that Hecate cannot touch them can she?' Brother Ralph was clearly troubled by the alchemist's mutterings.

Wenceslaus glanced up and laughed again, a cold, cackling sound that made his Adam's apple convulse and dance. 'There are spells and riddles of magic plentiful enough to protect them on their journey out of this life, good father. There is enough magic to confuse a graveyard full of gabares, but what about if they are reborn? Yes, yes,' he held up his hand to stop the questions, 'I know it sounds absurd, but what happens if their souls are reborn? Can you absolutely guarantee that this won't happen; after all the astrological clock predicts that this window will keep re-opening again and again, surely it wouldn't recur for no purpose.'

Brother Ralph's eyes flashed with anger as he opened his mouth to reply to this heresy but the alchemist raised his hand again and silenced him. 'It doesn't matter one jot what we believe, father, I know I can't prove that our souls are reincarnated and I do not care to convince you of my view of eternity – but doesn't it seem strange to you that Hecate has schemed and laid this curse to last for all time. And yet . . . and yet there are moments in the future when her curse can be broken and it is those moments I would somehow have us prepare for.'

'No more! I will have none of this heresy stain my children, do you hear, none of it!' Ilyer cried as the awful implications of what the alchemist had said sunk in. She fell to her knees beside the cradle and reached out a trembling hand to gather up the two babies. 'Protect them as best you can through this life, that is all I ask of you. We will journey on . . .'

'No! No, do not touch these children, Lady Ilyer,' Wenceslaus hissed, gripping her shoulder so fiercely that his fingertips pressed painful red weals into her skin even through the heavy weave of her robe.

'Although I have magic powerful enough to protect them for this life it is not enough, I feel it in my bones. There is no time for you to seek another's help. The Black Death stalks every highway and if it overtakes them on the road they will die unprotected. Is that what you want? Do you wish to sacrifice their souls to satisfy your own philosophies? Think! Think carefully on it, woman. But be quick about it, I sense the grave-wraiths gathering at my door!'

Ilyer hesitated and wrung her hands wretchedly, tears welling in her eyes. She sensed the warning in his words even though the thoughts went against everything she had ever been taught to believe in. She was afraid to leave the safety of the hermitage and the one person who might be able to protect them in spite of his heretical views. She was afraid of the dark phantoms that lay in wait for her. 'Do what you have to,' she stuttered, burying her head in her hands in despair.

'Lady Ilyer,' he whispered, putting his fingers gently beneath her chin and lifting her head until she was looking directly into his eyes. 'I do not trade in evil, nor am I a heretic, unless daring to believe that a greater landscape might exist beyond the narrow margins of our lives makes me one. But if I am to help you at all you must put aside your doubts and trust me. You must trust me completely and stay silent; you must not distract me again until I have discovered a way to protect your children's souls beyond this life, if it is at all possible.' The alchemist's face became serious and he drew the monk aside. 'Brother Ralph, I do not ask this of you lightly, but for the space of this night alone I want you to forget the doctrines and the teaching of your Bishops and Popes. I want you to put aside your faith and become a man of science, a man of discovery. Concentrate your mind; focus it upon the dark shroud that I believe clouds our perception and forbids us to know what may lie beyond the world we know and understand. Try to peer beneath this mantle and tell me; if you were going to be reborn, if there was even a remote chance of such a future existence, how would you try to hide from those who would pursue your soul?'

'I . . . I . . . I don't know. It is impossible to answer

that, it is a condition so unnatural, so . . . so.' The monk's words trailed into an apprehensive silence as he began to pace slowly across the chamber, his wooden sandals clattering noisily on the stone floor.

'Think, father, think! Use all your ingenuity.'

'It's impossible,' Brother Ralph muttered angrily, throwing up his hands and coming to a shambling halt. 'You have the scientific mind, the imagination . . . so much knowledge at your fingertips, but you press me for an answer. I am a simple shepherd of men's souls, a wandering guardian of the flock. If I were to think of hiding from a band of robbers or villains on the road then I would hide in a cave or in the secret glades of the forest. I would vanish into the labyrinth of the dark places between the trees, or I would crouch down . . .'

Wenceslaus cried out, cutting short the monk's explanation. He turned quickly back to Ilyer, whispering, 'The hallowed labyrinth, the maze of secrets! I have been a blind fool for not thinking of this most ancient of hiding places, this secret that has endured from the beginning of time despite our feeble efforts to discredit it. It is a place so wrapped in its own mysteries that none have ever truly been able to define it.'

Ilyer frowned uncertainly and picked at the embroidered hems of her cloak. Somewhere buried deep in her memory she felt the echo of a childhood fear and remembered the frightening story of a dark and secret underground world that her tutor had terrified her with. But surely that wasn't the same magical place that this alchemist was talking about? Surely he wouldn't condemn her children to live in the darkness? She opened her mouth to question him, forgetting her promise of silence, but then hesitated, confused and afraid of showing her ignorance.

'But such a place cannot exist in the real world. It is

a thing of ancient myth, of fairy stories and pagan legends,' the monk protested.

Wenceslaus threw back his head. 'Is it? Good father, are all your judgements of what you cannot comprehend to be herded together and labelled as myths and fairy tales? There are so many rumours and wild stories of what may lie beyond the horizon. Tell me, is the world flat or round? What shape and colour is the wind? How does it exist at all if we cannot see it? Are the stars that we see at night merely candles in the sky or are they, as I suspect from my astrological studies, other distant worlds that revolve with the night? You seem to have forgotten too easily, father, that I implored you to be a man of science, a man of vision, until cock-crow. I begged you to throw off the dogma and narrowness of your doctrines for the space of one night.' Wenceslaus paused, placing his hand on top of the mountainous piles of books and scrolls that littered the long tables. 'There are too many references to the labyrinth in its many guises, its seven circles of secrets and its sacred spaces, its hidden mazes and places of sanctuary for me to doubt its existence.'

'But if that is so, where is the labyrinth?' Brother Ralph tried to argue only to be hissed into silence.

'It is not a physical thing!' Wenceslaus snapped. 'It is not a place you can measure any more than you can measure or touch a soul. Surely if you can believe in a soul then it must also be possible to believe in the labyrinth. I believe it is a secret place, a fortress against evil, and it is all around us, an essential, elemental part of the fabric of the universe. But the problem is how on earth can I find a way for these children's souls to enter and leave it whenever they die and before they are reborn. How can we discover a doorway, or . . .'

Wenceslaus' voice faded into silence as he began to rummage with a more singular purpose through his books. Suddenly he gave a cry of delight. 'Yes, of course! I can find it by using numerology; the magic square of Mercury must lead me to the classical labyrinth. If Mars and Jupiter are in alignment, if . . .' He grasped the quill from the ink-well and splattered ink across the parchment as he drew the squares of Mercury, filling each tiny space with its special magical number – eight, fifty-eight, fifty-nine, five, four – until all the one hundred and twelve numbers were complete. He repeated the process four times and then began a lengthy series of calculations. Eventually he started to link the numbers in sequential order beginning first with the number one then nine then seventeen and finally the number sixty-four.

'Golden thread, I need golden thread!' Wenceslaus muttered, shuffling along the tiers of carved shelves and throwing open the cupboard doors as he searched. 'I can turn base metals into gold – that's easy enough, but there is no time for that now and I must have some threads of spun gold.' He turned and paced across the room, stopping at the hearth as he threw up his hands in exasperation. 'To be thwarted so . . .' Suddenly he caught his breath as he looked down at the two infants and saw their golden hair reflected in the firelight. 'By all the saints!'

Quickly he instructed Ilyer on the exact number of hairs she should cut from each child's head which she did gently without waking them. Then, with infinite care and patience, the alchemist laid the hairs, one by one, upon the squares of Mercury to create the magical flow of numbers. Brother Ralph began to move closer but Wenceslaus motioned him to halt.

'Not a breath, not a movement, lest you disturb the flow and break the magic.'

The spidery numbers began to shimmer and fade beneath the golden threads, each tiny box drawn upon the parchment seeming to swell and become transparent, to blend together and grow, gradually engulfing everything in the chamber with a strange, echoing, blackness. A log toppled out of the fire and spilt a blaze of bright sparks, briefly illuminating the wall of swallowing darkness.

Ilyer stifled a gasp of terror and clutched at the throat of her gown. Everything around her had changed: the familiar clutter of the alchemist's chamber had vanished and in its place she was surrounded by a shadowy, half-seen landscape of twisted, tortured forms. She blinked and in the light of the crackling flames she glimpsed a myriad of moving shapes, merging, trapped inside the transparent wall of darkness. They gave the impression of a thousand towering archways, endless walls and echoing passages. She imagined she could see them filled with an endless procession of ghostly figures and humped-backed mythical beasts. The translucent blackness seemed to shiver and move towards her before hovering over the two infants where Adzine had laid them in a shawl near the hearth.

'Stay still. Do not disturb the labyrinth,' Wenceslaus hissed, his voice tight and shrill with tension as Ilyer tried to reach out a protective hand towards her babies. She heeded the warning immediately and scrambled backwards into a corner of the hearth.

'Of all the magic I have ever tried to weave . . .' the alchemist murmured, taking a tentative step closer to the two children, but the wall of the labyrinth shrank back from him, dissolving as coldly as hoarfrost on his fingertips. Gently he lifted both the babes, whispering spells and chants over them before trying to push them through the translucent wall, but each time their tiny bodies touched it the wall shivered and drew away before returning to hover over them once again.

'It is no good – I cannot find a doorway, not even

the slightest crack. The magic is somehow incomplete,' he grumbled as he lay the infants back down upon their shawl. His voice fell to a whisper as he carefully went over everything he knew twice more, checking every one of the numbers and all the words of magic he had used. Finally he threw up his hands in exasperation.

'My calculations are correct: they must be, or the flow of magic would not have revealed the ancient labyrinth. Yet it has no entrance and that is impossible, for every maze must have an entrance, it serves no purpose otherwise.'

The alchemist stared thoughtfully at the shimmering, spidery numbers he had drawn upon the parchment. The paper had dissolved but the numbers were still clear, though grown to a giant's height. 'By my calculations the entrance should have been where the number eight touches . . .' His voice faltered – in the half-light the numbers had twisted and wound themselves into such a complicated, three-dimensional maze that it now filled the room and it was impossible to separate them or tell which was which.

'Perhaps . . . perhaps the labyrinth senses the evil that haunts these children and hides its doorway,' Father Ralph offered in a small, hesitant voice.

Wenceslaus turned and stared for a moment at the simple monk. 'Yes, yes of course. Thank you, father, for showing me the obvious. There must be a link, something that binds the souls of these children, an essence that makes them a part of the labyrinth. But do I have the stuff of such magic here in my hermitage?'

He glanced anxiously across the darkened chamber to where the tiers of shelves and cupboards should have stood against the far wall. 'I must risk disturbing the labyrinth and pray that everything is still in its place beyond this darkness,' he whispered as he stole on tiptoe towards the translucent wall of shadows. It gave way easily, melting with the feel of cold silk against his skin and letting him pass through it before silently closing in around him.

Ilyer half-rose from where she crouched in the corner of the hearth and called out Wenceslaus' name, afraid that he would vanish forever. She stared intently at his shadowy form, afraid to lose sight of him as he rummaged through his store of magic. Suddenly he reappeared, breathless with excitement and haloed with a blue-white fire. His flowing gown crackled with frost and his arms were loaded down with his most secret and treasured artefacts.

'Something came out of the labyrinth – I felt it brush against me and it seemed to guide my hands as I chose the magic that would help us. There were voices, faint whispers in the darkness, which revealed a thousand sacred secrets. Quickly, Lady Ilyer, before I forget the wisdom that I heard, quickly give me the blade you carry concealed beneath your gown. I know now that I must use its sharp point to mark both of the infants, to bind them to the labyrinth through the squares of Mercury.'

'No, I can't let you cut my babies, never!'

'But I must, there is no other way,' Wenceslaus hissed, cutting across her protests. 'I must tattoo them with the flow of the magic numbers and cast the symbols of time yet unborn over them to unlock the labyrinth in this and their future lives.' The alchemist reached out his hand for the knife and Ilyer felt an invisible tug, as if ice-cold fingers were clawing at her arm, and she found she couldn't resist, couldn't stop herself from loosening the dagger from its sheath and offering him the hilt.

Father Ralph took an angry step towards the alchemist but Wenceslaus raised his hand to stop him. 'I promise you, father, that no harm will come to them and that there really is no other way.'

Gently, he lifted each infant and with the point of the blade carefully scratched the squares of Mercury onto their skin. Both babies screamed and tried to thrash their tiny arms as the blade left its red weal but Wenceslaus held them firm.

'Now, magic, reveal the hidden door.'

He lay the babies side by side upon their shawl and gathered together the claw of a grey wolf, a black crow's beak, the splinter of a unicorn's horn wrapped with the threads of a leper's winding sheet, glass pebbles, blood-red berries of blackthorn and grains of sand and threw them all into the air above their heads. The magic symbols swirled and hovered before falling into the shape of the powerful number two thousand upon the edge of the blanket. The raw weals on the infants' arms glowed blue-white and merged together forming two perfect halves of a labyrinth in miniature.

The shimmering wall of darkness convulsed and split apart as a howling wind tore through the chamber, over-turning chairs and scattering books and papers, sucking some of them through an echoing doorcrack that had opened into the labyrinth.

'What is happening?' Ilyer cried as the wind tore at her hair and sent red-hot ash and sparks from the hearth swirling through the room.

'It must be the hidden doorway,' the monk answered, as the wind pulled at his robes and twisted and turned him round until he lost his balance and toppled forward, throwing out his hands to save himself. In his panic he accidentally touched the translucent wall of shadows and, as it shivered and drew shut, snarls and growls erupted through the closing gap. He had a brief glimpse of huge, strange beasts with armoured scales and curved talons that prowled and guarded the inner side of the entrance, and then nothing.

Wenceslaus grabbed at the monk's robe and dragged

him away. 'The way is barred to us, father – those creatures would tear you apart if you try to enter. But I wonder . . .' The alchemist paused and looked thoughtfully down at the two infants. He considered for only a moment before bending and gathering them up, offering them up to where the doorway had been.

'No!' Ilyer cried, leaping up to prevent him. 'Those creatures that dwell in the darkness will seize them.'

But she was too late: the translucent darkness quivered as the hand of one of the babies touched it, and then it sighed and a tiny gap appeared in the wall of the labyrinth. Wenceslaus tried to push the infants into the gap and the shimmering wall shrank away from them and began to melt and fade away. The alchemist breathed a sigh of relief and handed the children back to Ilyer.

'The magic is done. They have a safe haven now, a refuge from Hecate's evil, a secret doorway into the labyrinth that I am sure will open and admit their souls each time they die.'

'But the labyrinth, the only place in which my children will be safe has disappeared, vanished! What have you done with it?' There was a hint of suspicion in Ilyer's voice as she peered into the corners of the gloomy chamber and looked for the slightest trace of the magical darkness.

Wenceslaus laughed softly and shook his head as he slowly bent to retrieve the scattered artefacts of his magic. 'You have such little faith, my lady, do you think that the labyrinth was only an illusion, some clever trick, an image of entertainment that I conjured up to while away the night hours?'

There was a strength of purpose and a hard edge beneath the alchemist's laughter that made Ilyer turn quickly towards him. 'No, no of course not, I meant, how can they ever find that hidden doorway if they can't see it?'

Wenceslaus sighed and spread his hands. 'Surely it would be truly burdensome if we had to see everything that was vital to our lives? Think, if you had to see the air we breathe or the wind that rustles the leaves of the trees – we would be condemned to live in a perpetual fog, blind to everything else around us. Imagine if that towering hall of translucent darkness were to follow your children everywhere they went in the form in which the magic revealed it.'

'Then where is it? What has happened to it?' Father Ralph asked, making the alchemist pause, his eyebrows crinkled into a troubled furrow as he tried to explain.

'It's everywhere – it's all around us – just like the air we breathe. I think it vanished because tonight isn't the children's time to die. But I do believe that it is still there and will appear again at the time of their deaths.'

'And those numbers that appeared – what was their significance?' the monk questioned.

Wenceslaus threw up his hands in exasperation. 'You cannot expect me to know the answer to every riddle in the universe, father, but perhaps . . .' The alchemist stared thoughtfully into the embers of the fire before he answered. 'Perhaps it means that the labyrinth will protect them until the year two thousand and that they will have until that far-off time to break the evil curse that Hecate has laid upon them.'

A trickle of soot fell down the chimney and ignited into a shower of bright sparks on the hearth, making the alchemist pause and glance anxiously at the dying fire. 'But how will Lady Ilyer's children know the words of the curse or what to do with them in another life? Surely they cannot carry such knowledge beyond their graves, and none of us will be there to help them will we?'

'Yes, yes, you're quite right, father.' Wenceslaus turned reluctantly away from the monk, a feeling of apprehension prickling the hairs on the nape of his neck. 'You must school them when they are grown, Lady Ilyer. They must know the nature of this curse and its antidote. And we must prepare for every future they might be born into by leaving clear instructions: we must show them the words of the curse and the books of knowledge that explain the antidote . . .' He stopped abruptly and spun towards the fire as the overpowering stench of sulphur and corruption filled his nostrils.

'Gabares!' he hissed, grabbing a handful of quickfire and hurling it into the glowing embers: but it was too late – shrieking, eerie voices split the night and echoed before vanishing into the chimney sending a shower of hot soot cascading into the room.

'The grave-wraiths have been listening! I was a fool to allow the fire to burn so low. I wonder how much they overheard.'

The quickfire burst into a brilliant whirlwind of flames that roared up the chimney and drove Hecate out into the darkness.

'I must protect them in their moments of death and rebirth . . .' Wenceslaus turned thoughtfully towards the long tables but his mouth fell open in a silent cry of horror. His clutter of books and scrolls, everything that he treasured and had spent a lifetime accumulating, had been scattered across the floor. The alchemist fell to his knees and began frantically to rifle through the remnants of torn papers and pieces of parchment, fragments of spells and medicines, remedies and scraps of knowledge. Breathing a sigh of relief he gathered together everything connected with the curse, his most precious books and oracles, everything he needed to protect and arm them against the evil was miraculously still there.

'Remember, you must teach your children the words of the curse. School them how to calculate Galea's chart. You must teach them well.'

'Zoros, Delmusan, Surmy . . .' Ilyer stuttered, committing the curse to memory.

'I shall cast a spell against the beast Cerberus. He shall always remember how he suffered from Solomon's fangs and will fear the dogs of this world and they shall always be drawn to protect the souls of your children. By the powers of numerology the mantra will lengthen with each new life they live . . .'

'But how?' Ilyer cried out, overwhelmed by the shadows that hung over her children's futures and she bowed her head and wept. 'It is hopeless, hopeless, there is so much to remember . . .'

She gathered up her two infants and held them tightly, her shoulders trembling from her sobs. 'But what if I forget to tell them everything? What if the grave-wraiths seize them before they reach the safety of the labyrinth, what then? Will they be condemned to eternal torment?'

'Weep not so harshly, good lady,' Wenceslaus whispered as he tried to comfort her. 'Hope must kindle the flame of their futures and show them the door to the labyrinth. But there is one last thing I can do to protect them: I can weave the power of fire and water around your babies. Yes, they will become children of the flame and it will always protect them as they enter and leave the doorway.'

He lowered his voice and put his lips close to her ear. 'Remember, witches cannot abide fire and cannot cross water. Your children will be safe.'

'Will they?' Ilyer asked him bleakly. 'Can we really be sure of anything?'

'No, my lady, the future has yet to be written. But we have done all we can,' Wenceslaus murmured softly and looked away.

Death in the Sky

CHRIS OSTIC BLINKED and raised his hand to rub at something that brushed, ice-cold, against his face and settled on his eyebrows. He gradually became aware of faint noises in the darkness, the crackle of flames and the whisper of the wind in the branches overhead. Somewhere in the distance he heard the sound of a car approaching, grinding through its gears as it climbed Bovingdon Hill. But they were alien sounds that intruded upon the vivid images inside his head, sounds that broke up the bright pictures, scattering their meaning into the surrounding darkness. He screwed his eyes tightly shut; he had to cling onto those vanishing whispers of the past. He had to try to grasp their meaning and find out why he felt so much a part of them. But reality crowded in harshly and the stink of burning rubber filled his nostrils, sharpening his awareness. The sound of the approaching car was getting louder.

He opened his eyes and for a blurred, disoriented moment stared through the light snow flurries to the burning wreck of Stephanie's car. The awful reality of what he had done struck him in the pit of his stomach and he cried out, clenching his numb, cold hands into fists of rage. Tears of devastation streamed down his face as he climbed painfully to his feet, staggered and almost lost his balance.

'Stephanie, oh Stephanie, what have I done?'

Mingled with his cry of despair he thought he could hear the wail of a child's voice. He turned and hunted for its source as the sound gradually faded away to merge with the mournful sound of the wind. Fragments of images came flooding back, the reek of death and sulphur, the monstrous, three-headed beast and the black, ragged hags dancing and leaping in the firelight, calling out chants and words he only half understood, then he remembered Stephanie begging him to burn her body so that she could escape from the evil grave-wraiths who were trying to take her soul. It all came flooding back – the weird figures circling the burning car, goading their monstrous dog to leap through the flames and seize Stephanie's body, the huge, salivating creature knocking him off his feet. He spun round, searching for them, his mouth drawn into a bitter line of hate and anger, but hesitated, confused and unsure of what had seemed so real only a moment ago. Not a single footprint, not a scuff or mark of any kind marred the fresh thin covering of snow upon the grass around the car. He was alone, completely alone beside the guttered wreck.

The sound of the car stopping with a squeal of brakes in the gateway of the field made him look up. He heard the doors opening and saw the indistinct silhouettes of two figures climbing out. A voice shouted at him, asking him if he was all right, if anyone was injured and telling him to stay where he was until they reached him. A flashing light swept the field and Chris realized that it was the police. He looked back at the charred remains of Stephanie's body in the passenger seat of the burning car and his throat tightened in panic, the palms of his hands breaking into a cold sweat. How on earth could he ever begin to explain to them – nobody would ever believe him.

'Get away from the car, sir. Get away in case it explodes.'

Stephanie's corpse suddenly seemed to jerk upright, engulfed in a swirling hail of sparks.

'Jesus Christ!' Chris gasped as he backed away from the car and caught the briefest glimpse of a huge dog inside the vehicle, its maggot-ridden hide a mass of sulphurous, yellow flames as it mauled and savaged the charred body, tearing violently at the crumbling flesh and bones.

'Run! Run for your life, it's going up!' shouted one of the policemen, throwing up his arm to shield his face as the blistered, twisted body of the car glowed white-hot and seemed to swell, its rivets popping, its welded seams cracking and buckling apart. Moments later it exploded, sending up a billowing column of smoke and debris thirty feet into the overhanging branches.

Chris was thrown violently backwards by the force of the blast, his eyebrows and the hairs on the backs of his hands singed by the intense heat. But as he fell sprawling into the snow he could have sworn he saw the darkness beyond the car split apart and for an instant reveal a hidden dimension, a labyrinthine landscape of shadowy, half-seen forms. A blazing ball of fire no bigger than his fist seemed to detach itself from the rising column of smoke and flames and descend in a flaming cone to vanish through the closing tear in the darkness.

'What the hell were you carrying in that car, sir?' The policeman's voice was suspicious as he played the light of his torch onto Chris's flying jacket and then his face.

'I . . . I . . . I don't know, officer,' he stuttered, stalling for time and rubbing his hand through his hair. His mind was racing, searching for a plausible explanation. Jesus – he was finding it difficult enough to understand what he had done himself, without trying to explain it to anyone else. He felt a cold sweat break out on his forehead and the colour drained from his face as he realized what they would think.

'Go easy on him, George, I think he's suffering from

shock,' the other policeman said softly as he moved closer to the wreckage of the car.

Chris looked helplessly past him and stared at what was left of Stephanie's Humber, holding his breath and expecting the officer to see her body at any moment.

'You're lucky you weren't trapped in there, sir!' the policeman called out over his shoulder. 'That explosion destroyed everything – there's nothing left but a mass of twisted metal.'

Chris let his pent-up breath escape silently between his teeth, feeling at once weak at the knees with relief and quite light-headed.

'Flares!' he blurted out suddenly. 'There was a packet of target flares on the front passenger seat.' The rest of the lie came easily off his tongue. 'I lost my way somewhere a way back, when I turned off the London road. Your English lanes are so narrow and without the signposts I thought that gateway was the turn for the airfield. Anyway the car was bumping so much over the rough ground I dropped my cigarette and I couldn't find it. I'd got out of the car to get a torch to try and look for it and find out where I was when the car suddenly caught fire.'

Chris paused, inhaling a shallow breath and watching the closest officer, trying to gauge his reaction.

'It must have been the cigarette. I'm sorry, there wasn't a damn thing I could do once it had ignited one of those flares.' He spoke quickly, fumbling in his jacket pocket for the crumpled packet of cigarettes.

'You should have been more careful. You're lucky it didn't go up while the raid was on. We could see it burning miles away.' The policeman was abrupt as he pulled out his note-book. 'You had better give me some details, your name, rank, number and where you are based.'

'Why don't we do it in the car?' the other policeman

interrupted as they turned away from the wreck. 'There's nothing else we can do here and this chap looks half frozen to death.'

Sergeant Kovak shivered and cursed the bitter English weather under his breath, stamped his feet and pulled up his collar against the icy flurries of snow that had begun to swirl silently around him. It felt colder than the North Pole out on the perimeter track of the Bovingdon Airfield where the maintenance crews were working through the night, repairing and servicing the line of Flying Fortresses after the battering they had taken on their previous mission. He stopped in front of *Carolina Lady*, shielding his eyes against the uncertain glare of the hurricane lamps suspended from the gantry and picked out the two fitters hunched over the right-hand, inboard engine.

'Are you guys gonna be all night fiddling with that goddamned engine? You still gotta check the hydraulics on the ball turret and flush out the fuel lines!' he demanded through the chewed stub of his unlit cigar.

One of the fitters looked up, squinting against the light. 'We're working as fast as we can, chief, but we've still got to test the magnetos and run a compression test. Remember – you wrote it on the maintenance sheets . . .'

Suddenly he dropped his spanner which clattered noisily onto the gantry on its way to the ground.

'Chief – behind you! Look, there's something running across the airfield towards us. What the hell . . .'

Kovak spun round at the warning shout just in time to see a huge shadow vanish into the swirling snow between the aircraft. 'What in God's name was that?' he hissed, clenching his teeth on the cigar butt as he took a hesitant step after the fleeting shadow.

'Say, chief, was that a big dog or something? It ran out underneath me a couple of minutes ago,' called out one of the ground crew who were working in the open bomb bay.

Kovak glanced up at the mechanic and shrugged. 'I don't know what it was but I sure as hell am gonna find out . . .' he muttered grimly, unclipping the flashlight that hung from his belt and stopping to pick up the heavy spanner the fitter had dropped. Gripping it defensively he moved back along the aircraft, playing the light from the torch underneath the fuselage.

He paused and scratched his head when he reached the tailplane: there wasn't a single scuff or mark in the fresh covering of snow.

'That's crazy, everybody saw something.'

He swept the pencil beam of the flashlight away beyond the edge of the area illuminated by the hurricane lamps; suddenly an enormous shape, a bounding dog or fox, crossed the torchlight, but it was moving so fast it vanished before he had time to be sure what kind of creature it was.

'Jesus Christ, what the hell was that thing?' He tried to chase it with the light, catching only empty, swirling flurries of snow in the inky darkness.

'What have you found back there, chief?' one of the ground crew shouted anxiously.

'I don't know for sure – whatever it was has gone – there's nothing here now,' he answered, but as he turned, his skin began to crawl and the close-cropped hair on the back of his head began to prickle. He had the unnerving sensation that something out there in the darkness was watching him, following his every movement.

Kovak stood his ground, his eyes narrowed, and he worked the cigar aggressively between his teeth. His fingers tightened around the spanner. 'You want trouble? Whoever you are, buddy, I'm ready for you.' The sense of being watched began to shrink and Kovak took one last, careful look before turning and walking nonchalantly back to where the maintenance crew were working.

'I don't know what it was,' he shrugged, interrupting the babble of voices all eager to give differing descriptions of what they thought they had seen. 'It couldn't have been much of a creature if it hasn't even left a paw print. Now, let's get on, we've got to have these aircraft ready by first light.'

Chris sat hunched inside his heavy sheepskin flying-jacket, shivering despite its warmth. He was on his own in a corner of the crowded mess canteen, oblivious to the breakfast clatter, the cigarette smoke and noisy speculation about where the day's target was going to be or if the threatening weather fronts containing even more snow and ice would ground the squadron. He didn't care one bit whether they flew today, tomorrow, next week or not at all: the war had shrunk in significance to him after the events of the previous night. He hadn't dared shut his eyes since the police dropped him back at the base some time after one-thirty in the morning: the pain of Stephanie's death was clawing at him, churning up his guts, and it didn't matter where he looked he kept seeing her – the flames in her hair, her beautiful skin blistering and turning black. He shuddered with revulsion and pushed the congealing plate of bacon and eggs away from him.

'Skipper, hey – Skipper!'

Chris vaguely became aware of someone trying to get his attention and felt a light touch on his shoulder. He frowned at the unwelcome intrusion and looked up to see Joseph Kranski, the youngest member of his crew, their tail gunner, grinning down at him.

'Spiro reckons the target is going to be the marshalling yards in Alsace. Where do you think it will be?' Joseph hesitated, his grin collapsing into an anxious frown.

'You don't think they'll send us back to Stuttgart do you, Skip? Only I heard from Buddy Dewsbury up at Deenethorpe that the 401 took a hammering there yesterday. Buddy says there's no way anybody's gonna get close to those munitions factories.' Joseph waited for Chris to answer and while he paused he noticed the untouched breakfast. 'You ain't sick or anything, are you, Skipper?'

Chris tried to smile to reassure the tall, thin young gunner. Today would only be the lad's fourth mission over enemy territory and he didn't need to read the wrong messages in his private misery, but all he could manage was a tight grimace that stretched his lips across his teeth. 'No.' He shrugged, giving up the attempt. 'I've got a lot on my mind, things you wouldn't understand. But you eat it if you want to, it's a pity to waste it.'

'Thanks, Skipper.' Joe's grin spread back across his cheeks. He didn't need asking twice, he quickly grabbed an empty chair, straddled it and reached for the plate. Joe Kranski's bottomless appetite had already become so much of a standing joke with the other members of the crew of the B17, *Carolina Lady*, that they had christened him 'Gannet Joe'. Suddenly he stopped eating, the second forkful of egg half way to his mouth.

'There's something I've been meaning to ask you, Skipper. Why do we always get real egg to eat in these pre-mission breakfasts instead of that awful powdered muck?'

There was an air of innocence in the question that caused the ghost of a smile to hover around the corners of Chris's mouth. He pushed back his chair and rose to his feet. 'Perhaps it's just the way of it – they're making sure their gladiators are ready for battle.'

The spark faded from Joe's eyes as he reached out with his free hand and gripped at the sleeve of Chris's flying jacket. 'You mean it's like a hearty breakfast for the condemned – for those about to die!'

'No, Joe, I didn't really mean that. I don't know what I mean any more. Just eat it, live for today and be grateful because . . .' Chris fell silent, the words hanging unfinished in the air, his eyes clouding over with a haunted look. Through a mist he heard a familiar voice shouting from the doorway of the mess and the sudden scrape of chairs as everyone began to get up.

'The briefing starts in two minutes.'

Joe crammed the last greasy slice of bacon into his mouth, wiping it with his sleeve as he quickly rose to his feet to a chorus of laughter from the rest of the crew who were gathering around the table. 'Come on, Gannet, hurry up, you're always the last!'

The crew were more subdued as they left the briefing, the jokes over.

'Snow's beginning to melt on the runway,' Big Mike, Chris's co-pilot muttered.

'Yes, but I hope the clouds are as thick as chickenshit over the target,' Spiro, their navigator, added morosely.

'What? You mean so they'll let us go back to bed? No chance, we could never get that lucky,' John, one of the waist-gunners, grumbled as they began to drift towards the doorway.

'Stuttgart – I knew it would be Stuttgart!' Joe kept repeating as the jeep ferrying them out to *Carolina Lady* bumped over the melting ruts in the snow and ice on the edge of the runway.

Chris spun the wheel of the jeep, skidding slightly on the soft snow as he turned off the runway. He didn't care where they went, he didn't care much about anything right now except Stephanie's death and what all those dreams, or visions, he had experienced the previous night during his vigil beside her burning car meant. He knew he had to bite back the anger and the despair and concentrate on the job in hand or he would kill them all. He accelerated alongside the line of Flying Fortresses parked on the perimeter track in readiness for the day's raid but their still, silent propeller blades and gun turrets appeared as dark sentinels, messengers of death silhouetted against the early morning sky and in amongst them he half-expected to catch a glimpse of those black-ragged hags. He had a tingling, prickling sensation at the top of his spine: they were out there somewhere, shadowing him, following him along the track.

'Skipper, look out!' Mike's warning shout came just in time to make Chris brake and curse under his breath as the bonnet of the jeep slewed sideways to stop only inches from a petrol bowser.

'Are you OK, Skip?' Mike asked anxiously from the front passenger seat.

Chris tried to laugh. 'Sorry, the freeway is a little busy this morning with all this extra traffic.' He waved his hand vaguely at the cluster of maintenance trucks, petrol bowsers and the procession of slow-moving tractors that were towing away the empty bomb trolleys from beneath the line of waiting aircraft.

'We're getting full gas tanks today, Skipper!' Elco, the flight engineer, shouted from the back of the jeep, trying to make his voice heard above the noise of the wind and the engine.

'Yup, it's going to be a long day. The weather reports tell us that there are strong head winds all the way to the target. We're gonna need every drop of that extra fuel!' Spiro shouted back.

'Stuttgart, why did it have to be Stuttgart?' Joe muttered to himself, absently watching the ground crews busily making last-minute checks and adjustments to the line of bombers they were driving past.

Nobody said much else on the remainder of the short,

bumpy ride. Big Mike raised his hand a couple of times and shouted to men he knew in the other crews as they passed and suddenly they were there, pulling up beneath the nose of *Carolina Lady*.

'OK, it's show-time, you guys. I'll just check we've had a full service and a new set of wipers.' Mike laughed, trying to lighten the brooding atmosphere that seemed to have settled over the crew. He jumped out of the jeep and called over to the ground crew.

'Hi, fellas, everything OK? Are we all gassed up and ready to fly?'

'Sure, she's as ready as . . .' Kovak, the chief mechanic hesitated. Today his usual, pessimistic shrug seemed to be for real.

'Did you check out that vibration and loss of power I reported in number three engine?' Mike asked, ignoring the mechanic's apprehension.

Kovak glanced back to the dark, silent bulk of the aircraft before answering. Last night shouldn't have been any different from all the other nights working in the freezing cold and uncertain glare of the hurricane lamps. It should have been straight-forward, a routine job patching up the damage, servicing the engines and giving the Fortress a thorough check-over before re-arming and re-fuelling her. But after they had seen that shadow, or whatever it was, they hadn't been able to shake off the feeling that something haunted them in the darkness. It hadn't been anything you could put your finger on, more a silent, malevolent presence powerful enough to stop their usual noisy banter and tuneless whistling. They had talked about it most of the night as they worked and they were still none the wiser about what it could have been – a huge, misshapen dog was the closest they came to agreeing and they all thought they had caught the faintest reek of sulphur mingling with the smells of hydraulic oil, cordite and cold metal while they worked in the fuselage. He didn't want to upset the flight crew with it.

'Yes, yes, of course we did,' he muttered, trying to shake off his sense of apprehension. He didn't believe in the supernatural – he didn't have the time to indulge in such fantasies – but last night had unnerved him.

He shivered and nodded his head towards two of the ground crew who were replacing the final section of the cowling on the right-hand, inboard engine. He thrust a thick wad of maintenance sheets into Mike's hand. 'We've checked the magnetos and run a compression test, we can't find anything wrong with it. We've flushed out the fuel lines to make sure that the loss of power wasn't caused by a blocked filter. Anything else you want to know?'

Mike detected an unusual, defensive tone in Kovak's voice. He looked past him to the rest of the ground crew who were clearing away their tools and realized that their normal jokes and string of quick one-liners were missing: they seemed morose, almost sullen in their silence as they stowed the equipment in the maintenance truck. Chris hadn't seemed to notice the atmosphere and was already swinging himself up through the hatch beneath the flight deck followed by the rest of the crew. Taking hold of Kovak's sleeve, Big Mike drew the mechanic underneath the outboard engine.

'What the hell's going on? What's the matter with everybody today? Is there something wrong with this plane?'

'No, sir, no, it's nothing like that.' Kovak shrugged, wiping the back of his oily hand across his tired face and leaving a smudge of grease on his cheek. He opened his mouth to tell him about it but thought better of it and shook his head. 'You'd only laugh and think we'd all gone crazy.'

'What is it? We're about to risk our lives in this heap of metal, you've got to tell me!'

Kovak shrugged again. 'I don't know really – it was odd, at times during the night we felt as if something was haunting us – no, that's not right, it's just everybody seemed to sense something while we were working but it's probably only this atrocious weather. I don't know, we're all so exhausted. I'm sorry, I shouldn't run off at the mouth . . .'

'Are you gonna stand down there all day just shooting the breeze?'

Big Mike glanced up to see Chris's head upside down in the hatchway.

'Come on, I can't run through the checks if you're down there!' he called impatiently.

'Yes, we're all tired. I'll be glad when this war's over,' Mike muttered under his breath to the mechanic. 'Even our Skipper's in a black mood this morning, all we need is some wild story about your mechanics seeing ghosts – it'll be enough to give them all the jitters!'

'Ghosts, who needs them when there's a war going on?' Kovak grinned as he watched the co-pilot throw his 'chute up through the hatch and climb up into the belly of the Fortress after it.

Mike struggled into the cockpit and eased his lanky frame into the cramped co-pilot's seat. He pulled on his headset and reached forwards to switch on the intercom; through the crackle of static he could hear the crew calling in and starting to run through their pre-flight routines. Earl, their radio operator, called up the tower. 'Army 375 to tower – requesting a radio check. Charlie, Alpha, Tango . . .'

Chris adjusted his headset and listened absently to the babble of voices and then suddenly tensed – he could have sworn he heard Stephanie's voice whispering his name. He pressed the headset against his ear and listened intently, but the sound of her voice had faded.

'Skipper?' He felt a touch on his arm and heard Mike's voice beside him. 'You ready to run through the checks? Skipper, are you OK?'

'Yeah, sure, why not?' Chris nodded as he tried to smile. He had to concentrate, he had to put Stephanie's death out of his mind. 'Brakes . . .' he muttered, looking bleakly at the bank of instruments without really seeing them.

'Brakes set,' Mike answered.

'Intercoolers.'

'Intercoolers set.'

Chris stopped and sniffed the air. 'Do you smell something odd?'

Mike shook his head. They worked their way through the pre-flight routine checking. They made sure the oxygen was OK, the fuel booster pump was set, the transfer valves were shut off and the tail wheel was locked into position. A green flare fired from the control tower and lit up the pre-dawn darkness with a livid glow and put an end to any more speculations.

'Everybody ready?' Chris called into his headset, closing his fingers over the master switches. He spoke directly to Mike now. 'Fire guard left and right, master switches on, number three switches ready, booster pump on, gills fully open.'

Big Mike glanced out through the cockpit window and watched the inboard propeller begin to turn slowly. The engine whirred and he counted six blades before flicking down the ignition switch. The engine coughed as thin blue smoke puffed out of the engine vents. It caught and roared into life. Mike trimmed the mixture lever to rich and locked the gills, listening as the engine note settled to a steady roar. They rapidly primed the outboard engine and fired it up.

'Number two inboard, switches on. Ignition!' Chris

shouted above the thunderous roar. The propeller blades of the last, outboard engine began to turn and Mike flicked on the ignition switch. It coughed and caught sending a thin, blue cloud of exhaust smoke pouring across the wing. Now the huge aircraft was shuddering from nose to tail, its four sets of propeller blades scything silver arcs into the darkness.

Chris put his thumbs up to the ground crew and drew them apart giving them the signal to pull the wheel chocks away and one by one they ran the engines up, watching the rows of gauges as they did so, checking the cylinder head temperatures and the hydraulic and oil pressures.

'She's running as sweet as a bird!' Chris shouted as he eased the throttles back and set the propeller pitch for take-off.

Mike nodded but he found his eyes constantly straying back to the gauges for number three engine as they ran through their final checks. He had a bad feeling about that engine despite all Kovak's assurances.

The planes ahead of them on the perimeter track were slowly moving forwards and turning onto the main runway before taking off at forty-five second intervals. Chris released the brakes and let the *Carolina Lady* roll gently forwards along the track. He glanced out of the side window to the bleak dawn landscape. The thin covering of melting snow was stirred up into a swirling blizzard by their slip-stream and images of Stephanie's car engulfed in flames began to fill his mind. He ground his teeth together, his knuckles whitening on the throttles as he fought to shut the pictures out. A single tear trickled down his cheek as he turned the Fortress onto the main runway and put on the brakes.

'Here we go, boys. Right crew, assume positions for take-off!' he shouted over the intercom as he opened the throttles and the engines roared up to full power.

The great bird of war shuddered and strained forwards, the wet concrete runway stretching ahead of them, its icy puddles touched with liquid gold reflections of the rising sun.

'You ready?' he shouted above the thunder of the engines as he glanced across to Mike.

His co-pilot swallowed – he had always hated take-offs – the knot of anxiety tightening in his stomach. His eyes fixed involuntarily onto the gauges for number three engine. If it faltered now with two thousand gallons of fuel in the tanks and a full bomb load in the hold, if . . . But he knew there could be no turning back now, his life was in the hands of fate. 'Shit or bust, let's do it!' he shouted back, his mouth widening into an anxious grin as Chris released the brakes and the plane gathered speed.

The engines were straining on full power. Joe screwed his eyes tightly shut and crouched in the tail end of the fuselage, clinging onto a strut as they bumped and rattled along the runway. The cold wind howled and whistled through the waist-gunners' windows, the noise from the engines was deafening. It made him feel sick: he hated take-offs. Suddenly he felt the floor beneath him lift and, scrambling forwards to peer from the draughty window, he saw the hedgerows and stark winter trees that criss-crossed the snowy landscape which slipped away beneath them. They were airborne.

Mike let a breath of relief escape through his lips as they crossed the boundary fence and the undercarriage retracted. Chris held the plane level with the throttles wide open as the heavily-laden Fortress climbed steadily away from the airfield on full power, gaining altitude in a long widening arc north of London, leaving the smoke and the scars of the previous night's raids behind it as they headed towards the formation's assembling point over Harwich.

'Looks like everybody's coming on today's picnic,' Mike exclaimed as he made a rough count of the other aircraft in the sky around them converging on Harwich. They took their place in the rapidly-growing formation of bombers.

'Jesus! It's sure going to be some day out!' Elco whistled in agreement as he glanced up from the instrument panel.

'I reckon there must be over two hundred of us in this part of the formation alone.'

'Bombs armed!' their bombardier called through.

'Rallying over Harwich in five minutes; setting the course now, Skipper.' Spiro's voice crackled over the intercom.

Chris throttled back and trimmed the flaps as he eased the Fortress into close station between *Big Dipper* and *Frisco Moon*. He checked the altimeter and spoke to his crew. 'Ten thousand feet, switch onto oxygen and keep your suit heaters plugged in and your masks free of saliva – it's thirty degrees below out there. Stay sharp, you guys, test your guns and keep alert for enemy fighters.'

Chris yawned and rubbed his hand across his tired eyes, shivering despite the warmth of his suit.

'Do you want me to take over for a while – you look all in, Chris. I looked for you in the mess last night, where did you get to? Are you sure there's nothing the matter?'

Chris pulled the mask off his face. He had a real need to talk to someone about the previous night and to try to come to terms with the horror of it all but he hesitated: he was afraid to face it and unsure of Mike's reaction. Eventually he shrugged his shoulders. 'No, really, it's nothing, I caught a ride into town. I'm just tired, I didn't sleep last night. Thanks anyway – you can take over for a bit.'

Mike looked down out of the cockpit window with a sense of apprehension. Harwich and the snowy fields and rooftops of England were slipping away beneath the starboard engines and he had a brief glimpse of the irregular line of surf breaking onto the shingle beaches, and then the blue-grey, gunmetal sea stretched away into the morning light. The hot exhaust gases from their engines were beginning to leave tell-tale, white vapour trails, clear sign-posts in the sky of their route, as they climbed higher into the frigid air towards the French coast. There was some small comfort in their escort of fighters but it wouldn't be long before they had to turn back with empty fuel tanks.

'You're pretty keen on Stephanie, aren't you?' Mike smiled. 'Do you think you'll marry her and take her back to Cleveland after this war's over?'

Chris's mouth tightened and he quickly looked away while tears brimmed in his eyes. He pressed his headset hard against his ears as he fought to keep control of his emotions. He could faintly hear the waist-gunners arguing about something trivial over the intercom and Joe was singing tunelessly to himself in the rear turret. He could hear Spiro telling Earl about some girl he'd met after the dance – the thought of the previous night brought a lump to his throat, fragments of the images he had seen in the light of the burning car began to fill his head and he scratched at his flying jacket where it covered the small birthmark on his arm. He wondered what it all meant. Certain words were now fixed in his memory – Zoros, Delmusan, Surmy – words he didn't understand but he had the overwhelming urge to repeat them over and over again.

Images, memories, began to fill his head. He saw two people running through dark, overcrowded alleyways and felt the burning band of pain across his chest as he gasped for breath. He could hear voices crying out, their voices, as they tried to repeat the words. He felt the overwhelming terror of pursuit as they forced a passage through the crowds. He saw their pursuers, two shadowy, black, ragged hags with their huge, misshapen beast, gaining on them, getting closer and closer. Ahead, between the rickety wooden hovels and crude canvas shelters that clung to the walls of the dark alleys, he saw bright flames and a deep rooted instinct told him that the fire was their only escape. He felt a hand claw at his shoulder as it tried to pull them back from the flames and prevent their escape but the choking, smothering shadows were folding over them both. He couldn't breathe . . . he couldn't run . . .

'Chris, Chris, pull your mask on properly, it's come unclipped.'

He blinked as he gasped at the cold, thin air in the cockpit and started awake. Mike was shouting at him and shaking his shoulder fiercely. Chris instinctively clamped the mask over his mouth and inhaled deeply. 'Thanks,' he mumbled apologetically, pushing it aside after he had taken a few deep breaths. 'I'm sorry, I must have dozed off. I don't know what's wrong with me today, the moment I stop concentrating on what I'm supposed to be doing I keep going into these strange daydreams.'

'You should have got a proper night's sleep, I've told you before.' Mike frowned with concern as he adjusted the elevator trim control to keep their place in the formation.

Chris shivered. 'Yes, I know I should, but I'm afraid to close my eyes, afraid of what I'll see next. Last night . . .' He hesitated, he really wanted to confide in Mike, they had grown up together, he was his best friend, but he still couldn't find the words. He still wasn't even sure what he had done himself. A part of him was sickened, appalled that he had cremated

Stephanie's body in that car, yet there was another, more subterranean self that celebrated her release, that knew her soul had escaped through the flames. But why? Inside he knew he had done the right thing but he was damned if he could even begin to explain.

The sound of Big Mike's laugh broke into his train of thought. 'Go on, shut your eyes, snatch forty winks while you can. Remember, they're only dreams for God's sake. I'll wake you before we reach the French coast.'

Chris nodded bleakly. Only dreams – Mike didn't know the half of it. He stared out of the cockpit window to the grey, featureless sea below and ignored the voices of the crew. He let the roar of engines and the vibrations of the aircraft wash through him. The reasons for what he had done were in those peculiar dreams, he knew they were; the sensation of having done it all many times before was getting stronger, Stephanie's death had brought it all so tantalizingly close. It was so near the surface that he could almost reach out and grasp at why. Memories of an astrological chart, full of strange signs and symbols welled up; there were lines and numbers drawn across it all leading to windows in the sky. A voice he recognized began to chant those secret, magic words he kept remembering and the birthmark on his arm began to itch painfully.

'Zoros, Delmusan, Surmy . . .' he whispered, echoing the voice as a shimmering, translucent wall of darkness suddenly filled his vision. Huge, armoured beasts who prowled and guarded the wall paused to stare at him, flexing their claws and howling at the night. The figure of Stephanie began to appear behind the guardians of the labyrinth, she lifted her arms and reached out, calling his name as she tried to warn him about something.

'Stephanie!' he cried in his dream as he tried to reach

out to her, pulling hard against the safety straps of his seat harness.

The dream began to dissolve, the translucent wall to shrink, but as it did the shadows of the two hags who had danced around the burning car, goading their monstrous dog to pull her out of the flames, swelled up in his subconscious. He shuddered and started awake but the reek of them lingered, making him remember fragmented images from other lives, tumbling the pieces of the jigsaw into place. He knew what the magic words meant. He knew how to break the curse. He knew everything, but a sickening knot tightened in his stomach as he realized the implication of that chart. The calculations upon it had pointed to a future time for breaking the curse. A cold wave of fear swept over him; that faint smell of sulphur, of corruption and decay, that he had noticed when he had first boarded the plane meant that those two creatures must have got into the craft somehow. They had followed him, they had to be hiding back there somewhere, haunting the shadows. His skin began to crawl and tingle in anticipation. He was afraid to turn his head. They were there, waiting for death to stretch its smothering veil over him; waiting to steal his soul. He was powerless.

The aircraft suddenly jolted violently and Chris flinched as he looked across at Mike who was anxiously scanning the sky above and ahead of the formation. Dirty puffs of smoke were exploding all around them from the anti-aircraft batteries stationed along the French coast. 'Looks like we're getting a big reception committee today!' Mike shouted, his mouth widening in an anxious grin as he held the plane level.

'Bandits eleven o'clock, high – dozens of them!' Elco shouted.

The sound of rapid bursts of machine-gun fire echoed through the plane as the gunners got the 109s in their sights as they swooped down through the formation.

'It's behind us, it's behind us!' Joe shouted. 'It's right . . .'

The Fortress shuddered as a hail of cannon shells struck its metal skin. The violent impact of the aerial attack shattered the kaleidoscopic images crowding inside Chris's head. The sudden noise and smoke along with the shouts and screams of his crew as they fought for their lives overwhelmed his fragile grasp on the new-found secrets of his past and the images broke up, they were sucked away from him into the faltering roar of the Flying Fortress's engines. He blinked dizzily; he was disorientated and his face was drenched with cold sweat. The reek of cordite filled his nose, machine guns rattled and anti-aircraft shells exploded with a dull thump all around them. Splinters of shrapnel were puncturing the fragile skin of the Fortress and the plane was bucking and wallowing like a roller coaster; through it all he was aware that Mike was shouting at him, trying to get his attention. He shook his head and like a diver emerging from deep water he broke through the surface of reality to find chaos filling the cramped cockpit.

'We've been hit, Chris. For Christ's sake help me!' Mike was shouting as he wrestled with the control column.

Chris cursed himself for letting his attention wander, grabbed at the controls and began fighting to hold the stricken Fortress level. His eyes swept automatically over the banks of instruments to check for damage as it began to lose its place in the formation.

'They're coming back! Bandits nine o'clock. Nine o'clock, two of them, they're on our tail. Joe, they're right behind you. Joe. Joe can you hear me?' Elco was shouting over the intercom, trying to make the dead gunner hear him and cursing as his boots slipped on the spent cartridge cases that littered the floor beneath his feet.

'Come on. Come on, you bastards,' Earl muttered through clenched teeth as he swung the mid-turret, Browning machine gun towards the approaching fighters. His fingers tightened on the triggers as they loomed large and menacing in his sights. 'Die, you bastards, die!'

Flames flicked from the muzzles of the Messerschmidts as they attacked and Earl watched, paralysed. His fingers locked onto the triggers and he began firing wildly into the air as death crept relentlessly towards him along the fuselage in a ragged line of bullet holes. He tried to shout, he tried to curse but the words were sucked away as the perspex dome of the turret shattered into a million pieces around him. The alloy frame buckled and broke up as the hail of bullets struck him squarely in the chest and fragments of blood, bone and flying suit peppered the bulkhead below with pieces of shrapnel. The stream of cannon shells smashed the radio and tore through the cockpit narrowly missing the two pilots. Pieces of radio, broken glass and fragments of metal flew everywhere; live wires arced and clouds of smoke erupted from the battered, twisted instrument panels. The plane shuddered and lurched violently to the right and began to heel over, black smoke streaming over the wing from number one engine. Instinctively Chris reached through the haze of smoke, shut off the engine and searched for the fire extinguisher switch. Miraculously he found it amongst the smashed, bullet-ridden panel and turned it on. Icy wind howled through the broken windows, clearing the smoke and scattering the check sheets and navigation notes into a blizzard of paper that flew back into the fuselage. Both pilots fought with the controls and gradually levelled the plane out.

'Jesus Christ, what a mess!' Mike muttered bleakly as he glanced back over his shoulder and looked along the length of the plane.

'Crew, check in, crew, check in,' Chris repeated into his headset, punching the intercom button as he opened the throttles on the three remaining engines and looked up to find their place in what remained of the ragged formation. Slowly the bomber began to climb back into position.

'Crew, check in – goddamn it, answer me, report the damage!' he shouted more urgently against the empty hum and crackle of static in his headset. 'Joe, Earl, John, Elco – can you hear me?'

Number four engine suddenly coughed and back-fired. The plane began to lose power and lurch sideways. Chris cursed and throttled back looking anxiously out past Mike across the bullet-riddled wing to see a thin ribbon of blue smoke escaping from the engine vents.

'The oil line must have been ruptured!' Quickly, he shut down the engine and flicked the fire extinguisher switch. 'Earl, make radio contact with the lead plane and tell them we're dropping out of formation. Elco, get up here and start transferring fuel right now, the oil line's been cut. Spiro, give me our position. Spiro, answer me, I need to know where the hell we are!'

Beads of perspiration were trickling down Chris's forehead. His hands were shaking as he fought to keep the Fortress level but they were still losing height and slipping backwards out of formation. The propeller of number four engine began to windmill and threatened to shake the engine loose. Chris hit the feather switch and hauled on the controls as the propeller stopped spinning. Number three engine missed a beat and then resumed its steady roar.

'Jesus, where the Hell is everybody? We need some help up here!' he shouted angrily.

Mike gripped his arm to get his attention and shouted against the howling wind, 'It looks as if everything's been shot to pieces back there but I can't see much through this smoke.'

'Go back and find out what's happened. Take an extinguisher with you and tell me what damage we've suffered. I'll try to gain some height.'

Mike nodded and clambered out of his seat, grabbed the fire extinguisher and vanished aft into the smoke. Chris thought that he had learned all about emergency procedures; the *Carolina Lady* had been badly shot up on previous missions – he'd even lost an outboard engine before and made it back home, but something deep down inside told him this time it was different. This time all the practising he had done in training, flying on two or even one engine, didn't matter one damn bit – doing it for real with your instruments all smashed to pieces and the plane threatening to break up around you over enemy territory was a different ball-game. Thankfully, some of the gauges were still working: the altimeter was unwinding its hands rapidly as it marked off their descent – they'd already lost ten thousand feet and they were still going down.

'Come on, baby, come on, don't quit on me now,' he urged, easing the throttles of the two inboard engines open as far as he dared. His hands were wet and slippery inside his gloves as he hauled on the controls, his breaths came in short ragged gasps. The handset crackled with static and he reached up to tear it off but Stephanie's voice stopped him as it whispered to him through the ether, warning him that the gabares were drawing close, urging him to remember that he was a child of the flame.

The engine note changed, rising to a thunderous roar, obliterating her voice and Chris shook his head, listening intently, but the crackle was merely static. The crippled Fortress shuddered and shook from end to end, its propellers clawing at the air. The spinning hands of the altimeter slowed and stopped as the nose of the stricken aircraft began to lift. Chris pulled off his oxygen mask to breathe a deep sigh of relief but frowned as he smelt the icy air that was rushing through the cockpit. The hairs on the nape of his neck started to prickle. The smell of sulphur was getting stronger, it was all around him. Logic told him it wasn't possible – the air howling through the broken windows and the bullet-ridden fuselage should have carried any smells away – no matter how strong they were they should have been sucked into the slip-stream. Chris sensed a movement behind him and knuckled his fist in anticipation. He twisted around in his seat to see Mike scrambling through the bulkhead doorway and collapse in his seat. He was about to let a breath of relief escape through his lips but the shadow of a huge, three-headed dog momentarily filled the entrance. Stephanie's warning was right: those creatures were on the plane. He looked anxiously at Mike; his face was white and drawn, his lips were trembling with shock.

'What's happened back there? Where's the crew?' Chris shouted, grabbing his arm and staring back through the doorway, expecting the creatures to appear at any moment.

Mike shuddered, his mouth silently opening and closing as he tried to answer.

'Speak to me for Christ's sake, tell me what you saw!' Chris shook Mike's arm violently.

'They're dead – all of them – they've been shot to pieces, Chris. They must have taken the full force of that last attack. It looks like an abattoir back there.' Mike paused as he remembered the feel of the sticky slip of blood beneath his boots and saw again the splintered bones and mix of guts and flying suits sprawled together across the inside of the fuselage. He wiped his hand across his mouth, trembling as he looked anxiously behind him.

'What about the dog?' Chris shouted. 'What was it doing? Is it savaging the bodies?'

'Are you mad? You must be seeing things.' Mike paused and took shallow breaths, trying not to vomit but he was unsuccessful. He looked up at Chris as he wiped his mouth. He'd chosen a hell of a time to go crazy. 'Everybody's dead back there, we've got to get out of this heap. We've got to jump before this wreck disintegrates,' Mike urged, reaching for his parachute behind his seat.

'No, no, I can't do that. There's no escape for me, not now,' Chris said, fiercely shaking his head. There couldn't be any doubt in his mind now, Stephanie had warned him and he had seen that diabolical creature in the shadows. It had to be that same huge, three-headed beast that had followed the car the previous night, and he was sure the two evil hags would appear at any moment. Every nerve in his body was crying out, warning him. Stephanie's voice was in his head: 'remember you are a child of the flame'. The words kept going round and round but what had she meant? What was she trying to tell him? He frowned: the answers seemed to be on the edge of his consciousness, so tantalizingly close he could almost touch them.

'Chris, listen to me, we don't have a choice, we've got to jump – it's our only chance,' Mike shouted angrily, making a grab at his sleeve to get his attention.

The plane was beginning to vibrate dangerously and the engine temperatures of the two remaining engines were rapidly rising. They had to get out fast; every second counted. Mike wrestled with the controls, trimming the flaps and throttling back each engine as much as he dared.

'Look at the instruments! For Christ's sake, Chris, everything is shot to pieces, the crew are all dead and we're dropping further and further back behind the formation. We're losing height, we're never going to make it to the target. Even if we manage to turn this wreck around it's going to shake itself to pieces before we reach the coast. Chris, listen to me – get up, get out of that seat and put your 'chute on.'

Chris turned his head and stared blindly at Mike. Fragments of buried memory suddenly gelled together into one coherent ribbon. The words of Hecate's curse echoed inside his head – words that had followed him through the centuries. Suddenly he understood Stephanie's dying moments. He heard the voice of the alchemist revealing the magic he had woven to protect them – he was indeed a child of the flame: it was the only chance he had to escape, to reunite their souls again.

'No, Mike, I can't jump, it's too dangerous. I've got to burn up, it's the only way I can be sure . . .'

'Shut up, you crazy bastard! Put that 'chute on – we'll both be killed if we stay here!' Mike screamed at him, his face almost purple with rage and fear.

'Listen, Mike, you've got to listen to me,' Chris begged, breathless with the effort of trying to make Mike understand. He hesitated, staring back into the fuselage; there was an edge of panic in his voice. 'There are two ghosts, grave-wraiths, I don't know what to call them – they're back there somewhere with their monstrous dog. I haven't got time to explain it all to you and I'm not sure I understand it all myself but I know they're here waiting to steal my soul.'

Mike opened his mouth in disbelief but Chris carried on before he could interrupt.

'You've got to believe me, those creatures have been pursuing Stephanie and me for hundreds of years, through different lives, we never seem to find out about the curse until it's too late to break it. The timing's not right now, our only way to escape is through the fire. I have to burn up the way Stephanie did last night.'

'What did you do to Stephanie, you crazy bastard?' He was getting angry enough to leave Chris there, to jump on his own and let him rant and rave until the plane blew into a million pieces.

'She was killed in an air-raid. I got to her flat moments after the bomb hit it, just before she died. She begged me to burn her body, she warned me I'd have to do the same thing myself or those creatures . . .'

Shrieking laughter suddenly echoed through the rattling, juddering fuselage followed by a blood-curdling, howling sound that made Big Mike cry out and reach for the service revolver that was strapped to his thigh. 'What the Hell was that?' he hissed, staring back through the haze of swirling smoke that filled the stricken aircraft.

'It's them. It's that monstrous dog and those two hags, they're back there waiting for me to die. It's no good shooting at them, bullets can't harm them.'

'You may be going crazy but I'm not!' Mike shouted, defiantly. 'If there's something back there I'm going to deal with it right now. Ghosts – I've never heard so much nonsense. Now put that 'chute on.' He wrenched his arm free and, drawing his gun, he turned towards the doorway.

A sudden barrage of loud explosions shook the bomber violently. Splinters of shrapnel tore through the cockpit all around them. Mike cursed, catching at Chris's shoulder for balance as he spun round and struggled back to his seat. The weird, inhuman sounds and Chris's insanity were momentarily forgotten as he grappled with the controls.

'Jesus Christ – we've flown straight into the middle of a fucking anti-aircraft barrage. They'll cut us to pieces at this height. Chris, come here, help me for Christ's sake. Bank right, put the engines on full power. We must be over Amiens, or Abbeville, or some place near there.'

'She's not responding. Nothing's happening. The controls are jammed. We're going to have to fly straight through it – we're trapped. We'll be blown into a million pieces if one of those shells burst in the bomb bay.'

Chris's shouts were lost against the deafening roar of the engines as the Fortress shuddered and shook while it ploughed relentlessly on through the darkening curtain of exploding shell bursts like a fragile ship being tossed about in a wild sea. Both pilots flinched and cursed as they clung to the controls while jagged pieces of shrapnel tore through the fabric of the crippled bomber. They caught glimpses of crowded rooftops, church spires and factory chimneys through the smoke as the town slipped slowly past below.

The barrage ceased as abruptly as it had begun and Mike let out a pent-up gasp of relief as he wiped his hand across his cold, sweaty face. He looked down out of the cockpit window; the town lay behind them and he saw they were flying low across bleak winter fields. 'OK, Chris, it's time to get out of here – fast, before this wreck disintegrates. We'll have to trust to luck that we've got enough height to make the jump. Now, put on that 'chute and no arguments.'

Mike started to climb out of his seat and struggled into his parachute harness. 'Come on, you crazy bastard – I can't leave you here!' He was angry as he paused in the doorway, but Chris still refused to move. Mike took a step towards him, knuckling his fists in frustration. 'Put on that 'chute now or, so help me God, I'll knock you out and strap it onto you myself, you son of a bitch. Now get up!'

Chris stared up at him, his face white and wretched with despair. 'Mike, you've got to believe me, I can't jump, I've got to burn, it's the only way I can be sure of escaping. Look, everything's coming together inside my head only it's too late to block the curse – anyway even if I could it wouldn't save Stephanie's soul, she'd still have those creatures pursuing her through her next life, and then, for the first time since the curse was laid she'd be all alone. No, I've got to burn up, it's the only way, we've got to stay together . . .'

Mike lifted his fist only to let it fall back to his side as he spun awkwardly around. A snarling howl echoed through the fuselage. 'What in Hell –' He almost knocked his head against the bulkhead as he crowded forwards to stare through the doorway and caught sight of three shadowy shapes hiding in the swirling smoke back along the fuselage. A huge, misshapen dog with three heads was mauling at the bloody body of one of the dead waist-gunners.

For an instant he hesitated, staring at the beast, the fingers of his right hand curled around the butt of his revolver. Logic told him it couldn't exist, that he had to be hallucinating. Suddenly one of the figures shrieked at the dog, goading it, prodding at its maggoty hide with bone-black fingers. The monster snarled and lifted one of its heads, letting the mutilated body fall forgotten amongst the spent cartridge cases that littered the floor of the fuselage. It snarled, baring its drooling fangs, fixing him with its wild, pitiless eyes as it advanced. Mike sucked in a short, terrified breath. This apparition assaulted his senses, it couldn't possibly exist, but it was there, bearing down on him, he could even smell and feel its hot, sulphurous breath on his skin. Chris hadn't been going crazy after all, there was truth in his wild story. The maintenance crew hadn't been imagining something while they worked during the night, this beast must have been hiding back there somewhere before they took off. Mike instinctively stepped back as he snatched the gun out of its holster. He fumbled to release the safety catch, his trigger finger jerking with panic as he pumped three shots into it at point-blank range.

The beast howled, its body convulsing from the impact as the bullets tore through it and sent it tumbling over and over along the fuselage; but it leapt back onto its feet, snarling and barking, before he had the time to draw a breath. The two shadowy figures reappeared, cursing and goading it forwards to renew its attack. Mike blinked as the cold sweat trickled into his eyes and he wiped a troubled hand across his mouth. The creature should be dead, he had pumped three bullets into its head, he could see the entry wounds, but it was coming back at him.

'Die, you bastard – die!' He took aim again.

'You can't kill it, Mike, it's no good,' Chris said quietly behind him.

Mike cursed and squeezed the trigger. The gun recoiled and the bullet sent the creature crashing backwards into the bulkhead. 'What the Hell is that thing?' Mike shouted as he retreated into the cockpit with the dog padding towards him again.

'It's Cerberus, the witch-queen's hearth-beast. It's here to prevent me escaping through the fire . . .' Chris suddenly stopped and stared up at Mike. In every lifetime the knowledge always came too late; now he saw a way, a fragile chance, to seed the future. He turned and reached up, gripping Mike's arm fiercely. 'I want you to listen, memorize every word I say. I'm going to whisper, I can't let them know I'm telling you this. Keep everything fixed in your head and if you get out of this mess alive I want you to write everything down, keep it hidden for me.'

Chris whispered, 'Zoros, Delmusan, Surmy, Dandalen, Sator – the words of the mantra have to be used in connection with Galea's chart; they must be recited backwards and forwards until the curse is broken, hundreds, perhaps thousands of times . . .'

Mike tried to interrupt as the beast began to make its way towards the doorway.

'No, there's no time for explanations, just remember, some day somebody's life, somebody who's not even born yet, but somebody's life is going to depend on you knowing this. You will write down exactly what I've just told you. Remember, you're my future. I'll find you in another life, I'll come back.'

The huge dog had reached the catwalk that led through to the bomb bay. Mike fired again, driving the beast back, the bullets kicked up sparks as they passed through the creature's body and struck the metal framework of the fuselage.

'Get out of here! Go on, jump while there's still time. We're losing altitude.' Chris pushed Mike forwards towards the hatchway.

'No, we could both get out. I'll hold the monster off while you get your 'chute.' Mike began to reload the gun and fired at the approaching shape through the smoke.

'Jump, Mike, jump for Christ's sake! You're not helping me by staying: that beast's only going to hurt you to get at me. If I jump all three of them will follow me down, they won't stop hunting me, they want my soul. Now jump, you bastard!'

He pushed Mike roughly out of the cockpit towards the lower hatchway. Mike stumbled on the steep steps down to the hatch and almost fell. He caught his first real look at the two, shadowy figures and their monstrous dog as they swarmed forwards across the catwalk. Their shrieking voices clawed at his ears. Their hands reached out, touching him with icy fingers, their flowing shrouds began to smother and engulf him in claustrophobic darkness. The huge dog lunged, snarling and mauling at his arms and chest, its claws gouging at his skin. One of its cavernous mouths reached out to close around his throat.

'Get off me, you ugly bastard!'

Frantically he fired the revolver, staggering beneath

the weight of the beast, but his foot slipped on the third step and he spun round as he toppled backwards. The gun flew from his hand and he hit the hatch heavily with his right shoulder. His fingers scrabbled with the handle of the hatch and for an instant he was staring helplessly down the monster's throat as its teeth snapped in his face. Its claws ripped through the sleeves of his flying jacket as the handle turned and the hatchway fell open beneath him. He was snatched away by the slip-stream and tumbled over and over in the clear morning sky for what felt like minutes before he reached for the D-ring with trembling fingers and pulled. He sobbed with relief as the 'chute cracked open above him.

Chris snatched up the engineer's clipboard and hurled it through the doorway at the approaching creatures. 'You don't frighten me any more, you can't touch me until I'm dead. I've remembered everything.'

Chris looked out through the cockpit window and a thin, triumphant grin stretched across his lips as he caught a glimpse of Mike's canopy billow open and drift away beneath the plane. But the euphoria of the moment was evaporating: it was a Hell of a long shot, he had no way of knowing if Mike would survive the jump, or if he would live long enough to write it all down. He wasn't even sure if Mike would believe what had happened once his feet touched the ground, and he wasn't sure he would remember Mike or be able to find him in a new life. He sighed wearily; he had done all he could, it wasn't much but it was better than nothing. But something still worried him, deep down in his subconscious he had the distinct impression that he had tried to do it before – and failed.

A sudden reek of sulphur made him spin round; the monstrous hound was crowding the doorway of the cockpit snarling, the two, shadowy hags behind it. His fists clenched in helpless anger. He remembered so many other times they had haunted his death and tried to reach him through the flames, he could see an out-turned circle of flaming spears set by his fellow warriors protecting his funeral pyre, the bright fire devouring his bones, the deck of a man-of-war engulfed in flames, the pitch bubbling between the planks it burned, an attic room a blaze of sparks; but this time it was going to be different, this time they had him trapped. He became aware that the stricken Fortress was shuddering more violently. A quick glance at the altimeter showed him they were still descending. No aircraft in the world could stand up to this sort of battering for much longer before it shook itself to pieces and fell to earth. He had to do something, but what?

Chris looked helplessly out across the starboard wing. The morning air was so cold out there he could see the prop-wash from the inboard propeller swirling in glittering ice crystals across the wing. He sensed the creatures were moving closer, they distracted him, the cockpit was alive with their whispers. Their foul, sulphurous breath ghosted his cheek. He twisted around in his seat and cried out. They looked real enough – terrifyingly real when they were this close and their shadowy, ragged robes threatened to engulf him, their demonic faces were almost touching his and he could see the red veins in their wild eyes. He could even see the blistered texture of their skin which was scorched and shrivelled, translucent where the flames had eaten through to expose the rotting sinews and crumbling bones beneath. Instinctively he brought up his hand to ward them off as they screamed and flew at his face, but their bony, charred fingers passed through him.

He shuddered as the dog mauled at his arm, its teeth snagging on the leather of his flying jacket. 'Get off me, you ugly brute!' he cried, tearing his arm free and lashing out and striking the dog across one of its muzzles. It howled and leapt back away from him.

'Think, dammit, think! There's got to be a way to set this wreck alight!' he shouted at himself, smashing his fist down hard onto the mixture controls.

The levers unexpectedly shifted backwards into the rich position. The steady roar of the two inboard engines changed dramatically, running rough, hunting for air and losing power. The *Carolina Lady* shuddered violently and lurched sideways as the nose dipped and the plane began a shallow dive. His eyes narrowed as he looked at the controls. A germ of an idea began to form in his mind. He remembered the bombardier telling him the bombs were armed and a quick glance at the fuel gauges told him the tanks were still half full. He was sitting in the largest, flying funeral pyre imaginable. All he had to do was to light the fuse, but how?

He reached forwards for the controls, his hands pushing through the grave-wraiths' shadowy forms. He felt a numbing, tingling sensation and he hesitated, his fingers hovering above the banks of shattered instruments. It wasn't only the uncertainty about which, if any, of the switches or levers amongst the bullet-riddled dials and gauges still functioned, or what, if anything, he could do to blow the plane out of the sky. His hesitation went a lot deeper than that – the instinct to survive, to live, was so strong it hurt. It locked and knotted the muscles in his arms, tightened his throat and made his fingers tremble. Beads of cold sweat broke out upon his forehead: he didn't want to die no matter what the risk to his soul. His headset crackled and faintly he caught whispers through the static. It was Stephanie's voice.

'Remember, you are a child of the flame: beyond it lies the safety of the labyrinth. Come to me, Chris, come to me.'

Chris swallowed and wiped at his forehead. The two

shadowy figures suddenly crowded closer to him, darkening the cockpit with their shrouds; Cerberus's snarling heads filled the doorway. They sensed the end was very near now and their wild, demented eyes were watching him closely, their voices chanting some meaningless dirge of magic. But he knew they couldn't touch him, not yet, not until the moment of his death, and he had to keep that thought sharply in focus while he worked out a way to blow the plane into a million pieces.

Something on the starboard wing suddenly caught his attention, something that would, under normal circumstances have set alarm bells ringing. He looked again and whispered a prayer of thanks. A thin, almost invisible ribbon of blue smoke was still escaping through the engine vents of the outboard engine and that could only mean the extinguishers had failed. The fire he needed had been there all the time, smouldering amongst the hot metal, undetected beneath the engine cowling, and he had the means to feed it. The fuel and oil lines were there, thick arteries lying hidden, threaded beneath the metal skin of the wing. When the Messerschmidts had attacked he had shut down the engine, cut the fuel and feathered the prop, his quick reactions preventing it from bursting into flames. His hand stretched towards the fuel cut-off switch but he stopped. He suddenly realized why they had never been able to find the clues they had left for themselves in each past life. The knowledge of how to break the curse was only a part of it, he had to implant something deep in his subconscious so that he could find Mike in his next life. Something so indelible it would trigger the memories; something that would make him remember – but what? Then he saw it, staring up at him in white, stencilled letters on the instrument panel – the aircraft call sign, Army 375. They both must have used it to call up the tower a hundred times or more, it was so simple, something you would never forget, something you would probably remember all your life, and beyond. And it would live on in the airforce records for years, maybe forever.

The altimeter warned him they were getting dangerously low. He would have to flick that switch now or it would be too late. He wiped a trembling hand across his mouth and blinked at the sweat trickling into his eyes. He had to concentrate, to make sure the plane exploded into a fireball. He had to open the two inboard engines into full power moments before he tried to restart the outboard engine. If he tried to fire up both engines simultaneously and failed . . .

There was no more time for regrets, no more hesitation, he had to believe the doorway to the labyrinth was just a touch away. He had to believe in everything his memory had resurrected. He knew there would be no second chance to reach its safety.

'OK, you bastards, it's show-time,' he hissed through clenched teeth as his fingers punched every switch and pulled every lever he could reach on the shattered instrument panels. The stricken Fortress wallowed and shuddered, the two inboard engines roared to screaming pitch and vibrated on their mountings as he threw the throttles fully open on high rpm. The glass on the manifold temperature and oil gauges exploded, red warning lights blinked on and alarm bells began to ring. The air speed indicator revolved wildly around the dial. The two grave-wraiths shrieked and cried out for his soul. Cerberus leapt at his shoulders trying to pull him out of his seat. Chris managed to switch the fuel shut-off valves for the two outboard engines to open and unfeathered their propellers. Slowly they began to turn, scything through the air, the stream of blue smoke escaping through the engine vents on the starboard wing grew thicker as oil and fuel reached the engine. Chris stabbed the dog violently with his elbow, shaking it off as he reached towards the turbo super-charger levers, pushed them forwards and held them there. It was now or never. He flicked the ignition switch. Nothing happened. He cursed. The damn thing should have caught alight. Sweat was pouring off his forehead and into his eyes, the dog was lunging forward again.

The mixture control . . . he had forgotten to set it in the auto-rich position. He lunged forwards with his right hand, stretching for the lever, pulling it so violently that it twisted and cut painfully into the palm of his hand. The outboard engine coughed and backfired and then caught, puffs of smoke became a thickening stream and red flames were already licking across the engine cowling and gushing out of the vents, speeding along the wing towards him. It had worked, the fuse was lit. Suddenly, in that last frantic moment as a series of rapid explosions on his left shook the aircraft violently from end to end he remembered he had to keep repeating 'Army 375', he had to burn it into the depths of his subconscious. He had to remember it.

'Army 375 . . . Army 375 . . .' he shouted over and over as the stricken aircraft lurched to the right and began to heel over.

Chris kept on shouting the plane's call sign even as the inboard engine exploded, tearing itself free from its mountings and rupturing the fuel and oil lines. It disintegrated in an expanding blaze of white-hot metal.

Flames licked along the fuselage and poured in through the broken windows and bullet holes. The grave-wraiths howled and cursed with rage, their clothes and skin a mass of livid sparks as they clawed fruitlessly at his chest. Their bones began to crumble in the flames as his jacket caught alight. Somehow through the pain as his skin blistered and the mark of the labyrinth on his arm glowed white he kept on repeating 'Army 375 . . . Army 375 . . .'

A flash of blinding white light filled his last conscious moment as the bombs exploded just behind him.

Ahead in the swallowing darkness a doorway opened up and the shrieking cries of the grave-wraiths grew fainter and fainter. His soul passed effortlessly into safety and the labyrinth closed silently. The memories of his life as Chris Ostic began to merge with memories of other lives and were absorbed into his soul; reality blurred, shadows blended with shadows and his soul was safe once more in the womb of eternity.

February 21st 1972

D R GEORGE O'KEEFE yawned and rubbed his hand over his face trying to shake off the tiredness and concentrate on driving the car. It had been a hell of a day in the hospital; they were understaffed, as always, and almost overwhelmed by a string of emergencies. He hunched forward over the steering wheel of the old Bentley, gripping it with both hands in an effort to stay awake and stop his mind drifting back to an emergency appendectomy that he had performed earlier in the evening or the forestry worker's fingers that he had attempted to sew back on after they had been severed in an accident. But the warmth of the car and the quiet hum of its engine with the rhythmic swish of the wiper blades cleaning away the splattering raindrops on the windscreen was becoming mesmeric, drawing his thoughts back to worrying over his patients. The big car began to accelerate and drift towards the verge.

'George . . . George . . . are you all right?' His wife's anxious voice and her hand lightly touching his arm brought his mind sharply back into focus. He braked and straightened the car, mumbling his apologies.

'I'm sorry, Jean, I'm a bit preoccupied at the moment – it's that forester – I was worrying, it's been a rotten day . . .'

'You look tired out. Why don't you take that short cut home through Malsbury Woods; we can't be far from the turning, it will save a good ten minutes.' Jean twisted round in her seat and reached back through the gap between the seats to scratch their bull terrier under his chin.

Barnos growled softly, wrinkling his lips in ecstasy as he stretched out along the back seat, his tail thrashing the leather upholstery. Suddenly he sat bolt upright. George saw him, ears upright, in his rear view mirror and grinned. He always loved it when Jean brought the dog to the hospital with her to collect him. He had been their constant companion for years, and there was something so infectious about the way he grinned as he strode along beside them, and he always took the shortest route across the hospital grounds to his office. The dog rarely hurried but moved in such a determined fashion that he wouldn't give anybody much chance of stopping him: he was very single-minded; there was never any doubt about who owned who.

George felt his mind begin to drift again. He blinked and shook his head; he didn't want to end up in a ditch. He peered through the rainy darkness illuminated by the car's powerful headlights and caught sight of the pitted and rusty signpost at the entrance to the narrow, overhung lane that led through the centre of Malsbury Wood. Jean was right, it would get them home quicker and there was less chance of meeting any other traffic on that road at this time of night. Making up his mind to take that route he braked and swung the car into the lane, its tyres stirring up a gale of wet leaves as they turned. The headlamps cut stark, moving shadows amongst the dense winter trees, their boughs and twigs glistening, dripping wet in the light. Trampled bracken and withered undergrowth rushed past on either side as George accelerated.

'George, be careful, there's something moving in the trees, look – over there on the right. I don't know what it is, maybe it's a deer, or . . .' Jean paused and twisted around in her seat, craning her neck to look back. She thought she caught a glimpse of a figure running through the trees, she had the briefest impression of a child's face.

Barnos suddenly spun round on the back seat, his hackles raised along his back. He leapt up, snarling and barking, his face pressed against the rear window as if he was trying to get out of the car and attack the figure they had just passed.

'George, George, I think that was a young woman – a girl, running through the wood. Don't you think we should stop and go back, she might be in trouble.'

'Barnos, stop that barking and get down from the window.' George slowed and looked over his shoulder towards the dense trees and undergrowth that crowded either side of the road. 'I can't see anything.'

Barnos growled and snarled, leaping up at the window in uncontrolled fury.

'The dog must have seen something to be making all this fuss. I think we should stop and go back – it won't take a minute. Please, George, I'll only worry all night if we don't.'

George sighed and eased his foot off the accelerator. 'All right, all right, but it was probably only a deer,' he muttered looking for somewhere to turn the big car around.

Judith Thornbury had struggled to get as far away from the lights of the railway station as she could, but no matter how fast she moved she couldn't shake off the sensation that someone, or something, was following her. She kept catching the rustle of footsteps, the sound of panting, a huge dog, close behind her. She could hear whispering voices, so close, but every time she turned round the sounds melted into the shadows. She took another exhausted step and stopped amongst the deep drifts of winter leaves and muddy puddles on the edge of Malsbury Wood. It was pitch dark and the night was full of the sound of pattering raindrops. She was lost and scared. She clutched at her swollen belly and her rain-streaked, childlike face became a mask of agony, her breaths short, strangled gasps. The contractions were coming more often now, hot fingernails tearing at her distended abdomen. She would never have believed that her body could survive this amount of pain. She felt an urgent need to push this unwanted intruder out of her. She searched desperately for somewhere hidden and secret in the tangled undergrowth where she could scream and force it from her body, somewhere so dark that she could bury it, smother it in the earth, and leave it in the woods forever with her shame.

She swayed dizzily as she tried to keep her balance. Her legs were wet and sticky, she was soaked with sweat and she knew her waters had broken. In the distance she heard a car approaching along the lane that bordered the woods, the swish of its tyres through the puddles sounding so very close. Its bright headlights were cutting fast-moving shadows through the overhanging branches as if they knew she was there, sweeping over her as she tried to run between the trees and escape deeper into the wood but her muscles spasmed and she fell heavily, pitching forwards onto the wet grass. Her pale face and school coat were caught for a moment in the glare of the lights as the car swept around a bend in the lane and carried on past. She lay on her hands and knees gasping, her forehead pressing on the mud and stones.

Through the pain she became aware that the sounds of pursuit that had been with her since the station were getting closer. She sobbed and struggled as she tried to rise, grazing her knees on sharp stones and kicking up wet clods of earth as she scuffed the toes of her shoes; but she couldn't get up. She sank back down as the car slowed and stopped further down the lane with a squeal of brakes. Her sobs became agonizing cries of despair. Surely nothing could hurt this much, those stories in her geography books about the tribal women giving birth in the fields where they worked made it all seem so straightforward, so ordinary. They must have been lies. She couldn't even find the strength to get up, to crawl between the trees. Her sobs became a scream as another contraction cramped and mercilessly squeezed at her abdomen, its grip so fierce that the pain consumed her whole body.

Suddenly the nature of the contraction changed to become an overwhelming need to push down. The monstrous thing inside her belly was fighting, clawing to get out, threatening to split her swollen body wide open. Judith's screams rose to a wild shriek as she convulsed and clawed at handfuls of earth and leaves, biting savagely at the mud and grass in an effort to force the baby out.

The pain eased momentarily and her screams subsided. Dimly through the haze of sweat and tears of agony the sound of twigs breaking underfoot intruded into her consciousness. She caught her breath and frantically searched the darkness, realizing that she hadn't managed to shake of her pursuers as she saw two shadowy figures closing in on her led by a huge, misshapen dog which was scenting the ground. Away to the right, beyond the approaching figures, she heard a car door slam and saw the flash of a torchlight comb through the undergrowth toward her. She crouched lower, grinding her teeth together in an effort to stifle her cries; hoping, praying that the two figures would never find her. The beam of the torchlight briefly illuminated them, picking out their ragged shrouds and winding sheets they wore as robes. Judith felt a shiver of unnatural terror run down her spine. There was something odd, sinister, about those figures – and the dog appeared to have three heads. They paused and looked back to where the car had stopped as the light struck them, their voices became urgent, hissing whispers as they began to beat the undergrowth furiously in their effort to find her.

Suddenly the huge dog lifted one of its drooling heads and snarled as it caught her scent; Judith was filled with a terrible dread as it began to bound towards her. At that moment she heard two ordinary voices calling out, shining the torch into the undergrowth as the owners of the car began to look for her. She could do nothing to escape – she could only try to hide by wriggling her body deeper into the leaves and mud, stuffing her clenched fist into her mouth to try to stop the screams that the next contraction was forcing up out of her throat. She sensed a diabolical evil in the looming, snarling creature with its two shadowy keepers and suddenly she knew that she must shout, cry out and let whoever it was who had got out of their car know where she was before the monstrous dog reached her. Some instinct deep inside warned her that her life depended upon spitting out pieces of grass and earth. She hunted for the breath to scream but it was too late, the dog was suddenly straddling her, saliva dripping down from its hideous jaws. The two figures squatted beside her, smothering her with their black robes. She struggled and fought to get free but the dog moved down her body, tearing at her clothes with its teeth. The two shadowy figures cackled and hissed at her to be quiet. She shuddered with terror as she glimpsed their cruel, haggard faces and pitiless eyes and she could smell the reek of death they carried on their breath.

'Be quick, Cerberus, get to the child, somebody is coming,' Aglia hissed urgently at the dog as it tore Judith's coat open and shredded the front of her dress to ribbons in an effort to reach her swollen belly.

The sound of footsteps was almost on top of them and their voices were so close that Judith could have reached out and touched whoever it was. 'I'll swear I saw a child stumble and fall, the headlights picked it out quite clearly: whoever it is must be here somewhere,' Jean insisted, moving further into the trees.

'I told you, it could have been a deer. You get a lot of them close to the road at this time of year. Come on, I'm getting soaking wet,' George answered, turning up his collar and making the light of the torch waver as he swept it across the grave-wraiths' shadowy robes and moved away. 'You see, there's nothing here. Come on.'

Judith made a last desperate bid to shout, to scream and tell them she was there lying at their feet but her voice choked and gagged at the stench of decay around her.

'Be quiet, you stupid fool, we're only here to help you rid yourself of this child,' Aglia hissed in a venomous, evil whisper.

'What was that? Did you hear something?' Jean asked, tilting her head as she tried to catch the faint, echoing sound she heard mingling with the drip and patter of the raindrops in the undergrowth.

Cerberus quickly mauled at Judith's distended belly, slicing through the swollen wall of her abdomen, splitting the skin with long, blackened claws which poisoned the blood that welled up around the wound. Judith convulsed violently and lost consciousness just before her belly split open and the head and shoulders of a tiny baby appeared, still protected from the world by the birth-sac.

'Your soul will be ours forever and you will die, here in the dark with nothing and no one to protect you. Bring the child with you, Cerberus.'

The hound moved to obey, lunging forwards, his salivating jaws wide, ready to snatch the baby from the womb, but a torch beam interrupted the hags' moment of victory, illuminating Judith's face.

'Wait! Keep the torch steady, I think there's something right in front of us. Oh my God, look at her, George, how could we have almost missed her?'

George stared down the sweeping beam of light and was suddenly sure that he saw a huge, misshapen dog jump back from the girl and slink away into the shadows. He dropped to his knees to make a rapid examination of the young mother. 'My God, it looks as if somebody's attacked her – she's bleeding badly, and there's a baby – they're both barely alive. Quickly run back to the car and get my bag – and the blankets from the boot. Hurry, run, this girl's bleeding to death – and stop Barnos's infernal barking.'

George stripped off his jacket and quickly spread it over Judith's chest and arms in an attempt to keep her warm, barely noticing the icy downpour as he fought to save her life. The tiny infant moved feebly, rupturing the membrane that surrounded it.

'You just wait a moment,' George muttered as he tried to get hold of the baby, cursing softly that his hands were slippery with blood. The girl's skin was turning deathly white and her limbs shuddered uncontrollably. She was going into shock. The damage to her abdomen was so severe he hadn't a hope of stopping the bleeding and as the precious seconds ticked away he knew he was losing her.

'Hurry up, what the hell's keeping you?' he shouted as Jean appeared through the undergrowth behind him.

Suddenly the car rocked violently. 'Barnos, keep quiet, we're busy!'

At once the bull terrier's barking rose to a howling snarl and the dog hurled himself at the rear window, shattering the glass. The dog was snarling viciously, his fangs barred, as it charged past the kneeling doctor, almost knocking him over the girl's body, and vanished amongst the trees, howling as if going into battle.

Judith regained consciousness for a moment and her eyelids flickered and half opened. Her mouth twitched, then stretched to emit a thin, empty scream as her hands beat weakly against George's bloodied arms.

'It's all right, don't struggle – we're here to help you.' George spoke softly as he tried to comfort her.

She fought to focus her eyes, she tried to warn him, and he bent lower and pressed his ear close to her lips. 'They followed me – they wanted to take my baby. You mustn't let them touch . . .' Her head sank back onto the ground, her unfinished words dying on her lips to mingle and wash away with the splattering raindrops that speckled her mud-streaked skin.

'Quickly, Jean, give me the forceps and the scissors, and bring me that sterile blanket from my bag. I'm going to try to save this baby. We've got to get to the hospital and get it into an incubator as soon as we can.'

His shoulders seemed to tremble slightly as he pulled the baby free from the ruptured womb and immediately cut and clamped the umbilical cord. He blinked to try and clear the raindrops from his eyes, but they were tears that blurred his sight. Jean felt his emotion but said nothing as she unwrapped the blanket and held it out to receive the baby. She knew how he hated death's victories especially one as brutal and as senseless as this one. George quickly cleared the mucus from the baby's mouth and windpipe and gently struck it between the shoulder blades. It waved its tiny arms before exhaling a shallow breath and then letting out a small, almost inaudible, cry. A smile softened the doctor's face as he laid the baby girl out on the waiting blanket before rising slowly to his feet.

Barnos came breaking his way back through the undergrowth, panting heavily. His muzzle was torn and bloody as if he had been fighting with something and he circled them slowly, his hackles raised, and then kept watch, looking out into the darkness surrounding the little group.

Jean wrapped the blanket around the crying baby and lifted her, cradling her in her arms. 'Fate has stretched a long arm into the darkness to rescue you tonight, my little lady. You're a very lucky girl, we hardly ever drive through Malsbury Wood these days.'

'We'd better get going, Jean,' George interrupted softly. 'We have to get both of them away from here. The baby won't survive at all if we don't get her to the hospital quickly and I must inform the police. Whoever mutilated this poor girl can't be far away.' He knelt to spread out one of the blankets, moving the girl's body onto it, and made himself ready to pick her up.

A long, howling, baying cry cut through the rain-swept darkness and the undergrowth all around them shook and rustled. Jean cried out in fright and tightened her arms protectively around the tiny bundle of life. Barnos snarled and moved closer, his ears flattened along the sides of his head and his body poised to defend them.

'What in God's name . . .' George hissed in alarm. Dead leaves and twigs were swirling across the wet ground towards them, lit up by the wavering light of the torch, they were spinning, gathering momentum and forming into two shadowy, menacing shapes. An enormous, deformed dog, its jaws salivating and snarling was advancing out of the wet undergrowth.

'Get to the car – run, Jean, run for your life!' he shouted, hurling his torch at the advancing monster.

Barnos charged past him and leapt at the huge beast, sending it crashing to the ground, savaging it with his jaws. George ducked down and quickly wrapped the blanket around the girl's body and then picked her up and ran for the car. With trembling fingers he turned the ignition key, the engine fired at once and he slammed it into gear. The tyres spun on the wet leaves as he pulled away.

'The dog! Don't forget Barnos!' Jean cried, looking back out of the broken rear window.

Almost immediately the bull terrier ran out onto the road behind the car. George cursed as he stamped on the brakes and the big car slewed sideways. Jean opened the passenger door without waiting for the car to come to a stop and the dog leapt up onto the seat, springing around to snarl and bark furiously at the darkness outside.

'Are they following us?'

Jean looked anxiously back to the leaves as they blew across the road. 'I don't know. It's too dark to be sure.' But she found she was shivering as if somebody had just walked over her grave.

'We have to give her a name, George,' she added in a small, quick voice as the car sped away into the night. 'In case . . .' Her words trailed off.

There was a moment of silence before George answered. 'Amy,' he whispered, swinging the car across the oncoming traffic into the hospital car park. 'Yes, Amy,' he added more firmly.

Amy had gradually become aware of her existence in the warm, cramped darkness that surrounded her and in the core of her consciousness the image of the labyrinth receded, burying itself in her memory, its doorway to safety silently shutting, pushing her towards the moment of her birth. Nature's instincts were about to turn her head first into the birth position when the walls of her womb had contracted violently, squeezing her, crushing at her. Tremors of fear had travelled through the umbilical cord warning her and triggering her instincts for survival. She had kicked and twisted, pushing feebly against the fierce contractions that were trapping her by twisting her the wrong way. Suddenly the darkness had been torn apart and the world, with all its violence and noise, had rushed in towards her as she was thrust helplessly upwards by the dying, weakening contractions.

Blurred images, hooded figures and the savage, snarling jaws of a monster had loomed over her, threatening to engulf her. Harsh voices, words she didn't understand, had screamed and rent the air, hurting her ears. She had tried, vainly, to ward them off, her fingers weakly rubbing at the inside of the birth-sac that still surrounded her but it had distorted everything, making them more frightening. A beam of brilliant light had scattered the darkness, illuminating the glistening tree-trunks and driving the dangerous images away. Then she had been surrounded by a myriad of colours, soft reds and crimson hues, and she had heard a dog barking and felt gentle hands lift her. The snip of the umbilical cord had filled her with a sudden loss, and then that first, ice-cold shallow breath of air had crystallized her senses and awoken her memory. It had brought all those other lives she had lived sharply into focus. She had cried out in terror and tried to fight against the hands that held her, had tried to twist around and look for the grave-wraiths she knew were haunting the shadows. She had realized that she was weak and utterly helpless, completely vulnerable, unable, at that moment, to stop them from stealing her soul.

The phantoms' voices had howled through the dark wood with renewed hatred, whipping the leaves and undergrowth into a frenzy. They were coming back, closing in with a murderous vengeance. The sounds had filled Amy with terror. She had known that the demon-hound would kill the doctor if it needed to, they would stop at nothing, and she had been powerless to prevent it. Images of the monstrous dog pursuing her soul to the thresholds of her previous lives had been vividly clear to her. She had screamed and thrashed her arms fruitlessly, trying to warn him, to make him run for his life and get away from the dark, lonely wood. She had wanted to tell him about the grave-wraiths, tell him that they couldn't abide fire or the touch of holy water on their skins. Her head was full of the knowledge that could banish the evil creatures forever, send them back into Hecate's darkness, but shouting until her lungs were about to burst and beating her tiny fists at their smothering, shadowy forms had been to no avail.

Her words had become feeble infantile cries, lost in the warm folds of the blanket that had been hastily wrapped around her. Already the clarity of her memory had begun to blur. She had cowered down in the woman's arms, hiding in the blanket and had tried to cling onto the knowledge as the car had accelerated away from the wood. Gradually she had become aware of the huge dog that sat beside them on the seat. For an instant, panic had seized her and her tiny heart had beaten wildly as she heard it growling and snarling at the darkness outside. The dog had paused, put its head down and had gently licked her face until she realized it was guarding her. Suddenly she had felt safe and the warmth of the blanket and the motion of the car had begun to lull her to sleep and as her eyes closed she had heard the doctor call out her name: 'Amy, Amy.' The word had blended with her dreams. Reality was changing, the past slipping away with each living moment.

Tweed Heads, NSW, Australia
February 24th 1972

JOEL STIRRED FITFULLY in his cot, disturbed by a distant sound in the night and a fleeting shadow that momentarily blocked out the moonlight and then vanished silently, smoothing itself away across the window-pane. He blinked and woke in a cold panic, reaching out to touch the unfamiliar darkness with fingers he couldn't quite control. He tried to discover who and where he was. Confusing words and rhymes of magic were muddled together in his head and the expanding tunnel of his consciousness was full of shifting images that he couldn't understand.

The shadow slowly recrossed the window, scratching softly at the glass. The sound sharpened his senses. Fragmented memories of his other lives drew rapidly together, bringing the terror of the moment vividly into focus. He remembered it all now – there could be no doubt. He recognized the rub of dead fingers on the glass – the grave-wraiths. They belonged to the creatures of Hecate's evil who haunted the door of the labyrinth and waited to seize his soul and they had found him.

Joel tried to sit up, to shout the words that would break the curse, secret words that were so clear in his memory, but his voice was a wailing cry. The sound that had woken him was getting louder, drawing closer, drowning out the persistent night hum of insects. It was a lorry. It was the sound of a lorry accelerating down Razor Back Hill towards the house.

The door of the nursery opened and light spilled

across the room, banishing the shadow at the window. Joel's mother bent over him and lifted him up gently, whispering and soothing him, rocking him in her arms. The roar of the lorry grew louder. She heard the sound and spun round as the glare of the headlights shone through the window, throwing her shadow against the wall. Her look of interest turned to an open-mouthed stare of surprise. She took a backward step and cried out in terror as the window shattered into a million, glittering fragments and the wall exploded inwards as the cab ploughed through the verandah, its wheels riding up over the furniture, crushing everything in its path. Joel had the briefest glimpse of the driver's bloody, mutilated face and the huge, three-headed dog savaging him as he clung wildly to the steering wheel trying to fight it off.

His mother barely had the time to turn and claw at the door handle in a desperate attempt to escape from the path of the runaway juggernaut before it ploughed through the room towards her. She screamed as the fender struck her back hurling her forwards. The floorboards beneath her feet buckled and broke, rearing up like jagged waves in a wild, frozen sea. The walls splintered and broke apart before the ceiling and roof collapsed in clouds of slates and plaster. Joel's world abruptly turned upside down as his mother was flung to the floor but her body smothered and shielded him, protecting him as the front off-side wheel crushed her to death. His cry of terror was cut short as the breath was squeezed out of him and he was forced down, wedged between two of the broken floorboards by the weight of his mother's body. He felt her heartbeat against his chest: he listened to it as it stumbled and faltered: he felt her shiver and watched her fingers twitch before she lay still on top of him.

The rending, splintering sounds of the crash gradually

faded until all he could hear in the claustrophobic darkness was the hiss of air escaping through a ruptured brake pipe above him and the drip of diesel trickling out of a fractured fuel tank. The crackle of hot metal cooling joined the sound of the night insects who had resumed their monotonous hum oblivious of the tragedy. He heard another sound, a sound that struck panic into his heart – muttering, cursing voices. They were voices he recognized and they were getting louder. The grave-wraiths were picking their way over the wreckage searching for him and he was helplessly trapped. Then came another, more terrifying, sound. The three-headed beast was scenting for him, getting closer and closer. The snuffling stopped and he heard the snarl of the monster as it savaged his mother's body and dragged her roughly aside.

Desperately he tried to raise his hands to ward off the hideously drooling mouth of the demon-hound that loomed menacingly. He remembered the reeking stench of corruption that was flooding over him – it was engraved in his memory as deeply as the rhymes and chants of magic that would banish it forever. He began to shout the words that filled his memory, trying to speak them clearly, but they poured out in a rush of infantile wails, a meaningless jumble of sounds that made the grave-wraiths cackle with laughter. Cerberus's fetid breath choked him as the creature's fangs closed on his arm and tried to pull him free.

'Die quickly, child, and our long wait will finally be over: your soul will be ours. You cannot escape from us this time. Hamace, Achabahe, Hamace.'

Joel screamed, his face darkening with frustration. He felt so alone, so helpless against this momentous evil, the fear was smothering him.

One of the wraiths leaned over him, her wild, demented eyes boring into him. 'Keep quiet!' she hissed as she tried to smother his mouth with her fingers; but her fingers melted on his skin, scattering a fine trickle of grave dust and ash onto his skin and into his eyes. She couldn't stop him crying out. The pain made him scream louder.

'Leave him be, sister, if he wails any louder somebody will find him. Remember the other one would not have escaped if that useless cur, Cerberus, had been quicker. If we had not goaded the dog to tear her mother's belly open and release her she would have strangled herself with the birth cord and choked to death in the womb. If only those cursed people hadn't come along! We must not fail again.'

Joel listened to the wraiths' whispering voices and a surge of reckless hope filled him. He heard how his sister's soul had escaped their evil clutches and knew he must survive: somehow he had to find her. Joel's voice rose into a lung-bursting cry for help. The two shadowy creatures goaded and prodded at Cerberus to snatch the child and kill it as they muttered impatient snatches of black magic to try to muffle the baby's cries, squatting on their haunches on either side of Joel, anxiously watching the darkness. The dog worried at the splintered floorboards, trying to tear them with its powerful claws so that it could get enough room to crush the baby in its jaws.

'Kill the child, kill it quickly!' Aglia hissed in alarm, frantically beating the dog as the wailing sirens of rescue vehicles grew steadily louder and headlights breasted the top of the hill, then swept down towards them, flooding the wreckage of the house in brilliant white light.

The two wraiths backed away, cursing and muttering in rage, afraid of the rescuers and shrinking away into the darkness as the child's cries grew louder and he threshed his arms around. Suddenly Joel was surrounded by firemen who were tearing at the rubble to free him. Powerful beams of torchlight shone down, illuminating him as a doctor picked him up. Cerberus snarled, baring his fangs and then cowered away into the darkness.

A priest who had been visiting the neighbourhood scrambled through the ruins of the house and fell to his knees beside the doctor. 'How badly is the child hurt? Will he survive, doctor?' He unscrewed a spiral of holy water.

'I don't know, father – it looks as if he's been crushed. You had better say the last rites just in case.'

The priest trickled the holy water across the baby's forehead and as he made the sign of the cross with his index finger, a howling cry of rage split the darkness and then faded into silence. Joel felt a sudden warm sense of safety flow through him. The grave-wraiths and their monstrous dog-demon had vanished. He looked up into the priest's eyes and feebly waved his hands. There was so much he had to tell him but the memories were fading, blurring together. The past was slipping away.

A Chance Meeting
London 1994

T HE BELL ON the door of Wicken's Gallery
jangled softly. The lunch-time hum of the traffic
crawling nose to tail along Bond Street was
momentarily amplified as the door opened and a tall
figure entered and let the door swing shut behind him.
Amy Thornbury instinctively glanced up at the sound
of the bell and lost her place in the catalogue of contem-
porary watercolours she was compiling for the gallery's
forthcoming exhibition. She sighed and pushed the book
aside. It had been one of those mornings, full of inter-
ruptions, it always seemed to happen when the other
assistant was off sick and she was left to look after the
place on her own.

'I'll be right with you,' she called, rising gracefully
from her desk, pushing back the stray strands of dark
auburn hair that had fallen across her face and smoothing
out the creases in her skirt before walking across to greet
the hesitant figure who was silhouetted against the
sunlight as he hovered in the doorway.

'Good morning, sir,' she smiled easily as she picked
up a programme of the work on show. 'Is there something in our current exhibition you wish to view, or
perhaps . . .' Amy let her words tail off and her smile
stiffened slightly. Her manner became a little crisper
as she neared the entrance and saw the dishevelled
appearance of the young man as he stood awkwardly
on the threshold of the gallery with a folio of artwork
tucked under his left arm. She realized that he was most

definitely not in the prospective purchaser category.

'Yes, can I help you?' she asked defensively.

From the look of his clothes he was either a student or had recently been one. He couldn't be much older than she was, probably down on his luck and struggling to sell a talent that nobody wanted. There was always a steady trickle of young unknowns approaching the gallery, coming in off the street in the hope of that first exhibition, that lucky break. And it never got any easier watching the disappointment in their eyes when they were turned away. Sometimes, in the year she had worked in the gallery, Amy had wondered how anybody ever got started in the art world.

Mr Wicken, or the gallery manager Mr Hargraves, usually dealt with these situations personally but today they were both in Birmingham attending a sculpture exhibition. It was with a sinking feeling that Amy realized that she would have to send this young man on his way herself. She cleared her throat carefully and slowly began to choose the words. She didn't want to hurt his feelings or dismiss him too abruptly. Looking past him, avoiding his eyes, she opened her mouth to speak, but he spoke first.

'G'day, miss, my name's Joel, Joel Goudor. I'm sorry to barge in like this but I was wondering if you've got a moment to spare. If you wouldn't mind I'd like you to give me a little of your expert advice on my work.'

Joel paused and stared intently at the beautiful girl standing in front of him. It was uncanny – he could have sworn he knew her, that he'd met her before, but he'd only been in London for the past three months. Joel's soft Australian accent and his request took Amy completely by surprise. It made her look beyond her first impression. His smile was disarming, his face open and honest, framed by a mass of blonde, curly hair. His startling blue eyes held her gaze and made her forget what she was about to say. There was something in his manner – she couldn't explain it, but it seemed to touch a hidden chord deep in her, to awaken something in her subconscious. It was as if she already knew him, but that just wasn't possible: she would have remembered if they had met before. She stepped back away from him, was uncertain and a little afraid of the half-seen images he stirred up in her mind.

'I'm sorry, I've startled you,' he apologized quickly, seeing the shadow of doubt that crossed her eyes. 'Let me start again and I'll try to explain a little more clearly. I recently started a course at Goldsmiths' but I'm finding my Art tutors very confusing. They want me to change everything, they say I will never expand my talent if I cling onto the repetitive images that fill my work. But the pictures are so vivid inside my head I just can't shut them out. That's why I would really value your expert opinion.'

Amy smiled and recovered her composure as she gently shook her head. 'I'm only Mr Wicken's secretary – I couldn't give you an expert's opinion of your work. He isn't in today I'm afraid, perhaps you could come back another time. I'll tell him you called when he gets back but I had better warn you not to expect too much: the gallery doesn't usually give assessments of students' work, not unless it's part of an exhibition we're putting together. You did say that your name is Goudor, didn't you?'

'Yes, yes, Joel Goudor,' he stammered. His sun-tanned cheeks were flushing hot and darkening a shade, his easy manner was dissolving. He couldn't understand the effect this girl was having on him: he wanted to gather her in his arms and swing her around and around, to shout with joy and tell the world he had found her again; yet logic told him that they had only just met and he was on the verge of making a complete fool of himself. There were a thousand things he wanted to say to her but his tongue felt as if it was tied in knots. When he spoke the words came out in a rush. 'I'd . . .I'd much rather you looked at my work yourself, Stephanie.'

'No, I'm sorry, you must have the wrong person, my name's not Stephanie.' Amy's smile faded. The sunlight in the busy street outside seemed to dim fleetingly and she shivered as she shook her head more firmly and pushed the folder away.

The telephone on Amy's desk began to ring and its persistent double tone cut through the awkward silence. 'You must excuse me for a minute,' she murmured as she hurried across to her desk.

Joel felt his face burning with embarrassment. He didn't know why he had called her Stephanie: it was almost as though someone else had been talking. He had to get out of there before he said or did something even worse. 'No worries. I'm sorry I barged in like that,' he apologized softly, turning and moving quickly towards the door. On impulse he stopped and opened his folder, selected two of his drawings and left them on the gallery table before slipping out into the lunch-time crowds that thronged Bond Street. He didn't know why, but something told him they would meet again – they had to.

Amy heard the doorbell jangle and glanced up, cupping her hand over the mouthpiece of the receiver. 'Chris – no, I mean Joel, wait!' she called out, but he had vanished and she frowned as she reached for the programme of the current exhibition and rapidly read the details to the caller, thanking her for the enquiry before hanging up.

For a long moment she sat there staring at the door wondering why she had called him Chris: she didn't know anyone called Chris. Joel's sudden entrance into her life had been like a pebble dropped into a still pond:

ripples of disquiet were travelling through her subconscious and jolting forgotten memories, stirring up images that she didn't understand. Sighing, she glanced at her watch – ten to one, almost time for her to take a lunch break. She stood up and absently began to tidy the programmes that lay on the table close to the door when she noticed the two drawings the Australian boy had left.

At a first, cursory glance both the drawings were little more than a mass of abstract scribbles, meaningless, jagged lines and heavily overworked smudging of graphite which, in some places, had scored and torn through the surface of the cartridge paper that he had used. Here and there, vivid splashes and pinpoints of colour were visible through the dirty blur of light and shadow he had created. Amy could see from the gloomy, depressing smears of black and grey why his tutors wanted him to try something new. She was about to tidy them away and put them into one of the print drawers ready for when he came back for them when she hesitated and picked up the larger of the pictures. She looked at it, wondering what persistent image it was supposed to depict from his imagination, what it was he saw within the maze of scribbled lines. Curiously she looked at it on its side and then turned it upside down. Suddenly she caught her breath and dropped it back onto the table as if it had burned her fingers.

As she had turned it the right way up the mass of incomprehensible scribbles and jagged lines had seemed to shiver and merge together. The darker tones had blended deeper into the shadows and had revealed two hooded, sinister figures wrapped in shrouds with a huge, misshapen, dog-like creature at their feet. Their bony, black fingers were etched in careful detail and piercing eyes stared out from their withered, worm-eaten faces. She shuddered and brought her hand up to her mouth to stifle a cry of terror. The hairs on the nape of her neck began to prickle – she knew those hideous faces. Seeing them had triggered something in her mind and suddenly the sounds of their demonic voices seemed to echo through her subconscious. The hum of the traffic seemed to fade, the sunlight outside the gallery appeared to dim and the shadows closed in around her. Her memory seemed to open up and then she was running, trying to escape from something dark and terrible. The clatter of footsteps over cobbles followed her through a maze of dark alleyways, the screeching of her pursuers getting closer and closer.

Amy bit on her clenched knuckles and the sharp stab of pain banished the dark thoughts, scattering them into the background. She blinked and looked anxiously around the empty gallery. It felt cold and inhospitable. She shivered as she caught sight of the picture where she had dropped it on the table. The figures' penetrating eyes still seemed to be staring at her. In a moment of panic she grabbed the picture and turned it over, but she couldn't erase those withering, hunting eyes from her thoughts. She thrust it into the print drawer and reached for the other picture, grabbing at it, trying to shut it away without looking at it, afraid of what it might reveal. But her eyes were drawn irresistibly towards it. To her surprise it didn't frighten her at all – on the contrary it filled her with a sense of safety, a feeling of quiet peace. Yet she found difficulty describing what she saw: it seemed to change, to blend and merge together leaving only the vaguest impression of a far-off, secret place, a labyrinthine maze of towering archways and endless walls and passageways crowded with ghostly shapes. She thought she could see numbers of strange, hieroglyphics hidden in the picture but when she looked for them she couldn't find them.

She sighed with relief, grateful that the second picture

hadn't frightened her like the first, and slipped it into the drawer with the other one before pushing it firmly shut. She turned away and gathered the gallery keys before locking up on her way to lunch. Joel's visit had certainly given her something to think about.

In the hot summer weeks that followed their encounter in the gallery Amy found herself thinking more and more about Joel, finding it difficult to shake off the feeling that they had met somewhere before, that she knew him. But that was impossible – there hadn't been any Australian girls at her boarding school and foreigners, to the people of Malsbury where she had grown up, were people from the next village. Even in the two years she had worked for her father in the local hospital she had only met two real foreigners: one a houseman from Nepal and the other an anaesthetist from Italy. And as for the friends she had made while working in London, she could count them on the fingers of one hand, and none of them were Australian. And yet she had the uncanny sense of knowing him and the feeling didn't diminish as the days went by, rather it increased, strengthened by the oddest fragments of dreams and memories that kept rising to the surface of her consciousness. They were never clear enough to really comprehend the brief, vivid impressions of distant landscapes but he was always part of them, riding beside her through a dark, shadowy wood, holding her close as the sun rose, wreathed in fire. These strange dreamscapes would spring on her in unguarded moments filling that time of unreality between sleeping and waking, or when the swaying movement of the crowded commuter train that took her from her small flat in Blackheath into work lulled her into daydreams. Always the images seemed so real but as the world around her invaded her consciousness they melted away as quickly as soft sand would slip through her fingers.

Amy began to brood on their brief meeting, often waking in the darkness of her tiny bedroom, troubled by haunting dreams. There wasn't anyone she felt close enough to in London to share these strange experiences with, and there never seemed time enough during her brief telephone calls home to discuss it. She repeatedly took out the two drawings that Joel had left in the gallery and tried to see what it was that had frightened her but this only made them so familiar that she was unable to make out anything but a blurry pattern.

Mr Wicken had glanced over her shoulder at the two drawings and dismissed them with a wave of his hand as immature scribbles. Yes, he agreed, they showed a little talent but it would need a lot of hard work to develop it. He had frowned at the dark rings forming under Amy's eyes and her pale, drawn complexion and had complained that she was spending too much time indoors brooding.

'It's time you got out more, met new people,' he would say firmly.

One hot, airless Thursday afternoon towards the middle of July he called her into his office and gave her a gilt-edged invitation.

'There's a private view tonight at the Hondo Gallery in Chelsea Harbour. I'm afraid I am already booked to go somewhere else but I wonder if you would go and represent us.'

Amy paid off the taxi and reluctantly watched it pull away in a haze of blue diesel fumes. With a feeling of apprehension she turned towards the brightly lit entrance of the Hondo Gallery. She wasn't quite sure what was expected of her or even if she should be there at all. Mr Wicken's jocular laughter and his instructions to enjoy herself seemed quite daunting as she watched the noisy throng of people crowding into the gallery entrance. She hesitated: perhaps it would be better to wait until the crowd thinned.

She let her gaze wander across the harbour, shading her eyes against the low evening sunlight that shimmered like liquid gold on the river, casting a forest of thin shadows across the quay from the masts and rigging of the boats moored there. It was a beautiful evening with the hint of a breeze that ruffled her hair and carried with it the cry of swallows that wheeled and skimmed across the molten, sluggish surface of the water. There was a scent of Oriental cooking and rich eastern spices on the air and she breathed in deeply, savouring the atmosphere. Her mind began to drift to far-off places and she took a step towards the Embankment, drawn by the setting sun across the river. Suddenly a burst of laughter and noisy voices in the gallery entrance broke through her thoughts and made her glance back. She knew she would have to put in an appearance no matter how brief. She would have to go and see the private view and sign the visitors' book, she would have to look at the work on show so that she could discuss it with Mr Wicken, but then she would escape as quickly as she could. She smiled grimly and, straightening the sleeves of her silk jacket, she walked into the gallery.

The buzz of voices, the lights and the bustle of the crowd inside the art show almost made her turn back but it was too late for that now. She signed the visitors' book and collected a glass of wine from the waitress at the top of the steps before weaving her way through the crush and picking up a catalogue of the artist's work. Gradually she made her way into the main part of the gallery. She didn't know much about the artist, Marshall, or which of his works the gallery was exhibiting, but she remembered Mr Wicken telling her that his work was too 'rich' for his taste. She was so intent on not spilling all of her drink as the crowds jostled her that she hadn't given the catalogue more than a quick glance before she caught sight of the first two canvasses in the main hall. They stopped her in her tracks. They were huge, elongated slashes of colour that reached from floor to ceiling and were entitled *Slaughterhouse 1 and 2*. The brutal scenes of dissection and dismemberment revolted her – they seemed so startlingly real, so voyeuristic and almost pornographic in their detail.

The pictures assaulted her senses and brought the acrid taste of bile to the back of her throat. Quickly she turned away and pushed through the jostling people, only to find that wherever she looked more of the equally disgusting images adorned the walls. She was about to retrace her footsteps and leave the gallery when she sensed somebody stop and hover beside her and heard a soft Australian voice ask, 'Can I get you another glass of wine, miss?'

Amy felt a smile pull at the corners of her mouth as she recognized the voice and she turned towards him gratefully. The smile turned into a look of surprise and then embarrassment – it wasn't the dishevelled art student she had expected to see. She began to shake her head when Joel grinned that unmistakable smile of his and she realized that she hadn't made a mistake after all but had almost been fooled by the waiter's uniform and his newly trimmed hair.

Joel moved closer and whispered, 'Go on, have another drink, it's on the house.'

She took a sip from the glass she was holding and laughed softly as she made a face. 'Oh, it's horrible, it's much too sweet. No wonder it's free.'

She looked at him quizzically over the rim of her glass. Meeting him again like this had taken her completely by surprise. She hadn't expected to find him there serving drinks: he had told her that he was a student, studying at Goldsmiths', and she had taken to scanning the straggle of passengers disembarking at New Cross Station on her way to and from work in the hope of catching sight of him.

'Yes, I really am a student,' his grin widened as he spoke, answering as if he had read her mind. 'But I always go after the waiting jobs at the private views. Catervac, who usually do these events, advertise at the college for their temporary staff. The money's not much but the food and drinks are free, and if I'm lucky I can eavesdrop on the critics, listen to their opinions and get the inside track on all the new exhibitions before everyone else. This one's got some real punch, hasn't it?'

Amy shivered slightly and shook her head. 'No, well, yes – I mean, I don't like it at all, I think it's quite revolting, it assaults the senses. I was about to leave when you offered me that drink.'

Joel's smile dissolved into a look of disappointment. 'But you can't leave yet, I . . . I . . . I felt too nervous to come back into the gallery to see you. Won't you stay for a little longer, I'll be finished in . . .' He hesitated, feeling the colour rise to his cheeks: he was doing it again, letting his eagerness to get to know her make a fool out of him.

'There's a buffet out on the balcony overlooking the river. There aren't any paintings out there and the view of the setting sun is very beautiful.' He changed his approach quickly to cover up his embarrassment. 'I could bring you a fruit juice, mineral water, or something.'

Amy was about to turn him down and look for somewhere to deposit her half-empty glass before leaving when, to her surprise, she found herself smiling and accepting his offer of a mineral water as she followed his directions towards the balcony. She didn't know what had made her accept – suppressed desire to find out what it was that intrigued her about him perhaps, a moment of impulse or a tug from the hidden memories buried in her subconscious. A smile of anticipation hovered on the corners of her mouth as she threaded her way through the crowded gallery. It was a moment she would look back on and remember for from that minute onward her life was to change dramatically. But for now she felt only an odd tingle of excitement at meeting Joel again, something she hadn't experienced with anyone before. She was aware that something had changed: the lights strung along the balcony seemed brighter and the idle snatches of conversation that drifted and washed around her while she waited for him sounded different, more detached and remote, as if their content didn't matter to her any more. And the colours of the sun as it sank, an orb of molten fire into the river, seemed to burn with a special intensity inside her head. What would stay with her forever was the sound of the swallows crying as they skimmed over the water into the thickening twilight, their voices haunting the darkness long after they had vanished. In a strange way she felt as if her real life was just about to begin.

'Dave's a real mate: he's agreed to cover for me here for the rest of the evening.' Joel's voice broke through her thoughts, it made her start and turn around. He had changed out of the waiter's uniform and was now wearing an open-necked shirt and a pale, well-worn jacket.

'It's a beautiful evening, where would you like to go?' he smiled.

'But don't you want to look at the exhibition? I thought that's why you came.'

Joel laughed softly and shook his head. 'I think I've seen enough of it – come on, let's get out of here. Have you eaten?'

Joel touched her arm as they reached the top of the steps that led to the gallery's entrance, making her pause for a moment. He swept his hand back towards the two huge paintings they had just passed. 'I reckon you were right when you said they assaulted the senses: they do, and I also have this unnervingly familiar feeling about them. I can't explain it, it's almost as if I knew where they were painted – as if I've been there. And . . .' He shook his head, leaving the sentence unfinished as they ran lightly down the steps. Then he turned and looked up, his face drawn and serious. 'And there's something else that bothers me even more, something that's been troubling me for a few weeks – I don't know your name.'

She laughed as they walked out into the warm night air. 'It's Amy, Amelia Thornbury.'

'Amelia, what a beautiful name . . .'

Amy laughed, 'Just call me Amy.'

'OK, let's eat, Amy, I'm starving. Which do you prefer Indian or Chinese?'

Amy didn't answer immediately, she thought about what he had said about the waiting job not paying much before she replied. 'You know, it's such a lovely evening what I'd really like to do is walk along the Embankment for a while.'

He nodded and fell into step with her as they walked into Cheyne Walk past the houseboats moored along the wooden jetty.

'It must be really strange having your home float up and down on the tide mustn't it? Very unsettling,' Amy said thoughtfully.

'I don't know, I suppose they get used to it. I suppose you can get used to anything if it happens often enough.'

'Yes, perhaps you're right, but there's something about boats, sometimes they seem so . . . familiar, it's as if I've travelled on them, or maybe . . .' Amy's words trailed off. The reflections of the lights on the river between the silhouettes of the houseboats seemed to create soft, oily, mesmerizing rainbows of colour. The sound of the traffic on the Embankment seemed to recede and even Joel's presence faded into the background of her thoughts as a sharp, salty smell pinched at her nostrils and the sound of water slapping, breaking against the prow of a ship filled her ears. The line of lights on the water was moving, getting closer to her – she could hear the creak of timber and the flap of the canvas. Gradually she became aware of someone on the deck of the ship beside her, someone she knew. A hand suddenly gripped her arm, a strong, restraining hold.

'Amy, stop, wait for the lights to change.' Joel's voice shattered the images and she blinked, dizzy and disorientated as reality pressed in around her. She found herself tottering on the edge of the kerb, inches from the stream of cars and taxis moving through the lights on their way from Battersea Bridge.

'What's happening?' she stuttered. She tried to hold on to the images she had just experienced but they were fleeing back into the labyrinth of her subconscious, leaving her with a sharp sense of loss and regret.

'I don't know,' he smiled, relaxing his grip on her arm. 'You were looking at the reflections on the river and said something about them which I couldn't quite catch. I don't think you even noticed the traffic lights.'

'But that's crazy,' she muttered, more to herself than to him. She knew she often daydreamed quite vividly on the train to work, and had done so at school: but she had never lost all sense of where she was, at least never before this.

'I shouldn't worry, Amy.' Joel tried to laugh it off and put her at ease. 'I think there's something magical about lights reflecting across water. I reckon they make it easy to forget where you are. Sometimes if I look at them long enough I imagine I'm standing on the deck of an old sailing boat heading towards the harbour lights of a town across a bay. I've even sketched the scene a couple of times.'

Amy frowned and brushed the hair out of her eyes as she looked past him to the shimmering reflections on the water. It was a little unnerving: twice now he had described what she was thinking and she was sure she hadn't prompted him on either occasion.

Something moved in the shadows at the edge of her sight, making her jump. A cold shiver ran up her spine and she glanced anxiously over her shoulder. Joel sensed something too and spun round, digging instinctively into the pocket of his jacket for the box of matches he always carried. He quickly withdrew a match, striking the red head against his thumb hard, sending it spinning away into the shadows beneath the closest tree. A muffled howl echoed along the Embankment and a fleeting, shadowy shape disappeared amongst the evening traffic. Joel's face was drawn and pale beneath the street lamps as he reached into his pocket for another match. The nightmares from his childhood had followed him to England.

'What the hell was that? Why did you throw that lighted match?' Amy's voice had shrunk to a tight whisper.

'I suppose you think I'm silly, flicking a lighted match at the shadows but it's something I used to do as a kid. Whenever I was frightened by something in the dark I would light a match to scare it away. It always worked. Look behind, there's nothing there now, is there?'

'No, there isn't,' Amy agreed. 'And I don't think you're silly, there's nothing silly about being afraid, but it's a little dangerous throwing lighted matches about, isn't it? What if you had started a fire?'

'Yes, I know, I almost have done a few times.' Joel grinned a little sheepishly.

Amy still couldn't shake off the feeling that they were being watched, only 'watched' wasn't the right word to describe the sensation she was experiencing, it was more intimate than that, as if something had touched her. The reflections on the water seemed to dull and even the silent silhouettes of the houseboats had taken on a hostile atmosphere. There was the faintest smell of sulphur on the evening air.

'Come on,' she urged, shivering again. 'Let's keep walking and you can tell me about your life in Australia. I'll bet you weren't frightened all the time. I expect you grew up near one of those beaches, you know the ones I mean, the ones in all the adverts with waves breaking over a reef and miles of pure, white sand.'

'Yeah, sure thing,' he laughed. 'The ones with shrimps the size of lobsters that we cook on the barbie and palm trees growing on the beach.'

Joel paused and glanced back over his shoulder. The shadow had unnerved him and it still felt as if someone was watching them. It was a sensation he had experienced a lot while he was growing up, the feeling that something was haunting the shadows, and it had made him an expert at striking a match between his finger and thumb and using the flame to search the dark spaces behind doors and probe inside cupboards. Although there was never anything there, he had sometimes found what looked like a huge paw print in the damp earth or tears in the flyscreen on the outside of the door frame as if a huge animal had been prowling in the night. Such sensations had made him start sketching, to try and capture the shapes he sometimes thought he glimpsed around him in those quiet moments when he was on his own, and to draw the figures that persistently plagued his dreams. As they walked further the sensation gradually began to diminish and Joel shrugged, thrusting his hands into the pockets of his jacket. He wouldn't mention these phantoms to Amy – the last thing he wanted to do was to frighten her.

'I'm afraid there isn't much to tell. My parents were both killed when I was a baby and I grew up in a children's home in Boundary Street, Coolangatta, but it was only twenty yards from the beach at Rainbow Bay.'

'Oh, I'm sorry, I didn't mean to pry,' Amy apologized.

'That's OK, no worries. I don't remember anything about the accident – I was only a few days old when it happened. The priest who runs the home, Father Joseph, told me all about it when I was fifteen years old. He had helped to dig me out of the wreckage of our house and he gathered together a box of photographs and personal things which he gave to me.'

'What sort of accident? It destroyed your house?'

'It was a bit of a freak really, something you'd never expect to happen. A truck driver fell asleep at the wheel of his lorry and it careered out of control down Razorback Hill and ploughed straight through the house. It killed my mother and father instantly but I must have been thrown out of my cot and landed in a gap between the shattered floorboards. Father Joseph said it was a miracle that they found me, let alone that I survived. He blessed me with holy water and said the last rites over me and tells me I've been a thorn in his side ever since.'

Amy smiled as he talked affectionately about Father Joseph. 'What did you feel when he gave you the box of photographs?' She looked across at him hesitantly: perhaps she shouldn't have asked him such a question.

'I really don't know. In a way I suppose I expected them to jump up out of the box so that I'd get back something I'd lost all those years before, but they were just faces, people I didn't recognize. There was a ring and a brooch, a cigarette case and some family papers, but none of it really meant anything to me except perhaps it awakened a loss I had never really felt before . . .'

Joel fell silent for a moment and watched a pleasure boat cutting a glittering wave of lights through the shadows of Chelsea Bridge. 'But I'm glad now that Father Joseph kept it for me. It's good to know where my life started, better than just knowing that my birthday is in February.'

'February? My birthday's in February. Which day?'

'The twenty-first, the 21st February 1972,' he replied as they came to Chelsea Bridge.

Amy stopped abruptly and looked up into his eyes. 'But that's an incredible coincidence, that's my birthday too. I mean I was born not just on the same day but the same year as well.'

'Then that must make us almost twins.' He laughed. 'Almost twins, except for the twelve thousand miles that separated our births. Obviously fate always intended that we meet.'

'Well, yes, but there's another, even stranger, coincidence.' Amy hesitated and bit her lip before looking away. She wished she hadn't spoken quite so quickly but he had that effect on her, he made her want to confide in him, share everything with him, but as the words reached the tip of her tongue they seemed such a betrayal. It seemed wrong to tell him the little her father had revealed about the circumstances of her birth, secrets she hadn't told anyone else, not even her closest friends.

'Oh, it's nothing really,' she began as she started the tissue of half-truths she had invented years before to hide the real truth. 'My mother died in childbirth so I'm a sort of orphan as well.'

'I'm really sorry. Does your father ever talk about her? Have you seen photographs . . .'

'No!' she interrupted quite fiercely. Something deep inside her compelled her to tell him the truth. 'No, there were never any photographs, nobody knew who she was or ever found out where she came from. The police never even found any dental records. The only clue to her name was a name-tag sewn inside her raincoat which said "Thornbury". I would never have survived the birth if Dr O'Keefe and his wife hadn't accidentally stumbled on my mother as she lay, half dead, in Malsbury Woods. My father said somebody remembered seeing her get off the evening train from Reading but she could have caught a train from almost anywhere, Reading connects with dozens of lines. They think she was trying to reach the hospital but she lost her way and wandered into the woods where she collapsed.'

'But why wasn't your father with her?' Joel frowned. 'Why was she on her own? I don't understand – surely he must have known you were due to be born – he could have called an ambulance or something.'

Amy shook her head, her eyes were sad and there was regret in her voice. 'Nobody knows who she was, she seemed to be completely on her own. The O'Keefes adopted me and they've been the most wonderful parents. They have never tried to hide the facts about my birth from me: they even had Thornbury put on the birth certificate. They told me all about it once I was old enough to understand.'

'So we are both orphans – what an amazing coincidence,' Joel murmured.

Amy glanced at her watch: it was much later than she imagined. 'We'd better hurry and get a taxi or I'll miss my train back to Blackheath.' She raised her hand and quickly hailed a passing black cab.

Joel hesitated to follow her. He could catch the same train, it stopped at St Johns, but he wasn't sure he had enough money in his pocket to cover the cab fare.

'Come on, get in,' she smiled as she told the driver to take them to Waterloo. 'The gallery's paying the fare.'

Joel insisted on staying on the train for the two extra stops so that he could see Amy home to the door of her flat. They talked easily in the crowded compartment, their conversation seeming to open up hidden avenues in each other's minds and uncover a thousand things they had in common. A warm breeze with the scent of honeysuckle blew against their faces as they walked across the heath towards the Paragon and bright summer stars were strewn across the night sky above their heads.

'I've been meaning to ask you about those two pictures you left in the gallery . . .' Amy's voice fell silent.

Joel grinned in the darkness. 'I was hoping you'd take a look at them and give me an opinion. Tell me if you liked them.'

Amy shivered slightly. 'No, I found them rather frightening, especially the one of the two hooded figures with that creature at their feet. The other one had a sense of . . .' She paused as if searching for the right word to use. 'A sense of peace – no, tranquillity, and safety. But the strangest thing about both of the pictures was that I'm sure I've seen those images myself . . .'

Again she paused and frowned slightly. 'No, that's not what I meant, not really, but seeing them seemed to trigger memories – perhaps they were dreams, or something like that, connected with those pictures, which I know is ridiculous because I've never seen either you or them before you walked into the gallery.'

'In a way you did exactly the same thing to me when we first met. It was like receiving an electric shock, a sudden jolt that awakened something deep down in my memory, but the silly thing is I don't know what it is. The images and dreams it has stirred up are so disjointed. All I really know is when I first saw you there seemed to be something so familiar, it was as if we had known each other before, met each other somewhere else, yet we were strangers. That's why I left those drawings, so

I could come back . . .' Joel hesitated, feeling that he was on the verge of making a fool of himself again. He was about to tell her that they must have met in a previous life but even as the idea formed in his mind it seemed ridiculous and far-fetched.

Amy stopped when she reached the gates of Glebe House, on the corner of Pond Road. 'This is where I live.' She waved a vague hand towards the imposing Regency façade before rummaging in her shoulder bag for her front door key.

'Would you like to come out for a drink tomorrow evening? I think a folk group are playing in the Three Tuns,' Joel asked quietly.

Amy shook her head. 'No, I'm sorry, I've already made plans for tomorrow night.'

'What about Saturday?' he asked quickly.

Amy glanced up, about to tell him that she couldn't see him over the weekend, that she had promised her parents she would be going home, but the look of disappointment in his eyes made her hesitate. There was an historic country fair setting up on the heath for the weekend and she had intended to have a quick look around it before driving down to Malsbury, but perhaps if she left later they could visit the fair together and have some lunch before she left.

Joel had to concentrate hard to stop a grin of delight from spreading across his face as she suggested visiting the fair together. 'That's great! I'll call here for you at about nine o'clock.'

Warnings in the Tarot

A THIN, BLUE HAZE of wood-smoke and the smell of meat slowly roasting over the open fire-pits hung in the clear morning air over Blackheath. Long queues of cars were slowly converging on the entrance to the car parks while crowds of people walked in noisy groups from the railway station in the centre of the village up Montpelier Row towards the straggling rows of tents. Booths with brightly-coloured flags, awnings and gaudily-painted caravans occupied the high ground on the heath, and a troop of Cossacks were exercising their horses away to the right, cantering in circles, each one in turn leaning low out of their saddles to pick up brightly coloured handkerchiefs that had been laid out on the ground.

Joel and Amy stopped beside the pond as they waited for a space in the traffic to cross onto the heath. 'This reminds me of a great siege, the Crusaders encamping outside the walls of Jerusalem, horsemen preparing to charge . . .'

'Yes, and when the siege-engines are in place the attack will begin,' Amy answered quietly.

The bark of a car horn broke the illusion and made them both blink as they looked at one another.

'I suppose it's the colours, the noise and the milling crowds that give it that odd atmosphere – it just made me imagine it was something else, somewhere else.' Amy tried to shrug it off but although Joel nodded in agreement he couldn't shake off the feeling it had left with him.

'Don't you think it's really weird that we both imagined the same thing?' he asked as they crossed the road.

'Well, yes, I suppose it is, but then everything seems to be a little different when we're together, doesn't it? Come on, let's have a look at the herbalist's tent, and look over there – a candle maker and next to it there's a fortune teller – how wonderful. Hurry up, I love these old-fashioned fairs!'

'No, wait, let's go across and see the horses first, before the crowds get too thick. They're only over there.' Joel took her arm and guided her through the knots of people towards the area where the Cossacks had picketed their horses.

For Joel there had always been something about horses that had stirred up his imagination. He felt a peculiar sensation of familiarity that he had never really understood and was difficult to explain because he had never had much to do with horses and rarely had the opportunity to ride in the children's home. He reached out a hand and caressed the nearest horse. Its skin felt silky-soft beneath his fingertips, its muscles rippled with elastic ease, but the familiarity was more than this casual touch. The sweet smell of the sweat drying on its coat, the creak of the saddle and the jingle of the bit rings as it fidgeted on its halter rope triggered hidden memories. The noises of the fairground seemed to fade, the air grew colder and ruffled his hair, and a new sound began to invade his consciousness. There was a swelling rhythmical thunder of hoofbeats rushing over frozen ground, a low winter sun shining in his eyes, blinding him, making him blink at the forest of swaying shadows cast by the lances of the riders on either side of him. A faint, familiar voice was calling out his name, reaching out to him through the thundering hoofbeats. The image began to fade and fell in and out of focus as he became aware of Amy's voice and the music and laughter in the crowd all around him. But there was something else, a dark, sinister shape moving through the crowds on the edge of his sight. The horse sensed it and its muscles tensed.

'Joel, look at me, Joel, I'm trying to take your photograph!' Amy pressed the shutter. Suddenly the horse neighed, squealed out, its eyes white with terror, and then it reared, breaking the halter rope as its near foreleg struck Joel's shoulder and sent him sprawling on the ground only inches from the other horses' hooves.

One of the grooms rushed forwards and managed to grab the broken rope before the horse galloped off through the crowds. He stroked its sweating neck, talked to it and calmed it down before turning round to Amy in anger. 'There should be a sign stopping people like you frightening the horses. You're lucky that nobody was really hurt!'

Joel climbed slowly to his feet, brushed at the grass stains on his jeans and rubbed his shoulder gingerly. He was aware that a small crowd of curious onlookers had begun to form around them.

'Come on, let's get going.' He grinned self-consciously as he walked with Amy towards the rows of tents.

'I'm sorry, I shouldn't have done that, I didn't realize it would frighten the horses. Are you sure you don't need something for that shoulder?' There was concern in Amy's voice but Joel shook his head, glancing back across the heads of the crowd. The horse was still throwing its head about and neighing wildly.

'It wasn't the camera that frightened the horse,' he muttered.

'What did then?' Amy followed his gaze back towards the Cossacks and felt a tremor of fear flood over her.

Joel shrugged. He didn't want to tell her, didn't want to talk about the dark, canine shape that he had sensed. 'Oh, I don't know, horses are sometimes very unpredictable, perhaps something in the crowd, a noise, a movement, anything can upset them. Now which tent do you want to visit first?'

'The herbalist. They might have something for your shoulder.'

When they entered the tent the noise and the bustle of the crowds seemed to fade into the background. Instinctively they both paused and breathed deeply, inhaling the heady, aromatic atmosphere and gazing at the muted sunlight that filtered down through the hundreds of bundles of dried herbs and wild flowers that had been strung across the sagging canvas roof. The misty light reflected a warm kaleidoscope of colours from the thousands of antique drug jars, blue glass bottles and phials of ointments and ancient medicines that crowded the rickety, temporary wooden shelves and glass cabinets filling the herbalist's tent.

'Madwort and lavender infused in a cup of mulled wine, that would draw out the vile humours in your shoulder, and if the skin is broken it would clot the blood and reduce the risk of fever,' Amy whispered, pointing up at the bunches of lavender and madwort that were hanging above their heads.

'Yes, but essence of liquorice, maidens hair and figs would taste sweeter and ease the stiffness,' he answered, picking up a dusty drug jar with a spidery Latin inscription scratched into the glass. He tipped the jar slightly to one side and the thick, muddy-brown, viscous liquid inside it flowed towards the sealed neck to reveal the wrinkled faces of the pickled figs buried in the sludge at the bottom.

Amy made a face and shook her head. 'Pennywort would be more wholesome and purge the evil vapours just as well.' She paused, a puzzled frown puckering her forehead as she looked at Joel and wondered what had made her say that. How could she have known the names, let alone the old-fashioned remedies that these bunches of dried herbs were used for?

'That's weird, really weird, I couldn't possibly have known this. What's going on?' Joel shivered, it felt as if a cold door in his memory had creaked open and he hastily put the bottle back on the shelf.

'I don't know, but it's giving me the creeps.' Amy began to edge her way towards the door. 'I grew up in a doctor's house so I suppose some of it must have rubbed off on me; but I never remember seeing anything remotely connected with these herbal remedies. Come on, let's get out of here,' she urged. Her momentary familiarity with the medicines that crowded the shelves sent a shiver up her spine. How could the knowledge of all these old remedies be locked up inside her head? How could she possibly know these things?

'Good morning, good morning, would you like a catalogue of our exhibition, it's only sixty pence? Or is there something special you're looking for? Perhaps a scent for the young lady would interest you – I can recommend our essence of nightflower, it's distilled from an ancient recipe.'

The voice of the herbalist startled them both. 'No, no, thank you, we were just leaving,' Amy answered tensely.

'That's such a pity,' the herbalist smiled, 'it's taken Culpers years to assemble this collection of medicines and herbs and you'll probably never get the opportunity to see them under the same roof again. There are examples here that range from the medieval times to the present day – we've collected them from medical schools, dispensaries, universities and museums throughout Northern Europe. Culpers have even prepared a special perfume and toilet water recreated from the old recipes. You get a complimentary sachet with each catalogue.'

'I don't know, Amy, maybe we should have a look round first.' Joel tried to smile but he found he couldn't. This discovery of a knowledge he had been unaware of had shaken him and he wanted to get to the bottom of it. Wherever he looked images, fragments, disjointed memories of familiar things, stared back at him. He was looking at a past he couldn't remember.

As they walked slowly through the exhibition they found that neither of them needed to use the catalogue or read the neatly written legends beneath each exhibit. Many of the things on display seemed to prompt and resurrect scraps of lost memory. They instinctively knew what the purges, liniments, embrocations and, often vile-coloured, drenches were originally used to cure. They reached a section labelled 1300–1375 and paused in front of a squat preserving jar. Leaning forward and peering through the thick, greenish glass they could see half a dozen shrivelled, greying objects lying in the bottom. A sweet, sticky smell seemed to tickle at their senses and far off in their subconscious they heard the drone and buzz of flies and the single, mournful toll of a bell.

'They're sweet-apples, aren't they?' Amy whispered, a tremor of fear in her voice.

Joel nodded bleakly, his memory sharpening and bringing cold beads of sweat to his temples. 'Yes, I remember the alchemist used to make them to ward off the plague. He mixed them with black pepper, red and white sandal, rose petals and camphor, then he pounded the mixture into a paste and added gum arabic before moulding it into the shape of apples, sweet smelling apples to keep the Black Death away. Because . . .' Joel suddenly fell silent and pressed the palms of his hands hard against his forehead as he tried to force out the frightening images of unburied dead and fly-blown corpses from his mind's eye. Waves of dizziness swept over him and he grasped at the open neck of his shirt. It felt so hot and airless in the stifling atmosphere of the tent.

'I need some fresh air. I'll wait for you outside,' he muttered thickly, stumbling unsteadily towards the open canvas exit.

Amy felt a cold tingle of dread creep up her spine. The stench of death filled her nostrils and the rumble of cart wheels mingled with the tolling of the death bell which was growing louder inside her head. Panic seized her; she had to get out of there. She followed Joel out of the tent and the images dissolved abruptly as she blinked in the bright sunlight. She breathed a deep sigh of relief as she pushed the folded catalogue into her bag and glanced anxiously back to the herbalist's tent. She didn't understand what was happening to her or where those crazy thoughts were coming from. She felt scared, really scared, she looked around for Joel. He was only a couple of paces away, standing on the edge of the milling crowds, gently massaging his injured shoulder and staring at something far away across the heath.

'Joel, it really frightened me in there. I don't understand, I've never experienced anything like that before. What's happening to us?'

'I don't know, it frightened me too. Those last memories of the Black Death were so vivid it's as if I had been there, as if I had really experienced it.'

'Yes, I know, it was as if I had been there too. The smell, the noises, everything, I felt everything,' Amy said gently. The awakening of those memories, the discovery that there was a part of herself that she knew nothing about, filled her with an uneasy foreboding of what else might rise, unbidden, to the surface of her consciousness.

The experience in the herbalist's tent had drained the colour and enjoyment from her exploration of the fair.

She was about to suggest that they give the rest of the tents and sideshows a miss and walk back into the village for coffee at the Three Chimneys delicatessen when something she recognized, familiar but out of place, caught her eye in the noisy Saturday morning crowds that were streaming past them. It was little more than a fleeting glimpse of a large dog, a blur of movement, and then two dark, indistinct figures were slipping soundlessly towards them, causing only a ripple of attention as they approached. But the sight of them sent a chill warning scrambling back from her subconscious.

'Joel! Look, over there in the crowd, what's that?' she gasped, gripping his arm.

But Joel was already turning, his eyes narrowed as he hunted the crowd. He hadn't needed the warning in her voice or the bite of her nails in his arm: he had sensed the approaching figures and the hideous beast that strained to slip its leash and he had felt their malice, so raw with hatred that it had made the hairs prickle on the nape of his neck and had sent a shiver of dread down his spine. As he turned he caught a brief glimpse of them, making his breath escape in a hiss of surprise. They were the ghosts of his childhood, creatures from his dreams, persistent images that he had tried so often to capture with pencil and paper, only this time they seemed much more real.

Joel grabbed Amy's hand and pushed his way through the crowd, tripping over prams and children's tricycles in an attempt to reach the open heath. Angry voices shouted at him, telling him to take more care and he apologized and tried to keep closer to the tents but he couldn't seem to make any headway against the thickening flow of people entering the fair. He glanced anxiously back across his shoulder and saw that their pursuers were getting closer, effortlessly weaving their way through the people as they made their way towards them, appearing and disappearing in the blink of an eye but always getting menacingly closer.

'Quickly, in here, we'll hide in here!' Amy's voice hissed at him and he felt a sharp tug at his hand that almost pulled him off balance. He turned and stumbled through some loosely hanging canvas into a tent and followed her inside. He just managed to catch sight of the brightly painted board advertising 'Madam Corvo – Astrologer and Clairvoyant'.

The noise and bustle of the crowds and the terror of the pursuit seemed to fade once they were inside the booth. The air was cool and scented with the fragrance of juniper and balsam, the muted whisper of drums was no louder than a heartbeat, but it filled the silence. An inner curtain of midnight velvet shot with symbols of the planets rustled and was pulled aside as Madam Corvo looked out, disturbed by their hurried entrance.

'My hour of meditation is not yet complete. It clearly states on my board that readings will not commence until half past eleven. Perhaps you would be kind enough . . .' She paused and frowned. Her fingertips began to tingle and her pulse quickened. Her second sight, her hidden eye, detected their desperate need to hide from a pursuing evil. A dark shadow seemed to pass over the entrance to her tent and the sharp, acrid reek of sulphur crept beneath the canvas walls. Madam Corvo shuddered: it felt as if something foul had trampled on her soul.

'Quickly, come in here, you have great need of sanctuary,' she whispered as she beckoned them forwards with her heavily ringed fingers and shut them in her inner sanctum.

Neither Amy nor Joel needed to be asked twice. They sensed the two shadows stop outside the entrance and felt them begin to search through the line of tents on either side of the fortune-teller's booth. Without daring to look back at the doorway or make a sound they both slipped through the gap in the velvet curtain that Madam Corvo was holding aside. Her inner sanctum was like an Aladdin's cave of light and darkness. The thick, dark-blue velvet curtain which separated the inner tent completely shut out the daylight and sounds of the world outside. The gold and silver symbols of the planets were woven through the cloth and shimmered in the dancing light thrown by the many candles. Two nine-footed pentagrams, each one drawn in inch-wide wands of beaten silver, one set inside the other, had been laid out upon the trampled grass. Between the two pentagrams, iron-stone letters and ancient words had been placed at all the points of the compass. A double square of beaten copper two inches wide surrounded the pentagons and at each corner circles were engraved with the names Abni, Agla, Itt and Al. In the centre stood an ebony table surrounded by chairs inlaid with magic signs and symbols. Upon the table stood a crystal ball and a worn set of tarot cards just in front of a pile of astrological and magic books. The scent of juniper was heavy in the air.

'Clear your minds of all evil. Let nothing but the purest thoughts cross the threshold of my sanctuary,' Madam Corvo instructed as she motioned them to sit at her table. She entered the pentagram with the rustle of soft silk, her azure robe shimmering in the candle-light as she sat opposite them. She whispered a rhyming chant under her breath and caressed the crystal while looking intently at both of them. She reached out her hands. 'Give me the date and time of your birth and then turn up the palms of your right hand.'

'I don't have a clue what time of day I was born, but the date's the 21st February, 1972, and I was born in Tweed Heads, Australia. Amy was born on exactly the same day only here in England.' Joel grinned and leaned forwards expectantly, resting his right hand palm upwards on the inlaid, ebony table. He had never plucked up the courage to visit a fortune teller before although he had always wanted to, and he held his breath as he wondered what hidden things she would reveal from the lines on the palm of his hand.

Amy was hesitant. The thought of knowing the future intrigued her but she felt a knot of apprehension tightening in her stomach. She had always been afraid that she would not like the secrets it unveiled, afraid of seeing that which she would rather remain hidden. Deep down there was a real curiosity about who she really was mixed with the fear that the turn of a card or the soft creases that time had worn in her palm would reveal a past she could not bear to own.

'There is no need to be afraid: my child, give me your hand.' Madam Corvo's voice broke through her indecision, making her jump and focus on the intense, penetrating gaze of the fortune teller. 'Let the hidden eye of the crystal reveal your fears and the second sight of the cards show you the evil that pursues you. But first let me see your hands.'

Madam Corvo bent forward theatrically. She wanted to read their hands and dispel the fear she had seen in their eyes but the façade of showmanship quickly evaporated and the muscles of her jaw trembled slightly, betraying her genuine concern. The intricate maps of their lives were so complicated, and so similar they were almost identical. They could, at a glance, have been twins, and she would have gambled on that fact, yet she knew they had been born in different parts of the world.

'Extraordinary, most extraordinary. I've never seen anything like this before.'

A faint noise from outside the tent made her pause and glance up with a frown before returning her attention to their life-lines. She traced them repeatedly with her fingertip, searching every crease and ridge, every contour. They were so long, or rather so old, much too old to be etched in the hands of those so young; and there were so many breaks, indications of deaths and reincarnations in identical places in each life-line. Yet, if she peered closely, she could see a tiny, almost invisible thread that always carried their lives forwards. She frowned again as she tried to unravel what she saw and interpret the meanings of such unusual life-lines.

'What's the matter? What have you seen?' Amy's sense of uneasiness was growing.

Madam Corvo looked up, her penetrating eyes searching Amy's face. 'I don't know, your palms reveal so much and yet they're very confusing. You both have typical water hands but they both show strong fire signs as well. It is as though you have both passed through flames and then started again many times. But you are both so young, too young for these hands. It is as if . . .' She paused, hearing another sound beyond the curtain, louder this time. She straightened her back, her grip upon their hands tightening as she twisted to turn her head to listen intently. 'Did you hear anything?' she whispered.

Joel half-turned in his chair and saw the heavy velvet material of the inner tent ripple along one side and then billow and sag as if the wind had touched it. A cold draught of air ghosted his cheek and ruffled his hair, setting the slender candle flames dancing madly on their wicks. 'I think the wind must have risen across the heath,' he answered, turning back to face her.

'That's no natural wind.' She gathered her tarot cards protectively to her chest. 'There's a reek of evil in the air.' And indeed, a hint of sulphur was seeping into the juniper-scented atmosphere of the booth.

Amy smelt it and half-rose to her feet. It was similar to the foul odour she had noticed that first time they walked together along the Embankment. 'What's happening to us?' she cried, clutching at the clairvoyant's hands, her fingers gripping the edges of the cards she was holding. 'I don't understand why we're seeing things that aren't there. And we're remembering things we don't know anything about. You've got to help us, tell us what's going on!'

Madam Corvo could feel an overpowering evil encircling her tent and she tried to pull away, to break free from Amy's grasp. The tarot cards slipped from her hands and Amy caught at them as they fell. They cascaded through her fingers, scattering on the floor but some of them fell face-up in a pattern upon the table. Madam Corvo stared down at the cards and her face drained of colour. The evil wind was howling around the inner tent now and the velvet was flapping and straining at its guy ropes like a sail in a storm. She could see at a glance that all the cards that had landed on the table were from the major arcana – the Magician, the Hanged Man, the Devil, the Chariot, Death – powerful cards that couldn't possibly have fallen haphazardly, and they shouted a warning at her. They told of an ancient curse that was pursuing these two young people's souls through eternity. It showed their lives cloaked in fire, it showed them fleeing, always running before a black, shadowy shroud that threatened to engulf them. The cards foretold of a bleak, desolate future and their hope merely a shrivelled creature, barely visible.

The crystal ball in the centre of the table suddenly caught her attention. The cloudy, blue-green glass was changing colour. She could see images in the glass, getting larger, filling the crystal, reaching out to clutch at her.

Madam Corvo tried to rise and staggered backwards, throwing her hands up in terror and overturning her chair. 'Your souls are shadowed by a black curse. You must try to escape. There is an evil that has pursued you through all your previous lives and stalks you now.

You must run, flee before the darkness overwhelms you. Find a way to break the curse before it's too late . . .'

Wild chanting shrieks and savage growls assaulted the tent, drowning her voice, and huge claws began to tear at the velvet, splitting and ripping it to shreds. A howling wind rushed in, swirling around them, gathering up the tarot cards into a whirlwind. The crystal ball glowed white-hot and shattered into a million, spinning fragments. The candles exploded one by one. Amy screamed and hid her head in her hands as the wind tore at her hair. Joel leapt to his feet and grabbed his chair, ready to hurl it at their attackers, but all he saw before the last candle was snuffed out were the two pentacles beginning to glow silver against the evil darkness, and silhouetted against the fabric of the inner tent, the shapes of two shrouded figures and a huge, savage dog. They seemed to run backwards and forwards, their shadows shrinking and elongating, as they searched for a way in. The guy ropes of the inner tent suddenly gave way and it collapsed, smothering them in its heavy fabric.

The howling wind and the demonic assault it had carried against them vanished as abruptly as it had appeared. The inner tent shrouded them in silent darkness. The folds of velvet seemed to cling and wind themselves around them, isolating them from each other, every frantic movement they made seemed to entwine them even more tightly, preventing them from getting free. Joel could hear the panic mounting in Amy's muffled voice – her voice was so close, he could feel her kicking and clawing at the fabric, but he couldn't reach her. Somewhere in the mess of folds in front of him he could hear the fortune teller's incoherent screams and cries. The smell of sulphur was fading but Joel suddenly became aware of a new smell in the darkness. Candle-wax and the stench of smouldering cloth became very evident and his own panic began to rise as he realized what that meant. The terror of being burned alive clawed at the inside of his skull and beads of cold sweat oozed out of his forehead, his back and chest. He shuddered and clenched his fists. Nausea swept over him; he ground his teeth and fought to overcome his panic.

'Think, you silly bastard, think!' he shouted at himself. There had to be a way to get out. The material wasn't very heavy, there had to be an opening – and then he remembered.

'Amy, listen!' he shouted. 'Stop struggling. Stay calm, it's only the inner tent that collapsed on us. That opening we came through was right behind your chair. Try to locate it, it'll be the easiest way to get out.'

He heard her shout something back at him but her voice was so muffled he couldn't make out what she said. Moments later he felt the material that covered his face being pulled aside and a chink of daylight appeared. In another moment he saw Amy's fingers pulling at the material, dragging it off him. He sucked in a deep breath as he struggled free only to pause and stare out through the opening. He could hear the noise and bustle of the fair, it was going on as though nothing had happened. It was as if everyone was oblivious to the shrieking attack they had just suffered.

Amy sat on the grass, trembling with shock and relief. Then she looked around. 'Come on, something's burning. We've got to get out before the velvet bursts into flames and sets the outer tent alight.'

'No, wait! We can't leave the fortune teller trapped in here. We have to get her out!'

Together they trod out the mass of smouldering sparks until they could free Madam Corvo from the tangled mound of heavy velvet.

'My God, what's happened to her?' Amy hissed as the clairvoyant lifted her head and they saw her face in the sunlight.

Her raven-black hair had been bleached white, her body trembled violently and her slack lips dribbled as they babbled some incomprehensible chant. Her hands were gesticulating, making repeated jerky signs of the cross. But it was her eyes that had made Amy recoil with horror; the pupils had shrunk to wild pinpoints of madness and, for a moment, she imagined she could glimpse the terrible phantoms that the old woman had witnessed before the last candle was snuffed out.

Amy shuddered as she and Joel each took an arm and guided the terrified woman slowly towards the doorway of her tent. A snarling growl stopped them in their tracks. A large, grey-haired lurcher appeared in the entrance, its hackles raised and its yellow canine teeth bared in a snarl. It came towards them, crouching, ready to spring in attack.

'Bazaar, come here, leave them alone!' A small boy was hanging onto the dog's lead, shouting and struggling to restrain it as he was dragged into the tent.

Joel took a backward step and knuckled his free hand into a fist, searching around them desperately for something to hurl at the crazed animal.

'No, don't hurt it!' Amy cried as she sensed his fear. She used soft words and the dog, reassured by her voice, stopped barking and eventually began to wag its tail. She moved slowly towards it and began to stroke its coarse-haired head. Something about the dog reminded her of how Barnos, her father's old dog, had protected her when she was a child, always snarling and barking at shadows. He had always stayed with her at night, lying at the foot of her bed, protecting her while she slept. She had grown up without the slightest fear of dogs.

'I'm sorry, miss, Bazaar doesn't normally go mad like that. Something must have frightened him.' The small boy pulled the dog out of the tent as he apologized. 'My

Dad told me to wait here by the fortune teller, he's going to have his palm read or something. Suddenly the stupid dog went crazy, snarling and biting at the tent like there was a cat in it. I dunno what's wrong with him.'

'I think your Dad's going to be out of luck today, mate,' Joel answered as he helped Madam Corvo out of her tent and sat her on one of the chairs that had been set up on the grass near the entrance. He looked back into the tent to check that all the sparks were extinguished. 'Come on, let's get out of here before someone wants us to explain what happened in there,' he whispered to Amy.

Already knots of people had begun to stop and stare at the incoherent woman who was still gesticulating and chanting.

'But we can't just leave her sitting there – anything could happen to her,' Amy protested.

'What do you suggest then?' Joel asked her bleakly. 'You think we should take her to the first aid tent and tell them she's been frightened out of her wits by some monstrous shadowy apparitions that tore her tent to pieces and made it collapse on top of her.' He shrugged and thrust his hands into his trouser pockets. 'I don't know what really happened in there myself but there's one thing I'm certain about, whatever's happening to us is sure scaring the hell out of me. I don't want to stick around and wait for it to happen a second time, do you?'

Amy followed his gaze back to the hazy interior of the tent and a cold shiver tingled her spine. She hadn't understood what had happened to them either, she hadn't even begun to grasp what the fortune teller had been saying before all that noise, the howling wind, the snarls of the savage beast attacking the tent had over-powered her reason. How could it all have gone unnoticed? Surely somebody in the crowd must have heard something, or seen whoever had done it.

'No, I suppose you're right,' she muttered. 'But we'll stop off at the first aid tent and tell them that Madam Corvo's had a fit or a stroke or something. We'll send them back to the tent, at least that way she'll get some proper medical attention.'

'Let's get right away from this place, it's giving me the creeps,' Joel muttered as he followed Amy out of the first aid tent.

Amy nodded, glancing anxiously around at the passing crowds, half-expecting those two shadowy figures to reappear. She had to get down to Malsbury and she didn't fancy driving down in the dark, not after what had happened. 'I'd better get going right away, Joel.'

'Sure thing, I reckon the further you can get away the better. I'll walk you to your car. I wish I was going with you.'

Their experience in the fortune-teller's tent had thoroughly shaken him – he didn't want to stay there on his own a moment longer than was necessary. He was wondering what he was going to do with himself after she had gone when he remembered. 'I promised the Harrisons that I'd help them paint some scenery this afternoon – it's for the new production of *Hamlet* at the Erith Playhouse.'

Joel felt an overwhelming sense of relief as they left the crowds behind and crossed into Pond Road.

'Your flat's near New Cross, isn't it?' Amy asked him as she stopped beside an electric-blue sports car parked outside Glebe House.

'Yes, it's in Brockley – Wickham Road. Hey, that's a great car, a Honda, isn't it? Is it yours?' he asked as she sorted through her bag for the keys.

'Yes, it is, thank you, my father bought it for my last birthday.' She grinned as she released the locks that held the roof in place. 'I'll give you a lift home, I'll be going through New Cross. I think it's quicker to cut across town on a Saturday afternoon and get onto the M4 at Chiswick rather than going all the way round the M25, don't you?'

'Sure, I suppose it must be,' Joel said as he helped her remove the roof and stow it away in the boot of the car. He really hadn't a clue which way would be quicker and he only had the vaguest notion of where Malsbury was in the West Country.

'Great car,' he repeated breathlessly as they accelerated away from the kerb and the wind tugged at his hair.

Amy drove quickly across the heath, dodging confidently in and out of the gaps in the stream of traffic. She wanted to get away from the fair and put as much distance as she could between herself and those spectres that had hidden in the crowds: only it didn't seem to matter how fast she drove, or where she looked, the images were still with her. The memories they had stirred up were still there, hovering on the edge of sight, tantalizing and tormenting her. She couldn't get rid of them.

'You want to go left at the next traffic lights, there's a short cut,' Joel warned, breaking through her thoughts.

She threw the car into second gear and jumped the lights just as they were turning amber, accelerating around the corner, still lost in thought. The car held tightly to the road in spite of the sudden change of direction but the tyres squealed on the hot tarmac.

'What's happening to us, Joel? What's going on? What the hell were those shadowy figures in the crowd and what caused that wind in the fortune-teller's tent?' she asked grimly, braking hard and cutting in front of a bus as the taxi ahead of her suddenly decided to stop and turn right without indicating.

'It beats me, I haven't a clue.' Joel hesitated and he looked away from her to the blur of bright shop fronts and the procession of Saturday shoppers who jostled and crowded the hot dusty pavements of Loampit Vale. The moment he uttered those words he knew it wasn't the truth and lying to her made him feel wretched. He swallowed and turned to face her – he had to make a clean breast of it. 'No, that isn't the truth, not really,' he muttered shame-faced. 'I . . . I . . . I think I have an idea what those things in the tent and those shadowy figures in the crowd really are.'

Amy braked with a screech of tyres, half-raising her hand in apology to the red-faced, angry driver in the car behind who had almost rammed her.

'Well, I'm not completely sure, but I think it's the same ghosts who haunted the children's home where I grew up. I think they must have followed me here.'

'But that's crazy, Joel, ghosts can't follow people around, well not for thousands of miles or from one continent to another. No, it's no good, there must be another explanation.'

'Why can't they? Who says it's impossible?' he continued bleakly, indicating that they had to turn left into Wickham Road after the next crossing. 'Listen,' he added fiercely, almost angrily. 'You didn't have to grow up haunted by those things did you, but I did, and there was no escaping the sensation that someone, or something, was watching me. Odd things happened. I remember once at a picnic we discovered enormous paw prints in the sand, only there wasn't a dog anywhere to be seen. Things like that happened all the time, I was always scared. I would do almost anything rather than go back into the empty dormitory on my own. I used to imagine whatever it was would be there, waiting behind half-open doors, hiding in cupboards, lurking on the stairways. Waiting and watching, always on the edge of my sight, elusive shadowy shapes. I know it seems crazy but inside I felt I knew them, they were haunting me, waiting for something to happen to me. I never really figured it out but if ever I caught sight of them they would melt in the moonlight. They were vague, evil things, frightening, ghostly figures. You have no idea how many nights I hid under the bed clutching that box of matches. Mostly I was too terrified to strike the things in case I burnt the place down but sometimes I'd light them, cupping the flame in my hand to give me courage in the dark; then I'd have to stuff my knuckles in my mouth to stop myself from screaming. I think it would have driven me mad if I hadn't started drawing the shadows, trying to capture them with my pencil. Somehow it made them less frightening for me, as if knowing what they looked like prevented them from hurting me. Anyway it shrunk my fear of them. As I grew up they seemed to fade into the background. They were still there but they were less of a threat.'

He paused for a while. This was the first time he had ever really talked to anyone about those childhood nightmares and it had made the palms of his hands wet with sweat. 'I thought I had escaped from them,' he continued flatly. 'At least I did until the other night on the Embankment and after what happened just now. I know they followed me here: there's no mistaking that huge dog-like creature, it's exactly the same as the one in my drawings. I'm sorry, Amy, it's all my fault and I don't know why they're following me or how to stop them appearing.'

Amy felt a shiver of fear run through her. 'No, Joel, that's ridiculous,' she started to reassure him but he recognized the fear in her voice.

'Is it? I wish I could be so sure.' He paused. 'I live at number 131, that tall red brick Victorian house on the right, the one with the untidy hedge and the broken gates.'

'But why did I see them as well? Why did they terrify

that fortune teller out of her wits? I don't understand any of this.' Amy glanced in her rear view mirror before turning her car across the road and stopping at the kerb outside the gates he had pointed at.

'I don't know why it's happening. I don't know why they choose to haunt me, I'm really sorry they frightened you . . .'

A shout from the entrance of the overgrown driveway interrupted Joel. A short, balding man wearing a T-shirt, ragged shorts and broken-down trainers had appeared between the gates, carrying a rusty pair of gardening shears.

'You're back early, Joel, we weren't expecting you until late this afternoon. You must be Amy – Joel's told us all about you.' He grinned and stretched out his dirty, grass-stained hand in welcome before realizing how filthy it was and laughing as he wiped it across his sweating forehead. 'It's far too hot for gardening today – come in, come in, Marjorie's just brewing some coffee. You'll both join us, won't you?'

'This is John Harrison, my landlord.' Joel smiled as he introduced him to Amy and climbed out of the car. 'Will you come in for a moment and have some coffee?'

Amy glanced down at the clock on the dashboard and shook her head. 'No thanks, Mr Harrison, it's very kind of you to ask but I really must be going, it's a long way to Malsbury.'

'When are you getting back? Can I see you next week?' Joel asked quickly as he tried to hide his disappointment.

'Yes, if you give me your number I'll phone you when I get back,' she replied, but her voice lacked any real promise and she quickly wrote the number down on a scrap of paper and put it into the glove compartment without a second glance. She couldn't disguise her wish to get away. She smiled and raised her hand as she slipped the car into gear, revved the engine and pulled away in a roar of noise and exhaust fumes.

Joel raised his hand to acknowledge her brief good-bye. The small, blue car accelerated fast into the corner, the brake lights just flicking on before it slipped into a gap in the stream of traffic heading towards New Cross.

'Did anything unpleasant happen to you at the fair?' John asked in a soft, thoughtful voice as he watched the car vanish amongst the traffic. 'Only Amy looked anxious, as if she was trying to get away from something.'

'Yes, it was really weird – we were chased by ghosts . . . no . . . that's not really what I mean . . .' Joel hesitated as he searched for the right words. He didn't know how to begin to explain, all he knew was that Amy was running away, terrified by the ghosts that had haunted his childhood and he didn't know why or how they had appeared. They had followed him to England and he didn't know how to stop them. Miserably, he thrust his hands into his pockets and walked up the driveway.

Amy breathed a sigh of relief as she worked her gear-box hard, driving fast, dodging in and out of the heavy traffic in the centre of New Cross, trying to beat each set of lights as if they were gateways to escape. She could have stayed for a coffee but the experiences at the fair had frightened her and she needed to shake off the sense of dread, the feeling that something was following her. She needed to get home as quickly as she could, to get to the place where she had always felt safe. A knot of fear had been winding itself tighter and tighter in her stomach as Joel had talked about the nightmares that had haunted his childhood because deep down inside her she began to realize that they had been with her too, only hidden in her subconscious. The fears had been a dark, silent, cancerous growth waiting to be uncovered, waiting for the catalyst that would make their terrifying evil flower. And the worst of it was knowing that Joel was that catalyst.

A Whisper from the Past

IT WAS A beautiful afternoon to be driving. The hot, azure sky stretched away forever, scarred only by the occasional spidery vapour trails of transatlantic jets. She had escaped, got clean away, and she laughed with relief as she nosed her car out into the fast lane of the M4. 'White Boy Blues' was thundering out of the car's speakers, the wind was tugging at her hair and the hot sun was shining on her face: it was great to be alive and to feel the effortless sense of speed that she commanded.

It was only after Reading when the traffic had thinned out that the uneasiness began to creep up on her again. She found herself glancing repeatedly into her rear view mirror searching for something that she sensed was behind her but never quite in sight. The feeling was making her jittery and her hands were cramped with tension where they gripped the steering wheel by the time she reached junction fourteen and turned off on to the familiar, almost empty, network of country lanes that led to Malsbury.

'Catch me now,' she muttered through gritted teeth as she pressed her right foot hard to the floor, sending the rev counter racing around to the red. The sleek blue car clung to the narrow winding lanes, its tyres squealing in protest around the tighter bends. The roar of its engine echoed off the high banks and hedges on either side of the road but still she couldn't shake off the sensation that there was someone following her. Her eyes were drawn irresistibly back again and again to check the road behind her, but it was always empty except for the rush of leafy summer shadows that, having dappled her face, spread out in diminishing perspective across the road she had just left.

Or was it empty? For an instant she thought she caught a glimpse of a darker shape bounding along behind her, spilling through the hedgerows, rippling and smoothing itself over the high banks. Some instinct, some second sight screamed a silent warning to her. She tore her eyes from the mirror just in time to see the hairpin bend rushing towards her. She slammed the gear stick down into second and stamped on the brakes and the engine screamed in protest. Just before it was too late she took her foot off the brakes and back on the throttle, holding the steering wheel with grim determination. The hedges and steep banks became a blur of light and shadow, her stomach lurched sideways as the car skidded and sent up clouds of burning rubber. The rear bumper kissed the verge but the car held the line she had put it on, just. She prayed nothing would be coming the other way as she forced herself to keep the power on until the far side of the bend appeared and she straightened out. Her heart was pumping as she looked back and saw the curved, black tyre marks imprinted in the tarmac.

'Jesus, that was close, much too close.'

She was cold, chilled by the surge of adrenalin, and her hands and back were wet with perspiration. She sensed that, for all her rashness, she hadn't shaken off whatever was following, but she was determined not to be so stupid again and changed up through the gears smoothly and drove thoughtfully towards Malsbury. She couldn't afford to allow her imagination to run away with her again: she realized that whatever it was pursuing her she had almost allowed it to push her into killing herself. She passed a signpost and knew that in another three miles she would be safe.

A straggle of houses and cottages began to appear on either side of the road as she entered the outskirts of the town and slowed to thirty miles an hour. The feeling of being followed seemed to lessen as she passed the church, but it was still in the background, a constant shadow, as she turned in through the open gates of Crow Hall and drove slowly up towards the old Elizabethan house. Amy relaxed and eased her grip on the wheel. The old hall looked so safe, so permanent. The late afternoon sunlight glistened and reflected from the tall mullioned windows and picked out the warm colours of the climbing roses that had spread their tracery of branches across its walls. White doves cooed and strutted on the steep thatched roof while swallows wheeled and soared beneath the overhanging eaves. Billiard-table-smooth lawns vanished between the banks of rhododendron bushes and flowerbeds full of sweeping sprays of summer colour. Beyond the hydrangeas, berberis and japonica bushes, conifers, oaks and walnut trees grew amongst the woodland hedges, ancient sentinels that stood, watching over the bordering fields and woodlands standing knee-deep in their own silent shadows.

Something caught her attention. A large dog came bounding towards her along the drive, barking wildly. She braked hard kicking up a shower of gravel as the car slithered to a stop. 'Borso!' she shouted in delight, throwing open the door and bracing herself as the heavy bull terrier leapt up, licking her face in greeting, its stump of a tail wagging furiously from side to side. The fear of the pursuit had almost made her forget that Borso always dashed out to greet her the moment he caught the sound of her car. Once, in his excitement, he had actually crashed through a plate-glass window in the conservatory. She had almost run over him many times and now drove more slowly as she came near home.

'Borso, if only you had been in the car with me I wouldn't have been so afraid. You would have protected me!' she laughed, pulling at his ears and caressing his hard, muscular shoulders.

Suddenly the dog froze, the hackles prickling along his back. His noisy barking became a snarling growl, his ears flattened along the sides of his head and he backed away from her scenting the air. Suddenly he turned and raced towards the open gateway.

'Borso, come back, don't go out into the road . . . the traffic!' she shouted, running after him.

The dog reached the gateway well ahead of her and ran straight out across the road, leaping and running backwards and forwards along the verge, barking furiously at the low blackthorn hedge that bordered the lane.

'Borso, come back here at once!' she cried angrily, stopping only to check if the road was clear before she ran across and made a grab at his thick, leather collar. 'You're lucky you didn't get yourself killed. Now, walk to heel.'

Borso's wild barking gradually subsided to a low, throaty growl as he followed her back reluctantly, stopping at intervals and almost pulling her off-balance while he turned his head and barred his teeth, his growl deepening. His hackles were still ridged up along his back when she got him back into the drive and closed the gates. The moment she released her hold on his collar Borso rushed back to the gates barking furiously again, after a moment he began to chase up and down along the inside of the high brick wall at the front of the garden.

Amy paused by her car and watched the dog for a long moment, wondering what he could have seen beyond the hedge, what could have worked him into such a savage fury. A cold shiver prickled at her skin. Surely the creature that had attacked the fortune teller couldn't have followed her all the way to Malsbury. She shook her head at the idea and tried to laugh, tried to banish the spectral images that meeting Joel had stirred up. She was home, she was safe and she could stop letting her imagination run away with her. Nothing could have followed her. She looked down at Borso and remembered his father, Barnos, and how he had watched over her constantly during her childhood. He had been too attentive at times, threatening to attack her friends, and even her father, if the games of rough and tumble became too much for his sensitivity. For a moment sadness clouded her eyes as she remembered his last days and how he had refused to leave her side even as his breath rattled in his throat. His passing had left her feeling alone and unprotected.

'Borso, come here, come here and ride up to the house in my car. Come on, boy,' she called, rubbing away the tears that were misting her eyes and making a big fuss of Borso as he climbed up into the passenger seat. In many ways she loved this dog just as much, probably because he was so indifferent to the example Barnos had set for him.

Her mother appeared at the front door as she parked her car, her face pale and drawn with anxiety. 'Amy, thank God you're safe. I was coming out to investigate – I thought the dog might be barking at the police.'

'Police?' Amy echoed, climbing out of the car. 'What's happened? What's wrong?'

'Didn't you see anything on the way here?' There was relief in her mother's voice as she realized that Amy was safe.

'Why? What's happened? Where's Daddy?'

'He had to rush off to the hospital – there's been the most awful crash on the motorway. I was so worried, knowing that you were on your way down here. I've been watching all the news bulletins on the television with my heart in my mouth.'

'Crash? Where? When did it happen?' Amy frowned.

'Oh, it must be under an hour ago, dear, just the other side of Reading. It looked really terrible, all those cars and lorries all pushed into one another. It's closed both carriageways.'

Amy could hear the news announcer on the television in the breakfast room and she hurried in to see the Police Superintendent being interviewed.

'The cause of the accident hasn't been established yet but there are reports from eye witnesses of a sudden fog, or a cloud of dense smoke, that momentarily blanketed the whole motorway.'

'Were motorists driving too fast for the sudden change of conditions?' the interviewer asked as an aerial camera swept slowly across the black pall of smoke that hung over the motorway and the mass of burning, twisted metal and crumpled wreckage lying beneath it.

'Yes, speed was a possible factor but it is really too early . . .'

A loud explosion drowned out the officer's voice and sheets of flame erupted from an overturned fuel tanker on the westbound carriageway, suddenly illuminating the scene. Another officer interrupted the Superintendent and spoke quickly and quietly, pointing towards something in the thick, choking smoke.

'You'll have to excuse me!' the Superintendent shouted over the roar of the fire. 'The emergency services are stretched to the limit and we are still trying to reach people trapped in the wreckage. I'll talk to you again later . . .'

Amy turned away, almost tripping over the dog who had settled at her heels. She was dizzy and the flickering of the pictures on the screen had made her feel sick. Waves of nausea swept through her – what if she had been the cause of that dreadful accident? It must have happened moments after she had driven along that stretch of motorway. What if the drivers behind her had been distracted by whatever it was she had sensed was pursuing her? 'Oh my God,' she whispered to herself in horror as the awful possibility struck home.

'Are you all right, dear?' Jean asked with concern, gently putting her arm around Amy's shoulders as she staggered and reached out to steady herself on the arm of the sofa. 'You've gone as white as a sheet.'

'No, it's nothing, I'm OK.' Amy shook her head and regained her composure. She wouldn't know where to begin if she were to try and talk to her mother about what had happened. She didn't even understand it herself. 'Really, I'm all right – I think it must have been the shock of seeing how close I came to being involved in that terrible accident. It's made me feel quite giddy. I think I'll take a walk in the garden and sit out there for a while – a breath of fresh air will do me good. Really, I'll be fine, Mummy.'

Amy smiled but the haunted look did nothing to reassure her mother as she walked unsteadily out of the room through the conservatory and into the garden. Borso followed her, sticking like a shadow to her heels. She needed to be on her own for a while, to think, to try and find the explanation for what was happening to her. She felt as though she would go mad if she couldn't find the answer.

Amy was barely aware of Borso who was tagging along at her heels and didn't notice which direction she took as she walked across the lawn. 'Why? Why me? What have I ever done?' Her murmurings turned into a startled cry as she almost collided with the drooping, gnarled branches of an ancient mulberry tree that had stood for centuries alone on a low mound of mossy grass in the centre of the west terrace. A smile softened her drawn expression as she ducked beneath the branches and saw that the stone kissing-seat still leant drunkenly against its trunk. A forgotten relic of an earlier age, that the wind and weather had scarred and painted with mossy velvet, it had been her childhood hiding-place, her secret camp, where she had felt safe curled up on the dark, mossy earth. Only Barnos had ever joined her there, and the hard-shelled, slow-moving snails that clung to the underside of the stone seat.

She sighed and swept away the leaf and twig litter and the unripened mulberries that had fallen on the seat, and then sat down and rested her back against the rough pattern of the bark on the trunk. It had been a long time since she had last sat there but she could see the distant hills through the canopy of branches as they mellowed into a blue-grey misty line upon the horizon and they looked reassuringly familiar. The sounds of evening were the same, the soft cry of the swallows wheeling overhead, the muffled shouts of the village children playing on the green, the cry of waterfowl on Malsbury Dyke, dogs barking and the church clock striking out the hours. Yes, it was all reassuringly the same, but as she sat there watching the shadows lengthen across the garden she realized that something was different – an almost imperceptible change had taken place, overshadowing those familiar things as the twilight deepened. She had the sensation that something ominous was waiting, watching in the darkness and the feeling was growing stronger.

She shivered – it seemed suddenly to become very cold and her skin began to tingle as if a thousand icicles had touched it. Borso sensed it too, as if something was drawing closer to them, moving silently through the tangled undergrowth beyond the garden wall. His ears pricked, his nose twitched and he scented the fragrant twilight air. A low growl rumbled in his throat and he snarled, baring his teeth and crowding protectively closer to Amy.

'What is it, boy? What have you seen?' she whispered in alarm, her grip tightening on Borso's collar: her childhood hiding-place beneath the mulberry tree didn't seem so safe any more and she didn't want the dog running off into the gathering darkness leaving her there on her own.

Borso barked furiously, staring and snarling, pulling at her hand, and it hardly took her a moment to realize that he was trying to pull her towards the open door of the conservatory and the safety of the house.

Amy moved the salad aimlessly around her plate before pushing it away from her. Borso paced restlessly backwards and forwards beneath the windows of the dining room, growling up at unseen shadows in the night outside. Jean frowned irritably at the dog. 'Borso, sit down! Go to your basket or I'll shut you out in the woodshed.'

'No, I'll take him to my room, he'll settle there,' Amy cried, rising quickly from her chair. 'I've got such a headache from the drive, Mummy, I think I'll lie down for a while. I'll come down later for something to eat.'

The last thing Amy felt like was resting and she paced her bedroom, glancing repeatedly out of the window, pulling her curtains shut and then opening them again. The sense of threat had diminished but it was still there, haunting the darkness beyond the window pane. She sat on the edge of her bed stroking Borso's head and pulling gently at his silken ears. His behaviour was another thing she couldn't understand, all he had ever been any good at before was catching dog biscuits or chasing postmen and now, suddenly, he was guarding her as if his life depended upon it.

It was well past midnight before the twin beams of the headlamps of her father's old Bentley swept slowly across the lawns chasing the shadows in and out of the topiary hedges and between the trees, lighting up the house. Amy heard the reassuring crunch of gravel beneath the tyres as the car drew up and stopped beside the front steps. She smiled and felt a surge of relief flood through her as she watched the car door open and saw her father climb out. She hadn't realized how much she wanted to see him, how much she needed his strength. She was once more the frightened little girl with her nose pressed against the windowpane waiting for him to make everything safe again, to banish the evil and protect her. But the smile dissolved into a worried frown as soon as she saw him in the light from the doorway. He looked so old, so weary, his face thin and haggard, lined with tiredness, his distinguished, greying hair looked silver-white and he seemed to stoop, lifting each foot with an effort as he mounted the steps.

She resolved to say nothing of what worried her until he had rested. She was about to leave the window and go down to greet him when she heard her mother speaking to him in urgent whispers from the hallway below and twice Amy thought she caught the words 'Malsbury Wood' and 'Barnos'.

Suddenly an eerie, blood-curdling howl erupted from the undergrowth beyond the garden wall. The sound froze her with panic, stirring up images of the huge dog-like creature that had torn the fortune-teller's tent to ribbons. Amy cried out, too terrified to move, and Borso snarled and leapt in front of her, ready to spring to her defence. She heard her father shout to her mother, telling her to lock all the doors and windows, and moments later she saw his shadow elongated by the light from the hall lamp behind him, stretch out across the front steps into the driveway below. From the shadow cast upon the stones she could see he was carrying a shotgun, which he must have taken from the gun case in the hall. Her father stood there, quite still, for what seemed like an eternity, watching the darkness. Without any warning he threw the gun up against his shoulder and fired twice, then stepped back into the hall and slammed and bolted the door.

Amy heard him reload the gun and walk across the hall to his study, heard the soft click of the latch as he opened the door and then again when he shut it behind him. She sat down on the bed and pressed her hands over her ears. She was trembling from head to foot, and the sound of that eerie howl echoed in her mind, ploughing up terrible images inside her head. Getting to her feet she fled from her bedroom, running down the stairs two at a time, Borso flying at her heels.

'Daddy, I've been so afraid!' she cried, throwing open his study door.

Her father hurried to meet her, putting his arms protectively around her as he quietly pushed his study door shut and sat her down on the couch beside him. 'Your mother's told me that you've become afraid of something all evening, and that Borso has been acting very strangely since you arrived.' He paused and reached down to stroke the dog's head, softly telling him to sit. 'Now, tell me all about it from the beginning.'

Amy buried her head in his shoulder, tears forming in her eyes.

'Amy, it's important, you must tell me.' He gripped her shoulders and pulled her away to make her look at him.

'But it's all so ridiculous, really, you'll think I'm going mad. I . . . I . . . I don't know where to begin.'

George O'Keefe looked at the gun lying on his desk and then to the dark night pressing against the windows of his study. 'Tell me about the huge, shadowy creature, the one I have just shot at,' he prompted grimly.

Amy stared at him speechless. 'How on earth do you

know about that?' She gripped his arm. 'How could you possibly know what happened in the fortune-teller's tent – it only happened this morning!'

Her father frowned and, after a moment of silent deliberation, rose from the couch and, with the aid of the library steps, took down a long, stout, wooden box from the top shelf of the bookcase. Unlocking the box he brought out a bundle of old photographs and selected six of them to pass down to her. They were close-ups of wet, trampled ground. Amy looked carefully at them but was none the wiser. She was about to pass them back but her father stopped her. 'Look again, more closely this time, and then tell me exactly what you see.'

'Leaves, broken twigs, mud, stones, and . . .' Her voice trailed away into a shocked silence. Her lips thinned and trembled as she saw the huge paw prints, monstrous clawed impressions that had been left in the soft, wet earth.

Dr George O'Keefe rubbed a hand across his tired eyes and gently took the pictures back. 'We had hoped we would never have to show these to you, Amy. We hoped that the creature who had made them had gone for good when you were three years old. We knew we were wrong tonight when we heard its howl in the darkness.'

Amy reached out and took the pictures back for a closer look. The shock of what her father had just told her and the sight of those old photographs had opened a well of memories, released fleeting images that she didn't understand. She trembled with confusion. Her father frowned: he'd gone too far now to go back and he just hoped he had made the right decision. He called his wife into the study before picking up the long wooden box from his desk bringing it across to the couch and putting it down on the floor. He sat down beside Amy and Jean and rested his hand on the lid. For a moment he wrestled with the revelation he was about to make, his fingertips pressing hard down and white on the lid of the box. Finally he sighed and spoke.

'We never meant to hide this from you, Amy. There was nothing for you to be ashamed of, but there were things about your birth that would have frightened you when you were a very young child.' He paused, his frown deepening as he moved his fingers towards the catch on the lid. 'God knows they terrified us at the time, but . . .'

A noise outside on the gravel made him stop and half rise, reaching down for his gun as he did so. Borso growled and ran across the room, leaping up on to a chair beneath the window to growl at the night outside. Dr O'Keefe sat down again and carried on in a quick, breathless voice as if he was racing against time.

'These photographs are of the place where we found your mother in Malsbury Wood. You were born late at night in the pouring rain – the police took them later the next morning. There was a big enquiry but they never found out who your mother was or who had attacked her. Jean thought she had seen something move in the headlights of our car, a child running through the woods. I turned the car and drove back – we began to search through the undergrowth, it was dark and pouring with rain: I was about to give up when your mother heard a noise, I swung the torch round and we saw a girl laying on the ground. I could see straight away that she was in a terrible state. In the weak light from the torch I could have sworn I saw a huge dog crouching over the girl, trying to pull you out of her womb, but I couldn't be sure – everything happened so quickly – you know the way shadows shift when you move a beam of light. Anyway, I didn't have a chance to see what it was or where it went – I was too busy fighting to save your life. The girl, I mean your mother, was in a terrible mess, her clothes torn to ribbons and her abdomen gouged open. The shock of the assault had probably started the labour: you weren't in the right position, you were a breech birth, and your mother was almost unconscious. The umbilical cord was strangling you – another minute and we would have been too late to save you. But the most frightening thing was the moment you were safe that monster . . . creature or whatever it was, came screaming and howling at us, charging through the undergrowth as if to snatch you away.'

'If it hadn't been for Barnos smashing his way out of the car and chasing it off I don't know what would have happened,' Jean interjected quickly. 'That's why I was so worried about Borso's behaviour this evening – it's brought the whole thing back. I thought all this was buried in the past.'

Dr O'Keefe nodded seriously, glancing up at the dog which was standing on the chair at the window with his front feet on the sill and his teeth bared in a silent growl.

'Barnos refused to leave your side from the moment you were born: even when we got you to the hospital he insisted on guarding you day and night. In fact, he made a thorough nuisance of himself and we were going to keep him locked in a kennel in the garden but when we realized that those creatures from the wood had followed us here we were glad we had the dog. For the first two years of your life we were plagued with frightening, almost bizarre, incidents. Sheep were mutilated in the adjoining fields, cats were killed on the lawn and there were dozens of sightings of a huge, misshapen dog padding through the lanes of the village – all the local people were talking of it. We'd sometimes catch glimpses of it in the undergrowth around the house. If we took you out Barnos would become quite savage and wouldn't let anyone near you except us. But gradually, during your third year, the sightings became less frequent, and then one day they just seemed to vanish altogether. Gradually our life returned to normal, you went off to school – although I did have a lot of difficulty persuading your headmistress to allow Barnos to go with you . . .' For a moment there was a hint of laughter in his eyes as he remembered but a shadow soon clouded over and he clasped her hands firmly in his.

'I don't know what abomination we disturbed that night twenty-two years ago or what claim it thinks it has on you but we love you just as much now as we did that first moment. Remember, Amy, no matter what happens, we will do anything we can to help.'

He eased his grip on her hands and bent forwards lifting the lid of the box and pulled out a bulky, black plastic bag and broke the police seal before tearing it open. He withdrew a pale, crumpled coat and carefully laid it in Amy's hands. 'This is the coat your mother was wearing when we found her that night.'

Amy stared. She never expected to hold anything that had belonged to her real mother. She felt the material of the coat and was surprised how thin it felt. Leaning forward, she found that it held a faint stale, almost musty, odour, probably the result of lying sealed up in that bag for years. There were irregular brown blood-stains all over it and she lifted the coat and let it fall open. She inhaled a sharp, shallow breath as she saw the tears, long, gouged slits all across the front, exactly like the ones that the creature had torn in the fortune-teller's tent. Shuddering she folded the coat quickly but she couldn't help seeing the small name-tag that was sewn inside the collar and the word 'Thornbury' neatly written in faded ink. She looked up at her parents, her lips trembling with emotion as she wondered who her mother had been and what had driven her to flee into Malsbury Wood all that time ago.

'Did she say anything? Did she know who had attacked her?'

Her father slowly shook his head. 'I did everything I could but I couldn't save her. The only words she whispered were "They followed me. They wanted to take my baby."'

'But why? What could she possibly have done that was so terrible that it brought those creatures up out of Hell to come after me? Why do I have to suffer for something that she did?' Amy's voice was choked with anger and tears of self-pity glittered in her eyes. She crushed the raincoat, violently screwing it up in her hands before throwing it on the floor. 'I never wanted any of this to happen never . . . never . . . never!'

'No, Amy, none of us did.' Jean spoke softly as she put her arms around her daughter's shoulders. 'I don't for one minute think your mother wanted it to happen either – you mustn't forget that she was little more than a child when it happened, much younger than you are now, poor helpless thing. Think of her running away through those dark woods on her own.'

'I only wish we had spotted her earlier. I would have given whatever it was chasing her a thorough beating,' her father added in his down-to-earth way. 'I would have shown them what-for.' He bent forwards stiffly to retrieve the coat and return it to its plastic bag.

Amy looked at them both and realized how lucky she had been and suddenly felt very ashamed of her outburst. 'I'm sorry, I've been very silly,' she whispered as she gathered up the photographs of her birth place that lay scattered on the couch beside her. She felt a compulsion to touch them, to reach back through their matt surface and touch the past to find out what really happened. Her eyes were drawn to the mess of trampled leaves and the huge paw prints. The familiar objects in the study seemed to diminish into the background and the ceiling became a canopy of branches; she could smell the cold, wet earth and hear the desolate patter of rain, she could feel it tingle and sting as it touched her skin. Something was strangling her, tightening around her throat; there were sounds in the undergrowth all around her, frightening, terrifying noises, and two shadowy creatures and a huge, three-headed dog were looming towards her.

Suddenly hands were holding her and she heard a snip and felt a rush of cold air scald her lungs; a bright light was shining in her eyes and there were voices, shouts in the darkness. The sounds of a dog snarling, leaping and fighting against the advancing shadowy figures. Suddenly she knew what they were, she knew the words that would banish them. She opened her mouth and began to recite 'Surmy, Delmusan, Zoros . . .'

'Amy – what is it? What are you trying to say?'

She felt her mother shake her arm and heard her voice as it broke through the images that had formed around her. She blinked, trying to hold onto everything she had just seen as she reached out her tiny infant hand, only it was large again and it suddenly and painfully struck the arm of the couch.

'Amy, what happened? You seemed to go into some sort of trance,' her father frowned.

She shook her head, pressing her hands against her temples as she tried to catch hold of the elusive fragments of memory, but they were gone, racing from her like a dream in the morning. 'I don't know – when I looked at those pictures it was as if I was back there, back in Malsbury Wood. I think I remembered my birth, I must have done – I knew what those creatures were, I know I did. I even remembered the words that would drive them away. What did I say? Did I call out anything?'

'Well, yes, you did, but it wasn't anything intelligible,

dear, it was most strange, like a baby crying really,' her mother answered.

'Those creatures, you saw them? Could you describe them?' her father pressed.

Amy thought hard, struggling with her memories. Vague, shadowy, cloaked images formed in her head. 'Yes, I'm sure they were the same figures that we saw moving through the crowd at the fair and the creature that made those paw-prints has to be the huge dog-like beast who tore the fortune-teller's tent to shreds. But I don't know why – there were other memories of places and people – it's all so confusing.' She stopped suddenly and brought her hand to her mouth as the awful realization struck home. They were exactly the same, the same as the ghosts that had haunted the children's home in Australia where Joel had grown up. Her mind was racing, they were the figures in his drawings and they had been a part of her childhood too.

'Joel – he's a part of this . . .'

Amy hesitated and looked away as she felt the colour rising in her cheeks. She realized that she was on the verge of inventing a past for Joel, creating a background for him that would match up to her parents' expectations. It was something that she had never felt necessary to do for any of the other friends she had brought home and it made her realize how different he was, and how far apart their upbringings had been. It didn't seem to matter much in London but here at home it was important that her parents liked and accepted him. She didn't know how to begin to tell them about him or how much he meant to her.

'There's a young man I met recently at the gallery, a student at Goldsmiths' College, an Australian. He's experienced something very similar to this.'

'I'm sure he's a very nice young man, dear – you must bring him down for the weekend.' Her mother's warm voice filled the uncomfortable silence that had been created.

'Yes, he is nice but . . .' She thought carefully about what to say next. 'He's penniless, he's an art student, an orphan who grew up in an Australian children's home. I'm not sure you'd really approve of him.' The truth came out in a breathless rush, but she felt a sense of relief.

To her surprise her father laughed and clasped her hand. 'The luggage, Amy, is always more important than the label it carries. God knows the journeys we make through our lives are difficult enough without having to always justify how we started. Bring him down and let us make up our own minds about him.' He winked and added, 'He's got a pretty good head-start if he's made this much of an impression on you. Now tell us all about him and about why you think he is a part of this.'

Smiling with relief she told them both how they had met and how special he felt to her and how being with him seemed so natural, but anxiety clouded her eyes as she related the incident in the fairground and the unnerving feeling she had that despite being born twelve thousand miles apart they had been haunted by the same evil creatures during their childhoods. It seemed that there were too many strange coincidences and parallels in their lives to be put down to chance.

'You don't think those creatures could have caused the dreadful accident on the motorway, do you? I sensed something weaving through the traffic, following me . . .' Amy's voice trailed away and her face was deathly white as the horror of the television pictures was brought back to her.

'No, of course not, don't be silly, Amy,' her father reassured her, but a shiver of apprehension prickled his skin. There had been so many reports of wild sightings by those involved in the accident that the rescue services were buzzing with the story. There were tales of a huge, shadowy shape, that it appeared to be a creature bounding through the traffic. One moment it had seemed to be a large hound and the next it had transformed itself into a smothering cloud, a dense black fog that obliterated everything. 'No, now don't think like that – from the report I received in the hospital it was caused by a freak weather pattern or smoke from a field-fire blowing across the motorway.'

'But . . . I feel so responsible: that howling cry in the darkness outside, the sense of evil surrounding the house wouldn't be here if I hadn't brought it with me. Even Borso's behaving strangely and it's all my fault.'

'No, Amy,' he replied firmly, getting to his feet and retrieving his gun from the desk. 'You are as much an innocent victim now as you were all those years ago when we disturbed that creature crouching over your mother's body in Malsbury Wood.'

'But what is it? How can we drive it away?' she asked in a small, frightened voice.

Her father sighed and checked his jacket pocket for shotgun cartridges. As he called the dog away from the window his face was haggard and drawn by tiredness. 'I don't know. We tried to find an explanation for it years ago. We had a priest perform an exorcism in the hope of driving the beast away and we consulted the leading experts in witchcraft and devil worship, but all to no avail. Perhaps there isn't an answer . . .' He paused and watched the dog cross the study to sit at his daughter's feet. 'There is one thing though: the creature seems to be afraid of dogs so keep Borso with you at all times. Now I think we should all try to get some sleep.'

As he walked to the door she called after him. 'Will you show me where I was born in Malsbury Wood tomorrow morning?'

He paused with his hand on the doorknob and a smile

appeared at the corners of his mouth. Perhaps after all the people he had approached in search of an answer it was Amy herself who would be able to get to the bottom of it, to exorcize the creatures that had plagued her childhood. 'Yes, of course, we'll go straight after breakfast.'

Malsbury Wood seemed to brood, wrapped in its own ancient and private silence once they had left the road behind and followed the narrow animal track in amongst the trees. Thick leaf mould softened and deadened their footsteps while unruly banks of ferns and tangled brambleheads that drooped across the path snagged at their clothes. Amy's father hesitated, finding it difficult to locate the exact place where she had been born – it was many years since he had last walked through the woods and it looked so very different from that rainswept, February night.

'Here, boy, stay close!' Amy called anxiously as Borso ran ahead scenting the air and chasing butterflies, crashing through the undergrowth, startling the foraging squirrels and sending them scrambling up into the branches of the tall oaks and elms. He frightened away the squabbling blackbirds and song thrushes between the trees and after he returned, panting for breath, the only sound that broke the cathedral quiet of the wood was the drone and hum of clouds of hovering insects, their iridescent wings caught by the shafts of misty, morning sunlight that filtered down through the dense summer canopy of leaves.

'We must be very close to the place now,' her father murmured, stopping where the path divided. 'We couldn't have come much further from the road that night.' Slowly he checked his bearings. 'Yes, I remember noticing the split trunk on that elm tree in the torchlight – that's the place – directly ahead. Of course the undergrowth had died back during the winter – you can see much further when the branches are bare of leaves.' Dr O'Keefe trampled and beat down the ferns and under-growth in a broad circle with his walking stick, stopping only when he had cleared the area. 'This is the place. When we found her your mother was lying exactly where you're standing. The creatures, or whatever they were, fled towards those trees and bushes away to your left.'

Amy let her eyes travel slowly across the dappled shadows between the trees and then looked down at the trampled ferns beneath her feet. She wasn't really sure what she had expected to happen or what she would gain by coming back. She wasn't sure if it was morbid curiosity or merely clutching at straws in a vain attempt to reach back through the shrouds that clouded her memory and remember inhaling those first, frantic breaths on that dark February night.

Nothing happened to break the whispering silence of Malsbury Wood. She sighed and crouched down, feeling a great sense of loss, a sadness she couldn't define. She pulled aside the trampled undergrowth, closing her eyes to sharpen her awareness as she touched the cold, damp earth. Something moved and wriggled beneath her fingertips and she cried out as she snatched her hand away, only to see a beetle, a devil's coach-horse, its black back and pointed tail arched in defence against her alien touch as it scuttled away through the dense mass of broken fern stems. Borso heard her cry, snarled and crowded forwards, almost crushing the beetle to death with his nose as he followed its retreat through the undergrowth.

'It's all right, it's not going to hurt me, it's only a tiny beetle.' She hauled on his collar and stood up.

Her father saw the sadness in her eyes and though he wanted to put his arms around her shoulders and make everything right again, he knew she would have to face this moment alone.

'It's as if she never existed. The world's forgotten and the trees have all grown over where she lay.' Tears glittered in the corners of her eyes. 'There's nothing here to remember her by: it's as if that terrible night of suffering never happened.'

'She's not forgotten, Amy,' her father answered gently as he took her hand and walked her back towards the car. 'We set up a trust to equip the maternity ward with two incubators and all the ancillary equipment they will ever need. There's a brass plaque on each of them telling her story and one over the door. We thought that helping other desperate mothers was a better way of remembering her than a lonely cross in the wood. I'll show them to you the next time you come to the hospital.'

Amy paused and turned to look back at the small, trampled circle: already the ferns were straightening, the wood claiming back its territory. 'I must get back to London, to see Joel – there's so much we have to talk about.' She shivered despite the warm morning sunlight.

'Take the dog – keep him with you at all times,' her father said quickly as she climbed into the car.

Amy reached down and helped Borso to scramble up onto her lap, liberally covering her clothes with mud as he did so. She smiled and pulled at his ears. 'But you'll miss him, won't you?'

Dr O'Keefe glanced back into the soft, leafy shadows of the wood before he nodded. 'Yes, of course we will, but we'll sleep easier knowing that he's looking after you.'

He sighed as she started the car and then smiled across at Borso. 'You know, in a strange way, I think he inherited the task of protecting you. I know he'll never let this creature hurt you if he can help it.'

An Attack in the Dark

A WAVE OF NAUSEA tightened in Amy's throat when she caught sight of the thick haze of smoke and the stench of burnt rubber that still hung over the wreckage on the motorway, she had to concentrate on the diversion signs which sent her through Woodley and Whistley Green and around the east of Reading. A part of her would always feel responsible no matter what natural explanations her father or anybody else produced; she knew deep down inside her that the horrific accident hadn't been caused by any freak weather or smoke blowing across the motorway.

'We have to stop those creatures, whatever they are. We have to destroy their power before they can do anything like this again,' she muttered fiercely to Borso who lay curled up asleep on the passenger seat beside her.

The dog growled softly, his ears twitching at the sound of her voice. He stretched but stayed sleeping, his head resting heavily against her left arm. She glanced down and smiled as she eased her arm away from him. Borso had a Herculean appetite for sleep, but it made her wonder if he would ever wake up in time to defend her if any real danger threatened.

'You're a good boy,' she murmured softly. 'Even if you're not much like Barnos.'

The diversion route around the crash site followed a maze of narrow, intersecting country lanes and minor A roads that converged on the outskirts of London and they soon became snarled up with the thousands of weekenders and holiday-makers returning to the city. It was a slow, frustrating journey as they crawled from junction to junction and it seemed to take forever. To make it worse, a solid mass of low, dark thunder clouds crept relentlessly across the sky, blotting out the sun and bringing with them a stifling, muggy heat. Thunder rumbled and stamped along the horizon line, flashes of lightning split the darkening sky and large raindrops began to splatter irregularly on the windscreen before the slow, seemingly endless, procession of caravans, buses and cars had driven through Cranbourne. Amy yawned and rubbed her eyes, easing the clutch in to creep forward another dozen yards. It was going to take hours to reach London at this rate and lack of sleep the previous night was beginning to catch up with her. Her concentration was starting to drift, lulled by the mesmerizing, rhythmic swish of the wiper blades and the drumming of the rain on the roof.

She glanced sleepily in her rear view mirror and instantly snapped awake. The briefest glimpse of a shadow, a huge, canine shape that dissolved and merged with the raindrops sliding down the rear window, sent a shiver up her spine, adrenalin pulsated through her. Borso seemed to sense her fear and sat up, snarling and turning his bullet-shaped head from side to side. Amy depressed the automatic door locks and carefully searched the line of cars and vans ahead and behind her. But she couldn't see anything out of the ordinary. She breathed a sigh of relief but it made her realize that she couldn't afford to drop her guard or relax for a minute. It made her glad she had the dog with her and she scratched him under the chin.

'It's OK, Borso – there's nothing there – go back to sleep.' But the feeling that something sinister was following her back towards London, somewhere out there in the shadows, sharpened her senses and kept her alert.

It was dark and raining heavily by the time she passed the bus station on the New Cross Road. Her eyes were sore and gritty with tiredness and the shimmering reflections from the neon shop signs on the wet road were becoming hallucinatory rivers of liquid colours swirling beneath the wheels of her car. She blinked and shook her head, braking hard to prevent herself from overshooting the pedestrian traffic lights on the small, humped-back bridge outside the railway station. She watched a group of people huddling beneath their umbrellas cross in front of her – another few feet and she would have run them down. The palms of her hands were damp with perspiration. It wasn't far now: she was close to Joel's flat and she had to concentrate, to remember exactly where to turn off the main road – it couldn't be more than a couple of miles. She slowed the car and pulled onto the crown of the road, indicated and waited for a gap to appear in the steady stream of traffic heading in the opposite direction before turning into Wickham Road.

She didn't want to go back to her empty flat, to face having to open the door on her own, without first talking to Joel and trying to work out what was haunting them both. She was sure he had written his phone number down on a scrap of paper but she couldn't find it. She searched through the glove compartment, her foot riding the clutch: she ought to telephone him first. What if he had someone with him? Wickham Road looked so desolate in the rainy darkness, so empty and forbidding despite the glare of the sodium lamps spaced irregularly between the flowering cherry trees that grew along its vanishing length. She wasn't sure if she could find the house where she had dropped him off the day before. She hadn't taken that much notice of the number then, or exactly where it was, and they all looked so similar in the lamplight. Headlamps momentarily dazzled her, reflecting into her rear view mirror. She felt the car rock and saw the blurred image of a black taxi-cab as it drove past inches from her wing mirror, its tyres spraying up water from the puddles lying in the road and throwing it against her windows. She flinched instinctively and it made Borso growl.

'It's no good, Borso, we can't sit here blocking half the road while we dither – it's got to be here somewhere. It must be further up on the right-hand side.' She took her foot off the clutch and accelerated forwards, peering out at the gateways through the driving rain.

Suddenly she caught sight of a broken white-painted gateway and remembered seeing it on her previous visit. She braked and spun the wheel before driving up into a shallow, gravelled drive. Borso was out of the car at her heels before she could shut him in the car and she smiled to herself as she ran up the front steps and rang the bell; there were odd, reassuring moments when he was a lot like Barnos.

The house stood wrapped in silent darkness. The sound of the front doorbell sounded shrill as it echoed through the empty hallway. Amy stepped back and half-heartedly pressed the bell a second time. An overwhelming sense of emptiness rushed over her as she paused on the top step, listening to the rain gurgling in the gutters and drumming on the roof of her car. In the distance was the persistent hum of evening traffic and the darkness smelt of passionflower, jasmine and wild raspberry, fresh-washed fragrances that awakened long-forgotten memories of other nights beneath the stars, memories that scattered and melted away into the night as she tried to hold onto them. They left her with a feeling of losing something she might never truly touch again.

'Come on, Borso, there's no one here,' she sighed. Then sound from inside the house made her turn back. A finger of light appeared in the hallway, picking out the intricacies of the etched, glass panels in the front door as an inner door opened and a figure hurried towards her. She hoped she had chosen the right house as she listened to the rattle of the chain and the click as the lock was turned but her apprehension vanished as the door opened and she saw Mr Harrison's smiling face appear.

'I'm sorry to bother you, Mr Harrison, but I was just passing and I wondered if Joel was in.'

'Why, yes, of course he is. He'll be delighted to see you. Come in, come in. Please call me John, everybody else does.' The smile faded and he stepped quickly backwards as Borso followed her over the threshold.

'This is Borso – he's an English bull terrier,' she offered in an apologetic explanation as John pushed the front door closed behind her. 'He goes everywhere with me. You don't mind if I bring him in, do you?' Mr Harrison's anxiety reminded her of the reactions that Barnos' presence had caused when she was a child.

'Of course, bring him in, we like dogs.' John tried to laugh, but his voice betrayed an edge of nervousness as he looked down at the hard, unblinking, almost murderous gleam in Borso's eyes and the grinning, half-open mouth crowded with sharp teeth. He remembered reading somewhere that bull terriers had been bred as fighting dogs and that nothing, short of a rifle bullet, would stop them once they had it set in their minds to attack. He was definitely not going to put that theory to the test.

'Joel, you've got a visitor!' he called, hastily opening the inner door to the sitting-room and motioning Amy to go in.

Borso slipped past her before she could keep him to heel and she heard a growling yelp as he ran into the room. She hurried anxiously after him but her anxiety dissolved into a smile as she realized that the growl had, in fact, been a greeting as he bounded straight across the room to where Joel was sitting in a deep armchair. The dog had half-climbed onto his lap and was licking his face, his short stump of a tail wagging furiously.

'Borso, get down! I'm sorry, Joel, I didn't expect him to charge straight in here like that. Get down, you bad dog!'

'No worries, he's a great dog!' Joel laughed as he pulled Borso's ears and gently eased him off his legs so that he could get up. His look of surprise and relief at seeing her turned into a frown of concern as he noticed her distraction. 'Amy, are you OK, you look exhausted. What's happening? We saw pictures of the crash on the M4 yesterday and it was on television all the time, I was worried, it's on your way home, isn't it?'

She nodded bleakly, wringing her hands together, her voice sounding small and empty. 'Yes, it happened right behind me, Joel. The terrible thing is that I know I must have caused it. If only I hadn't tried to escape. If only I'd known.' Huge tears were forming in her eyes and she buried her face in her hands, her shoulders trembling uncontrollably as she sobbed. She hadn't meant to let her emotions get the better of her but carrying the burden of the accident, her lack of sleep and the strain of the long drive back had exhausted her.

'What do you mean "escape"? Who . . . what . . . were you trying to escape from?' Joel asked, grabbing her shoulders.

Slowly she controlled her sobs and looked up into his eyes. 'I had a horrible sensation that something was following me on the motorway. I thought it was that dog-beast – it was weaving in and out of the traffic behind me like a threatening black shadow so I accelerated to get away from it only . . .' She shuddered. 'That accident wasn't caused by smoke blowing across the road or by freak weather.'

'But that's crazy, it's impossible. Why should it have chased you? It's me those creatures have followed half way around the world. I'm sorry they've frightened you, Amy, but you mustn't blame yourself for that crash.'

She shook her head angrily. 'You're wrong, it's not only you they've haunted, they have been over here as well. Look, look at this . . .' She broke free from his grip and found the photograph of her birthplace in her bag and handed it to him. In a flat voice, almost drained of emotion by the strain of the past thirty-six hours, she quickly told him everything her father had revealed to her about her early life.

'You see we must have both been haunted by those things, the same things, Joel. There are so many inexplicable similarities. The only reason I didn't know anything about it was because my father's dog, Barnos, kept chasing them away. My father thinks they're afraid of dogs so that's why I've brought Borso back with me.'

Joel frowned and looked down at the dog. 'You know, you may be right, you've reminded me – I had a dog when I was very young, well it wasn't really my dog, it was a mangy, old, lame cattle dog, a blue-heeler. He sort of belonged to all of us kids, he didn't really have an owner, but we called him Blue on account of him having one blue eye. The dog warden hated him and was always setting traps but old Blue was much too clever.' Joel's face softened into a smile. 'The warden swore he had more fleas and ticks living on him than a flock of sheep. He probably carried the plague, but he was a great dog. We used to steal food for him and hide him in our dormitory. Most nights I'd hear him scratching and snoring under my bed.' He paused and after a moment's thought he laughed softly. 'He guarded me too, in a rather casual way – when he wasn't foraging in the bush. I remember some nights we had a hell of a job keeping him quiet – for no reason he'd start snarling and attacking shadows. The times we almost got caught . . .'

'But why is this happening, Joel? What had either of us done to these evil creatures to make them haunt us?'

'Perhaps it's because of something you did in an earlier life.'

Marjorie's voice made Amy catch her breath in surprise. She hadn't realized there was anyone else in the dimly-lit room and she had become so intent on telling Joel about her weekend she hadn't felt her presence.

'I'm sorry, I should have introduced you – Marjorie meet Amy, Amy this is Marjorie, John's wife.'

'I'm so sorry, I didn't mean to barge in like this,' Amy stuttered, feeling the colour rush to her cheeks as she turned towards the voice and saw a large, well-dressed woman with an embroidered shawl draped around her shoulders sitting in a high-backed chair close to the open French windows. She had a candid face with deep, intense, blue eyes and a smile that immediately dissolved Amy's embarrassment. Borso obviously hadn't felt that she was any threat and had walked straight past her chair to stand guard at the window.

'What did you mean?' Amy asked, her interest sharpening. 'What did you mean just now when you said those creatures may be haunting us because of something we did in an earlier life?'

She sat forwards on the edge of the worn sofa, waiting for her to elaborate.

Marjorie smiled. 'Well it really depends on whether you believe in reincarnation, you know – living other lives before this one – and perhaps after, maybe even on different planes of consciousness.'

'We've been sitting here all evening watching the storm through the open window and discussing the inner meaning of life,' Joel interrupted with a grin. He was delighted to see Amy so unexpectedly and he wanted to lighten the conversation and make her feel more at ease. 'Would you like something to eat, or perhaps a drink . . . coffee, wine?'

'Oh, yes, some wine would be lovely.' She took the glass that was offered but declined anything to eat as John closed the sitting-room door.

'You mustn't approach the mysteries of the universe so flippantly, Joel.' Marjorie frowned, leaning forwards in her chair. 'There's so much going on out there and we haven't scratched the surface – we don't even begin to comprehend the knowledge we have locked up inside our heads. Think about it, Joel, if only we could find the key to unlock those other planes of consciousness what might we have experienced?'

The wine almost spilt over the rim of Amy's glass as she listened intently to what Marjorie was saying, her whole attention focused on the possibilities she was unfolding. She remembered discussing reincarnation with her friends at school but it had never really interested her before, imagining that she were someone from an earlier life and fitting that into the well-trodden path of history. She hadn't pursued the idea beyond the shallowest daydreams and she had never seen the point in believing in earlier lives she couldn't even remember. It had been easy to dismiss the notion of reincarnation living, as she did, in the centre of her own universe, surrounded and protected by the familiar fabric of the world she inhabited. Ghosts, demons and past lives were all conjecture: none of these phenomena could really be proved: how could they be real? But now, in the light of what she had discovered about her birth, and about the creatures that were pursuing them, there were chilling implications in what Marjorie had just said. It opened up a terrifying, subterranean landscape of possibilities that might lay just beneath the surface of their consciousness – if it were true.

Amy took a slow, thoughtful sip from her glass and savoured the dry taste on her tongue. What if she was right? What if she could reach back into her own memories, beyond the world she knew: would she find the common threads of a whole tapestry of earlier experiences? Would she find the answers they needed through those glimpses and pin-hole peeps? Suddenly she shivered, and her mind filled with fragmented images, jigsaw pieces of sounds and colours, shouts and voices, disjointed noises and familiar, yet unknown, faces that crowded her vision. The glint of light on armour, the sound of hoofbeats, the smell of sweat and dirt and the rumble of wheels. An endless procession of figures moved through the dusty sunlight towards tall spires that stood out against the setting sun. Over all this she could hear the crackle of flames with mournful voices in the background and smell the overpowering reek of death.

'Amy! Amy, are you all right?' A voice, louder than the other sounds, cut through the pageantry of memories and began to draw her back. She struggled to hold onto the images, to fix them in her memory. Then she blinked and brought the room back into focus, steadying her glass; for an instant she looked vacantly at the three faces that were staring at her.

'Amy – are you OK? You seemed to be in a trance: your hands were shaking. Look at your dog, he's growling at the open window.'

There was concern in Joel's voice but before she could reassure him wind billowed at the curtains, swinging the ceiling lamps on their flexes and ruffling the Sunday newspapers that lay discarded on the floor. Borso's growls became a warning snarl and his hackles ridged up along his back as he threatened something that lurked in the darkness outside.

'Joel, that smell!' Amy hissed in alarm as she caught the faint odour of sulphur.

Marjorie watched the fear widen Amy's eyes and felt an icy coldness suddenly blanket the room. She rose quickly from her chair and pulled the French windows shut, locking them securely. 'John, switch on the electric heater, will you, it feels very cold in here,' she asked, scanning the garden for any sign of an intruder.

The glistening leaves of the laurel and wild raspberry bushes close to the house swayed and trembled beneath the steady downpour of rain, the lawns were empty and the far end of the garden was lost in shadow. All she could see beyond the fence was the stark architectural outline of the houses in Cranfield Road and the tree tops, etched black against the wet, sodium night sky.

'There's nothing out there to be frightened of,' she reassured Amy as she drew the curtains to shut out the darkness. But something caught her eye, a movement between the shrubs, silent, gliding shadows drawing closer to the house. Marjorie's eyes narrowed and her fingers tightened on the curtain: for an instant shadowy figures seemed to loom towards her. Borso leapt up beside her snarling, his teeth bared inches from the rain-streaked glass.

'For God's sake what is it?' Amy cried, half-rising from her chair.

Marjorie threw the curtains back to let a shaft of light stream out through the window and illuminate the lawn but the figures had melted into the rain. 'There's nothing there now, nothing at all,' she answered calmly, pulling the curtain shut. 'But a moment ago I would swear I saw two figures, two people and a large animal, and they were approaching the house.'

'Well, I'm glad they've gone.'

There was relief in Amy's voice. The supernatural seemed to be crowding uncomfortably close and it sent cold shivers up her spine. Marjorie stepped back from the French windows and let the curtains drop back into place. The hem creased and rumpled over Borso's head. He growled and shook it aside, keeping his nose pressed against the glass of the bottom pane as he watched the garden.

'At least the dog will warn us if anybody else comes prowling around the back of the house.'

'You don't have to see them to know they're out there watching, waiting.' Amy's voice was little more than a frightened whisper from the corner of the sofa where she had shrunk back to hide.

'This is crazy, it's giving me the creeps!' Joel rose angrily to his feet and strode to the window, defiantly throwing back the curtains. 'I'm not afraid of you, do you hear me, I'm not going to spend the rest of my life jumping at shadows. You're not going to make me afraid of the dark!' he shouted at the night outside, watching the raindrops splatter against the glass and merge into thin, liquid reflections of the light behind him. 'Damn you to Hell!'

When he turned to Amy his face was flushed with anger. 'It was bad enough having them haunt me when I was a kid: I'm not going to let it start again. I'm going to stop them, Amy – somehow I'm going to drive the bloody things away.'

'It's no good getting wound up, Joel, it won't solve anything.' John spoke firmly, crossing to the window to draw the curtains shut.

'But how will we find the answers? We don't even know what they are or why they're following us. We don't know where they come from.' Amy's voice was tight with the utter hopelessness of the situation. 'There's nothing we can do. We'll never get rid of them, I know we won't!'

'Calm down both of you,' Marjorie intervened. She'd had to deal with more than the occasional patient who had insisted they'd had some sort of brush with the supernatural and in a small way she considered herself an authority on the subject. Normally the patients were highly emotional, paranoid and verging on the hysterical and it hadn't been easy preparing their psychiatric reports for whichever local health authority had referred them to her. They had all shown an unnatural fear and hysteria very similar to the pattern developing right there in front of her.

'Sit still both of you and pay attention!' she spoke firmly, clapping her hands together. The sound echoed like a pistol shot. It was the only thing she could think of on the spur of the moment, but it caught their attention.

'Getting hysterical isn't going to solve anything, is it? You have both got to think calmly, approach this situation logically and compile a profile of these . . . these ghosts.'

'Logically?' Joel laughed harshly. 'You saw those drawings I did as a kid, didn't you? Well it didn't matter how many times I tried to tell myself there wasn't anything to be afraid of – they were illogically, terrifyingly real, and it never stopped my skin crawling with fear as I waited for them to touch me in the dark . . .'

'Joel, you're not listening to me,' Marjorie interrupted. 'I never said your fear wasn't real for you, did I? But think back, did they ever touch you – actually touch you?'

Joel frowned and after a moment's thought he shook his head. 'No, but I thought they were going to.'

'Exactly. It's the anticipated violation, the very unnatural appearance of the supernatural that creates fear and hysteria simply because it defies the logic of the world we live in.' Marjorie paused before continuing. 'I'm sure the only way you will ever be free of this evil power is to find out and understand its source and with that knowledge exorcize it.'

'You make it sound so easy; but where do we begin?

My father tried to find out and he didn't get anywhere, why should we do any better?' Amy answered uneasily.

'Because it obviously involves you two and not your father, Amy.' Marjorie paused and glanced uneasily around the room. She felt a heaviness in the air, an oppressive stillness that seemed to deaden her voice. 'Listen, both of you,' she continued urgently, moving her chair closer. 'If you have lived before and the ghosts come from that time then the answers to what they are must be locked in your subconscious. You have to think back, release the knowledge and bring it to the surface of your memories, put it together piece by piece like making a jigsaw. Why don't you start with what happened in the fortune-teller's tent yesterday. John, will you get some paper and a pen, and we'll write down everything that happened.'

'But that's crazy!' Joel protested.

'Think, Joel – haven't you ever felt that you have been somewhere before, seen people you think you already know but couldn't possibly have met?'

'Well, yes, I suppose so,' he answered, looking at Amy.

'Well, let's try reaching back into your memories. You've got nothing to lose, have you?'

'Don't you think we had better be careful. Isn't it dangerous meddling with the supernatural?' Amy asked anxiously.

'It wouldn't surprise me if these ghosts, or whatever they are, aren't involved with black magic and Marjorie's quite an expert in the occult. She'll help you get to the bottom of it if anybody can.' John began to rifle through the pile of magazines and newspapers, carefully moving the bottles of wine and glasses on the coffee table while he searched for the pen he had used earlier to complete the crossword. 'There's a notebook in the study, I'll just get it.'

'No! Don't go out of the room – stay exactly where you are!' Marjorie warned him as Borso suddenly spun round and charged towards the door snarling and barking furiously. 'Nobody must leave the room and don't touch the door whatever you do! The evil is drawing in around us; I can sense its presence. Everyone stay exactly where you are.'

'Marjorie – the door-handle – look at the door-handle!' John gasped, backing away.

The brass handle was glowing dull red and the layers of old paint around the lock and finger-plate had begun to bubble and blister. Thin, yellowing trails of smoke were curling up from a maze of cracks in the melting paintwork but his eyes were focused on the central panels as they darkened and the huge menacing outline of a snarling beast with three heads began to loom out of the reeking doorway, advancing pace by pace into the room. Amy screamed and shrank back; Joel made a grab at one of the wine bottles to hurl at the salivating, shadowy creature, but Borso had already sprung forward before Joel's fingers could close around the slender neck of the bottle.

With a snarling growl, Borso's jaws snapped shut on one of the huge beast's muzzles. There was a sharp crack of bone and a howling yelp of pain as he savaged the creature, violently shaking his head from side to side, clawing at its chest as it shrunk back and disappeared. The choking, sulphurous smoke thinned into a misty haze as the blackened blisters on the paintwork shrivelled and vanished as the door returned to its original state except for a deep, splintered scar across the central panel where Borso's teeth had sunk in.

Borso stood there for a moment growling defiantly at the door, his feet planted wide apart, the muscles tensed and knotted across his powerful shoulders. Blood trickled from three long claw gouges on the side of his head. John was staring, open-mouthed, at the door, his hands trembling, his face deathly white. Amy was the first to move, crossing the room quickly to kneel beside her dog and praise him for defending them. She used her crumpled handkerchief to dab at the blood flowing from the wound.

'Marjorie, what in God's name was that? Where on earth did it come from?' John whispered, taking a tentative step toward the door.

'That's the same creature that tore the fortune-teller's tent to pieces, it's got to be!' Joel gasped as he struggled to control his ragged breathing.

John reached out tentatively to touch the central panel of the door where Borso's teeth had struck it. The paint felt cold and glossily hard. 'I don't understand: a moment ago this paint was bubbling up about to burst into flames but look at it now, it's stone cold.'

'It was magic,' Marjorie answered, crossing to examine the door. 'Evil, black magic, and that creature we saw was the hound from Hell – an apparition sent to terrify us.'

'It was a lot more than an apparition – it was real enough to claw at Borso's head!' Amy shuddered, putting her arms around him protectively.

'It's difficult to define reality in magic, especially in evil magic – that is partly where our fear of the occult lies. Yes, we all saw the creature coming towards us, and it was real enough to attack Borso, but the door is barely damaged and logic tells us that is impossible, doesn't it?'

'Yes, but I swear I could smell its breath and I felt completely helpless. What made it stop? Why did it suddenly vanish into thin air? Why didn't it attack us?' Joel asked in confusion.

'Borso saved us,' Amy answered quickly. 'Remember my father said that these ghosts, or whatever they are, are afraid of dogs.'

'Yes, yes you are right,' Marjorie agreed, 'and I wouldn't have believed it if I hadn't seen it happen myself. Everything I've ever read would say that your dog couldn't have stopped that creature, nothing could have if the magic that created and animated it was as powerful as it seemed to be. It should have torn us all to pieces easily – but it was afraid of Borso and cowered away from him when he leapt at it.'

'I don't think that it necessarily came through that door to attack us,' John spoke softly, making the others turn and stare at him. 'No, I think it burst in to frighten us, or rather to frighten Amy and Joel – and to stop them from remembering.'

'You know, you could be right,' Marjorie murmured. 'It did appear at the very moment you were trying to remember.'

'Jesus Christ – that means that this evil can read our minds!'

Marjorie shook her head. 'No, Joel, I don't think their power is like that but they can probably pick up on our kinetic energy, especially on thought patterns directed at anything trying to get to the source of their evil.'

'Will it attack us again tonight?' Amy asked in a small, frightened voice.

Marjorie thought for a moment before answering. 'Yes, it is possible, but from everything I've read on witchcraft and magic I would guess that it took a tremendous amount of energy for that apparition to take on solid form, so it probably couldn't attack us so violently, at least not until it's renewed its power. Remember that creature wasn't living tissue like us.'

'But why now?' Joel muttered angrily. 'I've grown up with a sense of being haunted but it was never like this. Why after all this time are they now trying to attack us?'

'I think it's to stop you finding out,' Marjorie answered flatly.

'Finding out what?' Joel frowned, looking at her blankly.

Marjorie shrugged her shoulders. 'I don't know. You're hardly giving me time to think. Obviously your meeting with Amy was some sort of catalyst, it had to be because it awakened both of you to the existence of the evil, didn't it?'

'You mean if I hadn't walked into that gallery where she works none of this would have happened at all?' Joel interrupted.

'I don't think you had a choice, Joel.' John spoke softly. 'I think fate deliberately drew you two together. Anyway it's too late to pretend it didn't happen, you were clearly meant to meet and perhaps you've already done so many times before in different lives. Perhaps each time you meet you get a little closer to discovering a way to destroy the evil that's pursuing you both.'

'But that's crazy . . .' Joel began.

'Is it? Think carefully, Joel, all those memories, all those inexplicable fragments of ideas you've both been telling us about, all those glimpses of the past that have been drifting up out of your subconscious since you both met, it's got to be more than just a coincidence, hasn't it?' Marjorie urged.

'No, that's absurd. We grew up twelve thousand miles apart; the chances of us ever meeting must have been billions to one,' Amy disagreed.

'But you did meet, didn't you, despite the odds.' Marjorie thought for a moment and then added, excitedly, 'Just think, perhaps you were born apart deliberately to hide you from the evil – to give you both a chance to grow strong.'

Amy listened and then nodded slowly. 'Yes, maybe you're right: after we first met my head was full of inexplicable images, memories if you like, things I didn't understand. It made me realize that they've always been in the background, not as strongly as Joel's visions but I've always had the sensation that something – or someone – was watching me from the shadows. It's been with me all my life.'

'But neither of us had actually seen them properly until we went to the fairground. Why did they suddenly become so obvious and attack us in the fortune-teller's tent?' Joel interjected.

'I think it's because you were on the threshold of discovering their existence. The tarot and clairvoyance has so much power within their realms. It all points to the answers being buried in your subconscious. You both have to think hard and dredge deep – tell us what you remember. John and I will use the backs of these old envelopes and write everything down.'

'But they'll attack us again! You said they would!' Amy cried.

'No, I said they might but that their power would be greatly diminished. Now think, both of you, think!' Marjorie insisted, reaching for a pen.

A muffled voice echoed in the chimney and huge flakes of soot began to cascade down into the hearth, billowing out into the room and forming a choking black cloud as she plucked the envelopes from behind the clock.

'Borso, guard!' Amy commanded, releasing her grip on his collar. He leapt over the brass fender, knocking over a large vase of dried flowers on his way, then crouched and jumped up repeatedly, his jaws snapping at something high up inside the blackened chimney, his front feet dislodging the logs that had been piled up neatly in the fire basket. Fear paralysed Amy as she watched the dog vanish into the thickening cloud of soot and she blocked her ears to shut out the sound of his snarling growls.

'Think, reach back and unlock those memories. Do it now!' Marjorie urged, trying to break the spell of fear that gripped her.

Amy screwed her eyes tightly shut and tried to concentrate, to open up the dark well of her subconscious. Vivid, disjointed images immediately sprung up; she glimpsed sheer mountain walls, deep, silent, wooded valleys, she heard the cry of eagles soaring on the thermal currents and the hollow sound of wind chimes spinning in the breeze. She smelled the sweet aroma of wood-smoke and resin and ancient perfumes assaulted her senses. The images began to change swiftly, began to blend and merge together, each one coming to her with a separate flash of light. Now there were figures cloaked in armour, the sound of horses, the creak of leather boots, the smell of oil cloth and the tang of the sea. Through it all like an endless ribbon of pain she heard the roar and crackle of flames and smelt the reek of burning flesh. She could hear the death bell tolling and carts rumbling over cobbles, and somewhere on the edge of each fleeting picture hovered a huge monstrous dog and two shadowy, shrouded figures which seemed to reach out and try to snatch and smother her. Then they faded, cursing and cackling with howls of rage, vanishing into the drifting, confusing kaleidoscope of shapes and colours that filled her head.

She cried out, clutching at her temples in a desperate attempt to stop the blinding roar of noise and flashing blur of images that seemed to burst painfully against the inside of her skull. Her heart was pounding, keeping time with the wailing of air-raid sirens. Suddenly the room seemed to be changing, her clothes, the furniture, everything was different. It was dark and the air was full of the drone and throb of approaching bombers, searchlights stroked the sky as the shriek of falling bombs grew louder and louder. The room shook and ceiling plaster showered down, and suddenly the shrouded figures were all around her, smothering her with their robes, chanting and clawing at her with their bone-black, brittle fingers. She tried to tear herself free but they clung to her as she tumbled over and over and found herself falling dizzily into a black, bottomless void.

'Stephanie, help me, Stephanie!' Joel's voice cut suddenly through the nightmare images that had engulfed her. Amy sat bolt upright on the couch and stared at him.

'Stephanie?' she whispered, as the darkness melted away and new images began to form – drab pictures of burnt-out buildings, palls of dirty smoke drifting across flaking, terraced, Regency houses battened down for war, houses with their windows taped or blacked out beneath a floating forest of barrage balloons tethered in an empty, waiting sky. Crowds hurried through the streets, picking their way among piles of rubble, continually glancing up and listening for the sirens. Amy suddenly caught her breath as she saw a tall, slender woman emerge from the crowd and stop beside a large, old motor car. Instinctively she knew it was Stephanie. A cold shiver ran up her spine as she realized that she was seeing herself, that she knew which key would fit the door, how it felt to drive and even the smell of its leather seats. She tried to move closer to see the woman's face more clearly but the picture vanished abruptly. Suddenly Joel screamed and leapt to his feet, his body convulsed, his face contorted in agony. He struggled towards her for two steps, struggling, as if he was trying to fight off an invisible enemy tearing violently at his clothes.

'Burn! Burn in hell, you ugly hags, you won't get me, you're going to burn!' he shouted, but his voice sounded different, American, even though it was distorted by pain. He ripped open the front of his shirt as he collapsed, crumpling forward onto the edge of the couch.

Amy clutched at his arm to stop him from falling heavily to the floor. His skin felt burning hot and looked blistered, rupturing and shrivelling as she touched it. She shuddered but the illusion that his body was on fire vanished suddenly, the stench of his burning flesh evaporating before she had a chance to snatch her hand away.

'That's amazing – absolutely amazing!' John whispered to Marjorie. 'For a moment there Joel seemed to metamorphose, he seemed to almost become his memories!'

'Joel, wake up, Joel, speak to us!' Amy called, shaking his arm.

Joel's eyelids fluttered and he mumbled something about a fuel cut-off switch and worried about the throttles being fully open before slowly regaining consciousness.

'Wait a moment,' Amy whispered, her eyes widening in surprise. She gripped at Joel's shirt, roughly pulling it open to reveal a small, blue mark on his skin just below his right collarbone which she had glimpsed as the second button had come undone.

'What's the matter?' Marjorie asked anxiously, moving closer to look over her shoulder while Amy drew his shirt further open.

'That mark, look at it!' Amy's voice was shaking as she pointed to a small, circular blemish. 'I've got one almost identical: it's a birthmark. Mine's in exactly the same place, only mine is so faint that you can hardly see the pattern of veins. Look.'

Her fingers trembled as she fumbled at the buttons on her blouse, pulling it open to reveal a small, circular mark that lay in the shadow of her own collarbone.

'That's incredible!' Marjorie exclaimed, her interest

sharpening as she compared the two birthmarks. 'The pattern of lines is just as clear in both of them, I've never seen anything like this before. They're like . . .'

'A labyrinth.' Amy spoke quietly. 'That's what my father said it looked like sometimes when I was very small. He said the pattern of the veins formed an almost perfect labyrinth.' She paused and tentatively reached out her hand to touch the identical mark on Joel's chest. 'But why have we both got the same birthmark?'

Joel flinched as her fingers touched him. His eyes snapped open and he took a sharp intake of breath as he stared at her. 'That's impossible,' he muttered. He examined the small mark below Amy's collarbone, touching his at the same time. 'Does your birthmark fade sometimes and then at others become clear, and then itch so much you want to scratch at it until it bleeds?' he asked.

'Well, yes, it does now, and it did when I was younger, while I was at school, but it hasn't done for years.'

'This is getting crazier by the minute. What the hell does it all mean, Marjorie? What's happening?'

'I don't know, but it could be another indication that you are somehow bound together. Remember it's not uncommon for twins to have identical birthmarks.'

'Twins!' they both exclaimed.

'No, no, I didn't mean in the literal sense, but all your recollections undeniably point towards shared experiences. The only way to explain them is that you have kept on meeting in earlier lives, but neither of you have thrown any light on why those two shadowy, hooded figures and their monstrous hell-hound are pursuing you.

'Joel . . .' she began again, only to be distracted by the dog pulling the logs about in the hearth, sending up clouds of soot into the air around them.

'Borso, leave, sit!' Amy ordered.

'What were you going to say?' Joel asked, leaning forwards as the dog quietened down and sat, staring up the chimney.

Marjorie thought for a moment and then shrugged. 'I'm not sure, it was something about your birthmarks I think, I'll remember in a minute.'

'There's something I don't understand about all those people I remembered from the past.' Amy spoke slowly, interlacing her fingers. 'They were me, weren't they? I knew they were . . . but they couldn't really have been me, not really, because I'm me – now, I'm a different person.'

'It's your soul that lives.' John suddenly stopped. 'Of course – why didn't we think of it before – it must be your soul that those ghosts are after, it's your soul that's immortal, not your body.'

Marjorie felt an icy, tingling sensation in the nape of her neck, as if the evil presence was closing in, tightening its grip while John spoke. He must have accidentally touched on the truth of this haunting – these creatures were pursuing their souls through the fabric of time. Perhaps they were really twins, it would certainly explain why they were drawn together in each life time. But why was this happening, and what were they trying to escape from? Marjorie concentrated her mind on the idea of their souls being pursued and the more she thought about it the more it seemed to fit into the jigsaw.

'Yes, I've got it, listen: it must be your souls they're after and each time you're reborn your souls are weak and have to hide, or blend or in some way become invisible in their new life until . . .' Marjorie paused, shaking her head – the idea had seemed a good one until she began to expand it and she remembered that both of them had been haunted in their childhood. 'Perhaps if you both concentrate on the most recent memories, remember your closest lives. Was it Stephanie? If it was who was she, when did she live? And who were you, Joel?'

'Stephanie?' Amy repeated. Slowly her eyes narrowed as images of her filled her head. 'I think she lived during the war. Yes, I can see barrage balloons tethered in the sky, and . . . and . . . there's a permanent smell of burning rubble. She owned a large, old car, no it's not hers, it's her father's.' Amy paused and clenched her fist, her breaths coming in short, shallow gasps. 'There's going to be an air-raid – I know there is, shadows are forming all around me in the room. The . . .'

Howling, baying cries suddenly sounded in the chimney, drowning out her voice. Clouds of soot billowed out across the hearth and the door rattled violently on its hinges. The scattered rugs rippled and flapped as if caught in a gale and the wine glasses on the coffee table began to hum moments before shattering.

'My name was Chris, Chris . . . something!' Joel shouted against the rising bedlam, his voice thick with an American accent. 'I was an American, a pilot. I'm getting glimpses of an airfield: it's near London, there's a row of Nissen huts and a control tower, and I can see bombers waiting on the taxi-way in the dawn light. Wait, there's something else, something's here in the cockpit with me, Jesus Christ, it's . . . look out!' he shouted, ducking as vases, books, pictures and ornaments suddenly lifted up into the air and flew wildly around the room, smashing into fragments, the books breaking their spines, as they struck the walls.

Borso leapt after them, barking furiously and rushing around the room. The light-bulbs glowed white-hot, their filaments exploding one by one. Amy screamed as the walls and ceiling seemed to move and come alive in the brilliant flashes of light. The ceiling creaked and groaned as the room began to shrink and close in on top of them. The two hooded figures and their monstrous dog suddenly appeared, their winding sheets unravelling to smother them. Cerberus snarled and snapped at their legs.

'Joel, make it stop, help me!' Amy screamed in terror, thrashing her hands as the hags' shrouds fell over her face, muffling her voice as they filled the air with the choking reek of sulphur.

'Listen, both of you – this is important. You mustn't give up now, you must be on the verge of remembering something vitally important and you must keep trying to remember. Amy, they wouldn't be attacking so violently if you weren't a threat to them: try to remember, you've got to!' Marjorie tried to shout against the enfolding silence. She made a grab at Amy's hands and shook her fiercely.

Amy shuddered, her face a mask of disgust at the cold feel of the clinging fabric. The last light-bulb exploded, showering them with hot glass and plunging the room into utter darkness. Marjorie shuddered and fought to hold onto her self-control as Cerberus clawed at her skin. The wraiths were suffocating her and the ceiling was crushing her. Faintly, through the smothering darkness she could hear the others screaming.

'It's an illusion. The forces of evil are bringing these horrors, they are trying to terrify you out of your minds and drive you insane. You've got to fight back, you must remember this isn't real. Joel, Amy, tell us what happened when you were Chris and Stephanie, tell us how you died. This is really important, concentrate!' Marjorie shouted against the wailing howls and shrieking cries of the grave-wraiths.

'Everybody's dead, I'm losing control we're going to crash! The plane's catching fire – that vile dog is mauling at my arm. I can see those two shadowy figures – their faces are blackened, scorched – as if they've been burnt hundreds of times. Their skin is all withered and blistered . . .' Joel cried.

'The sound of the bombing is getting closer,' Amy sobbed, her voice close to hysteria. 'I can't escape – the ceiling is collapsing on top of me – the beast is trying to drag me towards two hooded figures. I must recite the curse . . . I must recite . . . I must . . .'

Joel suddenly laughed, his voice full of rage. 'You can't touch me, you ugly hags. You can't follow me into the flames. I'll find a way of defeating you, I'll find a way . . .'

'The words of the curse, Amy, what are they?' John called into the darkness. 'Can you remember?'

'Don, Dor, Surmy, Zor . . . Zoros . . .' Her voice trailed off. 'I know there's more, I can't remember, the words keep slipping away!'

Suddenly the inhuman sounds and the assault vanished. John managed somehow to stagger to the window and draw back the curtains and the pale sodium lights dimly illuminated the room.

'Strewth, look at this mess!' Joel gasped as he struck a match.

Amy cried out and recoiled in horror at the stench. She stared at the blackened, crumpled shrouds and withered, crumbling winding sheets spread over the mounds of dust and grave litter on the floor at her feet. 'I thought you said that the attack was only an illusion, that we were creating it in our imaginations.'

Joel cursed softly as the match burnt down and scorched his fingers but he quickly lit another and picked his way to the mantelpiece to light the candles.

'This is getting too dangerous and I don't want Marjorie or John, or anyone else, to get hurt. Look at this room, Joel: we've got to stop antagonizing this evil, we've got to find another way,' Amy urged, crouching down and making a fuss of Borso as he ran to her.

'But it was an illusion, an illusion created from things long dead, things and images that were bound to terrify us. Look around you again,' Marjorie insisted as the candleflames strengthened, filling the room with a soft, flickering glow.

Amy caught her breath. It was true, the rotting grave litter, the mounds of mouldering fabric, were all beginning to melt away, leaving only the shattered ornaments, the books and broken picture-frames littering the floor as their grip on reality strengthened.

'I think it is already too late to turn back: we have become involved and we know too much to stop now.'

'Are you mad? Look at this room, look at what they tried to do to you, what do you think they'll do next time, set the house on fire, blow it up?' Joel interrupted.

Marjorie stared at Joel: something he had said earlier about lighting matches and flicking them at the ghosts – and again just now at the height of the attack when he had imagined he was in a plane as it burst into flames – suddenly made sense to her and connected with dozens of their disjointed, collective memories that related to fire and burning. 'Of course! They definitely won't use fire against us: it is the one thing they are afraid of. Joel, you told us that Chris had set his plane alight, that it was the one sure way he could escape from them.'

Joel nodded slowly. 'Yes, and . . .' His face drained of blood as a new and vivid memory flooded through his consciousness. 'Oh my God,' he whispered, and he reached out and clasped Amy's hand. 'That car of your father's – I mean Stephanie's father's – that old Humber – I burnt your body in it. I know I did that, I remember you implored me to do it as you died and . . . and . . .' He shuddered, shaking his head – the images were so real. 'Those ghostly creatures couldn't reach you through the flames so they sent that huge dog to try and pull you out but it couldn't . . .' He fell silent, burying his head in his hands.

'It was the only way,' she answered softly. 'The knowledge always comes too late: we never have the time to find out or remember the words to break the curse. We have to pass through the fire to save our souls.'

Joel nodded grimly and stood up slowly. 'But this time it's going to be different: we have learned more about the evil tonight than we have done in any other life time.'

'It's a pity you couldn't remember more than those few words from the curse. I've written them down,' John murmured, glancing anxiously around the room, expecting a fresh attack, but all he could hear was the soft, persistent patter of the rain against the window-panes and the faint hum of the evening traffic.

'There's still so much to find out. Do you think we'll ever get to the bottom of it?' Amy sighed, picking up some of the books that had been thrown to the floor.

'You could start by following up on Stephanie and Chris. Find out everything you can about them: where they lived, who they were, you know, things like that,' Marjorie suggested.

'But how could that help – they've been dead for almost fifty years. Everything will have changed in that time.' Joel frowned. 'Anyway we have their memories, isn't that enough?'

'Fifty years isn't much more than a blink of an eye in relation to some of the things you two have remembered tonight. My advice is to use Stephanie and Chris's memories, let them take you back to the places they knew – you never know, there might still be people alive who knew them. Surely anything will help,' she urged.

Joel laughed. 'But that's a hell of a long-shot, isn't it? I can just imagine walking up to some old guy in the street and saying "excuse me, mate, but I knew you in another life!"' And he bent down and began to gather up the rubbish on the floor.

'No, leave everything exactly as it is,' Marjorie murmured as another idea occurred to her. 'I want to examine everything in the daylight, to see if our evil visitors have left us any clues that I can follow up.'

'Clues?' Joel questioned. 'What could you possibly find in this mess? I was just about to get a dustpan and brush.'

'Well, they may have left something, it must have needed a lot of kinetic energy to create this much mayhem. There's a lot been written about the paranormal, plenty for me to study. It's worth a look anyway.'

'I think I'd better be going, I've already caused you enough trouble tonight,' Amy apologized, looking at the state of the room but Marjorie laughed.

'It's been fascinating, really fascinating. You know, you don't have to go, dear: you're welcome to stay here if you want to. Joel will make you comfortable, there's a spare room.' Marjorie didn't look up as she made her offer: she was occupied with searching for something on the floor and consequently didn't see the smile that passed between Amy and Joel.

'What on earth are you looking for? I thought you said we weren't to disturb the mess?' John asked irritably.

'I've just remembered that book on magic, the one I bought in that secondhand shop in Deptford years ago, I thought I had put it in the bookshelf in here. Yes, there it is!' She pulled out a battered copy of *Givry's Sorcery, Magic and Alchemy* from the back of the couch.

For an instant Amy hesitated in the open doorway of

the room and watched as Marjorie became engrossed in the book, leafing through its pages. She wasn't looking forward to leaving Joel and going back to her empty flat: Marjorie's offer had been very tempting, but she had glanced down and caught sight of her dog's filthy coat and the blackened, sooty paw prints that were now all around the room and she shook her head. 'Thanks, it's a lovely thought but I really have to get back, there's a dozen things I've got to do and there's a couple of catalogues for the new exhibitions that I must take into the gallery with me tomorrow morning.'

Joel escorted her to the front door and, for a moment, they stood together on the porch listening to the steady beat of the rain and the swish of cars driving through the puddles. The wet, night air was heavy with the scent of wild raspberries and jasmine that grew around the front door and it reminded them both of a thousand other times they had spent together, eternal twins.

'Fate always draws us together,' Joel whispered.

'Yes, I know.' Amy smiled into the darkness.

'This time we must find a way to break the curse: it may be our only chance to put an end to the creatures and we can't afford to let it slip away.'

'But how? Where will we begin?' she asked as they ran down the steps to her car.

Joel stood silently by the passenger door and watched as Borso settled himself on the floor. 'Stephanie and Chris were here in London during the war – we know they were,' he answered slowly. 'I'm getting a picture of a clock on a railway station and of waiting for you underneath it.'

'It could have been Charing Cross. Yes, I'm sure it is,' Amy answered quickly. 'The station's crowded with people in uniforms and there's a smell of smoke, it's stinging my eyes. There's a noise, it's the sound of . . .' She shook her head and got into the car. 'It's no good,

I don't know what the noise was – the image has gone completely.'

'That's OK, I'll start at Charing Cross in the morning, I'll just get off the train and let my memory take me, who knows where I'll end up!'

Echoes in the Ether

THE CANVAS AWNINGS and bright, striped umbrellas set up over the cluster of pavement tables outside Luigi's Bistro in Avery Row flapped idly in the hot gusts of wind stirred up by the constant stream of passing cars and taxis. Joel shifted uncomfortably on the hard chair and stretched his legs underneath the table as he glanced at his watch. It had just turned three forty-five and he watched the passing crowds anxiously. Amy had said that she would meet him here soon after three because the gallery always closed early on Monday afternoons, and he was beginning to worry. He'd had the uneasy sensation that he had been followed all day and he was afraid that something might have happened to her. Pushing aside the quick sketch that he had done of the people sitting at the tables around him he sipped unenthusiastically at his second glass of iced tea, hastily putting it down when he realized that it had grown tepid and formed a scummy sheen on its surface while he waited.

He was about to get up and walk to the gallery when he spotted her hurrying towards him through the crowds that thronged the pavement. A smile tugged at the corners of his mouth as he watched people hastily step out of Borso's way as the dog trotted lazily along beside her.

'I'm sorry I'm late,' she said breathlessly, sitting in the chair that he had pulled out for her. 'There was an important buyer in from Japan and we had to wait until

Mr Wicken had taken him out for a late lunch before I could leave.'

'That's OK, no worries. Do you want a coffee, a beer or an iced tea?' Joel grinned, but the relief he felt that she was safe showed in his voice as he called the waiter over and ordered the drinks.

'Well?' she asked, her eyes sparkling with interest. 'What happened? Where did you end up?'

'You know, it was really strange.' Joel paused and glanced over his shoulder to make sure he wasn't being overheard. 'You won't believe what happened,' he continued, lowering his voice. 'It was really weird letting Chris's memory come to the surface and then trying to follow the directions he wanted to take. You don't realize how much London's changed in fifty years, but the oddest thing was I kept seeing it how it was then, not just the buildings – I saw the people, the cars and buses, the piles of smoking rubble from the Blitz, the sand-bag barricades – everything, it was all so real I could smell it.' He paused and frowned. 'The trouble was *I* was the ghost, I was the one who didn't exist: the crowds walked right through me, a bus ran right over me and I didn't feel a thing, and the worst of it was I really had to keep my wits about me crossing the roads because, apart from the age of the vehicles, it was difficult to tell at a glance which ones belonged to which reality.'

'But where did Chris's memory lead you?' Amy pressed impatiently.

'I'm not sure, I don't know London very well, but so many of the places have vanished – like Rainbow Corner in Piccadilly Circus – that when I asked people about an officers' club or a certain pub they just looked blankly at me, but I think I found the house where Stephanie lived.'

'Where was it? What is it like? Tell me, is it like the one I described last night, the tall, white, Regency terrace?'

'I've got a better idea, why don't you use Stephanie's memory and see if it leads you to the same place. If it does then it's got to be the right one, hasn't it?'

Amy glared at him darkly and her shoulders trembled slightly. 'I'm afraid to do that after what happened last night. If that creature tries to attack us, it could cause a terrible accident, there's so many people around us now.'

'I've sensed something following me all day but so far it hasn't caused me any trouble, it's just been there, hovering in the background. I really think you should risk it,' he answered firmly as he began to get up. 'Now which direction would Stephanie take? Where would she be trying to get to?'

Amy reluctantly closed her eyes and concentrated on Stephanie, reaching back into her subconscious to release her memories, willing her to lead them home. The sounds of the traffic changed imperceptibly, the air smelled different and a sense of anxiety gnawed and tightened in her stomach. She found herself listening, straining to hear that first, rising wail of the air-raid sirens. 'I must get home before the raid starts. I don't want to be caught out here on the streets.' She rose abruptly, almost upsetting the table.

'Where's home, Stephanie?' Joel asked quietly.

'In Drayton Gardens, off the Old Brompton Road. We can go by bus, it stops at the corner of Grosvenor Street, we'll change at Hyde Park Corner.'

Joel felt a cold shiver run up his spine: he'd already visited Drayton Gardens. 'I think it would be quicker to go by underground to South Kensington.'

Amy slowed and then stopped half-way along Drayton Gardens and stared at two modern town houses sandwiched in between the terraced, Regency ones. 'I used to live there,' she whispered, pointing a trembling finger across to the two modern steel-and-glass town houses that stood out as blatantly as amalgam fillings in a row of perfect teeth. 'I know my flat was there, on the second floor. I remember the furniture, the photographs on the piano, I even remember the tiny blue flowers on the curtains . . . and . . .' Her voice faltered. 'But it's all gone, Joel, everything from Stephanie's life, everything I can see so clearly now has gone, hasn't it?' She let her hand fall helplessly to her side and turned away, overcome by desolation. 'Oh, why did we have to come back? Why do we have to stir up the past?' Stephanie's memories suddenly welled up inside her, and the terror of those last, desperate moments possessed her. Cowering down, she clutched at the cast-iron railings beside her and dropped her bag on the pavement. Borso growled and moved close to her but she was oblivious to him. It was dark, but the sky was suddenly full of violent magnesium flashes of light from the anti-aircraft batteries and the sweeping fingers of the searchlights. She turned towards the sound. The rumble of the guns and the drone of the approaching bombers was getting louder and she knew instinctively from the whistling shriek of the falling bombs and the sounds of their explosions that the next drop would strike her house. There hadn't been a warning wail from the sirens, she knew she would never reach the shelter – it was too late. A deafening explosion shook the house followed by another and then another. The building shook violently, the floor beneath her feet creaked and swayed, vases toppled over, pictures slid down the walls and the chairs crashed onto their sides. She fell forward and staggered, trying to keep her balance as the ceiling crumbled and started to collapse, showering her with thick clouds of choking dust. Something struck her hard across the back, crushing her. She was falling, trapped in an avalanche of broken beams, furniture and bricks and mortar. She could still see the shells bursting in the sky and the flickering light of the fires all around her but everything had grown quiet.

She struggled but her arms were buried beneath her and her weakening cries for help were lost in the roar and thunder of the raid. Gradually, as death moved closer measuring her last, fluttering heartbeats, she became aware that two sinister, hooded figures and a huge, misshapen beast were approaching, gliding through the piles of burning debris. They seemed to be trying to smother the fires around her by throwing out yards of black, ragged cloth, but it shrivelled up into stinking, sulphurous clouds of smoke. Ice-cold terror clutched at her as she heard them hiss and curse and in one awful instant her dying memory blossomed and opened. She knew who they were and why they had come to possess her soul. She knew that her one and only chance to escape lay through fire, but she was trapped, helpless, and she could not crawl to the flames.

Suddenly another figure appeared behind them, haloed by the flickering light of the burning buildings across the road. She knew it was Chris even before he shouted her name as he ran towards her.

'Chris, Chris, you must burn my body! Promise me, you must promise me, burn my body!' she cried weakly as he found her and dropped to his knees, clawing at the wreckage in an effort to free her . . .

'Amy, are you all right? You had better get up – there's somebody coming!' Joel called out, gripping her shoulder and shaking it in agitation.

Joel's voice broke the trance. The terror of Stephanie's last moments blurred and shrank back into Amy's subconscious. She blinked and suddenly became aware of the sounds of the traffic and the houses on either side of her and she felt the colour rise to her cheeks as she saw a couple with their dog walking toward her. She rescued her bag and scrambled to her feet, smoothing down her skirt as she tried to regain some composure. 'I saw how Stephanie died. I made you promise to burn my body, I had to – it was the only way.'

Amy gripped Joel's hand as she fell silent, she was trembling with emotion. 'It was so awful, I was trapped, almost buried alive.' Her voice had fallen to a whisper and her face was a bleak mask as she stared across the road to where it had happened over fifty years before.

'I wonder if anybody still lives around here who would remember?' Joel murmured.

Amy frowned and tightened her hold on Borso's lead while the couple with the dog walked past. Reliving the horror of Stephanie's death, experiencing the sensation and then seeing the hooded figures face to face had shaken her and left her with an overwhelming sense of fear. 'Come on, Joel,' she muttered impatiently, eager to get away. 'We're not going to learn anything more; I expect most of the tenants who lived here during the war are either dead or have moved away. It was a long time ago.'

'I don't know. Perhaps it's just a crazy hunch but . . . Look, why don't you go and sit on that bench down there, it won't take me more than a minute to ring a few doorbells, will it?' Joel smiled.

'But you can't just knock on somebody's front door, what on earth will you say?' she asked anxiously.

Joel's smile widened into an infectious grin. 'Remember, I'm an Australian, I'll spin them a line pretending I'm over here trying to trace my relatives.'

'I think I had better stay with you,' she sighed, following him up the steps to the large front door of the Regency house on the left of the two modern ones.

'Well, which one?' she asked, her hand hovering doubtfully over the double bank of polished brass name-plates and bell-pushes.

'Any one, choose at random and then leave all the talking to me,' he grinned.

Amy pushed the second button on the bottom row.

'Why did you choose that one?' he asked as they waited.

'I don't know, Mr and Mrs Agate sounded . . . well, respectable.' She shrugged.

The intercom crackled and a faint voice asked who they were.

'G'day, Mr Agate, I'm sorry to be troubling you but my name's Joel, Joel Goudor and I'm over from Australia trying to trace my folks. My great-aunt Stephanie used to live next door at number eighty-eight, you wouldn't know what happened to her by any chance, would you?'

The intercom crackled and the voice laughed. 'No, I'm sorry, I don't know anybody called Stephanie. We've only lived here for five years.'

'Do you know if anybody still lives around here who might remember her?' Joel asked quickly but the crackle of the intercom went dead as it was switched off.

'Try another,' he muttered, clearing his throat in readiness.

'This is ridiculous – I told you nobody would still be living here who would remember. I'm going home,' Amy said crossly after more than half an hour of unsuccessful ringing and knocking on doors.

'Let's just try one more and then I promise I'll give up. Let's try that basement over there, the one with the roses growing up the iron trellis-work beside the gate,' Joel insisted, hurrying across the road.

Amy followed him dejectedly, Borso trotting at her heels, but her flagging spirits lifted as she descended the worn, stone steps and saw the small basement garden that was hidden from the road. The air was still and heavy with the scent of the old roses, bees hummed and swarmed lazily on the masses of summer flowers that grew in the numerous pots and hanging baskets crowding the flagstones around the front door. She paused, inhaling the heady scent of the roses and was barely aware of the front door opening and Joel launching into his string of questions until his excited voice cut through.

'She remembers, Amy, Miss Morston was living here during the war and she remembers Auntie Stephanie!'

Amy hurried down the steps to see a frail, white-haired woman wearing a flowered smock and an embroidered cap standing on the threshold.

'Well, I was only a young woman then, my mother wanted me to go and stay with friends in the country but I refused . . .' Her eyes sparkled with excitement at the memories, her arthritic fingers fumbling and crushing her white handkerchief as she recollected those hectic war years.

'Come and sit down, I'll make us some tea.' She indicated two stone benches. 'Yes, I remember the night your great-aunt Stephanie disappeared as if it was yesterday: the warning came too late for any of us to reach the shelter – oh, the smoke and the noise – the light from the fires raging all across the city made it as clear as day. There were fire engines and ambulances rushing everywhere.'

'Do you remember exactly what happened to my aunt that night?' Joel pressed.

A shadow seemed to cross her eyes briefly. 'It was a direct hit, you know, the sound of the explosion almost deafened us. At first we thought she must have been killed in the explosion. I remember peering out of that window above your heads as the whole building came crashing down.' She raised her hands in alarm, her eyes wide and round as she relived those terrifying moments. 'It was really terrible, you know, I thought we were all going to be buried alive. And the clouds of dust and debris – it was flying everywhere.'

Miss Morston coughed and inhaled a shallow, dry breath, delicately dabbing her handkerchief to her lips. 'It's very odd, you know, I thought I saw people with a large dog clambering through the rubble, but I knew they weren't wardens or anybody official. It was only a glimpse, mind you, as the dust began to settle, but there was something odd about them. Anyway, a few moments later Stephanie's car was suddenly driven away with a screech of tyres. It was all over the place, zigzagging through all the rubbish that was almost blocking the road. I thought perhaps Stephanie had somehow escaped – mind you, it would have been a miracle, I knew she was in that night, I'd spoken to her only half an hour earlier.'

Miss Morston sighed, her frail shoulders trembling slightly despite the still warm evening air. 'But sadly I was wrong, the police eventually found her car burnt out in a field miles away.'

'Do you remember where it was found?' Joel asked, trying to suppress the excitement in his voice.

'Well, yes, but it doesn't make any difference, they never found any trace of Stephanie. It was a week before we even discovered that the car had been found. It was in a field near Bovingdon, close to one of those American airfields. The police said that the car had been stolen and that was that. Of course everybody was so busy in those days, with the war going on, and nobody bothered with any further enquiries, but I've often wondered what really happened to Stephanie.'

Miss Morston paused and began to absently twist her handkerchief between her fingers, looking over their heads to the profusion of flowers growing in her potted garden. 'They're always drifting in when I'm not looking,' she muttered to herself as she rose stiffly to her feet and, moving slowly between the large, ornamental, stone tubs, plucked the thin, straggly weeds that had seeded themselves among the flowers. 'I am sorry, I was distracted,' she exclaimed suddenly, glancing at Borso and then at Amy and Joel. She frowned and seemed to think hard for a moment. 'No, I'm afraid that's all I can remember, there's nothing else I can tell you. I'm sorry, I haven't been very much help, have I?'

'Oh yes, Miss Morston, you've told us a lot about great-aunt Stephanie, it's been very helpful,' Joel reassured her, thanking her for giving them her time as he stood up.

'You'll stay for some tea, won't you? I'll get a bowl for your lovely dog. It's unusual to see an English bull terrier these days, they were quite common before the war you know.'

'No, thank you, it would be lovely but we really must get going or we'll miss our train.' Amy smiled as she stood up. On impulse she asked, 'Did Stephanie have a dog?'

'Oh yes – it had completely slipped my mind. She had an alsatian, a beautiful dog, he went everywhere with her. They found him crushed beneath the rubble when they cleared the street the following morning.'

'That must have been very sad,' Amy said softly.

'I don't suppose we'll ever know the truth about what really happened to her, will we. Thanks again for your time, it's been most interesting,' Joel smiled.

'Please call again. I'm sure I've still got a box of old photographs from the war years, I've put them away somewhere. There's some of Stephanie in there, you could take a couple home for your mother if you like. I could write to your mother about Stephanie if you'd like me to, I might remember more if I put pen to paper.'

'Oh, that would be wonderful, I'd love to see a photograph of her.' Amy rose to follow the old woman.

Joel swallowed and rose quickly to his feet, gripping Amy's arm. He hadn't given a moment's thought to anything like this happening. He smiled at Miss Morston as she paused, waiting for Amy in the doorway. 'Amy, we've got to get out of here. I can't go on lying to her,' he whispered before turning to Miss Morston. 'I'm really sorry but we have to get going or we'll miss our train,' he said awkwardly, trying to hurry Amy towards the steps and up to street level, 'but thanks, it's been wonderful hearing all about Auntie Stephanie.'

'I really would like to see those photographs. We'll come back and visit you, I promise,' Amy smiled, briefly clasping Miss Morston's frail hand before she followed Joel.

'Why did you promise to go back? It was embarrassing enough spinning her that line without going back for more,' Joel said once they were out of earshot.

Amy smiled and there was a far-away look in her eyes. 'Because we must have been friends once, back in the war years.' She paused, glancing at the traffic clogging the Old Brompton Road and looking for a place to cross. 'I mean, that part of me that will always be Stephanie wants her to know what really happened that night, wants to set the record straight. Oh, I don't know, Joel, she's a lonely old woman, maybe one day we can tell her, but there's a growing curiosity deep inside me that really wants to see what Stephanie looked like – to know everything there is to know about who I once was.'

'OK, I can understand that; I want to find out everything I can about Chris,' Joel laughed. 'I was just a bit embarrassed about lying to her, that's all, but it's great to have found all this out: my only problem is Chris's memories of that time kept getting stuck at pulling you out of the rubble. He felt there was something in the darkness and caught a glimpse of that huge dog, but he wasn't really aware of anything else . . . except images

of Stephanie's car. That's why I wanted to find somebody who might remember that night.'

Joel paused as they threaded their way through the
traffic to cross Gloucester Road. 'But it was a brilliant
stroke of luck to find out where Stephanie's car was
found. Bovingdon . . .' Joel turned the word over
slowly on his tongue, it conjured up so many half-
formed memories. 'I don't suppose you could drive us
out there tomorrow evening after work?'

'Slow down, Amy: you're driving too fast, I didn't have
a chance to read that sign we've just passed,' Joel complained letting the crumpled map slip off his lap as he
tried to look back. 'Damn this, it's so confusing, I'm
sure we're very close, if only I could remember . . .' He
fell silent, pressing the palms of his hands hard against
his temples as he tried to shut out all the distractions.
The throaty roar of Amy's CRX, the low, flickering,
evening sunlight that constantly dappled the car through
the passing hedgerows, were pushed into the background. Somehow he had to concentrate and hold onto
Chris's memories of that night.

Joel barely felt the bite of the seat-belt across his chest
as Amy stamped on the brakes and the car skidded to a
halt in a squealing cloud of burning rubber. She slammed
the gear stick into reverse and the engine screamed as
she accelerated back along the narrow, country lane.
'Look, there isn't a signpost, is there?' she insisted as
they reversed past a blocked and overgrown gateway
and she brought the car to a stop. 'Admit it, Joel, we're
lost. Surely it doesn't matter if you can't remember this
one place, does it? We've been driving around here aimlessly for the past half an hour. It'll be getting dark soon,
please can't we give this up and go home?'

'It matters to me,' he answered thickly as he opened
the door of the car and let Borso out before climbing

out himself. 'I brought your body here that night, there was an air-raid, the memories are getting sharper, I was driving your old Humber without the headlights, almost feeling my way along. I remember being really afraid of something that was following us in the darkness behind the car.' Joel shivered and, although it wasn't cold, he turned up the collar of his jacket before glancing up the lane. 'There's something scratching painfully at the inside of my skull, Amy, letters and numbers, I can't make any sense of them but I know I've got to find out what they are. I've got to find the key to unlock them from my memory. We've got to find that field.'

Joel walked along the hedgerow trying to remember, kicking at the tangled growth of summer weeds and nettles. He heard the noise of a car changing gear as it climbed up the winding lane towards him and he looked up, calling the dog to him and holding him close as the car roared past. Then he noticed something half-buried in the undergrowth. Breaking off an overhanging branch, he used it to beat down the brambles and nettles.

'What is it? What have you found?' Amy called, shutting her car door and hurrying to where he crouched, pulling at a broken signpost that had lain hidden in the undergrowth for years.

He brushed at the mud and leaf litter that clung to the old wooden sign, almost obliterating the writing, and revealed the words 'Whelpley Hill – 2 miles'.

Amy stared at the old broken sign. 'We used to come here together, didn't we? We would stand and watch the Blitz.'

Suddenly she gripped his hand fiercely as a chill, almost invisible wind seemed to touch her skin and send a shiver down her spine. It rustled the leaves in the hedgerow and combed through the tall grass and nettles at their feet. 'Joel!' she hissed in alarm as an unearthly howl broke the evening silence.

The hackles rose along Borso's back and he began to snarl and pace defensively around them. 'Joel, it's those creatures, I can sense them! Come on, let's get away from here, let's go somewhere safe before it gets dark. Come on!' Amy pulled at Joel's hand to make him follow her to the car.

'Wait! I know this is the place – this gate was open that night I drove your car, I mean Stephanie's car, through it.' The smell of the Humber's leather seats, the stench of the aviation fuel tickled at his nostrils; for an instant he was back in the driving seat and could see the silhouette of Stephanie's body. Instinctively he reached out to stop her from sliding off the seat then took a hesitant step towards the gateway, his grip tightening on Amy's hand.

'Joel, stop it, Joel, listen to me, I'm really afraid: if that huge monster has followed us we are defenceless out here on our own.'

Joel blinked and stared at her. 'But we've got to follow Chris's memory, we must be on the verge of discovering something really important here. We're not completely helpless – we've got Borso to protect us: tell him to guard us. We'll only stay for a moment, I promise.'

'We must be out of our minds!' Amy muttered, sticking very close to Joel and helping him to trample a path through the dense bank of nettles and tall grasses that had almost swallowed the rotten gate.

Joel felt a strange, tingling sensation in the nape of his neck as he paused, straddling the gate. The view ahead almost exactly matched his memory and he automatically reached inside his shirt to touch the small birthmark beneath his collarbone. The two gnarled oak trees where he had parked the Humber still formed an almost perfect, leafy arch and his memories began to stir and break the surface of his consciousness, sending ripples of awareness through his body. He could smell frost in the chill night air and see clusters of searchlights illuminating the thick cloud cover over London. He slipped to the ground on the far side of the gate and waded through the scrub and undergrowth, drawn by the vivid image of the flames that were engulfing Stephanie's car. Bright ribbons of sparks danced and swirled up to vanish amongst the winter branches overhead. As he drew closer he became aware of two shadowy, hooded figures cursing and trying to beat a way through the flames, their fingers crumbling as they caught fire, their shrouds smouldering and covered in sparks. Suddenly a huge, monstrous dog, an apparition from Hell, rushed at him out of the darkness. The two figures turned on him, their hoods falling back to reveal their withered, burnt and corrupted faces as they attacked. Joel instinctively raised his arms to protect his face but the creatures' charred and crumbling fingers disintegrated as they touched him, the beast's snarling jaws snapped shut on his sleeve but it howled and cowered away as he raised his other hand to beat it off.

'Joel, we've got to get away from here, the smell of that hound is getting stronger, it must be very close now, it's driving Borso mad,' Amy cried fiercely, shaking his shoulder to try and break the trance that he had sunk into.

'It's a coward! It won't hurt us if we stand up to it!' he whispered in amazement. His eyes were focused on her frightened face and he put his arm protectively around her as he drew her close while the spectre of the burning car was shrinking back into his subconscious. 'I can't explain why, I just know, for all its size and savage looks it's a coward and those figures can't hurt us while we're alive.'

'Yes, I know, somehow I know that, but please come away now, this place really frightens me,' she pleaded.

'In a moment, I promise, Chris is trying to tell me

something, I know he is. It's tied up with being here and it will lead us to discover who these creatures are, we must stay, just for a while.' He fell silent and lifted his head to look out across the still evening landscape and opened his mind to Chris, letting his memory rise back to the surface.

'Do you remember how we used to sit here and watch the formations of bombers building in the sky, how they gradually climbed in a great thundering arch as they headed towards the coast?' he murmured softly, pointing across the shallow valley. 'You could see the base from here, remember?' Joel sighed as a sad smile picked at the corners of his mouth. Chris's memories were taking over: the countryside was changing, frost and a thin covering of snow clung to the branches of the trees, whitening the bare blackthorn hedges and peppering the raw, muddy ridges of plough.

A bitter wind tugged at the collar of his flying jacket and he shivered, wretched at the loss of Stephanie, barely glancing up at the huge, black hulks of the line of waiting bombers that were silhouetted against the grey, dawn sky. Their names almost seemed to glow in the half light as he drove past, *Big Dipper*, *Frisco Moon*, *Angel*, *Carolina Lady*. The sudden thunder of aero-engines filled his ears, quickening his heart beat as he scrambled up through the small, open hatch in the belly of the Fortress. The air was full of the smell of oil and hot exhaust fumes, the lingering tang of cordite and stale coffee. He heard familiar voices as his crew ran through their checks and there was a crackle of static in his head-set. There was a large guy, a bear of a man, uncomfortably squashed into the co-pilot's seat, intent on the pre-flight checks. 'Brakes – set, intercoolers – set . . .'

'Mike . . .' he began, trying to get his attention he reached out to touch his arm when a green flame arched across the grey, dawn sky. The noise of the engines reached a thundering roar and the plane shuddered and vibrated as one by one the engines attained full power. They were moving now, creeping along the taxi-way, waiting their turn to take off. Earl's voice crackled over the headset. 'This is Army 375 to tower requesting radio check, Charlie, Alpha, Tango . . .'

For an instant the sound of Earl's voice repeating the radio check gave Joel's memories a sudden jolt. He inhaled a sharp intake of breath and tried to chase the memory down but the images began to fade, the steady roar of their engines grew fainter as one by one the rising Fortresses vanished into the sky.

Joel blinked and a single tear trickled down his cheek. He knew they had gone forever, that most of them would never come back. Slowly he became aware of the sounds of the birds settling down into the hedgerows for the night and he could see the low sun riding the horizon. 'The memories have gone, come on, there's nothing more for me here.'

He sighed dejectedly as he turned towards the gate. He had hoped for some startling revelation, something that would give them some answers, but there was nothing but empty memories and an overwhelming sense of loss.

'I don't know what you saw or remembered just now but it's made those creatures shrink into the background, look, even Borso isn't half as agitated now. What happened? What did you find out?' Amy asked expectantly as they retraced their footsteps.

Joel shrugged as he wrestled with the fragments of Chris's memory that had stayed with him, trying to put it into some sort of order. 'I'm not sure. On the face of it nothing – well nothing I could really put my finger on and say that's the key to why these ghosts haunt us. I think they disappeared just now because I realized that they can't hurt us. I saw Stephanie's car burn up, I know she was in it when I set it alight, and I saw those creatures, they were trying to get at her through the flames but they couldn't. I saw a lot of dead friends and heard their voices over the intercom. I know for sure now that Chris was an American pilot, I even know the names of some of his crew. I was at the controls; I felt his plane lift into the air and I saw the grey-white fields slip away beneath the wing, but then everything began to fade. The voices became softer and then the silhouette of Big Mike sitting hunched in the seat beside me became transparent and then vanished. Even the roar of the engines merged with my own heartbeat. But . . .' Joel hesitated, thrusting his hands deep into his jeans pockets. 'I keep hearing the radio operator's voice, it's so faint now but it's still there, little more than a crackle in the ether but it still keeps repeating "This is Army 375 to tower . . . this is Army 375 to tower . . ." Those ghosts were on Chris's plane and I knew that something was wrong when I took off but I'm afraid the memories are growing fainter and becoming very confusing. Everything seems to end abruptly with a screaming shout and a flash of white light. The plane must have exploded, perhaps it received a direct hit a long way from here, after that there's nothing, the memories stop as suddenly as switching off a light switch, the only thing left is that weird call, it's so persistent, "Army 375 to tower". I don't know what to make of it or why it's scratching so persistently at the surface of my thoughts,' he murmured as they reached the car.

Amy glanced back to the gateway and smiled. 'I can remember the summer nights when we were here together: it was so good not to be alone any more.'

'I reckon it'll get better.' Joel grinned back as they began their journey home. 'I reckon it probably gets better with every life, you know, practice makes perfect.' Joel paused as he looked out across the darkening countryside. 'But it's odd, isn't it, that coming here has awoken the memory of that radio call. I can't get the sound of it out of my head now.'

'Perhaps that's because it's like a beacon, a distress call, that's meant to guide you to the plane. Perhaps you're meant to find it, perhaps Chris found a way to break the curse during that last flight only it was too late for him. Maybe he tried to leave a message in the plane to forewarn us in this life,' Amy offered as she worked through the gears and accelerated for a gap in the traffic.

'Oh sure!' Joel laughed harshly. 'But you're forgetting that the plane blew up. It was probably scattered in thousands of tiny pieces all over France or Germany or somewhere.'

'Yes, but I bet Chris would have done anything to leave a message. I know if I found the answer I would try to write it down somewhere, I would try to leave it so that somehow I could find it in my next life no matter how hopeless it seemed at the time.'

The laughter died on Joel's face.

'Jesus Christ, do you realize the implications of what you just said? If Chris tried to leave us a message in his plane I'll bet he wasn't the first.' Gasping, he turned to stare at her, his mind reeling. He shivered – it suddenly felt as though a bucket of ice cold water had drenched the back of his neck.

'What on earth do you mean? Do you think we've left clues about this before? Why haven't we ever found them? Why do I get this feeling that we've been eternally stumbling around in the dark running away from these vile creatures?' she cried, glancing across at him, momentarily distracted.

The blast of a horn and a squeal of brakes snapped her attention back to the traffic. She cursed and hit the brakes, sharply turning the wheel, swerving the car and narrowly missing a taxi that had pulled across the stream of cars to pick up a fare on the opposite side of the road. She muttered something to herself under her breath and eased her car back into the flow of traffic. 'Well, I'm waiting, why haven't we found any of these messages before?'

'I don't know,' he answered slowly, struggling to grasp a firmer hold on the nagging idea at the back of his mind. 'Perhaps we have, perhaps they've been there all the time, staring at us in the face, perhaps . . .' His words trailed off. 'Of course! We might not recognize those messages, they might not mean anything to us, well, not until we knew an awful lot about those ghosts. Wait! Do you remember those drawings I showed you that first day in the gallery? Well, they were a sort of visual record, perhaps we did something like that before, perhaps dozens of times.'

'Do you remember Marshall's painting, the ones on exhibition at the Hondo Gallery? You don't suppose they were painted as a message, do you? There was something terribly familiar about them, I felt as though I had almost been inside the canvas, I even knew the things he hadn't painted into each picture.' She pulled away from the lights slowly.

'Yes, maybe, it's strange you should say that, I found those paintings really disquieting and I swear I was at the place where they were painted, which is impossible since they were painted over two hundred years ago. But I know I was involved with them somehow, perhaps during some other life. If only I could reach that far back into the old memories.'

'Wait a minute, something else has just occurred to me.' Amy broke off to concentrate on the junction ahead and pulled across into the filter lane to wait for the green arrow before turning across onto the Vauxhall Bridge. 'You'll probably think this is silly . . .' she continued as she accelerated, 'but I've experienced this sort of thing before and I've never given it much thought, it's happened with places as well as pictures. People call it *déjà vu*, sensing you've been somewhere or seen something that you couldn't possibly have known about. Strangely enough I've often been drawn to specific pictures in galleries and museums without knowing why, I'd stand in front of them for ages wondering what it was that caught my attention, I've spent hours leafing through old manuscripts wondering what on earth I'm looking for. I've even known scraps of the language they're written in although I've never learnt a word of it. This interest in pictures is what drew me to work in the gallery. But why, if I have been staring at vital clues or messages didn't I understand them? A part of me must have known what they meant, it had to be locked up somewhere in my subconscious, didn't it?'

'Well yes, I suppose it must have been but perhaps the signals to release the memories grow weaker the older they become . . .' Joel paused, his head was beginning to ache as so many new thoughts collided with each other, exploding in his mind like bright flashes of light. 'Of course, we wouldn't understand a lot of these messages, the world has changed so much, the things that were relevant in, say, 1520 wouldn't mean anything to us now. Just look how much everything's changed just in the last fifty years here in London, Stephanie and Chris would hardly recognize it, we've got computers, lasers, our clothes are different, people have even begun to travel in space.'

'But a curse is a curse, Joel, these creatures have been the same in all our memories, they haven't changed that much have they?'

'I don't know, I'm not sure what to think about them, it's a bit of a mystery,' he muttered miserably. 'I can sense them hovering in the background all the time like a brooding shadow, watching, waiting, I just wish that we could find a way to blow them away, make them vanish from our lives forever.'

Amy nodded, silently changing down the gears as the traffic was reduced to crawling pace along Camberwell New Road. 'Perhaps we'll never have the time to find a way to break this curse. From what we have discovered so far it seems that we're born in different places as if fate, or whatever it is that protects us through our childhood, is hiding us. Perhaps our meeting is the catalyst, you know, the first time we're together is when we start to become properly aware that something is haunting us, waiting to possess our souls. I know it seems weird but suppose these creatures have the power to control our lives, perhaps once we know about them it becomes a deadly race to find a way of destroying them. Perhaps we only have the time to paint a picture or write something down or, in Stephanie's case, utter a dying whisper to warn of the danger. Perhaps Chris only had time to scrawl a hurried message somewhere in that plane.'

Joel turned and stared at her, the colour draining from his suntanned face. 'Jesus, do you think we're about to die? Christ, our lives have only just begun.' His voice was angry and bewildered.

'Look, I'm guessing in the dark as much as you are, my head's spinning, clogged up with so many confusing ideas and memories, I hardly know whether I'm coming or going. It's something that fortune teller said at the fair when she was looking at our lifelines, it's made me think. She said they were identical and incredibly long, but broken, many times. I remember reading somewhere that it could mean that we have lived many times before but that our lives were always short, that they end abruptly, burning out like blazing stars. We've obviously never managed to break the curse so it could mean something entirely different, of course it might mean nothing at all. Oh, I don't know, I'd like to wake up, blink and banish the nightmare but I'm afraid it's real, brutally real.'

'Well, yes, I reckon you're right,' he nodded grimly. 'These creatures, demons or whatever they are have got us completely beat. I'd sort of been pinning a lot on Chris giving us some answers, but I'm pretty sure that the plane was blown into a million pieces and I just know he never came back. I haven't a clue what we can do now.'

Joel fell silent and stared morosely at the passing, brightly-lit shop fronts and the crowds that thronged the pavements of Camberwell. 'No, I haven't got a damned clue,' he muttered to himself, absently stroking Borso's head and gently pulling at his ears. Borso growled softly, wrinkling his forehead and looking up at him from the cramped space where he was sitting between his legs, sighing as he rested his head heavily on Joel's lap.

'I wonder if Marjorie's come up with anything?' Amy murmured as they stopped at the traffic lights in the centre of New Cross.

'That's odd, you took the thought right out of my head, I was just going to say that.'

'You know, sometimes it's almost as if I can hear what you're thinking, it's so clear to me,' Amy said softly.

'Marjorie really knows a lot about the occult, let's see if she's uncovered anything,' Joel laughed as she turned the car into Wickham Road.

'What on earth has been going on? Look at the house!' Joel cried as Amy slowed to turn across into the drive of number 131 and the car headlamps picked out dozens of strange signs and symbols, fluttering prayer flags and glistening spirit chimes that spun and rattled mournfully in the dark night breeze and festooned the front of the house. 'I don't like the look of it – something's wrong – there should be some lights on.'

'There's a torch in the compartment behind my seat, I'll get it,' Amy whispered, twisting around and reaching back for it.

Borso leapt out of the car the moment Joel opened his door, his hackles up and a low, threatening growl grumbled in his throat. Joel fished in his pocket for his door key and Amy stayed close to him, playing the beam from the torch across the drive as they hurried towards the front door.

'There's something painted on the door – shine the torch on it.'

Amy brought the beam across the front of the house and stopped it abruptly. 'What in God's name is that?' she gasped, trying to hold the beam of light still and stop it from trembling as it illuminated a crudely-painted design of five, interlocking rectangles and circles with five daggers painted beneath it. Inside each circle an ancient name had been daubed beneath a crown.

Joel reached out and lightly touched one of the daggers with his fingertips. The paint was still wet and it smudged. 'I hope John and Marjorie are all right.' There was anxiety in his voice as he wiped his hand clean and inserted his key in the lock, turning it firmly.

The front door swung slowly open. The unnatural silence in the inky darkness of the hallway seemed to amplify the creak of the hinges. Borso, his eyes reflecting red in the light of the torch, ran across the threshold towards the sitting room door. Cold beads of sweat prickled Joel's forehead and trickled down the back of his neck as they entered the darkened hallway. He feared that something terrible had happened to John and Marjorie, it was so quiet. The sounds of the grandfather clock near the bottom of the stairs, mechanically marking off the seconds, seemed muffled and far away. He remembered Marjorie warning him of the danger of letting his imagination run away with him and concentrated on finding a plausible explanation to dispel his fears. Perhaps the strange paraphernalia festooning the outside of the house was nothing more than something that John was working on for the college: he remembered him mentioning a paper he was preparing on obscure tribal customs. Perhaps the house was in darkness simply because they were out for the evening.

Hesitantly he felt for the light-switch and pressed it, but nothing happened. He tried briefly to cling onto the slender hope that it was nothing more than a power cut but Amy's sudden grip on his arm sent it scuttling away into the darkness. 'There's a light – I think I saw a flickering light in that gap beneath the sitting-room door, there must be someone in there,' she hissed, pointing the trembling torch beam at the door and catching the dog in its light as he sniffed at the gap, sending his shadow leaping up across the wall.

'There's only one way to find out,' Joel muttered grimly, gathering his courage and striding across the hallway. He gripped the brass doorhandle firmly and turned it, throwing the door open.

'What the hell?' he gasped, teetering on the threshold with Amy beside him. They both stared open-mouthed at the weird, chaotic scene that met their eyes.

John and Marjorie were huddled, chanting, in the centre of the room surrounded by lighted candles, piles of books, necklaces, cups, beakers and a silver chalice with a host of magic symbols and bones lying in a heap around them. The rugs and furniture had been piled up haphazardly against the walls and they were inside a pentagram that had been painted on the floor.

'John, Marjorie, what's going on? What's been happening here?' Joel cried, advancing hesitantly into the room.

Borso snarled, his ears flat against the sides of his head, his nose wrinkled as he sniffed the pungent scent that pervaded the room. A slight draught from the open door stirred the candle-flames, making them dance and sway, elongating and distorting their shadows as they leapt up across the ceiling.

'Nothing evil can tread here!' Marjorie cried out, rising to her knees, her eyes wild with fear. She was clutching a dagger, waving it threateningly at them. Its hilt was of ebony, carved into the shape of a crucifix and entwined with silver, scaled serpents that sparkled in the candle-light. She began to chant once again, her words running erratically and breathlessly together– 'Eko, Exn, Arazaks – I banish you, vile dimblewicks, I cast you back through the gates of night, you cannot enter, by the power of the shining moon, the bright sun, water, earth and fire, I cast you back amongst the dead . . .'

John's voice rose with hers, echoing everything she chanted, and he began to ring two handbells.

'Stop! Stop it both of you, don't you recognize us, it's us, Joel and Amy!' Joel tried to shout above Marjorie's frantic chanting and the rising clamour of bells as he stepped into the circle.

Marjorie screamed and rushed at him with the dagger raised above her head but Borso sprang forwards, his powerful jaws closing on her ankle as she lunged at Joel. She lost her balance and fell sideways giving Joel time to grab hold of her arm to stop her falling and force the dagger from her grip to fly harmlessly out of her hand across the floor.

'Marjorie, it's me Joel!' he shouted, shaking her hard. She blinked and stared at him and slowly the chanting died away.

'Joel?' she whispered with a surge of relief. 'Thank God it's you.'

'Thank God you're both safe.' John's chanting

faltered and he gradually let his hands fall to his sides and the sharp sounds of the clappers faded into silence. 'We thought they must have killed you. They came back in the dead of night, shrieking and howling through the house, throwing open all the doors, smashing everything in their path. That vile, three-headed beast tried to savage us – its teeth were snapping at our faces and its breath was enough to make you choke to death. Those hooded creatures cursed us into eternal damnation for helping you.'

'It was so horrible, far worse than when you were here, and we were utterly helpless to prevent it.' Marjorie shuddered.

'It seemed so terrifyingly real,' John continued, putting the handbells on the floor inside the circle. 'I'm still afraid to shut my eyes while it's dark. I'm terrified that I'll feel the sensation again that my blood is oozing away through the pores of my skin, trickling out of my eyes and ears, running down my nose and thousands of crawling insects are gnawing at the flesh of my bones, that I'm being buried alive, unable to breathe, that my mouth is full of choking earth and all the time dozens of bone-black fingers are pulling me down into the suffocating darkness . . .'

'That's enough, John, you'll have us all reliving it without those creatures having to come back if you carry on.' Marjorie frowned and looked down, feeling the warm trickle of blood and an ache of pain as she realized for the first time that Borso had bitten her ankle.

'I'm really sorry,' Amy apologized, offering Marjorie her handkerchief for the blood. 'He was only defending us, I'm sure he didn't mean to hurt you.'

Marjorie crouched and called the dog to her, making a fuss of him. 'It's all right, boy, I wish you'd been here with us last night.'

Marjorie rose to her feet, her face growing serious,

and she quickly closed the door and drew them into the circle with her. 'They're coming back, I know they are – I've been expecting them ever since it grew dark. They seem to have a powerful effect on the electrical system: somehow they have managed to fuse the lights of the whole house. We've had two electricians working here almost all day and they can't find a way to get them working – they've even tried bringing the power over from next door but as soon as they switch anything on the light-bulbs keep exploding: even the television blew up with a white flash. That's why we've done everything we can, the pentagram, the prayer flags, everything to keep them out.'

'They won't get it all their own way next time: we're prepared for them now,' John added grimly, indicating with a sweep of his hand the paraphernalia that cluttered the crude circle they had painted on the sitting-room floor.

'What are all these things? Why have you collected them into a circle?' Amy asked, her interest sharpening.

'They're to keep evil out,' Marjorie answered defiantly, wringing her hands in hesitation only a moment after. 'Well, we're not sure exactly . . .'

'Keep your voice down, Marjorie, don't go telling the world your doubts, they might be listening,' John interrupted her.

Marjorie swallowed and glanced furtively into the darkened corners of the room, listening for a moment to the brooding, unnatural silence that seemed to have enveloped the whole house. 'From those fragments of the curse and the earliest things you have remembered I have made a guess that these creatures originate from the medieval period. I've spent most of today scouring every book I could lay my hands on that had anything in it about the occult, witchcraft or medieval magic. It's all there in those ancient grimoires, everything we need to break the curse. The only trouble is that there's so much of it that it could take us a life time to go through it all. There are literally thousands of different spells and their antidotes and most of them are written in secret codes or in languages that have long since fallen into disuse. The other problem is that magic was so thoroughly woven through the lives of everyone in medieval society that we'll probably never be able to single out the particular curse that affects you – all we can tell is that the words you used pinpoint it as coming from Northern Europe. We're unlikely ever to find out why it was laid against you, let alone discover the antidote. But one very curious thing did come to light . . .'

Marjorie paused, lowering her voice to the barest whisper. 'I kept coming across references to a monstrous dog, a hell-hound, that was frequently seen during the medieval period and from its description I'm sure it's Cerberus. The creature first appeared in Greek legends and it's identical to that vile beast that accompanies those two hooded figures. Yes, it has to be Cerberus, the dog-demon.'

The colour drained from Amy's face the instant Marjorie uttered Cerberus's name. She sank to her knees, gripping Borso's collar as the candle-flames shrank, drawing the darkness over them. Vivid, terrifying images of the beast assaulted her, looming up out of the well of her subconscious to possess her.

'Oh, my God, they've come back – they're going to attack!' Marjorie cried, dropping onto her hands and knees and frantically scrabbling to find the dagger as the darkness thickened and the huge, diabolical shape of Cerberus and the two hooded women began to materialize on the outer margin of the circle painted on the floor.

Borso snarled and growled, straining to pull free from Amy's terrified grip, ready to defend them but she would not let him go. The two grave-wraiths began to move around the circle, spinning ever faster, their shrieking voices raising curse after curse to try and break the power of the pentagram. They goaded the dog-demon to hurl himself at the circle and try to burst through it. Loops of sulphurous saliva hung from his snarling, cavernous jaws and his pitiless, red eyes and vaporous breath glowed in the darkness as he sniffed and clawed at the floor.

'Look, our magic is working! It can't break through!' John snarled, furiously ringing the two handbells and calling out every chant he could remember.

Suddenly Cerberus stopped and moved quickly backwards and forwards over a small section of their painted line. The two hooded figures crowded there with him, scratching at the floorboards.

'Oh no, there's a gap!' John hissed in alarm, losing the rhythm of the bells and dropping them to his sides.

He barely had time to draw a startled breath before the monstrous apparition had clawed and splintered the floor, widening the gap. With a triumphant howl, the beast crouched back on its haunches and leapt into the circle, rushing at Marjorie. Marjorie stood her ground, her skin crawling with terror, her teeth chattering violently and her hands trembling as she clutched the hilt of the dagger and forced her arms upwards, pointing the blade at the heart of the creature as it towered over her. Cerberus reared up, its talons outstretched ready to rip and tear, its razor-sharp fangs open to bite at her face. Marjorie took a defiant step forward into the stinking, black shadows that boiled and clung to the beast's scarred and maggoty hide and plunged the dagger into its chest, crying out as the weight of the creature sent her crashing to her knees. 'By the power of Gibil, by the shining moon, by the east and west and the word of Baalag I sever the evil sinews that bind your body together. By the hammer and anvil that forged this blade, by the scourge of this sacred blade, Bashag, Achalane, I banish you back into the darkness you came from!'

Borso twisted himself free of Amy's grip and suddenly threw himself at the hell-hound in fearless attack. Cerberus's open, dripping mouths snarled and snapped as his head thrashed from side to side. His body writhed and convulsed as his corrupted hide began to split and his blackened, crumbling bones broke through his rotting flesh. Yellow, phosphoric slime oozed and bubbled out of the wound around the hilt of the dagger and he began to shrink. Borso leapt once again onto the floundering hell-hound, his powerful jaws tearing through the disintegrating flesh, splintering its bones as he drove the creature out of the circle to vanish in a howl of pain. The two figures screamed and cursed in impatient rage, clawing at the empty air as their shadowy forms began to fade. A sudden reek of sulphurous wind tore at the outer edges of the circle, sucking them away into the space where Cerberus's echoing howl still sounded.

A light-bulb in the standard lamp near the window began to glow softly, crackles of static and a blue-white light suddenly filled the blank television screen, illuminating the room with an eerie, fluorescent sheen. The mundane sounds of the outside world suddenly broke through the oppressive, heavy silence.

'You did it, Marjorie!' John cried, running to where she lay huddled, bruised and dazed by the ferocity of the beast's attack close to the centre of the circle and gently helped her to her feet. 'You destroyed that creature: I wouldn't have believed it was possible if I hadn't seen you do it with my own eyes!'

'No I didn't,' Marjorie interrupted wearily, making the others turn to stare at her as she reached down to retrieve the dagger where it lay near where the beast had vanished and held it up for the others to see. The ebony hilt was scorched, the silver scales of the entwining serpents had melted and fused together and the bright blade was blackened and pitted along its cutting edge. 'Don't let this small victory over the evil deceive you – you cannot slay the guardian of Hades. Remember he is Hecate's leash-hound and there is not the power on earth that can destroy him.'

'Hecate – the witch-queen!' Amy whispered, staring at the spot where the darkness had opened up and swallowed their pursuers and feeling her skin go ice-cold.

'But . . . but . . . we all saw you stab it in the heart. We saw it disintegrate right there in front of us, for God's sake!'

'No, Amy, have you forgotten: the creature doesn't have a heart. It doesn't have breath and it doesn't live as we do. It is a mockery of nature: a beast created and bound together with evil, perhaps the most ancient evil that exists.'

Amy shivered as old images of the dog-demon and memories that she would have rather stayed buried flooded her mind. She caught terrifying glimpses of its monstrous shape on the edges of the funeral pyres, she saw it illuminated by the bright ribbons of sparks swirling up against the darkening sky. It was always there, clawing at her as her flesh was shrivelled by the flames, trying to reach her, to pull her free. In the background the two shadowy grave-wraiths were goading and driving it on. The memories were sharpening, becoming more precise. She saw it now, following the plague-carts, feeding on the blackened corpses, padding through the darkened alleyways, picking over the detritus of every plague and pestilence.

'It has always been there haunting the shadows, gorging on the bodies of each new tragedy as it pursued us through eternity.'

'Yes, you're right, it is a creation of evil.'

'But that's ridiculous – I know what I saw!' John argued in dismay. 'Look! Look at the dagger you're holding, look at the splintered gouges in the floorboards – it wasn't an illusion – Marjorie drove that beast out of the circle . . .' he fell silent and threw his arms up in exasperation.

'No, I didn't drive it out. For an instant there was another figure on the edge of the circle, something more powerful than those two hooded creatures: it called the dog back.'

Marjorie's voice had sunk to a whisper. 'I know what happened because for one dreadful moment, as I hung onto the hilt of that knife, the weight of the monstrous thing was crushing me to death. I could feel my ribs creaking and the breath was being squeezed out of me. It was going to smother me, I was about to be suffocated, but just as everything was going black I heard her voice . . .' Marjorie shuddered and covered her ears with her hands. 'I can still hear that demented shriek of rage and see her fingers stretching for me through the shrouds that hid her wild eyes. I can still feel her hatred for me because I dared to hurt her creature.'

'Who? Who was it, who did you see?'

'Hecate, the witch-queen. Even to whisper her name brings a chill to my heart, and if it hadn't been for Borso it would have killed me,' she smiled and caressed the dog's head, 'I felt the creature shudder and loosen its grip on me. I felt it convulse as soon as Borso attacked.'

'But why is Cerberus so afraid of dogs?' Joel muttered almost to himself as he began to return the furniture to its rightful places in the room.

'Perhaps it's because they don't have imagination and so they can't be intimidated. Or maybe somebody in the past once wove a spell and gave all dogs a power against it . . .' Marjorie began to speculate.

'No wait! That's just triggered a memory, let me think. Yes, Stephanie had a dog – and there were others, I know there were, but I can't remember their names, but I know them, I remember them in the past, huge hunting-dogs. Perhaps they were always with us, perhaps they have always helped us.'

'We spent the best part of today putting up all those signs and symbols to protect us, but the one thing that could have really helped would have been a dog. First thing in the morning I'm going into Lewisham to buy the biggest and most ferocious-looking dog I can find,' John said, trying to laugh as he slumped, exhausted into one of the armchairs and pulled free a crumpled copy of the *Sunday Times* that had been pushed down beside the cushion. 'Yes, I've wanted a dog for a while anyway,' he murmured, as he smoothed and opened out the paper.

'I wish it really was as easy as that. I wish we could put an end to whatever haunts us,' Amy sighed. 'But I know that it isn't, even if Borso or a dozen other dogs kept them at bay for the rest of our lives they would come swarming back to follow us through the next one unless we can find out exactly what the curse is and how we can break it.'

'I know Chris tried to leave us a clue; if only his plane hadn't blown up!' Joel's voice was full of helpless frustration and he rubbed a tired hand over his forehead and told John and Marjorie everything he had remembered of Chris's last flight from Bovingdon.

'It's so tantalizing . . .' he muttered as he finished. 'To have been that close to finding an answer, and you know I can still hear the faint, persistent echo of his voice repeating over and over again "Army 375 to tower . . . Army 375 to tower . . ."'

'How can you be sure that the message from Chris was totally destroyed?' Marjorie asked as she busied herself around the outer edge of the circle, putting straight the five gilded and red-painted carvings of the watching eye that she had positioned to keep out the evil.

'Because it was in the plane when it was blown into a million pieces. I should know, shouldn't I, I was there, remember!' Joel muttered irritably.

The more they unravelled from the past the more he was growing to hate their utter helplessness, hate always being hunted and looking over his shoulder, knowing that the creatures would always be haunting the shadows, watching and waiting for that one opportunity to steal their souls. He hated knowing that one time they wouldn't escape through the flames.

'But was the message in the plane? Can you be absolutely sure – think back – think really hard, exactly where did Chris put that message? Did he put it in the fuselage or the cockpit? What did he write it on?' John pressed, looking up at him over the crumpled newspaper.

'I've already told you . . .' Joel's voice was full of exasperation but Amy intervened quickly, sensing that John was trying a different angle. Maybe there was something they had missed, perhaps they had overlooked a tiny detail . . .

'What are you getting at?' she asked, frowning.

'I'm not really sure,' John shrugged, rustling the newspaper. 'It just seems odd to me that Chris's last memory should be the plane's call-sign: it's as if he was intentionally trying to draw your attention to it, but why? Think back, there must be something else you can remember of those last hours. Where did you write that message?'

Joel slumped down on the sofa, his head buried in his hands. 'I can remember the smells – cordite, sweat, smoke – I can hear the thunder and roar of the engines:

I can sense those creatures, they were in the plane, but the memories are so vague, so jumbled. I can hear the rattle of the Messerschmitts' guns firing at us and I can feel the plane lurch and drop out of formation, it was helplessly out of control. There was somebody beside me wrestling with the controls, I can almost see my co-pilot . . .'

'Concentrate on that call-sign, Joel,' John whispered, his voice shattering the images, sucking them away from Joel's head.

Joel shut his eyes and pressed his thumbs hard against his temples, forcing everything else out of his mind as he tried to reach back across the years to that hostile sky over France. He had to concentrate, he had to understand why he had kept repeating that call-sign. He was bitterly cold – brilliant flashes of white light burst painfully against the insides of his eyelids – now he was on his own in the cockpit there – flames – fire all around him and he was shouting the call-sign. He was using up his choking breaths to imprint this last impression on his subconscious, it was important but why? Why was he sending this message into the ether?

Joel shook his head and blinked. Suddenly his eyes began to focus and he stared at the others. 'Of course! I wouldn't, I mean Chris wouldn't, have had the time to write down what he had learned about the curse in those last few hours. And even if he did he would have known better than anybody that it wouldn't have been much use leaving it in the plane, the chances of it surviving, or of his getting back home alive were pretty remote. But I know he tried to do something, he tried to pass this information on somehow. His memory is full of jumbled words, of fragmented images – they're too confusing for me to make much sense of them but I got the distinct impression that he was trying to tell somebody. I caught a glimpse of somebody, perhaps it's the co-pilot, I don't know, but there was definitely someone there and he was trying to make them understand what this curse is all about. After that his final memories are of being alone, engulfed in fire, with two shadowy figures and that hell-hound trying to claw out his soul.' Joel paused, tilting his head as he listened intently to that internal echo. His face grew ashen as he relived Chris's death.

'He intentionally destroyed that plane,' he whispered. 'He destroyed it so that his soul could escape through the flames. Shouting that call-sign, imprinting it in his memory, was the only thing he could think of in those last moments, somehow he had to leave a signpost, something that would stay for eternity and draw me to the plane in this life. And it's worked hasn't it, it's made me aware of the importance of that plane. But where on earth do I start to look? It all happened fifty years ago – the remains of the plane must have disappeared, perhaps they've even been ploughed into the ground somewhere in France ages ago. There's virtually nothing left of the airfield at Bovingdon. Can you think of anything?'

'I think I had best concentrate on these old books. One of the grimoires might give us a lead on breaking curses.' Marjorie busied herself with consulting a translation of the Magus and Amy yawned, glancing at her watch.

'Look, it's getting really late, I think we had better be going.'

'No, wait a moment, there is somewhere to start looking,' John cried rustling the pages of the weekend supplement. 'I noticed an article in the travel section called *The American Connection*, I did no more than glance at it on Sunday but I think it was about one of those wartime reunions. It was an old picture of American bombers flying over the Norfolk countryside in winter that caught my eye. Yes, here it is – the reunion's next

Saturday at Lavenham,' he smiled, scanning the article as he folded the paper and passed it over to Joel.

Amy looked curiously over his shoulder as he smoothed out the creases in the page.

'Jesus, it's like stepping back into yesterday,' he whispered, his skin prickling icily. He recognized the formation of Flying Fortresses instantly and it brought those times back to him so vividly that he could almost see the frost-sharp, white, winter fields and the miles of bleak, black hedgerows slipping away beneath the wing-tips in the old war-time photograph.

'It's going to be a big reunion, flying displays, exhibitions, old films and loads of other things going on. It says here they're expecting a lot of those airmen to come over,' Joel murmured as he quickly read through the article.

'You and Amy could go up to Lavenham on Saturday and ask around. You know, see if anybody remembers Chris,' John suggested.

'Are you crazy?' Joel exclaimed, pushing the paper aside. 'Do you realize that almost seven thousand of those guys were killed – what do you think the chances are of anyone remembering Chris? And there must be even less chance of anyone who does remember actually being there! No, I haven't the nerve to go.'

'I don't think you have to,' John murmured, reaching for the discarded paper: something in the article had struck a hidden chord. He read it through quickly and his smile widened to a grin. 'There's a permanent memorial museum at Lavenham. I'll bet they've got a proper record of Chris's plane – they've probably got one of every plane that ever took off from East Anglia during the war. That call-sign is important, because the plane might have disappeared but the record of it will always be there in the files. You might even find out where it crashed.'

'John's got a point there, you know: it would give us somewhere to start,' Amy agreed.

'Would it?' Joel frowned, shrugging his shoulders noncommittally. The thought of going back, actually touching his past, really unnerved him. And the worst of it was, he could already feel himself being pulled, unavoidably, like a moth to the flame.

Awoken Memories

THE LOW SUN seemed to balance amongst the leafy oaks and spreading chestnuts, silently brushing the tops of the hedgerows as it rose, momentarily appearing and disappearing, shrouded by thin ribbons of early morning mist. A faint, cool breeze ruffled Joel's hair as he got out of the car and made him turn up his collar. It tugged idly at the orange windsock that hung beside the runway and made the fragile carpet of dew-wet spiders' webs on the newly-mown grass tremble and shimmer. It sent swaying waves through the tall grasses and wild summer flowers that grew in abundance along the boundaries of Lavenham airfield. It was going to be a beautiful day.

Amy stretched as she got out of the car and looked at her watch. 'We're hours too early. I never thought we'd get here this quickly. Do you think there's anywhere open yet so that we can get a coffee or something to eat?' she asked, calling Borso to heel and checking that his lead was securely clipped to his collar. She'd promised the attendant at the gate that she would keep him under control.

'The mess will probably be open but we'll get something later, come on.' Joel walked slowly towards the small crowd of veterans who had gathered near the control tower.

'Why is everybody meeting out here so early – the reunion doesn't start officially until ten-thirty?'

Joel smiled and listened for a moment, savouring the

American drawl of their subdued voices and the odd burst of laughter with the familiar words and snatches of conversation from another life. The faint whiff of their cigar smoke seemed to stir up forgotten memories. 'This is something we always did. Whenever the planes were due back from a raid we'd come out and watch for them.' He stopped, suddenly feeling embarrassed and out of place as he reached the edge of the group.

The conversation had died away and silver-haired heads were turning in their direction, critical eyes focused upon them. Amy sensed that they had intruded into a very private party. 'Good morning. It's going to be a lovely day,' she smiled.

'Are you reporters?' a heavy-set man asked, barely disguising his irritation at their intrusion.

'No, we're nothing to do with the press. We only came over to watch the planes arrive. I'm sorry if we've interrupted you, we didn't mean to cut in,' Joel apologized.

The veteran's scowl gradually dissolved. 'That's OK, young fella . . .' he began, but a ripple of excitement in the crowd made him turn back quickly. Old heads were tilted, listening, their eyes scanning the sky.

'It was a sort of ritual,' Joel whispered as he drew Amy back a few paces away from the old men. 'I suppose it's the most important part of it for these old guys who've come back, a sort of pilgrimage – standing here where it happened – remembering lost friends.'

He knew they were listening for the first sounds of the returning aircraft, remembering how they used to pray that they'd all come back; counting the silhouettes in the sky as they appeared one by one over the tree-tops and watching for the flares that would tell them which planes had wounded aboard: he remembered breathing a sigh of relief as they saw their undercarriages locked down. But he hadn't forgotten how frequently the wail

309

of the ambulance sirens and fire trucks drowned the sound of the planes.

Joel instinctively tilted his head, Chris's memories were so clear. 'There! Do you see them?' His voice was tight with emotion and his finger trembled as he pointed to three slow-moving specks flying in formation, banking and turning towards the airfield, dropping for a second below the trees. The throb of the aero-engines suddenly grew louder as they levelled out and appeared in full view. The undercarriage of the leading aircraft, a Flying Fortress, locked down as the pilot eased the throttle back and touched down, bringing the plane to a trundling halt close to the tower. Its escort of two Thunderbolts roared low overhead, banked and climbed away on full power before returning to land.

The moment the Fortress's engines were shut down and the propellers had stopped turning, the group of veterans all began talking at once while they walked towards it.

'Do you remember the raid over Rechlin, when we lost the outboard engine?'

'I'll never forget Babenhauser . . .'

'But do you remember that Christmas party at Rougham Airfield?'

'Jesus, we'd been flying for so long we were sucking rust from the bottom of our tanks while we were looking for somewhere to land. The fog was that thick over England you could almost eat it. Then it was like a miracle, suddenly we saw an airfield – there it was – immediately below us with hundreds of aircraft parked up. We could see some guys signalling to us with hurricane lamps. Yes, that was some party.'

A group of them laughed as they noisily swapped reminiscences, gesticulating with their hands as they demonstrated angles of combat, smiling with relief as they recounted lucky escapes, happy to relive the youth that had slipped so quickly and violently away. They gathered around the hatchway in the rear of the fuselage where two members of the Fortress ground crew were securing a short set of aluminium steps.

'Are you guys ready to come aboard?' the pilot called out, ducking through the open hatch, grinning and shaking hands warmly with old friends in the group as he descended the steps.

'Ready? Are you kidding?' laughed one of the veterans who stood closest to the open hatchway as he reached up for the handrail and began to climb.

'You should know by now, Harry – we wouldn't miss this part of the reunion for the world. We keep on coming back, don't we?' a tall, iron-grey-haired figure who stood a good head above the others added. He pumped the pilot's hand vigorously in greeting as he waited for his turn to mount the steps.

Joel felt an icy tingle in the nape of his neck as he heard the tall man speak. There was something so familiar in his deep, gravelly voice – it stirred up old memories, filled his head with scattered, confusing pictures of a young, laughing face, a mane of tousled, auburn hair and penetrating eyes the colour of cornflowers. The memories began to fragment and cloud together as other voices in the group broke through his consciousness. He knew he had to get a better look at the tall figure.

'Wait here, I won't be a minute,' he whispered to Amy, moving quickly around the back of the crowd.

The tall figure mounted the steps slowly, ducking down to enter the aircraft.

'Damn!' Joel murmured, and was about to turn away when the tall figure stopped and glanced back to say something to the man following him up the steps before looking out across the heads of the waiting group. For a moment their eyes seemed to meet. The American frowned and stared at Joel as if he thought he should know him and then dropped his gaze and vanished into the aircraft.

Joel stared at the tall man's suntanned face and thinning hair, trying to look beneath the indelible lines and wrinkles that time had weathered there and imagine what he might have looked like fifty years before. But the harder he tried the more Chris's memories blurred inside his head and the face he almost remembered became indistinct and shadowy. Bleakly he realized that he couldn't be really sure of anything that had happened in Chris's life, not without something more substantial than those fragments of memory to rely on. He sighed and slowly retraced his steps to where Amy was waiting. He couldn't shake off the sensation of having once known the American veteran but how could he go up to him and tell him that they had once known each other in a previous life? It was impossible, the man would think he was a crank.

'You thought you recognized one of them, didn't you? Which one?' Amy asked as he reached her.

'I don't know. For a moment that tall American seemed so familiar, his voice – I know his voice, but everything inside my head is so confused. Maybe it wasn't such a good idea coming here after all,' he muttered, thrusting his hands into his pockets.

'Why don't you go over there and see if they'll let you into the plane? Mix with those veterans, they seem very nice, I'm sure they won't mind. You never know, it might trigger more of Chris's memories. I'll wait here with the dog.'

Joel looked at the short crocodile of old airmen as they waited to climb into the aircraft and shook his head. 'No, let's get some coffee now, perhaps I'll come back a little later, when I can be in the plane on my own for a while.'

Amy smiled and linked her arm through his as they

walked towards the low huts on the perimeter of the airfield. She understood how difficult it was trying to grasp and hold onto those fragile memories but deep inside her subconscious she knew they had to, that their future depended on finding a way to break the curse that haunted them.

Joel fidgeted with his empty coffee cup and let the noisy hum of conversation float from the tables around them in the mess hall and wash over him. When they had entered the canteen he had half-hoped that something – a voice, a face in the crowd – would stimulate Chris's memory, perhaps bring something to the surface and give them some answers. He even found himself keeping an eye on the door, watching for the tall American. They both felt ill at ease amongst the veterans, and were acutely aware of the curious glances they were receiving, the sudden ripples of silence and the polite but guarded smiles if they unexpectedly caught someone's eye.

'They're probably wondering what on earth we're doing here,' Amy whispered as she leant close to Joel.

He grinned and nodded. 'Yes, but I bet they would get a shock if we told them!' He glanced down at his watch and then stood up, pushing back his chair. 'Come on, the museum must have opened up by now, let's check out Chris's plane.'

Letting the door of the canteen swing shut behind them Joel looked across at the two Thunderbolts and the Flying Fortress parked near the control tower. There were only a handful of the veterans standing near the two fighters. There was no one near the old bomber and Joel felt himself drawn uneasily towards it.

'I . . . I . . . I think you were right earlier,' he murmured. 'I think I should take a closer look at the plane. I promise it won't take more than a couple of minutes.'

Amy smiled. 'Take as long as you like, Borso needs to stretch his legs after the journey.' She walked along the edge of the runway and listened to the skylarks, enjoying the sunshine on her face.

The attendant beside the hatchway scowled at Joel but after a moment's hesitation he reluctantly let him climb up into the fuselage though he couldn't resist calling up after him. 'Make sure you don't touch anything, I'm only supposed to let the veterans aboard.'

'I'll be very careful, mate!' Joel called back as he made his way forwards between the waist-guns. A broad smile began to spread over his face, his mind was alive with the smell and the feel of the old aircraft. It was like opening the door of a musky room and stepping inside. Instinctively, he reached up for the spar above the bomb bay to keep his balance as he crossed the narrow catwalk. Glancing at the radio equipment and the navigator's small table cluttered with his instruments, he climbed up into the cockpit. Joel stopped suddenly, his heart beating wildly: there was somebody sitting in the co-pilot's seat, the ghost of a familiar figure, the bulky silhouette of a bear of a man hunched over the controls.

'Mike,' he whispered. 'Is that you?'

The tall man sitting cramped up in the co-pilot's seat didn't hear Joel whisper his name or immediately become aware of his presence. He was staring up through the windshield, his head full of the roar and beat of the engines. His intense blue eyes were clouded with reminiscences and the fingers of his left hand were curled around the throttle controls. Gradually Big Mike sensed there was somebody with him in the cockpit, a figure so familiar that it blended into his memories, and he automatically glanced down to the instrument panel and began to read off the manifold temperatures. The sound of his own voice broke through the daydream and he hesitated, frowning as reality crowded back. He blinked and swung his head sharply round to see who was there.

'Who in God's name?' he gasped as he caught sight

of Chris standing just behind him, filling the entrance to the cockpit for a split second. Fear ran an icy fingernail up his spine and his face turned deathly pale as beads of cold perspiration prickled his forehead. 'Chris, it can't be . . .' His words were lost in the short intake of breath that crackled in his throat. The image was so real, so lifelike, that he could almost reach out and touch it, but he forced himself to stifle the movement of his hand. He knew Chris had died fifty years before – he had watched the plane explode and burn up. Mike slowly raised his hand and rubbed it over his eyes and up across his forehead, blinking and shaking his head as he took a controlled, deep breath before he looked up again.

'I'm sorry, young fella, for a moment there I thought you were somebody else. Come on in and sit with me for a while, I'll talk you through take-off if you like, I don't suppose anyone of your generation will get the chance to fly one of these old planes.' He smiled and gestured Joel into the pilot's seat.

Joel slipped into the seat and automatically rested his hands on the controls as he looked across at the old man. There was definitely something about him that stirred up Chris's memories. There were so many questions he wanted to ask, so much he wanted to know, but he suddenly realized that it was going to be a whole lot more difficult than he had imagined. How could he just ask about Chris? He couldn't pretend to be searching for information of a dead relative, he didn't even know his surname. Joel felt a peculiar, hidden rapport with the tall American but he still couldn't see a way to broach the question he really wanted to ask. He felt awkward and tongue-tied and he silently cursed Chris's elusive and fragile memories, here amongst the veterans Chris really was a living ghost.

'All these instruments probably make it look very

complicated but it wasn't.' Big Mike smiled, breaking through Joel's thoughts.

He glanced across to find the old man staring quizzically at him. Mike was frowning, rubbing his hand over his eyes again, unable to get the idea that he knew the young man from somewhere out of his head. 'Have you ever been to Cleveland?'

'No, I was born in Australia, this is my first trip abroad.'

'I'm sorry, my head's full of so much stuff, I'm getting distracted, it's the curse of old age you know, everything gets muddled up and you forget . . .' Big Mike's eyes drifted across the instruments. 'Oh yes, I remember, I was telling you about these old B17s. Almost flew themselves they did. There was a freezing January morning in 1942, we'd been grounded for a week with the fog – well HQ insisted that we take off although we couldn't see further than the wingtips . . .' Mike's voice was softening as he slipped back into his memories, his fingers brushing instinctively across the banks of dials and switches, his lips forming the words as he relived the take-off procedure. 'Fireguard left and right, master switches on, booster pump on, gills fully open, inboard switches on, ignition . . .' His fingers tightened on the control column and his eyes were staring, peering through the swirling fog.

Joel sighed and watched the old pilot's hands. The memories were as fresh in his mind as the day they were created: it was only the trembling flesh, the ravages of age, that told of the present. He quietly eased himself out of the seat without breaking the daydream. Big Mike didn't need him there to lift the nose of the bomber up above the fog.

'No, it didn't really help, if anything it confused me even more,' Joel murmured despondently to Amy as they walked hand in hand towards the museum building. Joel slowed and glanced back across his shoulder at the plane.

'Do you remember that tall guy, the one I pointed out to you earlier, the one I thought I recognized? Well, he was in the plane, I sat next to him in the cockpit, and the oddest thing was I could have sworn he was my . . . I mean Chris's co-pilot, Mike. If only I could find a way to ask him.'

'But why didn't you? You had the perfect opportunity,' Amy exclaimed.

'Because I knew it couldn't really be him – I know all the crew died in the explosion,' Joel answered flatly.

Amy sensed his frustration and misery and gently squeezed his hand. 'Come on, we might get lucky in the museum.'

The attendant glanced down dubiously at Borso as they entered the hallway and Amy had to promise to keep him strictly under control before he would let them in. They were directed to the archives through a second set of doors in the far corner. Joel gripped Amy's arm as the inner swing door sighed shut behind them. The silent atmosphere of the long, low, white-washed room crowded with display cases, photographs and hanging banners overwhelmed him. Minute specks of dust danced in the shafts of sunlight streaming in through the small windows and reflecting from the wooden polished floor but it was the memorial, the simple epitaph to the fallen that filled the centre of the room that had brought him to such a sudden halt. From floor to ceiling the plain white sculpture of a tail plane was covered with the thousands of signatures gathered from the families of the aircrews who had given their lives during the Second World War.

'Chris's name must be up there somewhere,' Joel whispered as he moved closer to read through the names of the dead.

Amy felt her eyes being drawn away from the memorial to the thousands of young faces that stared silently out of the faded photographs in the display cases that lined the museum walls. She shivered slightly as the atmosphere pressed in around her and she could imagine that she could hear the faintest echo of the pilots' voices, snatches of careless laughter, memories of a time forever frozen in the dusty shafts of summer sunlight.

'Come on, Joel,' she whispered, touching his arm. 'I feel like an intruder in here. Let's see what the archives can tell us, if anything.'

The archivist listened, slowly polishing his steel-rimmed glasses, as Joel related the story that he had made up, explaining that his father, who had flown briefly with the Eighth Airforce during the war, was very ill and was desperate to trace and find out what had happened to one of his friends from that time. Joel smiled and spread his hands in apology as he explained that they didn't have very much to go on as his father's memory had suffered badly during his illness but that his father's friend's name was Chris, they had been stationed together at an airfield near London called Bovingdon and his father kept repeating a call-sign – Army 375.

'We thought that it might be the radio call-sign for Chris's plane, do you think so? I'm sorry that it isn't much to go on.' Joel shrugged in embarrassment.

'I've had stranger requests for information before. Let's see what we can do.' The archivist smiled, pulled on his spectacles and jotted down the call-sign on his note pad. 'Now let me see, Army 375,' he murmured, tapping his teeth with his pen as he ran his hand along a bank of gun-metal, grey filing cabinets behind his desk and stopping at one labelled BG (Bombardment Group) B–17.B.24.1942/43. He pulled it open.

Joel felt a knot of curiosity tightening in his stomach

as the archivist's fingers rifled quickly through the card index in the drawer. Suddenly his hand slowed and stopped before withdrawing a small, yellowing index card covered with lines of numbers and letters. 'Yes, here it is, Army 375 was the official call-sign of the B17, Flying Fortress, serial number D23747 stationed at Bovingdon with the 483rd.'

'Can you tell us anything else? I mean – who were the rest of the crew and what happened to it? Is there anything else I can tell my father when I get back home?' Joel pressed, leaning forward and trying without luck to decipher the information on the card.

'Yes, of course,' the archivist nodded, punching the serial number of the plane into his computer keyboard and watching the screen flicker and change. He glanced up at them, a smile widening across his face. 'It would have taken me at least an hour to cross-reference the aircraft serial number against all the information stored here if you had asked me the same question a couple of years ago but we've almost finished transferring everything in those files onto disc. By the next reunion, hopefully, the job will be finished and all these cabinets will be stored away in a cellar somewhere. Ah, yes, here it is . . .'

Borso's ears suddenly pricked up, his hackles rising along his back. He tugged the lead out of Amy's hand and spun round to face the door as a low, snarling growl vibrated in his throat. The room immediately darkened and the door-handle rattled as if turned by an invisible hand. The curtains at the window stirred as if touched by an icy draught.

'What's the dog making such a fuss about?' the archivist cried, rising from his seat and backing away as Borso's growl turned into a threatening snarl.

'It's nothing, I'm sorry, the dog must have heard something outside in the museum, he's very sensitive to unusual noises but he won't hurt you,' Amy apologized, grabbing hold of the lead.

Joel sensed the two shadowy figures and their hell-hound were near, trying to prevent them from finding out what had happened to Chris's plane and discover who he really was. He used the moment as the archivist backed away from the dog to slip his hand into his pocket, withdraw the box of Swan matches he always carried and hide them beneath the table. He took two matches out of the box and struck them against his thumbnail, just as he had done so many times before to scare the ghosts away. The sudden, flaring flame didn't hurt the hard calluses that he had already burned on the tip of his thumb and first finger. He swept his hand behind him in the general direction of the door. The bright flame briefly flared, bending and scorching his thumbnail. Joel's eyes flinched at the pain and he smelt the thin, curling ribbon of blue smoke as the flame shriv-elled and died out. The evil creatures seemed to have been driven back for a few precious moments – he could hear their hateful mutterings fading away.

The archivist sniffed and looked dubiously at Joel as he stuffed his hands into his jacket pockets. 'No worries, mate, the dog's perfectly harmless. Now exactly what can you tell us?' He leaned expectantly forwards, trying to disguise the urgency in his voice as the archivist reluctantly resumed his seat and studied the screen.

'Well, let me see. The crew had christened the aircraft *Carolina Lady*, the pilot was Captain Christopher Ostic, the first officer/co-pilot was Mike Folberth and they were both from Cleveland; the radio operator, Earl Dunison was from Florida; the navigator was Spiro Shelsrighter from New York, the flight engineer was Elco Watts from California, bombardier Henry Smith was from Seattle, the waist-gunners were William Dowand from Brooklyn and John Snipe from Ohio;

and last but not least was Joseph Kranski, the tail gunner, from New England. It says here that Sergeant William Kovak was chief mechanic in charge of maintenance and ground crew for the plane.'

The information on the screen changed and the archivist scanned it quickly, sighed and looked up at them, pushing his glasses up onto his forehead. 'I'm afraid your father's friend didn't make it. *Carolina Lady* was lost with all its crew somewhere over France on February 21st, 1942 on their way to bomb the marshalling yards in Stuttgart.'

Borso's ears started to twitch and his lips began to curl back across his teeth. Amy rose quickly to her feet, motioning Joel to follow her and thank the man for his time.

'It's a pity I couldn't have had better news for you,' he smiled. 'But at least your father will know what happened to his friend now.'

They turned to leave.

'No, wait, there's something else,' he called out as the information on the screen changed again and he pushed his glasses back on.

Joel paused, his hand on the door-handle, and Amy turned expectantly.

'They didn't all perish. Mike Folberth, the co-pilot, managed to bale out. He was caught by the Germans a week later trying to cross the Massif Mountains. He . . .'

Dark shadows suddenly enveloped the room and the computer's keys began to jump and depress themselves. 'What's happening? My computer – it's going haywire – look at the screen!' he shouted in terror as the pages of information he had just called up began to merge and melt together. The lines of words and numbers, the carefully preserved files, were running into one another and then vanishing off the edge of the screen. 'Stop it!

Stop it!' he cried, reaching forwards to pull out the keyboard lead and try to save the disc as the screen glowed white-hot.

Borso snarled and barked furiously, rushing around the room, snapping his teeth at the shadowy forms that created the enveloping darkness. Joel struck another match and thrust it out into the swirling shadows. The attack ended as abruptly as it had begun. The darkness vanished in a malicious howl of demonic laughter leaving the archivist staring helplessly at the empty screen.

'Oh my God, everything has been wiped clean. The disc is ruined – everything has gone, all that work. How could it have happened?' He punched fruitlessly at the keyboard and stared at the blank, flickering screen.

'It must have been a freak surge of electricity. I'm sorry, really.' Joel retreated quickly through the doorway, almost dragging Amy with him.

'What's the hurry, Joel?' Amy frowned, struggling to keep up with him as he strode towards the outer door of the museum. 'We should really have stayed a little longer and tried to help that poor man; at least we could have calmed him down. It was our fault those creatures destroyed his records, wasn't it?'

'There's no time for that now.' He hurried her out of the door and away from the building and pulled her close to him. 'Listen, I'm sure now that Chris did manage to leave a message,' he whispered, barely able to conceal his excitement. 'He gave it to Big Mike, I know he did, but he didn't dare try to remember that in case those creatures discovered what he had done, that's why he fixed the call-sign in his memory – to draw us to the plane. Everything clicked into place in there when that archivist said that Mike had managed to bale out!'

Joel paused and looked back across to the B17 parked near the control tower. 'But Mike's in great danger, Amy. We've got to find him, and fast, before . . .' His words died away as the engines of the Fortress were started up one by one and it began to taxi towards the end of the runway to return to its home station.

'Damn, what a fool I was, if only I had spoken to him earlier when I had the opportunity. He could be anywhere now, we may never find him again!' Rage and frustration boiled in Joel's voice as he watched the aircraft gather speed. Its tail came up and it lifted into the air, climbing away across the boundary fence. The two Thunderbolts started their engines and took off, climbing after it.

'There are still plenty of people about and lots of things going on. The reunion doesn't finish until six o'clock – he must still be here somewhere. Let's start looking in the canteen. We'll ask around, somebody's bound to know where he's got to,' Amy suggested.

'He can't just have vanished, it's impossible, we've been through every display, every room, we've looked everywhere,' Joel muttered despondently.

As a last resort Joel asked at the main gate on their way out of the car park. The attendant pushed his peaked cap up onto the back of his head and watched thoughtfully as a group of veterans boarded their coach. 'Big guy you say? Yes, I know him, he comes over every year but he never stays for long. He spends the time touring the area, visiting old friends: they call him Big Mike, yep, he left hours ago.'

'Have you any idea where he was staying?' Amy asked.

The attendant shrugged. 'I don't know. The veterans stay in all the villages around here, but you could try Lavenham, it's the most popular.'

'Thanks for your help,' Joel smiled as they walked across to the car but he turned to Amy and in a quieter voice he said, 'I hope to God he hasn't caught his flight home already.'

Amy passed the map of East Anglia over to Joel before she waved to the attendant as she drove through the gates. 'Where to?' she asked.

Joel looked at the map hopelessly: he could be staying in any one of a dozen villages – finding him was going to be worse than looking for a needle in a haystack.

Amy slowed down when they reached the junction with the main road. 'Well? Where do you want to start looking?'

Joel shrugged helplessly as he looked at the signpost. Big Mike could literally be anywhere in that part of East Anglia. The sharp, impatient blare of a car horn cut through his indecision and he twisted round angrily in his seat to glare at the driver behind them.

'It's not his fault, it won't do any good taking it out on him,' Amy murmured, putting a restraining hand upon his arm as she edged the car closer to the double white lines. 'Which way?'

'Lavenham, we'll go to Lavenham in a large circle through Great Waldingfield and Washmere Green. Turn right and right again at the signpost to Acton.'

He felt better now he had decided but he realized that the likelihood of finding Big Mike was still very remote. He stared out at the isolated farmhouses barely aware of the slatted shafts of sunlight streaming through the high hedges or the patterns of serrated shadows that dappled the narrow, twisting, Suffolk lanes.

'If only I had spoken to him – he was so close. If only I had taken the chance when I had it,' Joel muttered as they left the Crown Inn at Little Waldingfield and walked back to the car. So far they had stopped at six country pubs and drawn a blank.

'Why don't we go on to Lavenham: it's got to be the largest village around here,' Amy suggested, taking a look at the map.

Joel felt the car slow up as they reached the top of a

shallow rise and glanced up to see rolling wheat and barley fields almost ready for harvesting spread out on either side of them, neatly bordered by blackthorn hedges. But it was the solid finger of a stone and flint church tower directly ahead of them up on the horizon that made him catch his breath. His interest sharpened as they breasted the crown of the hill and a curving street of ancient timbered weavers' cottages came into view.

'I recognize this place, I've been here before! I mean Chris must have been here before,' he whispered, staring at the sagging, medieval buildings with their overhanging galleries and tiny mullioned windows, some decorated with pargeting and others revelling in their blackened, exposed timber frames. They were driving past the half-timbered guildhall when Joel saw the gallows sign for the Swan Inn on the far corner.

He smiled. 'We used to drink in there. I remember the uproar we caused one Saturday afternoon when a whole crowd of us flew into Wattisham and came to the Swan. We drank the beer ration in two hours. Of course we didn't realize what we'd done until the *No Beer* sign went up outside. Let's stop, for old times' sake. You never know – it could be the one place he'd want to come back to.'

Amy pulled in next to the kerb and stopped, killing the engine.

Joel lifted the latch of the door of the Swan and pushed it open. The low hum of conversation, the clink of glasses and the ageless fragrance of malted hops, barley, pipe tobacco and tallow wax that pervaded the cool, gloomy interior drifted out around them as they entered. He had the fleeting impression of shadowy forms in the doorway behind them. Borso growled and turned his head, his ears flattening and his lips curling back. Amy tightened her grip on his lead – she didn't want the landlord to make her take him out, and she glanced back anxiously as Joel suddenly spun round and stepped out into the street, his eyes narrowing as he watched the shadowy form of the huge beast rush away along the outside of the ancient wool-hall. Amy heard the voices of the two grave-wraiths rising in cursing shrieks as they pressed against the mullioned windows looking for a way in. A couple on the opposite side of the road who had stopped to look into a gallery window were staring open-mouthed across at the apparitions. A pensioner further along the street was struggling to hold onto his dog as it snarled and barked furiously at the huge hell-hound as it disappeared down a narrow alleyway. With a fading howl the grave-wraiths vanished abruptly into thin air leaving behind them a faint odour of sulphur that hung heavily in the evening air.

Joel frowned and stepped in over the threshold before letting the door swing shut. 'That was very odd,' he whispered moving closer to Amy. 'For some reason they can't get in here, there's something stopping them, some power we can't see.'

Amy smiled and squeezed his arm. 'This building is so old there were probably all sorts of magic spells woven into it to protect it against evil. You know, they used to bury a child's body under the threshold and put witches' barriers in the chimneys, but I don't think that old magic will keep us safe for very long if Chris's friend is here. We had better find him as quickly as we can. Do you see him anywhere?'

Joel looked through the thin haze of blue smoke and scanned the crowded, low-beamed room, a smile softening his eyes. It was as if he had stepped back and was reliving a different time. There were echoes of familiar voices and laughter filling his head. He was in uniform, the heat of the roaring fire in the enormous inglenook was releasing the tang of wet leather from his flying jacket. The fire-light reflected in the long-handled brass and copper warming pans, the pot-bellied cauldron and steaming kettles hanging from the trammel. Bunches of dried hops, corn dollies from a war-time harvest, gin traps, pewter tankards and country bric-à-brac hung from every beam. Somebody brushed past Joel, a voice called out from the bar, the fragile memories were broken, the crackling flames shrank back into cold, grey ash, the bright reflections dulled into reality. Joel blinked and let his eyes travel slowly across the heads of the crowd. It felt like coming home – and then he saw him.

'He's there at the end of the bar. Come on,' he hissed suddenly, threading his way through the crowd.

Big Mike was engrossed, reading through the hundreds of autographs on the bar wall. His lips were silently forming the words as his fingers traced out old friends; *KL Buck, Pennsylvania, HJ Allen, 483rd, November 16th 1943, Kovak was here, Brooklyn*. His concentration was so complete that he didn't see Joel and Amy approaching him.

'Big Mike, 483rd.' Joel said it softly, pointing up to the barely visible, scrawling signature high above the others.

Mike jumped and stared as if an electric shock had passed through him, he rubbed his hand over his eyes. 'How did you know that I wrote that up there, young fella? Even I had trouble finding it just now.'

His voice had taken on a defensive tone, the slack muscles tightened in his jaw. When he had seen the young man earlier it had unsettled him, seeing him again had to be more than a coincidence.

Joel moved his finger across the wall and traced it across 'Chris Ostic, 483rd'.

'No, it can't be . . .'

'Our Fortress, *Carolina Lady*, was crashing. Our crew was dead – I told you to bale out, I gave you a message and I said you were my future. I said I would find you – remember?' Joel spoke breathlessly, his words almost blurring together in his haste.

Big Mike frowned, rubbing his hand over his eyes. He had to think straight, he had to clear away the muddle of his memories building up inside his head. He would be a fool to be taken in so easily by a complete stranger even if he had been waiting for this moment for a long time: and yet the boy did remind him so strongly of his long dead friend. But, after all, those signatures had been up there on that wall, preserved for anyone to read for fifty years, and it wouldn't be difficult to go through the records to find out that he and Chris had flown together, it would be easy to piece some story together – but how did he know this?

'Well, I'll be damned, is it you, Chris? Is it really you?' Mike's words choked in his throat and the colour drained from his face as he gripped Joel's shoulders and searched his face, blinking his penetrating blue eyes with disbelief. There was definitely something about the young Australian that reminded him of Chris Ostic, especially his eyes, but coming face to face with Chris reincarnated in the young man seemed too absurd, it wasn't something that could ever be proved – was it?

Mike shook his head, he had never forgotten those last frantic moments while he scrambled to escape from the cockpit of their stricken bomber, that enormous, hideous dog clawing at him to prevent it, howling, demonic screams and curses from the two shadowy figures were all around him and he remembered Chris shouting as he fought with the controls, urging him to get out while there was still time. He remembered him calling out, telling him that somehow he would come back from the dead and find him, urging him to remember everything he had just told him because his future in the next life depended upon it. Although he had written

328

down everything exactly as Chris had begged him Mike had never really believed it would happen. Well, not until thirty seconds ago.

'Why don't you tell me something personal, something that only Chris and I would know. If you want me to believe you convince me that you were once Chris Ostic.'

'There isn't time for a cross-examination . . .' Amy began when a baying, unearthly howl echoed in the street outside and the dark, shadowy forms again crowded at the windows, their blackened, razor talons scratching at the glass. People at the crowded tables began to rise, upsetting their chairs and spilling their drinks.

'What's happening? Those noises . . . it's getting dark.'

There was confusion and panic everywhere but Big Mike didn't need to ask what they were, even after fifty years the memories were so vivid and the echo of those howling voices had stayed with him, waking him up in the middle of the night, covering him with a cold sweat.

'I wrote it all down exactly as you asked,' Mike answered quickly. He didn't need to hear any more to convince him that Chris had made it back and those terrifying apparitions that had attacked them in the cockpit were still pursuing him. Instinctively Mike reached into the inside pocket of his jacket and pulled out a small, dog-eared note pad that he had been carrying around for almost fifty years.

'Everything you told me in the plane is in there. The curse, how it began, everything. But I don't think you're going to have time to read it, look!'

Joel heard the sound of breaking glass and the screams from the crowded room behind him. He snatched the book from Mike's hand and, clutching it to his chest, spun round to see the monstrous hound smashing its way through the window. It rushed across the room, upturning chairs and tables, scattering the frightened people. Borso leapt at Cerberus's throat, sending it backwards with a howling yelp of pain as his teeth sunk into its rotten flesh. The two grave-wraiths swarmed through the broken window, rushing through the crowd at Joel, their tattered cloaks streaming out behind them sending up choking clouds of sulphurous dust. A dark, claustrophobic atmosphere engulfed the Swan Inn as their eerie voices rose to ear-splitting shrieks of rage as they fruitlessly tried to tear the notebook from Joel's hands. They spun faster and faster, clawing at him with bone-black vicious fingers, their hoods flying back to reveal their hideous, withered, fire-scarred faces, but they could not tear, nor even touch, one fragile page of the book and their hatred boiled in their eyes as they spat and cursed.

'You can't touch us while we live, can you? There's a power greater than your evil and the key to it is in this book, isn't it?' Joel laughed in their faces. Suddenly he lifted his other hand, striking his thumbnail across the head of the match he had been hiding in his palm. The flame flared up and he thrust it out towards their spinning, shadowy forms.

'Burn, burn in Hell!' he hissed as their flying cloaks ignited into a blaze of sparks and with wailing screams they fled, folding their shadows about themselves to quench the sparks while they vanished up the inglenook, stirring up a gale of ashes from the hearth, their howling beast following them.

A shocked, paralysed silence briefly seemed to grip everyone in the bar as the wailing voices vanished up the chimney and the darkness gradually lifted. People began to cough, their eyes stinging and watering in the sulphurous fumes that hung heavily in the air. They blinked and stared at each other in disbelief, wondering what on earth had happened. They looked at the trail of wreckage, the upturned tables and chairs, the mess of spilt drinks and the broken glasses. They stared at the jackets and handbags that had been so violently flung onto the floor and now lay in a wide, trampled curve from the shattered window across the centre of the room, passing close to the wall of signatures at the end of the bar and into the centre of the inglenook. The iron trammel lay broken and twisted, the kettles and cauldrons were overturned, and a thick cloud of ashes was still swirling and spreading out across the hearth as it settled.

The landlord was the first to move, cursing and white with fright as he rushed out from behind the bar. He flung the outer doors open to clear the reeking stink and moved quickly amongst his customers, apologizing and checking that no one was hurt, expressing bewilderment as to what could have smashed the window and charged across the room with the speed of a tornado like that. Suddenly everybody was talking at once, giving a dozen different versions of what they thought they had seen.

'Poltergeists!' announced a fat woman in a high-pitched, hysterical voice as she retrieved her outlandish floral hat from the floor. 'I'm not staying in a place haunted by poltergeists – I don't care how good the food is. Come on, George, we're leaving!'

'It's never happened before – I'm sure you're quite safe now,' the landlord exclaimed in dismay as the majority of his other customers began to follow her example and gather their belongings together and head towards the doors.

'I tell you I saw a monstrous three-headed dog burst through that window and that smacks of the Devil! I'm doing my drinking in the Cock Inn in future,' muttered one of the locals as he led a group away from the bar.

'I'm sure it wasn't anything to worry about. There

must be a simple explanation,' the landlord called after them as he hurriedly set the chairs and tables upright and began to help his staff as they cleared up the mess.

He glanced up to see Big Mike brushing ash from his jacket and he hurried over. 'Mr Folberth, I'm very sorry, I don't know what to say. I hope your jacket isn't spoiled.'

His eyes flicked over Joel and Amy and lingered on the dog sitting close to her feet. He frowned and stepped back. He could have sworn there had been a huge dog in the middle of all that commotion just now, a ferocious-looking beast charging through the tables. He was about to ask the young woman to take the dog out when Big Mike laughed and asked him if ghosts in the parlour would interrupt dinner.

'I think my two young friends will be joining me and I'm sure you can find something in your kitchen for the dog, can't you?' Mike smiled.

The landlord glanced at his departing customers, it looked as though Mr Folberth and his guests would have the dining-room to themselves, and he nodded reluctantly. All it needed now was a visit from the health inspector to make the evening complete. 'Dogs aren't allowed in the dining-room I'm afraid, but I could serve your meal in the snug, they're allowed in there.'

'That will be just fine, we'll go through now and order some drinks in there.' Big Mike began to stand up.

Amy smiled at the publican and called to him as he was about to leave, 'Can we have our dinner by candle-light – it would be so romantic?'

'Why yes, yes of course, that's no trouble at all.' A bewildered smile returned to the landlord's face as he called over a waiter to attend to their drinks.

Big Mike waited until the door of the snug had closed and they were on their own before he smiled and gripped Joel's hand, staring into his face. 'You know something inside me always wanted to believe that you would come back, Chris, I suppose it's what made me keep coming back to these reunions every year.'

Joel smiled and shook his head as he gently pulled away. 'It isn't like that, I'm not Chris, well not the Chris Ostic that you knew. All I have of him are some of his memories and even they are as fragile as . . .' Joel shrugged, he could sense the doubts, the well of questions inside Mike and he didn't know how he was going to answer them.

'You see, Mike, it's our souls that are immortal, not our bodies. It's that special, elusive part of us that you can't measure or see, but you know it's there carrying our individuality through all eternity. Think of all the millions of thoughts and experiences, the hopes and the tragedies, that must go into making each one of us unique. It's crazy, isn't it: most of the time we're barely aware of the most important part of our own identity. I think the Chris you knew is somewhere inside my subconscious, along with all the other lives I must have experienced, that's why I caught your attention at the airfield earlier today.' Joel spoke softly as he tried to explain, to blunt the look of disappointment he could see developing in the old man's face.

Mike nodded. He knew he was talking sense and he knew he should feel elated, but he didn't. He had been wanting this meeting for fifty years but this proof, this illogical, impossible triumph over death that Chris had promised to make wasn't at all as he had imagined it would be. Yes, he had recognized something of Chris, but it was only an echo of his friend in the body of this young Australian, it wasn't the guy he'd grown up with, the one true friend he had fought and flown with and then watched die when the aircraft had exploded.

Mike released his grip on Joel's hand and turned slowly towards the window. His big frame seemed to sag, his shoulders to bow a little, as he watched the setting sun wreathed in misty fire sink beneath the distant hedgerows, pulling the mantle of night behind it across the darkening sky.

'So reincarnation boils down to a handful of memories, nothing more than that?' he sighed, trying to mask the regret in his voice.

'No, Mike, it's much more than that!' Joel exclaimed, moving to the window and making the big man sit down next to him. 'Just think about what we've done. I gave you that vital information in those last few hours of my life, I've come through eternity, just as I promised, and I've found you, and the book. I couldn't have done that if you hadn't written it down or kept the memory of Chris alive. If you hadn't kept coming back year after year I would never have found you.'

'You're damned right you wouldn't. It's fantastic. The more I think about it the crazier it is, but you always were the craziest son of a . . .' Mike suddenly laughed. Joel was right, dammit, Chris had beaten the most impossible odds and it really didn't matter how, or in whose body he had done it. The important thing was that Chris, or his soul, had made it back. He was right there beside him. Mike felt a deep sense of satisfaction: the long wait was over and he had kept that unlikely promise that he had flung back across his shoulder as he had scrambled free from that stricken bomber fifty years ago. The smile broadened across his face as he leant forwards and tapped the small, dog-eared notebook that Joel was clutching so tightly in his hand.

'That's one hell of a story Chris told me and it's all in there, every last detail, right down to the words that will break the curse, only I'm not sure how you're supposed to use them because Chris shouted something about not having enough time to recite the mantra. I looked them up some years later in the Imperial Library and it seems that some ancient spells or their antidotes were constructed in mantra form – it gives them special powers you know – you have to repeat a set pattern or words, either forwards or backwards, sometimes up to a hundred, thousand times, but . . .' Mike paused and frowned, rubbing his hand up across his forehead. 'We're jumping the gun a bit. How on earth did you know where to find me? I wasn't going to come over to the reunion this year, I only telephoned my reservation here at the Swan from the airport. I suddenly had this driving compulsion to be here, but it was a last-minute rush.'

'But we didn't know you'd be here.' Amy laughed softly and sat down on the corner of the window seat opposite. 'We didn't even know you were alive until this afternoon when the archivist in the museum at the airfield traced the plane and told us that you had baled out. In a strange way I think that Fate has drawn us together in the same way that it directed Joel to walk into the gallery.' Amy hesitated and glanced at the door as the handle turned. A quiet breath of relief escaped through her lips as she saw it was only the waiter pushing a trolley loaded down with their food. She waited until the table was ready and they had taken their places in the flickering candlelight before she told Mike of the weird series of events that had led them to the reunion at Lavenham.

'Discovering who we were in our most recent lives was the biggest breakthrough – it led us to Bovingdon and then to Chris's memories of that last flight,' Joel muttered through a mouthful of food, gesticulating excitedly with his fork, making the candle-flame dance wildly. 'I knew, I mean Chris knew that he had left a message, something really vital, and his last conscious memories were focused on the plane. I kept hearing him repeat the aircraft's call-sign, an endless echo, a distress beacon. We worked it out that he must have wanted us to find out something about the plane, that's why we came down here, to search through the records. It was quite a shock finding out that you had survived the crash, and I knew the moment the archivist told us, that Chris had given you the message. I just hoped and prayed we could find you before those evil creatures realized what you know.'

'This is an incredible story, and such a coincidence – if you had come down tomorrow for the last day of the reunion you would have missed me altogether, I'm flying back first thing!' Mike exclaimed as he poured the wine.

'I think Fate intervened to make sure we would meet,' Amy smiled.

'Listen to this,' Joel interrupted excitedly. 'It says here in the notebook that the curse originated in Aurillac during the plague of 1347, there were two women, the daughters of a healer . . .'

Borso growled suddenly, his ears pricked, as he paced around the room, bringing the conversation to an abrupt halt. Mike shivered and watched the dog as he stopped and stared up the cavernous chimney. He barked once and then returned to settle again at Amy's feet. Seeing Borso patrol the room triggered a memory from the war years. 'They are afraid of dogs, aren't they? Even that three-headed monster shrinks away from them,' his voice was barely a whisper.

'Yes, you're right, they're afraid of dogs,' Amy answered, reaching down to stroke Borso's ears.

A smile hovered on Mike's face. 'You know I have never thought of it before but I was a prisoner of war in Germany for a while and their dogs used to patrol the perimeter fence – I think they saved my life a dozen times. You see I had the distinct impression that someone or something was following me all the time I was on the run; I could always feel them, that second footfall, whispers in the dark, the sudden snap of a twig underfoot, shadows in the moonlight. At first I put it down to paranoia but after a couple of days I almost gave myself up – I was jumping at the slightest sound. The sensation of being followed was with me right up to the camp gates, but it never came any closer, it never got past the dogs that patrolled the perimeter day and night. Suddenly I had the sensation that whatever it was that was hunting me outside the wire had vanished. Eventually, by the time the war ended and I was released I had forgotten all about it. Funny thing though, since then I have always kept a dog, and I've slept better knowing it was there at the foot of my bed.'

Mike smiled and reached down beneath the table to scratch Borso under his chin and make a fuss of him. The dog stretched and yawned, his mouth opening into a wet grin of sharp teeth as he tilted back his head, enjoying the attention.

'Borso seems to be getting stronger. Did you see the way he despatched Cerberus earlier, when we were in the bar? The hell-hound was cowering back, howling with pain, the moment Borso attacked. It's never disappeared as quickly as that before has it. I wonder why?'

'Perhaps it had to use up so much of its power breaking in here: but don't forget,' Amy warned looking up from the notebook, 'it's so steeped in evil there's no knowing what it's capable of doing.'

'But the creature didn't seem so terrifying this time – and its attack was shorter.'

'I'm sure that's only because you know what to expect. Everybody else in the pub tonight, including me, was frightened out of their wits. Jesus, for an instant I thought the world was coming to an end, when that monster burst in through the window. And remember,

I've tangled with them before, even if it was fifty years ago,' Mike frowned.

Amy continued reading quickly through the notebook while Mike and Joel talked. Suddenly she shut the book and interrupted them. 'You know there's something that really bothers me, it's been there at the back of my mind like a persistent itch ever since we became aware of those creatures chasing us. Every time we try to fight back – when Joel throws a match at them or Borso attacks – they disappear. Well think about it, where the hell do they go – to heal their wounds or to recoup their strength? And something else has just occurred to me after reading through this book – you said the time had to be right to recite this mantra but you haven't told us when that is. And another thing, what's going to happen if we try to chant it, will they just disappear out of earshot only to reappear once we're out of breath? How are we ever going to keep them in one place long enough to destroy them?'

'It beats me,' Joel muttered, shrugging his shoulders. He hadn't given a thought to where the vile apparitions went, he was only too glad to see them disappear, but he could see what Amy was getting at. They'd never be rid of this curse if they couldn't pin them down, but how? They were afraid of fire but ringing them with it wouldn't work, he had set their robes alight enough times to know they merely vanished in a blaze of sparks. Borso could savage and hunt them down but he couldn't hold on to them.

'Wait a minute, the answer's staring us in the face,' Amy exclaimed. 'The curse was first uttered in Aurillac during the plague – it says so right here in the book – I'll bet that's where they vanish to. I'll bet they go to the source of their evil, it must be somewhere near there.'

'Aurillac,' Mike whispered. 'The Germans caught me

a couple of miles from Aurillac, no wonder I sensed the evil while I was on the run.'

'Of course! They can't escape from us when we're there, can they!' Amy waved the note pad at them.

'To think I've known it all those years. I even wrote it all down without realizing its significance,' Mike grumbled, rubbing his hand across his tired eyes.

Joel laughed and grabbed his hand across the table. 'No, Mike, you must never think that you've got it wrong. It was vitally important that you didn't realize the value of the knowledge that you carried. Don't you see, it was your ignorance that kept you alive.' Joel suddenly grew serious and leaned closer to him across the table. 'If those creatures had for one minute understood what Chris had done, if they had realized that you carried the seeds of the knowledge that could destroy them, that hell-hound would have killed you before your parachute had snagged in the trees and bushes.'

'We'll have to go to Aurillac. We have to follow those creatures to the source of the evil – there's nothing else for it,' Amy whispered. 'But when is the right time for us to recite the mantra, and how many times? Listen, it sounds like this "Zoros, Delmusan, Surmy, Dandalen, Sator". I wonder what it means?'

'I don't give a damn what it means as long as it breaks the curse,' Joel answered flatly, 'but Marjorie might know – if anybody does.'

Mike laughed softly, the sound of wheezing and cackling sounding dry in his throat. 'Listen to me, both of you, because I think I know a way you can nail those bastards once and for all, and if I'm right it won't matter one jot if you lose count while you're reciting that mantra or if you get distracted. It won't matter one bit.'

'How?' they both cried, staring at him.

Mike's grin widened across his face and his intense

blue eyes sparkled with a fire that time had failed to rub away.

'They're as old as dust, aren't they? Think about it, their clothes, their mannerisms, their spells and chants, everything about them is medieval, isn't it?'

Both Joel and Amy nodded. 'Yes, but how does that help us?'

'Well, it's simple, from everything Chris told me, and the way they look, I don't think they've advanced one day since they were burned at the stake for dabbling in evil all those hundreds of years ago in Aurillac. Their minds, their whole purpose of trying to possess your souls, Hecate's curse, everything is locked in that period. I don't think they understand our modern world and I don't think they have the slightest idea about our technology – and that's where your greatest power lies – you have the ability to harness everyday things that we take for granted, electricity, micro-chips, laser beams, anything. Jesus, the choice is almost endless, remember you have both advanced through each of your new lives but they have stayed frozen in their medieval times – even striking that match took them by surprise.'

Mike paused for a moment to take a shallow breath.

'But how can we use this advantage exactly? I don't see . . .' Amy frowned.

'Hey, it's easy, it's the simplest thing in the world. I've been working in communications all my life . . .' Mike hesitated, searching for the words to explain, and then rose from his seat. 'Wait here, it'll be easier to show you, I think I've got everything I need in my room. I won't be a minute.'

'Mike, wait!' Amy called, making him stop, his hand on the door handle. 'I don't know if those creatures will come back here tonight, but take Borso with you – just in case!'

Mike returned a few moments later carrying a large

leather travelling bag over his shoulder and with Borso trotting at his heels. He rummaged through his bag and brought out two small, black plastic boxes that looked like portable cassette recorders, he checked the batteries and laid them on the table side by side. Next he fished out a box of miniature tape cassettes and selected two blank tapes with identical running times and slipped them into the recorders. 'My company has been developing a new form of distress signal for the aviation authorities to be installed in the flight recorders. Once we've modified it it'll be reduced to the size of a micro-chip. Its function is not only to pinpoint the signal but to tell how long it's been activated. In its simplest form all it does is repeat a message, any message, over and over again and record the number of times it does it in this visual counter here.'

He attached a small microphone to one of the recorders and handed it to Joel. 'Now, recite the mantra just once, exactly as it's written in the notebook when I press this button.'

Joel swallowed, licked his lips and did exactly as Mike asked.

'Good, that was exactly four seconds,' Mike murmured, setting the spool to repeat every five seconds and making some fine adjustments to the machine before setting up the second recorder and making Amy recite the mantra backwards.

'Now listen to this. It should nail the bastards good!' Mike grinned, sat back and activated the transmitting signal, turning up the volume control so that they could hear their voices repeating the mantra forwards and backwards every five seconds. He inserted two specially coded keys to the recorders and switched them both off, adjusting the counters back to zero, and then handed the keys over to Joel and Amy.

'It won't matter how those creatures try to distract

you or how many times you're supposed to recite those words – those recorders are now programmed to do it for you twelve times every minute, seven hundred and twenty times an hour, seventeen thousand, two hundred and eighty times a day, and the special titanium power cells will operate them for a year at least. That's got to take care of the problem, you must be able to repeat the mantra way beyond the amount of times you need. It's designed to function at sixty degrees below freezing and to keep pumping the signal out until the plastic melts. I'd advise you to strap them to your waists, they have a strong reinforced strap on the back of each recorder, and once you think you've found that place in the forest above Aurillac – I've drawn you a map of where I landed, it might help you – you activate the transmitters and then sit back and watch them burn in Hell.'

The Power of Magic

MARJORIE PAUSED FROM comparing the open
notebook that Joel had handed to her the
moment they got back from Lavenham with
one of the old grimoires and looked up at them. She was
sitting cross-legged in the centre of an untidy pile of
books and old manuscripts that lay scattered on her sitting-room floor and was excited by the new knowledge
it had given her.

'Yes, yes, yes. This notebook is definitely the key!
It's fantastic, absolutely brilliant! Thank God Mike had
the good sense to write it all down while it was fresh in
his mind – and those tape recorders are such a novel
idea, I'd never have thought of them.'

'Yes, I know, they're great,' Joel muttered
impatiently. They'd been back in London for two days
kicking their heels, waiting to see if Marjorie could
throw any light on exactly when the mantra should be
recited before they caught a ferry to France.

'I may be wrong but I get the impression reading
through these notes that we can determine the exact time
we should begin to chant the mantra.'

'Yes, and I've seen a reference to that in one of the
grimoires,' Marjorie murmured, burrowing through her
books. 'Yes, I remember now, it was in this translation
of the *Grimoires of Mascous*, and there's a short chapter
in the *Oracles of Zoroaster* on spellbreaking. I marked
it the other day, I wondered if it would be of any use
to us. Let me see now . . .' Marjorie fell silent as she

found the relevant sections in both books and began to make quick, scrawled notes on a scrap of paper.

'Yes, yes, here we are. I was right, the timing of the reciting of the mantra would be set by one of the major star charts. It seems, from what is written in the Oracles, that for every spell or curse, no matter how severe or evil, there was an optimum time in the astrological clock for breaking it, now . . .' Marjorie's voice trailed off as she stared fixedly at a page in the grimoire. 'Listen to this: there was a belief amongst some medieval alchemists that the soul was immortal and if it was ever threatened by evil they could protect it by using their powers of magic to open a doorway into the labyrinth so that the soul could escape from danger between each life. There's a whole section here on how they created the doorway using numerical magic and objects invested with powerful magical properties like lepers' winding sheets, unicorn horn, wolf claws – and it even says that some alchemists went as far as tattooing the sign of the labyrinth upon the body of the person whose soul they were protecting.

'It seems that it would then appear somewhere different on the body in each new life, like a small, blue-and-white thumbprint in the shape of the labyrinth.'

'You mean like this?' Amy whispered, opening the top two buttons of her blouse with trembling fingers.

'Or this,' Joel added in an awed voice, revealing his identical birthmark.

'There's something extremely unnerving about all this. It throws everything we've grown up to believe in into doubt, I mean you never really expect to find out that all those medieval stories and beliefs were true, do you?' John frowned as he stood at the French windows watching Borso playing with the young alsatian he had bought to protect them.

'Now I understand why those creatures are so

desperate to possess our souls just at the moment we die, before we escape into the labyrinth!' Amy cried.

'Children of the flame – I wonder . . .' Joel murmured, almost to himself. 'Did that alchemist cast a spell to protect us so that our souls could pass through the fire?'

Marjorie looked up as she caught the importance of what he had just said and her voice was serious. 'Yes, but it can't protect you forever: it says here that the power of numerical magic created its own boundaries through the numbers it uses.'

'How long? How long can it protect us?' The dismay was obvious in their voices.

Marjorie re-read the passage and attempted to do some calculations but she gave up. 'I don't know, it's impossible to tell without knowing the actual numbers that were used originally, but we can assume that he meant the labyrinth to protect you for a long time, it's already lasted over six hundred years.'

'You said just now that there were special optimum times for reading the mantra. Is it possible to work them out?' Amy asked.

'Yes, it might be, but I'll have to hazard a guess at which planets the alchemist used to set against the chant at the ritual,' Marjorie murmured thoughtfully, going back to Galea's chart and poring over the mass of ancient mathematical formulae, running her finger slowly across the rows of astrological signs and symbols. With a growing feeling of helplessness she looked up. She hadn't realized how vast and complicated, and how confusing, the great astrological clock was as it measured the rhythms of their lives.

'It's impossible, I can't fix a time, there are so many possibilities, the chart is so complex. But I can't believe that the alchemist would have left Joel and Amy, or who ever they were in their previous lives, simply guessing in the dark – there must be a key. There must be something that's always been completely personal . . .'

'What about the time they were born? You can't get more personal than their natal charts, can you? Don't forget they were born at identical times, like twins, even though they were twelve thousand miles apart.'

'Yes, of course, we'll just have to assume that this echoes back through their other lives. How brilliantly simple!' Marjorie cried as she wrote down what they knew of the times, dates and places of their respective birthdays. 'Now, let's start with Amy since she was born in the northern hemisphere and we know the time of her birth. Ah, Scorpio rising; if we assume that Joel will have a similar chart we can use that to guess the time of his birth. You have the moon, Jupiter and Mars in the eighth house, Amy: the way they aspect your Sun is very significant . . .' She returned her attention to Galea's chart, moving her finger more purposefully along the rows of astrological signs and symbols. 'This is interesting, there is a moment almost every hundred years when these planets have a peculiar alignment . . .' She stopped and quickly rummaged through her books for *Solomon's Almanac*, scanning through it and comparing it with her own calculations and Galea's chart.

'It falls in August – exactly two days' time. The moon will be full and . . .' Marjorie laughed softly. 'The alchemist wouldn't have known this because they hadn't discovered the planet in his time, but Pluto will be exactly in conjunction with your mid-heaven. You must act now – there won't be a better time for you both.'

'I'll telephone and book a ferry for this evening: thank God my father had the good sense to have Borso fully inoculated – he must come with us.'

'I've got something else for you – it might just help!' Marjorie called, making Amy pause in the doorway and watch with curiosity as Marjorie picked up a small, crumpled cardboard box that lay amongst the books on the floor beside her. She broke the sellotaped seal and withdrew two, long, woven leather thongs each with a loop at one end and a shell engraved with the sign of an eye sewn into the other end to act as a simple fastening. Each one had at least twenty small pieces of gemstone, crystal, shells, beads and charms held in place by tiny silver clasps and knots of golden thread.

'What on earth are they?' Joel asked as he took the one she offered to him.

'They are talismanic necklaces for you to wear. The woman in the shop said they were probably two hundred years old. They are meant to possess great power against evil and they should protect you both,' Marjorie said, giving the other one to Amy. 'Each of the objects attached to the necklace was originally selected for its power to protect, to ward off evil, and it is meant to give its wearer strength. I've found so many references to talismans in all these books, there must be something in the belief. When I saw these two in the shop I thought you really must have them, I have even managed to find a chapter in *The Power of Magic* that describes some of the properties believed to be invested in this type of necklace.'

'But how do we use them, is there a special way?' Joel asked as he wove the leather thong between his fingers and let it lie heavily across the palm of his hand. The sunlight sparkled and reflected from every facet of the precious objects as he moved it in the sunlight.

'The woman in the shop said that you must recite the words engraved on the gemstones to invoke their power as you hang them around your necks and then you must never take them off. But there are many references to these talismanic necklaces in the grimoires and they tell how the wearer can use the gemstones and crystals to ward off evil by plucking them from the necklace one by one and throwing them at the evil shapes as they are being pursued.'

'There are times when I find all this very difficult to believe. I can't imagine how these strings of pretty stones will have any effect on those vile ghosts and especially that monstrous hell-hound,' Joel frowned, pushing the engraved shell through the loop at the other end of the necklace and pulling it tight.

The lights of Aurillac carpeted the valley floor below them and threaded away in thin, shimmering tentacles of silver light across the darkened countryside. Joel peered ahead through the windscreen, concentrating and comparing the narrow, switchback mountain road, its steep, wooded slopes and abrupt rock ravines, with the map that Mike had drawn for them before he left Lavenham. He yawned and rubbed his eyes, they had already stopped four times and clambered through the undergrowth at what had seemed to be likely places only to draw a blank.

'Slow down – stop! I think that bridge we've just crossed could be the one on Mike's map. We had better take a closer look!' Joel shouted above the roar of the engine as Amy expertly dropped down through the gears, accelerating out of a tight hairpin bend at the end of the bridge.

'There's a track or something on the right, you could park there,' he added, pointing to a wide break in the trees.

Amy slowed the car, spun the wheel and pulled across onto a narrow area of gravel before stopping beside a sign that marked it as a viewing point. She switched off the engine and sat there staring up at the dark shoulders of the mountains. The only sound that broke the night silence was Borso's panting breath from where he sat between Joel's feet and the tick of contracting metal in the engine as it cooled down.

'Are you afraid?' she asked Joel in a small voice, touching the smooth, cool fragments of crystal that hung from the necklace around her neck, hoping for its protective aura to enfold her.

'Yes,' he whispered, reaching across to take her hand, entwining his fingers with hers. 'It seems strange, doesn't it, to be so close to the end after being on the run for so long, hunted from life to life, always looking over our shoulders, listening for that footstep in the dark, feeling that blind terror waiting to possess us. Yes, I am afraid, afraid of being the hunter instead of the hunted, afraid of confronting those evil creatures, especially here where their power is the strongest. There's a large part of me that wants to run, that wants to try and hide . . .'

'No, Joel, we mustn't!' she interrupted him, gripping his hand tightly.

'I know. If we fail now . . .' Joel hesitated, the words strangling in his throat. He couldn't bring himself to speak of the terrifying, spectral forms and images that were rising in his head, breaking through the surface of his subconscious. To talk of them would make them real.

'Being here is bringing our memories alive, isn't it? It's releasing all the terrors that have ever haunted us,' Amy whispered, her fingers were beginning to tremble. There was so much to be afraid of – even the inky shadows amongst the trees seemed to move, to sway and stir threateningly as the night wind ran its fingers carelessly through their whispering branches.

'We must be strong, we don't have any choice,' Joel answered, glancing grimly at the clock on the dashboard. It was almost ten o'clock.

Borso shifted in the cramped space between Joel's legs, stretched and turned awkwardly as he clambered up to rest his front feet in Joel's lap. He licked at Joel's face making a soft, grumbling sound of welcome in his throat as he stared out unperturbed, his ears pricked, at the moonlit landscape. Joel frowned and pulled gently at the dog's ears and scratched him under the chin before opening the car door to let him out. 'It's got to be somewhere around, I can sense it . . .' He froze, the hairs prickling the nape of his neck. 'It's here, it's here somewhere.'

'But we only have two hours to find the exact place. What will happen if we don't find it in time? How will we know when we've found it? What will it be – a cave, a hole in the ground, what?' Amy asked, locking the car and following Joel and Borso to the edge of the steep, sparsely wooded valley that fell away from the road.

'We'll know, there'll be something, we'll just know.' Joel was searching for a way down. 'Let's just follow the feeling and see where it leads us. Come on, I can hear water running over rocks, there must be a stream.'

They both checked the straps that held their tape recorders secure around their waists and took a last, quick glance up at the silver-white mountains before plunging through the strangling undergrowth of tall ferns, brambleweeds and wild flowers that grew along the edge of the road. They followed the sound of the stream as it rushed and gurgled down in its deep cutting, catching elusive glimpses of it through the weeds where shimmering pools of moonlight were momentarily caught in the swirling water or thrown up in glittering plumes of spray before it vanished beneath the dense canopy of trees below. The steep slope became darker and the sense of evil grew more intense as the moon disappeared from their view. Joel cursed under his breath each time he slipped and lost his footing on the loose rocks and boulders that choked the valley. He was constantly grazing his knuckles as he scrambled for a better purchase on the path.

'Watch where you tread, this slope is treacherous!' he called up to Amy as the rocks he had disturbed clattered and vanished into the trees below.

'I know, you're making enough noise to wake . . .' she paused, biting her lip, even thinking of the dead stirred up terrifying images of the grave-wraiths. She shivered and tried to push the pictures back away from her consciousness but they crowded forwards, filling her thoughts. 'Wait for me, this whole slope seems to be moving beneath my feet. How anything manages to grow in this God forsaken place at all is a mystery.' She snatched at the trunk of a spidery rowan tree to stop herself from sliding past him.

Slowly they worked their way across the scree and breathed a sigh of relief when they reached firm ground where the trees grew more thickly. Borso scrambled down behind them, finishing his descent in a small avalanche of stones and rocks.

'Come on, we haven't got time to stop, we've got to find that place it's almost midnight already,' Joel warned, glancing at his watch but Amy hesitated.

'Joel, I'm scared. I'm really afraid – there's something so evil about this place, so stifling and suffocating. It's more powerful than anything I've ever felt before, even the silence is getting heavier as we get further down.'

'We must be getting close. There's no turning back now, you know there isn't.' Joel grabbed her hand tightly in his and led her quickly down through the trees.

The undergrowth thickened into impenetrable banks of brambles, elder bushes and blackthorn that forced them away from the stream, Joel picked up a branch and used it to beat a path. Amy was feeling dizzy with fear, she had lost all sense of direction by the time they reached tall, slender pines which filled the night air with the sweet scent of resin, the carpet of pine needles and leaf mould deadened their footsteps. It was utterly silent, as if the whole forest was listening and holding its breath.

'Hecate knows we're here. Those creatures are in the trees, I can sense them near us!' Joel warned, but his voice was sucked away by the silence.

Borso snarled and circled constantly, almost tripping them up in his efforts to protect them. 'Joel, for God's sake let's go back. Joel, I'm so afraid – listen to me!'

He felt her pull on his arm and try to turn him back and he tightened his grip on her hand. Faintly, somewhere in the well of his consciousness, beyond the terror that was enfolding him, he heard the fear in her voice. 'No, we mustn't give up now.'

Borso suddenly began to bark furiously, barging past his legs and leaping at a mass of brambles and high nettles that completely blocked the way ahead. 'What is it, boy? What have you found?'

Joel suddenly felt knots of terror tighten in his stomach: the atmosphere was heavy with threat and there was a reek of sulphur and a stagnant odour of corruption seeping through the undergrowth directly ahead of them, burning the nettle stems black just where Borso was trying to break through. 'Amy, that must be the place!' he shouted, pulling the dog away and beating at the nettles and brambles. He forced a way through. 'Amy, look!'

They came to an abrupt stop on the edge of a wide clearing which was surrounded by a mass of tall flowers. They hesitated for a moment and then picked their way cautiously through them before they stopped and stared at a huge, bare area of blackened earth where the only thing that grew was the encircling bank of fireweed. The plants looked like polished crystal, their leaves jagged fingers in the moonlight, their tall, pale purple flowerheads bending and swaying in the faint breeze.

Amy touched one – it felt brittle and its colours glowed luminously and spread from flower to flower.

'They're not real, they're magic, look how they glow and sound like windbells when they touch. They're acting like a warning; look at the earth, nothing can have grown here for hundreds of years.'

'This must be where Hecate was first summoned. We must go into the centre of the clearing, and remember – no matter what happens we must stand our ground once these recorders are switched on. This is the only chance we are ever going to get to break the curse.'

Amy swallowed and nodded. She knew he was right, there could be no turning back now – the evil presence that had shadowed their descent in the valley was closing in all around them, encircling the clearing. Her mouth went dry with fear as the fireweed stirred and the sound of their music reached a shrill clatter of warning. A hot, stinking wind began to fill the clearing and the leaves on the trees began to wither and turn leprously white in the moonlight as the bark glistened and cracked. The earth beneath their feet trembled and wreath tails of vapour began to seep through the soil as it rose to swirl against the fireweed. As it touched it evaporated in clouds of steam. Gradually the images of two hooded figures and then the witch-queen herself clad in livid, sulphurous flames emerged from a widening, reeking split in the ground on the far side. Borso snarled and crouched, ready to attack.

'Joel!'

She tried to warn him, her fingers hovering over the switch of her recorder, but he had already seen.

'Don't look at them. Don't give them any indication of what we are going to do. Stay close to me, we must reach the centre of the clearing by midnight. Press the switch when I say so.'

Amy screwed up her courage and called Borso

close to her as they walked out into the moonlight. The blackened, rutted ground felt unnaturally brittle beneath their feet. She shuddered, knowing that if she looked down she would be able to see right through the earth's scorched and shrivelled crust into the very depths of Hell.

Joel held his breath and watched the second hand creep funereally towards the midnight hour. 'Now! Press it now!' he cried as they reached the centre of the clearing.

The two hooded figures rushed forward, engulfing them in smothering shrouds of darkness, but it couldn't muffle the recording of their voices as they cut through the darkness evenly reciting the mantra. 'Zoros, Delmusan, Surmy, Dandalen, Sator.' Backwards and forwards it rang out as the shadowy figures screamed and cursed.

'You dare to enter my sacred place and challenge my power!' Hecate hissed as she advanced, stabbing her hand and throwing flame towards them.

A shrieking howl echoed through the darkness from beneath the ground. Cerberus stirred in his lair as he was beckoned by his mistress. The brittle earth began to crack open around their feet and the stench of sulphur grew stronger, making them gag and choke. Borso spun round snarling and barking. Amy clung to Joel's arm, gasping for breath, her eyes streaming. The stems of the fireweed were swaying wildly, their flowerheads glowing brighter and brighter.

Suddenly the ground around them teemed with every imaginable creature that burrowed and slithered on earth. Enormous centipedes, dung beetles and devil's coachmen disturbed by Hecate's evil magic were crawling up out of the cracks, running and wriggling up over their shoes, slithering and scuttling on top of one another in an effort to escape. The sight of them made Amy scream. The beetles rose in black clouds and whined around their heads, their iridescent wings shining in the light from the fireweed before they flew away. Borso leapt up, spinning around fruitlessly, snapping his teeth at their flying bodies. Amy let out a long, shuddering scream and covered her head with her arms. Somewhere beyond her revulsion she heard Hecate's pitiless laughter turn into a cursing howl as the witch-queen realized that Amy's screams of terror hadn't altered the even, monotonous rhythm of the mantra by one word.

She took a step closer, her mouth thinning into a cruel sneer, she would teach them what real terror was, she would stop their chanting. Stabbing her finger at the ground she invoked swarms of grave-beetles the size of blackbirds and commanded them to swarm up and smother them. Amy shrieked, thrashing her arms as they bit at her skin, and found herself crawling away as she tried to escape from them.

'Amy, come back, we have to stay here!' Joel shouted, tearing at the mass of insects as they tried to crawl into his mouth. He tried to grab her ankle and missed. Suddenly he remembered the necklace hanging around his neck. Marjorie had said something about using the objects tied to it to drive the enemies back. In desperation he clawed through the mass of buzzing wings, brittle legs and sharp, armoured bodies and found the talisman, his fingers closing on a splinter of black tourmaline. He wrenched it free from its silver clasp and threw it with all his strength high into the air above the clearing. It spun in the darkness, absorbing and trapping the light from the purple flowerheads and the pale moonlight. Each facet glistened like hammered silver before it slowly fell back on to the scorched, seething earth to explode in a flash of brilliant silver-white light that swept through the clouds of swarming insects, shrivelling them into dust.

It took both Joel and Amy a few moments to stop shuddering and to overcome their horror. Their racing heartbeats and ragged breathing took even longer to slow down. Joel barely had time to pull Amy to her feet and drag the back of his trembling hand across his mouth to wipe away the revolting taste of decay that the wriggling insects had left on his tongue before Hecate's voice shrieked the settling dust into a blinding whirlwind which swept in a gale around the edge of the clearing, shattering many of the fragile flowerheads as it beat a path through the fireweed, dimming its violet glow and stripping the leaves from the overhanging trees. It spun faster and faster in a black, whining cloud as it drew into the centre, enveloping them in a wailing, rising maelstrom that tore abrasively at their skin as it spun them round, filling their ears, their eyes and their noses, making them cough and gasp for air.

Joel made a desperate grab for Amy, locking his arms around her waist as the force of the whirlwind lifted them up off their feet. Through the swirling dust he caught a brief, fleeting glimpse of the witch-queen and the two grave-wraiths as they rose to stand on the outer edge of the clearing repeatedly lifting their arms to make the wind spout as they chanted their magic with their heads thrown back.

'Use the necklace before the wind carries us away from here!' Joel shouted urgently, his lips almost against Amy's ear.

She snatched at the leather thong around her neck, her fingers finding a piece of peacock ore. She tore it free and, forcing her hand out into the stinging maelstrom, she let it fly free in the wind. Blue and white ice sparks blazed as it left her fingers and cut a swathe of clear air through the eye of the whirlwind. The piece of ore fizzed and melted but the towering windspout faltered, swayed and collapsed in a rush of stinking air that knocked Hecate backwards and threw her two grave-wraiths off their feet, bowling them over and over into the dense, flattened banks of fireweed. They screamed as they tried frantically to cover themselves with their robes but the pale purple flowerheads brushed against them, bursting into brilliant, purple fire and withering their skin as it blistered their rotten flesh.

Joel and Amy landed heavily on the ground in the centre of the clearing. Borso landed with a jarring thump and a yelp. He lay there, his ribcage heaving with the shock of having the breath knocked out of him. Joel climbed painfully to his hands and knees and looked across at the witch-queen with a thin, hard smile hovering on his lips. 'I think they're beginning to realize they can't stop us from reciting this mantra. Look at the way they're hunting about, searching to find out where our voices are coming from.'

'I wouldn't be so sure they can't stop us – there's no way of knowing what they'll try next. I don't think it'll be too long before they work out that we're carrying our voices and try a different method of attack.'

'Yes, maybe, but we know they can't actually touch us while we're alive and we've got these talismans to ward off Hecate's evil. It's just a matter of sweating it out,' Joel muttered, grimly running his fingers over the smooth pieces of gemstones and crystal that hung around his neck.

Amy gave the visual counter on her recorder a worried glance. It read 603, which meant they hadn't even been in the clearing an hour yet and still had a long way to go to get anywhere near the figure of twenty thousand mentioned in those old grimoires. 'Joel, we've got to be careful how we use these talismans . . .' she began, when Hecate's voice cut as sharply as shattering glass from across the clearing silencing her. She was goading the two wraiths into action, making them raise blazing

357

storms by conjuring up brimming cauldrons of hail and ice which they shook violently, swinging them around their heads before emptying them onto the ground. They produced knotted lengths of rope from beneath their cloaks which were undone and cast down upon the scorched earth and up into the branches of the trees. Thick, black thunderclouds immediately obliterated the moon and stars and it became bitterly cold. A howling, wintry wind swept down through the steep valley coating the trees and ground with ice and covering the fireweed with a sparkling frost. Amy shivered, her teeth chattering as it began to snow. In minutes the outer edges of the clearing had vanished in the blizzard as the snow piled up quickly reaching their knees and before long they were buried to their chests.

Joel scooped Borso up into his arms and held him as high as he could. 'Use the necklace!'

'No, we dare not, we'll use them all up far too quickly!' Amy shouted back.

'Then we'll have to keep moving, keep treading a space, it's our only other choice.'

'At least let's make it into the second hour!' she shouted against the howling wind.

Amy fell silent and clung tightly on to Joel, her face pressed hard against Borso's side, but despite his warmth she couldn't stop herself from shivering as the bitter wind cut through her clothes and the cold gnawed at her bones and burnt her extremities. Every nightmare second seemed to last a lifetime and the minutes and hours merged into a white blur of numbing pain that was too real, too terrifying in its violence, to be an illusion. Exhaustion was making her light-headed, vivid, confusing images, memories from other lives, were all bursting through the muddled surface of her consciousness, trying to cocoon and protect her from the reality of a frozen death. Her life was fading away rapidly.

Vaguely, through the swirling, stinging blizzard, she began to be aware of the cloaked silhouettes of the two grave-wraiths. They were drawing closer, becoming more solid, more real, as she became weaker. They were spinning around and around, gesticulating and clawing at the wind, their evil voices intensifying the storm. Close behind them, goading them forwards, Hecate's fearsome shadow loomed.

'Joel, it's no good, I can't move my feet. I can't go on. My hands are so frozen I can't move them, I can't reach the necklace. It's all over, Joel, it's finished . . .' Her words sobbed and ran together as the black, merciful well of unconsciousness closed over her. She slumped heavily against Joel and began to sink to the ground.

Joel clenched his jaws together in anger and cursed himself for trying to hold out for so long before using the talisman. Bleakly he realized that Amy was right, their voices reciting the mantra wouldn't matter a damn if they died before it was completed, Hecate would possess their souls before the recording was over, she would drag them down into her black Hell despite all their efforts to break the curse. He tried to lift his arms to reach for the necklace around his neck but he couldn't move, he was trapped, one arm wedged around Amy, trying to hold onto her and the other supporting Borso who was lying heavily against his chest. Savage anger boiled up inside him as he stared helplessly into the hideous faces of the approaching grave-wraiths.

'You won't beat us that easily, you evil, ugly bastards!' he shouted, but his words were a futile, frozen stutter, a waste of breath that made the approaching hags cackle and shriek with laughter as they lit up the sky with jagged bolts of lightning.

Joel shook his head violently. He had to think, to stop shouting and find a way to reach his necklace and use it. Borso was snarling and struggling in his arms, barking furiously at the ancient, withered women. Suddenly Joel saw a way of doing it. 'Borso, listen, boy, fetch! Fetch me the necklace. Fetch it!'

He edged the dog up a couple of inches and gave it enough room to reach the leather thong without letting Amy slip any deeper into the snow. The dog growled at the shadowy figures and then licked Joel's face.

'There's a good boy, now fetch! Fetch me the necklace.'

He tried again, fighting to keep the panic out of his voice. Borso snuffled his frozen cheek. He felt the dog's cold, wet nose in the angle of his jaw along his upturned collar.

'Borso, the necklace – fetch it!'

Borso lifted his head, tilting it slightly to one side. The skin wrinkled between his eyes as his teeth closed over the leather thong.

'Gently, boy, gently – don't pull . . .' Joel cried out but it was too late, the leather thong snapped and he watched helplessly as the necklace fell apart. Sea pearls, fragments of tourmaline, amber, quartz, turquoise and amethyst scattered across the snow. The wraiths' voices hissed into a startled silence and they gathered their grave rags around them and watched the precious objects roll slowly towards them. Joel held his breath, as they cut small, deepening grooves in the snow. What if the magic in the talisman didn't work?

Suddenly one of the tiny pearls exploded in a puff of steam and the turquoises burnt with a bright blue fire, dissolving the snow around them. The collective power of the necklace sent up clouds of steam, breaking Hecate's spell and melting the snowdrifts in an instant sending a towering, tidal wave of icy water surging after the fleeing wraiths, sending them tumbling over and over as it soaked their tattered cloaks. Joel sank, exhausted, to his knees letting Borso go as he caught Amy in his arms. He looked up in time to see Hecate scream and curse, beating at the two bedraggled wraiths who were frantically trying to stop the water from scarring their skin. Hecate's face was livid with rage, her cloak of fire enveloped by clouds of steam.

The surge of water vanished through the stems of the fireweed, melting the frost on the flowerheads and sweeping them back, full of bright purple petals, towards the centre of the clearing. Joel realized the danger they were in and scrambled quickly to his feet, roughly pulling Amy up in his arms and catching hold of Borso's collar, lifting him up. But the tidal wave vanished abruptly, a gurgling whoosh taking the flowers of the fireweed down into the hundreds of fissures and cracks that zigzagged across the scorched and brittle surface of the ground. It was at once deathly quiet. Hecate turned and stared across the clearing. The two wraiths took a hesitant step forwards and stopped. For the first time Joel saw panic in their wild eyes.

'Amy, wake up, listen, something's about to happen.'

A faint, roaring noise from deep in the bowels of the earth was getting louder and louder. The air was suddenly hot and stank of sulphur, it made Amy cough and gasp as she struggled in his arms, quickly regaining consciousness.

'What's happening? What's that noise?'

Huge geysers of steam and boiling water spouts full of the debris of Hecate's evil shot up through the ground all around them, fogging the air with sulphurous fumes, scattering her diabolical secrets, covering everything with a scalding, stinking, drifting spray. The two wraiths screamed and tried to cover themselves as the spray scorched their faces, eating through their rotten flesh. Hecate stabbed her fingers at the ground, unleashing a torrent of spells to seal up the fissures, frantic in her efforts to stop her blackened magic from escaping. But for each one she closed another broke open sending the columns of steam hundreds of feet into the air.

A smile stretched across Joel's lips. 'I think whatever goodness there was left in that necklace and the fireweed is destroying a lot of Hecate's foul magic. Look how she's cursing and trying to stop it.'

A pale light shining from between the shoulders of the mountains caught his attention. He looked at the sky with surprise. 'Look, dawn's breaking, we must have been here for hours trapped in that blizzard.'

Amy glanced down at the visual monitor on her recorder. 'The mantra's been recited almost five thousand times, if we can just hang on . . .'

'No! Don't say any more, don't draw Hecate's attention to it . . .'

But it was too late: the witch-queen had followed Amy's eyes to the small, black object tied around her waist and she ran towards them erratically, her shadowy robes bursting into new tongues of fire as they fanned out, her vile body twisting and changing its shape. She was using all the diabolical magic she had ever created, her hand elongating into writhing tentacles as she attempted to touch the small, black boxes that contained their voices, needing to feel and understand their magic in order to be able to destroy it.

Amy shuddered at her touch which made her skin crawl, and instinctively she tore a fragment of aquamarine from the talisman and hurled it at the witch-queen's face. 'Get back, get away from me you loathsome creature!'

The precious stone shattered as it touched Hecate's skin, exploding with a searing blue-green light and the sound of the rush and thunder of waves breaking on a rocky shore. It sent Hecate flying backwards, tumbling over and over. Amy blinked and grabbed at Joel's arm as the flash of light momentarily blinded her. She heard the witch-queen's voice rise in shrieks of rage and felt the ground tremble beneath her feet.

'Now you've really made her mad. We'd better look out!' Joel warned. 'Have another piece of the necklace ready.'

Lightning was crackling from the witch-queen's fingertips and her eyes were blazing with rage as she lifted her hand and ruptured the wet ground, stirring up a gale of hot, choking ash and debris from the bowels of the earth. With ominous chants she summoned up the demons from the pits of Hell.

Huge fissures broke open in the ground in front of them. Asmodeus the Destroyer, Ashtaroth the Vile, Behemoth the Ugly and hordes of satyrs and hobgoblins began to rise up. But in front of them all, emerging from a reeking, yawning, sulphurous pit, its snarling voice making the ground shake and tremble, rose Cerberus, and here, at the very source of Hecate's evil, he had grown huge. His body was wreathed in shadow, his eyes glowed with pin-points of fire. Each of his cavernous mouths snapped open and shut, their jowls hung with strings of yellow slime.

Amy began to cower as the beast snarled and took a step towards them. Suddenly her mind was filled with an image of the creature from her childhood, memories of her first, strangled moments as the beast had clawed at her mother while she lay helpless in the undergrowth. Her fear turned to overwhelming anger.

'Go on, Borso, tear its throat out, rip it limb from limb, it can't escape this time! Destroy it once and for all, pay it back for what it did in Malsbury Wood! Kill, Borso, kill!'

A sudden surge of memories filled Joel's head as Borso leapt up to tear at the creature's throat. Centuries of suppressed terror, of pain and helplessness at Cerberus's relentless pursuit, bubbled up from the secret depths of his subconscious. In one flash of recollection he understood why the sight and the choking stench of the beast filled them both with such dread. They had been its victims, unable to defend themselves for so long, and the beast had become strong with feeding on their fear as it stalked through their nightmares. In the space of one shallow breath Joel realized that it had only ever attacked them while they were weak and vulnerable, it had only come like a thief in the night, Hell's scavenger, looming out of the darkness, to snatch them from the cradle. It had only hunted them while they were helpless infants, always slinking away to hide and wait, dwelling in the shadows until death had sapped their strength and they stood close to the threshold of eternity.

Joel clenched his fist as he remembered the times when the beast had suddenly appeared and savaged his dying body and how he had fought back, desperate to reach the flames to escape from its monstrous, shadowy shape, only learning in those last, frantic moments of the danger his soul was in. But this time it wasn't too late – this time he knew what it was that had haunted him through all his previous lives. He remembered, too, the tearing pain as the creature's teeth had sheared through the bright metal ringlets of his hauberk, puncturing the thick leather gambeson he had worn all those lives ago. He remembered how he had once kicked it with his armoured boots and driven it back into the shadows at spear point. He could hear the goading, shrieking voices of the two grave-wraiths rising to a frenzy when the animal had failed to pull him away from the consuming flames.

The memories merged and began to fold back into his subconscious, but not before he caught a fleeting glimpse of Cerberus mauling at Stephanie's body as she lay in the bombed-out ruins of her flat. With all the noise and confusion at the time it had been no more than the briefest of impressions, a dark shape seen through the flames, a movement in the swirling dust that had fled when he approached. Almost a trick of the light. Borso snarled and leapt up at the salivating monster; his teeth tore through its rotten hide but he couldn't bring the beast down. The first rays of sunlight sparkled and reflected from a splinter of clear quartz crystal that hung from the necklace around Amy's neck. Joel snatched it and advanced on Cerberus with it clutched in his hand.

'No, Joel, stay here, let Borso kill him. Stay with me!' Amy cried in panic, reaching out to grab his arm to try to stop him from charging recklessly at the monstrous hell-hound, terrified that he would be overwhelmed by the demons swarming up out of the ground. But her voice faltered and doubt crept into her as those same, suppressed memories awoke inside her and, for the first time in her lives, she saw the beast and all the apparitions that Hecate had summoned up against them for what they really were – vile mockeries of Nature whose bodies were created by magic, made from rotting skin and bone, tooth and talons, woven together and bound by her black evil. Cerberus was nothing more than a cowardly, scavenging jackal, a grave-curse corrupted and riddled with her black hate who preyed on helpless children and worried the bones of the dead. She saw him cower away as Joel brought his fist slamming down onto one of his skulls, the clear crystal slashing through skin and bone making the beast howl and its back arch as it convulsed with pain.

The first rays of the new sunrise were finding their way through the trees on the edge of the clearing, touching the broken stems of the fireweed, rekindling the colours in their fragile flowerheads and casting slender fingers of light across the seething mass of demons, breaking up the darkness that held them together. They

cursed and howled, spitting at the light, covering their
eyes with their claws as they milled about in confusion.
Amy saw a ripple of doubt pass through them and it
fuelled her courage and made her reach up to the talisman. Her fingers closed around a sharp, flint arrow head
bound to the necklace with golden thread.

Hecate saw the rout begin and screamed, weaving
spells in the air above her head, urging Cerberus to kill,
driving the demons into a fury against them, but they
wailed and hesitated in the strengthening light. One by
one they began to shrivel and disintegrate as they vanished back into the ground. Cerberus suddenly sensed
the magic was failing and, realizing the danger he was
in, he began to retreat, dragging Borso, his teeth still
clamped around his windpipe. Joel had his arm locked
around the beast's shoulder and was stabbing at his chest
with the splinter of crystal, inch by inch he was being
pulled towards the yawning, sulphurous pit the beast
had emerged from. Amy saw Joel's feet skidding and
slipping on the scorched earth and rushed to help him.

'You shall harm us no more, foul padfoot!' she
shouted repeatedly, slashing at Cerberus's flanks and
legs.

The huge beast howled with pain and its body shuddered and convulsed as the arrow head sheared through
its hide, severing the rotten sinews, spilling out the ruptured muscles. It covered her hands with oozing slime
as the creature collapsed, crashing onto its side. Joel
gasped, the breath knocked out of him as he was flung
aside. Staggering onto his knees, he saw Amy sprawled
on the ground close to him and heard a splintering crack
as Borso's teeth sheared through the windpipe. The beast
staggered and tried to rise to its feet but Borso hung on
grimly.

'Go on, boy, kill, kill!'

'It's the evil that's keeping it alive, nothing else, just

the evil,' Joel wept, stabbing the crystal repeatedly into one of the monster's heads as it clawed and tried to fight them off.

Borso, covered by his own blood, renewed the attack and inch by inch he pulled Cerberus away from the safety of his lair and towards a patch of sunlight. Hecate leapt at Borso, cursing and clawing at his head, trying to gouge his eyes out to make him release her beast but he held fast. Amy slashed at the witch-queen's hands with the arrow head, shuddering with revulsion as it scoured through the webs of her evil, sending shock waves up her arms. The flint blade shattered in a searing flash of light that blinded Amy and cut a white, livid weal across Hecate's knuckles making her snatch her fingers away from Borso's eyes. Hecate's face blackened with hatred.

'Your vile cur will burn, burn in Hell for daring to touch me and mine!' she hissed, her breath making Amy retch and choke. Hecate infested the broken carcass of her demon-dog with all the evil magic she could summon, making it jerk and convulse and claw violently at the ground in its effort to escape. Slowly it dragged Borso with it towards the gaping mouth of its lair. Borso's claws scarred the ground as he was pulled towards the fissure.

'Leave, Borso, leave!' Amy shouted as she realized what was happening, and grabbed at her dog's collar, locking her fingers around it and pulling him away only moments before the monstrous creature slithered over the lip of the reeking chasm and vanished in an echoing howl of defeat.

'You shall suffer a thousand agonies and I will bind you in evil and swallow you with the darkness for hurting my beast!' Hecate hissed as she advanced on them, her arms outstretched, her eyes burning with revenge, but two long, wailing, tortuous cries like fingernails on slate rent the morning air and made her hesitate and spin round.

'Amy, those ancient hags! Something's happening to their clothes, look!' Joel hissed, scrambling to his feet.

Amy looked up across the clearing, her trembling hand still locked around Borso's collar, and saw the grave rags and shrouds that they wore as robes melting and dissolving. They were crying out and clawing frantically at their winding sheets, but each time their fingers touched the shadowy cloth it shrivelled and unravelled, revealing more and more of their withered, shrunken bodies to the sunlight. Hecate ran around them, her voice rising into a continuous chant as she wove her blackest magic, but each spell she cast protected them only briefly, hanging for such an infinitesimal time on the morning breeze before it was blown away amongst the gently swaying flowerheads.

Amy felt the birthmark under her collarbone begin to tingle and burn and she pulled open her blouse. 'The sign of the labyrinth is fading,' she whispered.

Joel tore his shirt off and watched the blue mark fade. 'I think the mantra must be working. Mike was right: Hecate couldn't find a way to stop us reciting it, we're breaking the curse!'

There was a note of hope in their voices and she glanced down at the visual monitor on her recorder, listening and savouring the words as her voice evenly repeated, 'Zoros, Delmusan, Surmy, Dandalen, Sator.'

Joel nodded grimly. 'I reckon we must be pretty close now, we've recited the mantra almost eight thousand times.'

He fell silent, his mouth thinning into a determined line. He watched the witches' power crumble away as they cowered in shivering nakedness. This was the moment they had waited so many lifetimes for. A flood of memories rose up out of the well of his subconscious, memories of pain and the relentless pursuit into the ashes of each life.

'We're going to end it now. We're going to put them to the flame.'

Amy nodded bleakly. She knew what they had to do but the thought of it revolted her senses. Joel's hand reached slowly into his jacket pocket, his fingers closing around the crumpled box of matches. He took out a match and gave her the box.

'Strike your match at exactly the same time,' he whispered, gripping his between his first two fingers and pressing the small, red sulphurous head against the nail of his thumb. 'Are you ready?'

Her hand trembled as she held the matches and they advanced across the clearing towards the two wretched creatures as they huddled on the other side, wailing and crying out for mercy. Hecate saw their intent and rushed at them, flailing her arms, shrieking at the top of her voice and calling the demons, naming them one by one, commanding them to rise up and pull Amy and Joel under the earth. The ground trembled and shook and as it split open claws and talons broke through the surface, snagging and catching at their feet. But they shattered like empty, brittle husks whenever Amy or Joel trod on them, breaking apart in clouds of ancient dust.

Hecate spun round and round, sending her voice high up above the clearing in a last, desperate bid to summon ferocious storms and a deluge of floods to drown them but only the slightest breeze answered her and ruffled the broken stems of the fireweed and stirred the leaves on the edges of the clearing. Somewhere deep in the mountains lightning crackled and the faintest echo of thunder rumbled once before it died away.

'Your curse is broken, your evil power over us is destroyed forever!' Amy cried, snatching the remnants of the talisman around her neck with her free hand and throwing it at the witch-queen.

The last three remaining gemstones and fragments of crystal sparkled and blazed as the necklace struck her. Borso leapt at her swirling cloak as she shrank away.

'Now!' Joel cried as they reached the two cowering, pitiful, and now almost-naked creatures.

The matches flared brightly between their fingers. Amy shuddered, her senses reeling as the closest figure shrunk back away from her, its voice babbling, calling for Cerberus to save them. They were terrified of the fragile flame she held but nothing could save them, they were as helpless as they were on that day in Aurillac when the townspeople had forced them into the fire. The two lighted matches dropped through the air, flaring brightly as they touched the shivering women who tried to cover their faces and huddle deeper into the earth. Their tinder-dry skin and bones, their leathery sinews, burst into jumping, crackling columns of fire that drew them up in a swirling, twisting ribbon of sparks. For an instant their hands seemed to reach out one last time, clutching at nothing but empty air before they shrivelled and collapsed into a fine grey-white ash that scattered and blew away to nothing.

A movement out of the corner of Joel's eye and Borso's sudden barking from near the centre of the clearing made them both spin round to see the dog snarling and growling furiously at Hecate as she sank defeated into the ruptured earth, wreathed in stinking fumes.

'Quickly, Amy, give me your recorder,' Joel urged.

He was going to teach the witch-queen never to come back. Unclipping his own device and snatching Amy's he ran towards Hecate, hurling both the recorders after her as she vanished into the closing fissure in the ground. For a moment he stood there, inhaling short, ragged breaths, listening to their voices as they followed her down into the labyrinths of Hell growing fainter and fainter.

'Zoros, Delmusan, Surmy, Dandalen, Sator, Zoros, Delmusan, Surmy . . .'

Joel smiled and sank wearily down onto his knees beside Amy, putting his arm around her and drawing her close to him. Shafts of sunlight broke through the trees and warmly dappled their faces. The morning air seemed to sparkle and was heady with the scent of wild flowers: it was going to be a beautiful day.

'It's over, isn't it?' Amy whispered, entwining her fingers with his.

'Yes.' Joel nodded. 'It's finally over.'

Epilogue

THERE WAS A hint of autumn in the still, evening air in Miss Morston's small basement garden. The summer flowers were faded and past their best and the roses that grew around the gate had wilted to litter the flagstones with a fragile snow of scented petals. Joel wasn't sure why they had come back to visit the old woman: he knew there was a vague connection with their past but he couldn't remember what it was.

'I've found those photographs I promised to show you when you called earlier in the summer – the ones of your aunt taken before the war,' Miss Morston smiled as she bustled out through the kitchen door, carrying a tea tray with a box of old photographs balanced on top of the cups and saucers, and put them down on the garden table in front of them.

The old woman's hands were as quick as a sparrow as she sorted through the faded pictures. 'Yes, here's one of Stephanie with that beautiful dog of hers, and here's another taken only a few days before that dreadful air-raid.'

Joel took the pictures from her and looked at them. 'Who is that standing with her?' he asked politely. The picture stirred up something in his memory but he couldn't quite catch hold of it.

'Why, that's the young American pilot she was very friendly with.' Miss Morston sighed and passed the photographs to Amy.

Amy looked at the two young faces staring out of the

picture at her. Something in them seemed to stir her memory and hazy, indistinct images began to form inside her head. She sat back, trying to remember, and caught the faint sound of the traffic in the Brompton Road, voices in the street above and a dog barking in the distance. She shook her head and tried to shut out the sounds that had distracted her but the memories had gone, fading deeper into shadow.

Daggerspell

Book One of the Deverry Series

Katherine Kerr

Daggerspell is the first volume of an epic series
set in a fantastical world where even death itself is cowed by
the powers of passion and high magic

In a void outside reality, the flickering spirit of a young girl
hovers between incarnation, knowing neither her past nor
her future. But in the temporal world there is one who knows
and waits: Nevyn, the wandering sorcerer. On a bloody day
long ago he relinquished the maiden's hand in marriage – and
so forged a terrible bond of destiny between three souls that
would last through three generations. Now Nevyn is doomed
to follow them across the plains of time, never resting until he
atones for the tragic wrong of his youth . . .

'Katherine Kerr is one of my favourites in the fantasy field
and one of the few writers who have been able to grasp the
true essence of Celtic myth . . . when you open one of her
books, there's a great rush of sensory detail. For that reason,
combined with a wolf's nose of a sense for storytelling, I read
Katherine Kerr: and you should too.' John Gilbert, *Fear*

Other Deverry titles:
Darkspell
Dawnspell: The Bristling Wood
Dragonspell: The Southern Sea

ISBN 0 586 07315 9

Black Trillium
Marion Bradley, Julian May, Andre Norton

A massively successful collaboration by three of
the world's greatest fantasy writers

Late one stormy night three infant princesses are born. As
each baby is placed into her mother's arms, so the Archimage
Binah bestows on her a gift of great power: a pendant
containing a bud of the long extinct Black Trillium. One day
that power will be all that protects the princesses from certain
doom . . .

Marion Bradley, Julian May and Andre Norton – separately
each author has millions of books in print and a legion of
devoted fans. Now in *Black Trillium* they've combined their
formidable talents to produce a masterpiece of breathtaking
imagination which will captivate old and new readers alike.

ISBN 0 586 21161 6

☐	MAGICIAN Raymond E. Feist	0-586-21783-5	£6.99
☐	SILVERTHORN Raymond E. Feist	0-586-06417-6	£4.99
☐	A DARKNESS AT SETHANON Raymond E. Feist	0-586-06688-8	£5.99
☐	THE SILVER BRANCH Patricia Kennealy	0-586-21248-5	£4.99
☐	THE ELVENBANE À. Norton/M. Lackey	0-586-21687-1	£5.99
☐	MASTER OF WHITESTORM Janny Wurts	0-586-21068-7	£4.99
☐	THE DRAGON AND THE GEORGE		
	Gordon R. Dickson	0-586-21326-0	£4.99
☐	BLACK TRILLIUM May/Bradley/Norton	0-586-21102-0	£4.99

These books are available from your local bookseller or can be ordered direct from the publishers.

To order direct just tick the titles you want and fill in the form below:

Name: _____

Address: _____

_____

_____

Postcode: _____

Send to: HarperCollins Mail Order, Dept 8, HarperCollins *Publishers*, Westerhill Road, Bishopbriggs, Glasgow G64 2QT.

Please enclose a cheque or postal order or your authority to debit your Visa/Access account –

Credit card no: _____

Expiry date: _____

Signature: _____

– to the value of the cover price plus:

UK & BFPO: Add £1.00 for the first and 25p for each additional book ordered.

Overseas orders including Eire, please add £2.95 service charge.

Books will be sent by surface mail but quotes for airmail despatches will be given on request.

24 HOUR TELEPHONE ORDERING SERVICE FOR ACCESS/VISA CARDHOLDERS –

TEL: GLASGOW 041-772 2281 or LONDON 081-307 4052